CARAVAL

STEPHANIE GARBER

HODDER &
STOUGHTON

First published in the United States of America in 2017 by Flatiron Books
A Macmillan Publishers company

First published in Great Britain in 2017 by Hodder & Stoughton
An Hachette UK company

A CIP catalogue record for this title is available from the British Library

Hardback ISBN 978 1 473 62914 1
Trade Paperback ISBN 978 1 473 62915 8
eBook ISBN 978 1 473 62917 2

Printed and bound in Great Britain by Clays Ltd, St Ives plc

Hodder & Stoughton policy is to use papers that are natural, renewable
and recyclable products and made from wood grown in sustainable forests.
The logging and manufacturing processes are expected to conform to
the environmental regulations of the country of origin.

Hodder & Stoughton Ltd
Carmelite House
50 Victoria Embankment
London EC4Y 0DZ

www.hodder.co.uk

To my mom and dad,

for teaching me the meaning

of unconditional love

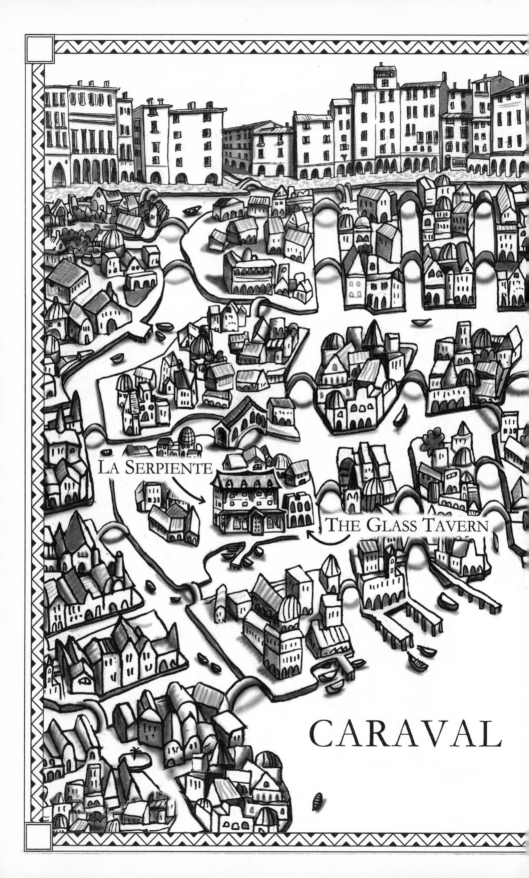

LA SERPIENTE

THE GLASS TAVERN

CARAVAL

HATTER AND
HABERDASHERY

DRESS SHOP

CAROUSEL OF ROSES

CASTILLO MALDITO

THE ISLE
OF TRISDA

I t took seven years to get the letter right.

Year 50, Elantine Dynasty

Dear Mister Caraval Master,

My name is Scarlett, but I'm writing this letter for my sister, Donatella. It's going to be her birthday soon and she would very much like to see you and your amazing Caraval players. Her birthday is the 37th day of the Growing Season and it would be the most wonderfulest birthday ever if you came.

Most hopefully,

Scarlett, from the Conquered Isle of Trisda

Year 51, Elantine Dynasty

Dear Mister Caraval Master,

It's Scarlett again. Did you get my last letter? This year my sister says she's too old to celebrate birthdays, but I think she's just upset you never came to Trisda. This Growing Season she'll be ten and I'll be eleven. She won't admit it but she'd still very much like to see you and your wondrous Caraval players.

Most hopefully,

Scarlett, from the Conquered Isle of Trisda

Year 52, Elantine Dynasty

Dear Caraval Master Legend,

I'm sorry I got your name wrong in those other letters. I hope that's not why you haven't come to Trisda. My little sister's birthday wasn't the only reason I've wanted you to bring your amazing Caraval players here, I'd love to see them too.

Sorry this letter is short, my father will be angry if he catches me writing to you.

Most hopefully,

Scarlett, from the Conquered Isle of Trisda

Year 52, Elantine Dynasty

Dear Caraval Master Legend,

I just heard the news and I wanted to send my condolences. Even though you still haven't come to Trisda or responded to any of my letters, I know you're not a murderer. I was very sorry to hear you won't be traveling for a while.

Most kindly,

Scarlett, from the Conquered Isle of Trisda

Year 55, Elantine Dynasty

Dear Master Legend,

Do you remember me, Scarlett, from the Conquered Isle of Trisda? I know it's been a few years since I wrote. I heard you and your players have started performing again. My sister told me you never visit the same place twice, but a lot has changed since you visited here fifty years ago, and I truly don't believe anyone would like to see one of your performances more than I would.

Most hopefully,

Scarlett

Year 56, Elantine Dynasty

Dear Master Legend,

I heard you visited the capital of the Southern Empire last year and changed the color of the sky. Is that true? I actually tried attending with my sister, but we're not supposed to leave Trisda. Sometimes I believe I'll never go farther than the Conquered Isles. I suppose that's why I've wanted you and your players to come here so badly. It's probably futile to ask again, but I do hope you'll consider coming.

Most hopefully,

Scarlett, from the Conquered Isle of Trisda

Year 51, Elantine Dynasty

Dear Master Legend,

This will be my final letter. I'm going to be married soon. So it's probably best you and your players don't come to Trisda this year.

Scarlett Dragna

Year 57, Elantine Dynasty

Dear Scarlett Dragna,
from the Conquered Isle of Trisda—

Congratulations on your upcoming nuptials.
I am sorry I cannot bring my players to
Trisda. We're not traveling this year.
Our next performance is by invitation only,
but I would look forward to meeting you and
your fiancé if you could find a way to leave
your isle and join us.

Please accept the enclosed as a gift.

From the pen of Caraval Master Legend

2

S carlett's feelings came in colors even brighter than usual. The urgent red of burning coals. The eager green of new grass buds. The frenzied yellow of a flapping bird's feathers.

He'd finally written back.

She read the letter again. Then again. And again. Her eyes took in each sharp stroke of ink, every waxy curve of the Caraval master's silver crest—a sun with a star inside and a teardrop inside of the star. The same seal was watermarked onto the enclosed slips of paper.

This was no prank.

"Donatella!" Scarlett plunged down the steps into the barrel room in search of her younger sister. The familiar scents of molasses and oak snaked up her nose, but her scoundrel of a sibling was nowhere to be found.

"Tella—where are you?" Oil lamps cast an amber glow over bottles of rum and several freshly filled wooden barrels. Scarlett heard a moan as she moved past, and she caught bits of heavy breathing as well. After her latest battle with their father, Tella had probably drunk too much, and now dozed somewhere on the floor. "Dona—"

She choked on the last half of her sister's name.

"Hullo, Scar."

Tella flashed Scarlett a sloppy grin, all white teeth and swollen lips. Her honey-blond curls were a mess as well, and her shawl had fallen to the floor. But it was the sight of the young sailor, with his hands wrapped around Tella's waist, that made Scarlett stutter, "Did I interrupt something?"

"Nothing we can't start up again." The sailor spoke with a lilting Southern Empire accent, far smoother-sounding than the sharp Meridian Empire tongues Scarlett was accustomed to.

Tella giggled, but at least she had the grace to blush a little. "Scar, you know Julian, right?"

"Lovely seeing you, Scarlett." Julian smiled, as cool and seductive as a slice of shade in the Hot Season.

Scarlett knew the polite response would be something along the lines of "Good to see you, too." But all she could think about were his hands, still coiled around Tella's periwinkle skirts, playing with the tassels on her bustle, as if she were a parcel he couldn't wait to unwrap.

Julian had only been on the isle of Trisda about a month. When he'd swaggered off his ship, tall and handsome, with golden-brown skin, he'd drawn almost every woman's eye. Even Scarlett's head had turned briefly, but she'd known better than to look any longer.

"Tella, mind if I pull you away for a moment?" Scarlett managed to nod politely at Julian, but the instant they'd woven through enough barrels to be out of his hearing she said, "What are you doing?"

"Scar, you're getting married; I would think you'd be aware of what occurs between a man and a woman." Tella nudged her sister's shoulder playfully.

"That's not what I'm talking about. You know what will happen if Father catches you."

"Which is why I don't plan on getting caught."

"Please be serious," Scarlett said.

"I am being serious. If Father catches us, I'll just find a way to blame it on you." Tella gave a tart smile. "But I don't think you came down here to talk about that." Her eyes dropped to the letter in Scarlett's hands.

The hazy glow of a lantern caught the metallic edges of the paper, making them blaze a shimmery gold, the color of magic and wishes and promises of things to come. The address on the envelope lit up with equal luster.

Miss Scarlett Dragna
Care of the priests' confessional
Trisda
Conquered Isles of the Meridian Empire

Tella's eyes sharpened as she took in the radiant script. Scarlett's sister had always liked beautiful things, like the young man still waiting for her behind the barrels. Often, if Scarlett lost one of her prettier possessions, she could find it tucked away in her younger sister's room.

But Tella didn't reach out to take this note. Her hands remained at her sides, as if she wanted nothing to do with it. "Is this another letter from the count?" She spat out the title as if he were the devil.

Scarlett considered defending her fiancé, but her sister had already clearly expressed her thoughts on Scarlett's engagement. It made no difference that arranged marriages were very much in fashion throughout the rest of the Meridian Empire, or that for months the count had faithfully sent Scarlett the kindest letters; Tella refused to understand how Scarlett could marry someone she'd never met in person. But wedding a man she'd never seen frightened Scarlett far less than the thought of staying on Trisda.

"Well," Tella pressed, "are you going to tell me what it is, then?"

"It's not from the count." Scarlett spoke quietly, not wanting Tella's sailor friend to overhear. "It's from the master of Caraval."

"He wrote you back?" Tella snatched the note. "God's teeth!"

"Shhh!" Scarlett pushed her sister back toward the barrels. "Someone might hear you."

"Am I not allowed to celebrate now?" Tella retrieved the three slips of paper hidden within the invite. Lamplight caught their water seals. For a moment they glowed gold, like the edges of the letter, before shifting to a dangerous shade of bloody crimson.

"Do you see that?" Tella gasped as swirls of silver letters materialized across the page, slowly dancing into words: *Admit One: Donatella Dragna, of the Conquered Isles.*

Scarlett's name appeared on the other.

The third only contained the words *Admit One.* Like the other invites, this was printed above the name of an isle she'd never heard of: *Isla de los Sueños.*

Scarlett imagined this nameless invitation was meant for her fiancé, and for a moment she thought of how romantic it could be to experience Caraval with him once they were married.

"Oh, look, there's more!" Tella squealed as new lines of script appeared on the tickets.

To be used once, to gain entrance into Caraval.

Main gates close at midnight, on the thirteenth day of the Growing Season, during the 57th year of the Elantine Dynasty. Anyone who arrives later than this will not be able to participate in the game, or win this year's prize of one wish.

"That's only three days away," Scarlett said, the bright colors she'd felt before turning to her usual dull shades of gray disappointment. She should have known better than to think, even for a moment, that this could work out. Maybe if Caraval were in three months, or even three weeks—*sometime* after she was married. Scarlett's father had been secretive about the exact date of her wedding, but she knew it would not be in less than three days. Leaving before then would be impossible—and far too dangerous.

"But look at this year's prize," said Tella. "A wish."

"I thought you didn't believe in wishes."

"And I thought you'd be happier about this," Tella said. "You know people would kill to get their hands on these?"

"Did you not see the part where he said we need to leave the isle?" No matter how badly Scarlett longed to go to Caraval, she needed to get married even more. "To make it in three days, we'd probably have to leave tomorrow."

"Why do you think I'm so excited?" The glimmer in Tella's eyes grew brighter; when she was happy, the world turned shimmery, making Scarlett want to beam along with her and say yes to whatever her sister desired. But Scarlett had learned too well how treacherous it was to hope in something as illusive as a wish.

Scarlett sharpened her voice, hating herself for being the one to crush her sister's joy, but better she than someone who would destroy even more than that. "Were you also drinking rum down here? Have you forgotten what Father did the last time we tried to leave Trisda?"

Tella flinched. For a moment she looked like the fragile girl she pretended so hard not to be. Then, just as quickly, her expression changed, pink lips curving once again, shifting from broken to unbreakable. "That was two years ago; we're smarter now."

"We also have more to lose," Scarlett insisted.

It was easier for Tella to brush aside what had happened when they'd attempted to go to Caraval before. Scarlett had never told her sister the entirety of what their father had done as retribution; she'd not wanted Tella to live in that much fear, to constantly look over her shoulder, to know there were worse things than their father's standard forms of punishment.

"Don't tell me this is because you're afraid it will interfere with your wedding." Tella gripped the tickets tighter.

"Stop." Scarlett grabbed them back. "You're going to crinkle their edges."

"And you're avoiding my question, Scarlett. Is this about your wedding?"

"Of course not. It's about not being able to get off the island tomorrow. We don't even know where this other place is. I've never heard of Isla de los Sueños but I know it's not one of the Conquered Isles."

"I know where it is." Julian stepped out from behind several rum barrels, flashing a smile that said he'd make no apologies for listening in on a private conversation.

"This doesn't concern you." Scarlett waved him away with her hand.

Julian looked at her strangely, as if a girl had never dismissed him. "I'm only trying to help. You've never heard of this isle because it's not part of the Meridian Empire. It's not ruled by any of the five Empires. Isla de los Sueños is *Legend's* private isle, only about two days' journey, and if you want to go there I can smuggle you onto my ship, for a price." Julian eyed the third ticket. Thick lashes lined his light brown eyes, just made for convincing girls to lift their skirts and open their arms.

Tella's words about people who'd kill for the tickets echoed in Scarlett's mind. Julian might have had a charming face, but he also had that Southern Empire accent, and everyone knew the Southern Empire was a lawless place.

"No," Scarlett said. "It's too dangerous if we get caught."

"Everything we do is dangerous. We'll be in trouble if we get caught down here with a boy," Tella said.

Julian looked offended at being referred to as a boy, but Tella went on before he could argue. "Nothing we do is safe. But this is worth the risk. You've waited your whole life for this, wished on every fallen star, prayed as every ship came into port that it would be that magical one carrying the mysterious Caraval performers. You want this even more than I do."

Whatever you've heard about Caraval, it doesn't compare to the reality. It's more than just a game or a performance. It's the closest you'll ever find to magic in this world. Her grandmother's words played in Scarlett's head as she looked at the slips of paper in her hands. The Caraval stories she adored as a young girl never felt more real than they did in that moment. Scarlett always saw flashes of color attached to her strongest emotions, and for an instant goldenrod desire lit up inside her. Briefly, Scarlett let herself imagine what it would be like to go to Legend's private isle, to play the game and win the wish. Freedom. Choices. Wonder. Magic.

A beautiful, ridiculous fantasy.

And it was best to keep it that way. Wishes were about as real as unicorns. When she was younger Scarlett had believed her nana's stories about Caraval's magic, but as she'd grown, she'd left those fairy tales behind. She'd never seen any proof that magic existed. Now it seemed far more likely that her nana's tales were the exaggerations of an old woman.

A part of Scarlett still desperately wanted to experience the splendor of Caraval, but she knew better than to believe its magic would change her life. The only person capable of giving Scarlett or her sister a brand-new life was Scarlett's fiancé, the count.

Now that they were no longer held up to the lamplight, the script on the tickets had vanished and they looked almost ordinary again. "Tella, we can't. It's too risky; if we try to leave the isle—" Scarlett broke off as the stairs to the barrel room creaked. The heavy tread of boots followed. At least three sets.

Scarlett shot a panicked look at her sister.

Tella cursed and quickly made a motion for Julian to hide.

"Don't disappear on my account." Governor Dragna finished his descent, the sharp odor of his heavily perfumed suit spoiling the pungent scents of the barrel room.

Quickly, Scarlett shoved the letters into her dress pocket.

Behind her father, three guards followed his every step.

"I don't believe we've met." Ignoring his daughters, Governor Dragna reached a gloved hand toward Julian. He wore his plum-colored gloves, the shade of dark bruises and power.

But at least he still had the gloves on. The picture of civility, Governor Dragna liked to dress impeccably, in a tailored black frock coat and striped purple waistcoat. He was in his mid-forties but he'd not let his body turn to fat like other men. Keeping with the latest fashion, he kept his blond hair tied back with a neat black bow, showing off his manicured eyebrows and dark blond goatee.

Julian was taller, yet the governor still managed to look down upon him. Scarlett could see her father appraising the sailor's patched brown coat, and his loose breeches tucked into scuffed, knee-high boots.

It said much about Julian's confidence that he didn't hesitate before offering the governor his own, ungloved hand. "Good to meet you, sir. Julian Marrero."

"Governor Marcello Dragna." The men shook hands. Julian attempted to pull away, but the governor held on tight. "Julian, you must not be from this isle?"

This time, Julian did hesitate. "No, sir, I'm a sailor. First mate of *El Beso Dorado*."

"So, you're only passing through." The governor smiled. "We like sailors here. It helps our economy. People are willing to pay a lot to dock here, and they spend more money while they visit. Now, tell me, what did you think of my rum?" He waved his free hand around the barrel room. "I imagine that's what you were down here tasting?"

When Julian didn't answer right away the governor pressed harder. "Was it not to your liking?"

"No, sir. I mean, yes, sir," Julian corrected. "Everything I've tried is very good."

"Including my daughters?"

Scarlett tensed.

"I can smell from your breath you weren't sipping any rum," said Governor Dragna. "And I know you weren't down here playing cards or saying prayers. So tell me, which of my daughters were you tasting?"

"Oh, no, sir. You have it wrong." Julian shook his head, eyes widening as if he would never do something so dishonorable.

"It was Scarlett," Tella broke in. "I came down here and caught them in the act."

No. Scarlett cursed her foolish sister. "Father, she's lying. It was Tella, not me. I'm the one who caught them."

Tella's face blazed red. "Scarlett, don't lie. You'll only make this worse."

"I'm not lying! Father, it was Tella. Do you think I'd really do something like this, weeks before my wedding?"

"Father, don't listen to her," Tella interrupted. "I heard her whispering about how she thought it would help with her nerves before the wedding."

"That's another lie—"

"Enough!" The governor turned to Julian, whose brown hand was still firmly grasped in his perfumed plum glove. "My daughters have the bad habit of being dishonest, but I'm sure you'll be more forthcoming. Now, tell me, young man, which of my daughters were you down here with?"

"I think there's been some sort of mistake—"

"I don't make mistakes," Governor Dragna cut him off. "I'll give you one more chance to tell me the truth, or—" The governor's guards each took a step forward.

Julian's eyes darted to Tella.

With a sharp shake of her head, Tella mouthed the name: *Scarlett.*

Scarlett tried to grab Julian's attention, tried to tell him he was making a mistake, but she could see the resolve in the sailor's face even before he answered. "It was Scarlett."

Reckless boy. He no doubt believed he was doing Tella a favor, when he was doing quite the opposite.

The governor released Julian, and removed his perfumed plum gloves. "I warned you about this," he said to Scarlett. "You know what happens when you disobey."

"Father, please, it was only a very brief kiss." Scarlett tried to step in front of Tella, but a guard pulled Scarlett back toward the barrels, grabbing her roughly by the elbows and yanking them behind her, as she fought to protect her sister. For it wasn't Scarlett who would be punished for this crime. Every time Scarlett or her sister disobeyed, Governor Dragna did something awful to the other as punishment.

On his right hand, the governor wore two large rings, a square amethyst and a sharply pointed purple diamond. He twisted both of these around his fingers, then he pulled his hand back and struck Tella across the face.

"Don't! I'm the one to blame!" Scarlett screamed—a mistake she knew better than to make.

Her father struck Tella once more. "For lying," he said. The second blow was harder than the first, knocking Tella to her knees as streams of red poured down her cheek.

Satisfied, Governor Dragna stepped back. He wiped the blood from his hand on one of his guard's vests. Then he turned to Scarlett. Somehow he appeared taller than before, while Scarlett felt as if she had wilted in size. There was nothing her father could do that hurt her more than watching him hit her sister. "Don't disappoint me again."

"I'm sorry, Father. I made a foolish mistake." It was the truest thing she'd said all morning. She might not have been the one Julian had *tasted*, but once again she had failed to protect her sister. "I won't repeat it."

"I hope you mean that." The governor put his gloves back on, then reached into his frock coat and retrieved a folded letter. "I probably shouldn't give this to you, but maybe it will remind you of everything you have to lose. Your wedding will be ten days from today, at the end of next week, on the twentieth. If anything gets in the way of it, more than your sister's face will bleed."

3

Scarlett could still smell her father's perfume. It smelled like the color of his gloves: anise and lavender and something akin to rotted plums. It stayed with her long after he left, hovering in the air around Tella while Scarlett sat by her side, waiting for a maid to bring clean bandages and medicinal supplies.

"You should have let me tell the truth," Scarlett said. "He'd not have hit me this badly to punish you. Not with my wedding in ten days."

"Maybe he wouldn't have struck your face, but he'd have done something else just as vicious—broken a finger so you couldn't finish your wedding quilt." Tella closed her eyes and leaned back against a barrel of rum. Her cheek was now almost the color of her father's wretched gloves. "And I'm the one who deserved to be hit, not you."

"No one deserves this," Julian said. It was the first time he'd spoken since their father left. "I'm—"

"Don't," Scarlett cut in. "Your apology will not heal her wounds."

"I wasn't going to apologize." Julian paused, as if weighing his next words. "I'm changing my offer about taking you both from the isle. I'll do it for free, if you decide you want to leave. My ship sets off from port tomorrow at dawn. Come find me if you change your mind." He divided a look between Scarlett and Tella before he disappeared up the stairs.

"No," Scarlett said, sensing what Tella wanted before she said any words aloud. "If we leave, things will be worse when we return."

"I don't plan on returning." Tella opened her eyes. They were watery but fierce.

Scarlett was often annoyed by how impulsive her younger sister was, but she also knew that when Tella finally set her mind to a plan, there was no changing it. Scarlett realized Tella had made her decision even before the letter from Caraval Master Legend arrived. That's why she'd been with Julian. From the way she'd ignored him as he'd left, it was obvious she didn't care about him. She just wanted a sailor who could take her away from Trisda. And now Scarlett had given her the reason she needed to leave.

"Scar, you should come too," Tella said. "I know you think your marriage is going to save and protect you, but what if the count is as bad as Father, or worse?"

"He's not," Scarlett insisted. "You'd know this if you read his letters. He's a perfect gentleman, and he's promised to take care of us both."

"Oh, sister." Tella smiled, but it wasn't the happy sort. It was the way someone smiles just before they say something they wish they didn't have to. "If he's such a *gentleman*, then why is he so secretive? Why have you only been told his title but not his name?"

"It's not because of him. Keeping his identity a mystery is another way of Father trying to control us." The letter in Scarlett's hands proved as much. "Look for yourself." She gave her sister the note.

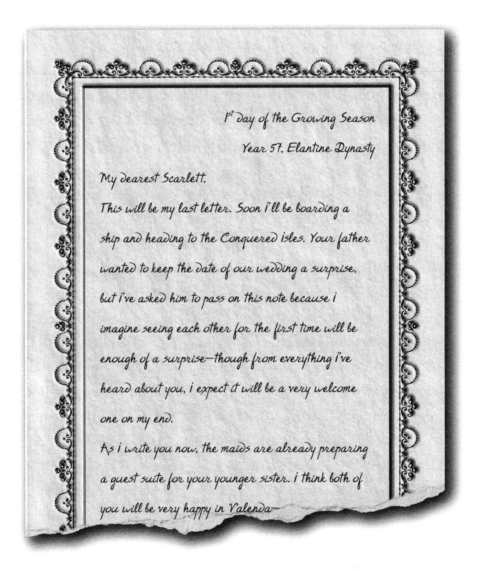

1st day of the Growing Season

Year 57, Elantine Dynasty

My dearest Scarlett,

This will be my last letter. Soon I'll be boarding a ship and heading to the Conquered Isles. Your father wanted to keep the date of our wedding a surprise, but I've asked him to pass on this note because I imagine seeing each other for the first time will be enough of a surprise—though from everything I've heard about you, I expect it will be a very welcome one on my end.

As I write you now, the maids are already preparing a guest suite for your younger sister. I think both of you will be very happy in Valenda—

The rest of the page was missing. Not only were her groom's words cut off, but her father had been kind enough to remove any traces of the letter's wax seal, which might have given Scarlett a further indication of who she was marrying.

Another one of his twisted games.

Sometimes Scarlett felt all of Trisda was under a dome, a large piece of glass that trapped everyone inside while her father looked down, moving—or removing—people if they weren't in the right places. Her world was a grand game board, and her father believed this marriage would be his penultimate move, putting all that he wanted within his grasp.

Governor Dragna had more fortune than most island officials, from his rum trade and other black market dealings, yet because Trisda was one of the Conquered Isles, he lacked the power and respect he desired. No matter how much wealth he amassed, regents and nobles from the rest of the Meridian Empire ignored him.

It didn't matter that the isle of Trisda, or the four other Conquered Isles, had been a part of the Meridian Empire for more than sixty years; the Islanders were still thought of as the uncouth and undereducated peasants they'd been when the Empire had first subjugated them. But according to Scarlett's father, this union would change all that, joining him with a noble family that would finally grant their own some respectability—and of course it would give him more power as well.

"This doesn't prove anything," Tella said.

"It shows he's kind and considerate and—"

"Anyone can sound like a gentleman in a letter. But you know only a vile person would make a bargain with our father."

"Stop saying things like that." Scarlett snatched the message back. Her sister was wrong. Even the count's handwriting illustrated thoughtfulness, neat curves and soft lines. If he were uncaring, he'd not have written her so many letters to ease her fears, or promised to also take Tella with them to the Elantine Empire's capital city of Valenda—a place where their father's hands could not reach.

A part of Scarlett knew there was a chance the count might not be everything she hoped, but life with him had to be better than living with her father. And she could not risk defying her father, not when his vicious warning still echoed through her head: *If anything gets in the way of it, more than your sister's face will bleed.*

Scarlett would not jeopardize this marriage for a mere chance at winning a wish during Caraval.

"Tella, if we try to leave on our own, Father will hunt us to the edge of the world."

"Then at least we'll travel to the end of the world," Tella said. "I'd rather die there than live here, or trapped in your count's house."

"You can't mean that," Scarlett scolded. She hated it when Tella made such reckless exclamations. Scarlett often feared her sister had a death wish. The words *I'd rather die* passed Tella's lips far too often. She also seemed to forget how perilous the world could be. Along with her tales of Caraval, Scarlett's nana had also told stories of what happened to young women who didn't have families to protect them. Girls who tried to make it on their own, who thought they were taking respectable jobs only to find themselves sold into brothels or workhouses with deplorable conditions.

"You fret too much." Tella pushed up from the ground on wobbly legs.

"What are you doing?"

"I'm not waiting any longer for a maid. I don't want someone fussing over my face for the next hour and then forcing me to lie in bed all day." Tella plucked her fallen shawl from the ground and wrapped it around her head like a scarf, concealing the bruised part of her face. "If I'm going to leave on Julian's ship tomorrow, I have things to take care of, like sending word to let him know I'll be meeting him in the morning."

"Wait! You're not thinking this through." Scarlett dashed after her sister, but Tella raced up the steps and darted past the door before Scarlett could reach her.

Outside, the air was as thick as soup, and the open courtyard smelled like afternoon—damp, salty, and pungent. Someone must have recently brought a haul of fish to the kitchens. The ripe odor seemed to be everywhere as Scarlett chased Tella under weatherworn white archways and through clay-tiled halls.

Scarlett's father never felt as if his estate was large enough. It was on the border of town, with more land than most, so he could constantly build more. More guestrooms. More courtyards. More hidden hallways to smuggle bottles of illegal alcohol, and who knew what else. Scarlett and her sister were not allowed in many of the newest halls. And if their father caught them running like this, he'd not hesitate to have their feet whipped. But injured heels and toes would be nothing compared to what he would do if he discovered Tella trying to leave the isle.

The morning mist hadn't burned off yet. Scarlett lost sight of her sister multiple times, as Tella ventured into the foggiest corridors. For a moment Scarlett imagined she'd lost her completely. Then Scarlett glimpsed a sliver of a blue dress, heading up a set of stairs to the highest point of the Dragna estate—the priests' confessional. A tall tower built out of white stones that gleamed in the sun, so everyone from town could see. Governor Dragna liked people to think he was a pious man, though in truth he would never declare his dirty deeds to someone else, making this one of the few spots on the isle where he rarely ventured—perfect for smuggling covert letters.

Scarlett picked up her pace at the top of the stairs, finally catching up to her sister in the half-moon courtyard right outside the carved wooden doors that led to the confessional.

"Stop," Scarlett called. "If you write to that sailor, I'm going to tell Father everything!"

The figure stilled immediately. Then it was Scarlett's turn to freeze, as the fog lifted and the girl turned around. Sharp sunlight streamed into the tiny courtyard, illuminating a young novice dressed in blue. With her head covered by a scarf, she had only looked like Tella.

Scarlett had to give her devious sister credit for being good at evasion. As sweat dripped down the nape of her neck, Scarlett imagined Tella pilfering supplies somewhere else on the estate, preparing to leave with Julian the following day.

Scarlett needed another way to stop her.

Tella would hate her for a while, but Scarlett couldn't let her sister lose everything for Caraval. Not when Scarlett's marriage could save them both—or destroy them if it didn't happen.

Scarlett followed the young novice into the confessional. Small and round, it was always so quiet, Scarlett could hear the candles flicker. Thick and dripping, they lined the stone walls, illuminating tapestries of saints in various states of agony, while dust and dried flowers created a stale aroma. Scarlett's nose itched as she walked past a row of wooden pews. At the end of them, papers for writing down one's sins rested on an altar.

Before her mother disappeared, seven years ago, Scarlett had never been inside this place. She didn't even know that to confess, people scribed their ill deeds on paper, then handed them to the priests, who set the notes on fire. Like her father, Scarlett's mother, Paloma, had not been religious. But after Paloma had vanished from Trisda, Scarlett and her sister had felt desperate, and with nowhere else to go they'd come here to pray for their mother's return.

Of course, those pleas had gone unanswered, but the priests were not entirely unhelpful; Scarlett and her sister had discovered they were very discreet about delivering messages.

Scarlett picked up a piece of sin paper and carefully penned a note.

I need to see you tonight.
Meet me at Del Ojos Beach.
One hour past midnight.
It's important.

Before handing it to a priest with a generous donation, Scarlett addressed the message, but she didn't sign it. Instead of her name, she drew a heart. She hoped that would be enough.

4

When Scarlett was eight, to keep her from the shore, her father's guards warned her about the sparkling black sand of Del Ojos Beach. "It's black because it's really the burnt remains of pirate skeletons," they said. And being eight, and slightly more foolish than now, she believed them.

For at least a year she didn't venture close enough to the beach to even see the sand. Eventually, Felipe, an older son of one of her father's kinder guards, revealed the truth—the sand was just sand and not the bones of pirates at all. But the lie had already buried itself inside of Scarlett, as lies that children are told often do. It didn't matter how many other people confirmed the truth. In Scarlett's mind, the black sand of Del Ojos Beach would always be burnt pirate skeletons.

As she walked there in the night, the speckled blue moon winking eerie light over the unnatural sand, she thought back to that lie; she felt it sneaking into her slippers and moving between her toes as she neared Del Ojos's rocky black cove. To her right, the beach ended at a jagged, black cliff face. To her left, a broken dock like a massive tongue jutted into the water, past stones that reminded Scarlett of uneven teeth. It was the kind of night where she could smell the moon, thick candle wax dancing with the salty scent of the ocean, full and glowing.

She thought of the mysterious tickets in her pocket as the smoldering moon reminded her of how their metallic scripts blazed earlier that day. For a moment she was tempted to change her mind, give in to her sister, and to the tiny part of her still capable of dreaming.

But she'd done that once before.

Felipe had booked them passage on a schooner.

She and Tella had only made it onto the boat's plank, and going that far had cost them so much. One of the guards had been especially rough with Tella, knocking her out as he dragged her back to the estate. But Scarlett had stayed conscious as she was pulled off the dock. She was forced to stand on the edges of the rocky beach, where water from glowing blue tide pools sunk into her boots, and she watched as her father took Felipe into the ocean.

She should have been the one to drown that night. She should have been the one whose head her father held under the water. Held until her limbs stopped thrashing and her body went as still and lifeless as the seaweed that washed onto the shore. Later people believed Felipe had drowned accidentally; only Scarlett knew the truth.

"If you ever do something like this again, your sister will suffer the same fate," her father warned.

Scarlett never told a soul. She guarded Tella by letting her believe she'd just become extremely overprotective. Scarlett was the only one who knew they could never safely leave Trisda unless she had a husband who could ferry them away.

Waves clapped against the shore, muffling the sound of footsteps, but Scarlett heard them.

"You were not the sister I was expecting." Julian strolled closer. In the dark he looked more like a pirate than an ordinary sailor, and he moved with the practiced ease of someone Scarlett felt it would be unwise to trust. The night dyed his long coat an inky black, while shadows lined his cheekbones, turning them sharp as two knife-edges.

Scarlett now debated how wise it was to risk sneaking off the estate to meet this boy so late at night on such a secluded strip of beach. This was the sort of wild, reckless behavior she was always warning Tella about.

"I'm guessing you've changed your mind about my offer?" he asked.

"No, but I have a counteroffer for you." Scarlett tried to sound bold as she pulled out the elegant tickets from Caraval Master Legend. Her fingers did not want to release them, but she had to do this for Tella. When Scarlett had gone back to her own room earlier that evening, it had been ransacked. It was such a disaster, Scarlett hadn't been able to discern exactly what her sister had made off with, but Tella had obviously been thieving things to prepare for this ill-fated voyage.

Scarlett thrust her tickets toward Julian. "You can have all three. Use them or sell them, as long as you leave here early, and without Donatella."

"Ah, so it's a bribe."

Scarlett didn't like that word. She associated it too much with her father. But when it came to Tella, she'd do whatever she had to, even if it meant giving up the last thing she still dreamed about. "My sister is impulsive. She wants to leave with you, but she has no idea how dangerous it is. If our father catches her, he will do far worse than he did today."

"But she'll be safe if she stays here?" Julian's voice was low, slightly mocking.

"When I get married I plan to take her with me."

"But does she want to go with you?"

"She'll thank me for it later."

Julian bared a wolfish smile, the whites of his teeth shining in the moonlight. "You know, that's exactly what your sister said to me earlier."

Scarlett's warning instincts kicked in too late. She turned at the sound of new footsteps. Tella stood behind her, her short frame covered in a dark cloak that made it seem as if she was part of the night. "I'm sorry to do this, but you're the one who taught me there's nothing more important than taking care of a sister."

Suddenly Julian clamped a cloth over Scarlett's face. Frantically she tried to push it away. Her feet kicked up black clouds of sand, but whatever potent potion laced the fabric worked its magic fast.

The world spun around Scarlett until she didn't know if her eyes were open or closed.

She was falling

falling

falling.

5

efore Scarlett lost all consciousness, a gentle hand stroked
her cheek. "It's better this way, sister. There's more to life
than staying safe. . . ."

Her words ushered Scarlett into a world that only existed in the delicate land of lucid dreaming.

As a room made of all windows came into view, she heard her
grandmother's voice. A pockmarked moon winked through the glass,
illuminating the figures inside with grainy blue light.

Younger versions of Scarlett and Tella, made of tiny hands and
innocent dreams, curled together in bed while their grandmother
tucked them in. Though the woman had spent more time with the
girls after their mother had left, Scarlett could not recall another
night she'd ever put them to bed; that was usually servants' work.

"Will you tell us about Caraval?" asked tiny Scarlett.

"I want to hear about Master Legend," chimed Tella. "Will you
tell us the story of how he got his name?"

Across from the bed, Nana perched upon a tufted chair as if it were a throne. Coils of black pearls circled her slender neck, while more covered her arms, all the way from her wrists to her elbows, as if they were lavish gloves. Her starched lavender gown was crease-less, adding more emphasis to the wrinkles etching her once-beautiful face.

"Legend came from the Santos family of performers," she began. "They were playwrights and actors, who all suffered from an unfortunate lack of talent. The only reason they had any success was because they were as beautiful as angels. And one son, Legend, was rumored to be the most handsome of all."

"But I thought Legend wasn't his real name," said Scarlett.

"I can't tell you his original name," said Nana. "But, I can say, like all great—and terrible—stories, his started with love. Love for the elegant Annalise. With golden hair and words made of sugar. She bewitched him as he'd done to so many girls before her: with compliments and kisses and promises he should have known better than to believe.

"Legend wasn't wealthy then. He mostly lived on charm and stolen hearts, and Annalise claimed it was enough for her, but that her father, a wealthy merchant, would never allow her to wed a pauper."

"So did they get married?" Tella asked.

"You'll find out if you keep listening," Nana tsked.

Behind her a cloud drifted over the moon, covering all but two tiny points of light, which hovered behind her silver hair like devils' horns.

"Legend had a plan," she continued. "Elantine was about to be crowned empress of the Meridian Empire, and if he could perform at her coronation, Legend believed it would bring him the fame and money he needed to marry Annalise. Only Legend was shamefully turned away, because of his lack of talent."

"I would have let him inside," said Tella.

"So would I," Scarlett agreed.

Nana frowned. "If you two don't stop interrupting, I'm not going to finish the story."

Scarlett and Tella puckered their lips into miniature pink hearts.

"Legend didn't have any magic then," Nana went on, "but he believed in the tales his father had told him. He'd heard every person gets one impossible wish—just one—if the person wants something more than anything, and they can find a bit of magic to help them along. So Legend went in search of a woman who had studied enchantments."

"She means a witch," Scarlett whispered.

Nana paused, and tiny Tella and little Scarlett's eyes grew as wide as saucers while the glass room transformed into the wooden walls of a triangular cabin. Nana's story was coming to life before their eyes. Yellow wax candles hung from the ceiling upside down, pouring creamy smoke in the wrong direction.

In the center of it all, a woman with hair as red as fury sat across from a boy made of lean lines, his head shaded by a dark top hat. *Legend.* Though Scarlett couldn't clearly see his face, she recognized his symbolic hat.

"The woman asked what he wanted most," Nana went on, "and

Legend told her he wished to lead the greatest troupe of players the world had ever seen, so that he could win his true love, Annalise. But the woman warned he could not have both things. He must pick only one.

"Legend was as prideful as he was handsome, and he believed she was wrong. He told himself if he were famous it would allow him to marry Annalise. So he wished for that. He said he wanted his performances to be legendary. Magical."

A breeze cut through the room, blowing out every candle but the one illuminating Legend. Scarlett could not clearly see his face, but she would have sworn something about him changed, as if he'd suddenly acquired an extra shadow.

"The transformation began right away," Nana explained. "Its magic was fueled by Legend's true desires, which were powerful indeed. The witch told him his performances would be transcendent, blending fantasy with reality in a way the world had never witnessed. But she also warned that wishes come with costs, and the more he performed, the more he would transform into whatever roles he played. If he acted the part of villain, he'd become one in truth."

"So does that mean he's a villain?" asked Tella.

"And what about Annalise?" Scarlett yawned.

Nana sighed. "The witch had not lied when she said Legend could not have fame and Annalise. After becoming Legend, he was no longer the same boy she fell in love with, so she married another and broke Legend's heart. He became just as famous as he'd wished, but he claimed Annalise betrayed him and he swore to never love again.

Some would probably call him a villain. Others would say his magic makes him closer to a god."

Both tiny Tella and little Scarlett were halfway on the path to sleep. Their eyelids were more closed than open, yet their mouths both moved into upturned crescent-moons. Tella's twisted at the word *villain*, but Scarlett smiled at the mention of Legend's magic.

6

carlett woke with the feeling she'd lost something significant. Unlike most days, where her eyes opened reluctantly
and she took her time stretching each limb before easing
out of bed and cautiously looking around, on this day,
Scarlett sat up the moment her eyes flickered open.

Beneath her, the world rocked.

"Careful, there." Julian steadied her, reaching out to catch her
before she tried to stand up in the boat—if the tiny tub they were in
could properly be called a boat. A raft was a more appropriate name.
It was barely large enough for the two of them.

"How long have I been asleep?" Scarlett gripped the edges of the
vessel as the rest of her surroundings came into focus.

Across from her, Julian dipped two oars into the water, careful
not to splash her, as he rowed through an unfamiliar sea. The water
almost looked pink, with small swirls of turquoise that swelled as the
copper sun crept higher into the sky.

It was morning, although Scarlett imagined more than one dawn had passed while she'd slept. Julian's face had been smooth when she'd last seen him, but now his jaw and chin appeared to be covered in at least two days of dark stubble. He looked even more disreputable than when he'd flashed that wolfish grin on the beach.

"You blackguard!" Scarlett slapped him in the face.

"Ow! What was that for?" A ruby welt bloomed across his cheek. The color of rage and punishment.

Horror filled Scarlett at what she had done. On occasion she had trouble taming her tongue, but she'd never struck another person. "I'm sorry! I didn't mean to do that!" She clutched the edges of her bench, bracing for him to strike back.

But the hit she expected never came.

Julian's cheek was a blaze of angry red, his jaw nothing but a series of tight lines, yet he didn't touch her.

"You don't need to be afraid of me. I've never hit a woman." He stopped rowing and looked her in the eyes. Unlike the come-hither gaze he'd worn inside the barrel room, or the predatory look she'd seen on the beach, he now made no attempts to charm or scare her. Beneath his hard appearance, Scarlett could see the ghost of the expression he'd worn as he had watched her father strike Tella. Julian had looked as appalled as Scarlett had been terrified.

On his cheek, the imprint of her hand was fading, and as it disappeared Scarlett could feel some of her terror slip away. Not everyone reacted like her father.

Scarlett's fingers unclenched from the sides of the boat, though her hands still felt a little shaky.

"I'm sorry," she managed again. "But you and Tella should have never—wait." Scarlett stopped. The awful feeling she'd lost something vital flooded back. And that something had honey-blond hair and a cherub's face with a devil's grin. "Where is Tella?"

Julian dipped his oars back in the water, and this time he did splash Scarlett. Icy drops of wet sprayed all over her lap.

"If you've done something to Tella, I swear—"

"Relax, Crimson—"

"It's Scarlett."

"Same difference. And your sister is fine. You'll find her on the isle." Julian tipped an oar toward their destination.

Scarlett was prepared to keep arguing, but when her eyes caught sight of where the sailor pointed, whatever she intended to say melted like warm butter on top of her tongue.

The isle on the horizon looked nothing like her familiar Trisda. Where Trisda was black sand, rocky coves, and sickly looking shrubs, this bit of earth was lush and alive. Glittering mist swirled around vibrant green mountains—all covered in trees—that rose toward the sky as if they were massive emeralds. From the top of the largest peak an iridescent blue waterfall streamed down like melted peacock feathers, disappearing into the ring of sunrise-tinted clouds that pirouetted around the surreal isle.

Isla de los Sueños.

The island of dreams. Scarlett had never heard of the isle before seeing its name on the tickets to Caraval, yet she knew without asking that she stared at it now. *Legend's private island.*

"You're lucky you slept on the way here. The rest of our voyage wasn't this scenic." Julian said it as if he'd done her a favor. Yet no matter how beguiling this isle was, thoughts of another isle weighed heavy on her mind.

"How far are we from Trisda?" she asked.

"We're somewhere between the Conquered Isles and the Southern Empire," Julian answered lazily, as if they were merely strolling on the beach next to her father's estate.

In reality, this was the farthest she'd ever been away from home. Scarlett's eyes stung as a spray of salt water hit them. "How many days have we been gone?"

"It's the thirteenth. But before you hit me again, you should know your sister bought you time by making it seem as if both of you were kidnapped."

Scarlett recalled the destructive way Tella had gone through all her things, leaving her room in shambles. "That's why my room was such a mess?"

"She also left a ransom note," Julian added. "So, when you return, you should be able to wed your count and live *happily ever after.*"

Scarlett admitted her sister was clever. But if their father figured out the truth, he'd be livid—especially with her wedding only a week away. The image of a purple, fire-breathing dragon came to mind, coating her vision with ashy shades of anxiety.

But maybe a visit to this isle is worth the risk. The wind seemed to whisper the words, reminding her that the thirteenth was also the date on Legend's invitation. *Anyone who arrives later than this will not be able to participate in the game, or win this year's prize of one wish.*

Scarlett tried not to be enticed, but the child inside her drank in this new world greedily. The colors here were brighter, thicker, sharper; in comparison, every hue she'd seen before seemed thin and malnourished.

The clouds took on a baked bronze glimmer the closer they drew to the isle, as if they were on the edge of catching fire rather than expelling rain. It made her think of Caraval Master Legend's letter, how its gilded edges almost seemed to flame when they captured the light. She knew she needed to return home immediately, but the promise of what she might find on Legend's private isle tempted her, like those precious early morning moments, when Scarlett could either wake up and face the ruthless reality of day, or keep her eyes closed and continue to dream of lovely things.

But beauty could be deceiving, as evidenced by the boy who sat across from her, rowing their raft smoothly through the water, as if kidnapping girls was something he did every day.

"Why is Tella already on the isle?" Scarlett asked.

"Because this boat only holds two at a time." Julian splashed Scarlett again with his oar. "You should be grateful I came back for you after I dropped her off."

"I never asked you to take me in the first place."

"But you did spend seven years writing to *Legend*?"

Heat rose to Scarlett's cheeks. Not only had those letters been something private she'd shared solely with Tella, but the mocking way Julian said Legend's name made Scarlett feel foolish, as indeed she had been for so many years. A child who'd yet to realize that most fairy tales did not end happily.

"It's nothing to be ashamed of," Julian said. "I'm sure lots of young women write him letters. You've probably heard that he never ages. And I've heard he has a way of making people fall in love with him."

"It wasn't like that," Scarlett argued. "There was nothing romantic about my letters. I just wanted to experience the magic."

Julian narrowed his eyes as if he didn't believe her. "If that's true, why don't you want it anymore?"

"I don't know what else my sister has told you, but I would think you saw what was at stake the other day in the barrel room. When I was younger, I wanted to experience Caraval. Now I just want my sister and me to be safe."

"Don't you think your sister wants the same thing?" Julian stopped rowing and let the boat drift over a gentle wave. "I may not know her well, but I don't think she has a death wish."

Scarlett disagreed.

"I think you've forgotten how to live, and your sister is trying to remind you," Julian went on. "But if all you want is *safety*, I'll take you back."

Julian nodded to a speck in the distance that resembled a smallish fishing boat. Most likely the vessel they'd used to travel there, since their current raft was obviously not built to combat the seas.

"Even if you don't know two coins about sailing, it shouldn't take you long to get picked up by someone else and returned to your precious Trisda. Or"—Julian paused and nodded toward the misty white isle—"if you're as brave as your sister keeps telling me, you can let me keep rowing. You spend this week with her on this isle, and see if she's right about some things being worth more than safety."

A wave rocked the boat, lapping turquoise water against its sides as they drifted into the isle's ring of chilly clouds. Scarlett's hair stuck to the back of her neck as Julian's dark locks curled into waves.

"You don't understand," she said. "If I wait to go back to Trisda, my father will destroy me. I'm supposed to wed a count in one week, and this marriage is our opportunity at another life. I'd love to experience Caraval, but I'm not willing to risk my only chance at happiness."

"That's a very dramatic way of looking at things." The side of Julian's mouth twitched, as if he were suppressing a smirk. "I might be wrong, but most marriages aren't pure bliss."

"That's not what I said." Scarlett hated how he kept twisting her words.

Julian dipped his oar in the water, just enough to splash her again.

"Stop doing that!"

"I'll stop when you tell me where you want to go." He splashed her once more as the boat sailed closer to the shore, and the brassy clouds began to tarnish, turning shades of green and chilly blue.

There was a scent in the air Scarlett had never experienced. Trisda always stank of fish, but the air here was mostly sweet with a bit of tangy citrus. She wondered if it was drugged, for although she knew what she needed to do—get to the isle, find Tella, and then return home as soon as possible—she was having a difficult time telling Julian this. Suddenly she was nine years old again, naive and hopeful enough to believe a letter could make her wishes come true.

She'd first written after her mother, Paloma, had abandoned

them. She'd wanted to give Tella a happy birthday. Her sister had been the most devastated when their mother left. Scarlett had tried to make up for Paloma's absence. But Scarlett was young, and Tella wasn't the only one who desperately missed their mother.

It would have been easier to let her go if she'd at least said good-bye, written a note, or left a tiny hint as to where or why she'd gone. But Paloma had simply vanished, taking nothing with her. She'd disappeared like a broken star, leaving the world untouched, save for the bits of missing light that no one would ever see again.

Scarlett might have wondered if her father had harmed her mother, but he'd gone rabid once Paloma had left him. Torn up the entire estate looking for her. Had his guards raid the towns under the guise of searching for a criminal, since he'd not wanted anyone to discover his wife had run away. If she'd been kidnapped, there were no signs of struggle, and no ransom note ever arrived. It seemed she'd chosen to leave, which made it all the worse.

Yet despite everything, Scarlett always thought of her mother as a magical person, full of glittering smiles, musical laughter, and dulcet words; when she'd been on Trisda there'd been joy in Scarlett's world, and her father had been softer. Governor Dragna had not been violent toward his family before Paloma had left him.

Scarlett's nana had taken more of an interest in the girls after that. She wasn't particularly warm. Scarlett always suspected she didn't actually like small children, but she told exquisite stories. She enchanted both Tella and Scarlett with her tales of Caraval. She said it was a place where magic lived, and Scarlett fell in love with the idea of it, daring to believe that if Legend and his players came to the isle of Trisda, they would return some of the joy to her life, at least for a handful of days.

Momentarily, Scarlett entertained the idea of experiencing not only a little happiness, but magic. She thought of what it would be like to enjoy Caraval just for a day, to explore Legend's private isle, before closing the door on her fantasies completely.

There was one week until Scarlett's wedding. This was not the time to embark on a foolhardy adventure. Tella had plundered Scarlett's room, and Julian said she'd also left a ransom note, but Scarlett's father would eventually figure out it was all a hoax. Staying here was the worst idea possible.

But if Scarlett and Tella stayed only for the first day of Caraval, they could make it back in time for Scarlett's wedding. Scarlett doubted her father would figure out the truth about where they'd been that soon. They'd be safe, as long as she and Tella remained for only the first twenty-four hours, and their father never found out where they'd really been.

"Time's almost up, Crimson."

The cloud encasing them thinned, and the rim of the isle came into view. Scarlett saw sand so fluffy and white, from the distance, it looked like icing on a cake. She could almost picture Tella running her fingers along it—and coaxing Scarlett to join her—to see if the sand tasted as sugary as it looked.

"If I go with you, do you promise there will be no more kidnapping attempts if I try to return to Trisda with Tella tomorrow?"

Julian put a hand to his heart. "On my honor."

Scarlett wasn't sure she believed Julian had much honor. But once they all made it inside Caraval, he'd probably abandon them anyway.

"You can start your rowing back up again. Just be careful with the splashing."

The corner of Julian's lips curved as he dipped his oars back in the water, this time soaking Scarlett's slippers with cold.

"I told you to stop splashing me."

"That wasn't me." Julian rowed again, more carefully this time, but water still soaked her feet. It was colder than even Trisda's crisp coast.

"I think there's a hole in the boat."

Julian cursed as water moved up to their ankles. "You know how to swim?"

"I live on an island. Of course I know how to swim."

Julian shucked his coat and tossed it over the side of the boat. "If you take off your clothes it will be easier. You're wearing some sort of undergarment, right?"

"Are you sure we can't just row to shore?" Scarlett argued. Although cold drenched her feet, her hands were sweating. Isla de los Sueños appeared to be about one hundred yards away; it was farther than she'd ever swum.

"We can give it a go, but this boat is not going to make it." Julian removed his boots. "We're better off using the time we have to undress. The water's cold; it'll be impossible to make it fully clothed."

Scarlett scanned the cloud-covered water for another sign of a boat or raft. "But what will we wear when we're on the island?"

"I think we just need to worry about making it to the island. And by 'we,' I mean you." Julian unbuttoned his shirt, revealing a row of brown muscles that made it clear he'd have no problems in the water.

Then without another word, he dove into the ocean.

He didn't look back. His strong arms cut through the icy current with ease, while arctic water rose around Scarlett until the bottom half of her dress floated about her calves. She attempted to row, but only succeeded in sinking the boat deeper.

She had no choice but to jump.

The air rushed out of her lungs, something cold and unbreathable taking its place. All she could see was the color white. Everything was white. Even the tones of the water had shifted from swirls of pink and turquoise to frightening shades of icy white. Scarlett bobbed her head to the surface, gasping for air that seared as it went down.

She tried to push against the current with the same ease as Julian, but he'd been right. The corset binding her chest was too tight; the heavy fabric around her legs kept tangling. She frantically kicked, but it did no good. The more Scarlett fought, the more the ocean battled back. She could barely keep above the surface. A wave of cold splashed over her head, dragging her all the way down. So cold and heavy. Her lungs burned as she battled to reach the surface again. This must have been how Felipe felt when her father drowned him. *You deserve this*, said a part of her. Like hands, the water pressed her down

down

down. . . .

"I thought you could swim." Julian wrenched Scarlett up until her head broke the surface of the water.

"Breathe. Slowly," he coaxed. "Don't try to take in too much at once."

The air still burned, but Scarlett managed the words: "You left me."

"Because I thought you could swim."

"It's my dress—" Scarlett broke off as she felt it dragging her down once more.

Julian took a sharp breath. "You think you can stay afloat for a minute without my help?"

He brandished a knife with his free hand, and before Scarlett could agree or protest, he darted under the water.

Scarlett felt as if forever went by before she felt the pressure of Julian's arm wrapping around her waist. Then, the tip of his knife pressed against her breasts. Scarlett's breath caught as the sailor cut away her corset, drawing a decisive line down her stomach to the center of her hips. The arm around her waist tightened, and so did something in Scarlett's chest. She'd never been in such a position with a boy. She tried not to think about what Julian was seeing or feeling as he finished slicing the heavy dress and pulled it off her body, leaving only her wet chemise clinging to her skin.

Julian gasped as he resurfaced, splashing Scarlett's face with water.

"Can you swim now?" His words were more labored than before.

"Can you?" Scarlett asked hoarsely, her ability to speak strained as well. It felt as if something very intimate had just happened, or maybe it was intense only for her. She imagined the sailor had seen lots of girls in various states of undress.

"We're wasting our energy with talk." Julian started swimming, this time staying close to her side, though she couldn't tell if it was because he worried about her safety, or if he was weak from helping her.

Scarlett could still feel the ocean working to drag her under, but without her heavy gown, she could fight it. She neared Sueños's gleaming white shore at the same time as Julian. Up close the sand looked fluffier. Fluffier, and now that she thought about it, much more like snow. More than she'd ever seen on Trisda. Resting clouds of magical white, a cold carpet stretched across the entire shore.

All eerily untouched.

"Don't give up on me now." Julian grabbed Scarlett's hand, tugging her toward the perfect tufts of white. "Come on, we need to keep moving."

"Wait—" Scarlett scanned the crisp snow a second time. Again it reminded her of a frosted cake. The kind she'd seen in bakery windows, perfect and smooth, without so much as a Tella-size footprint in the snow.

"Where's my sister?"

7

The island's gauzy clouds had sailed into a position covering the sun and casting the coastline in a haze of gray-blue shadows. No longer white, the untouched snow at Scarlett's feet winked up at her with periwinkle sparkles, as if it were in on some private joke.

"Where's Tella?" Scarlett repeated.

"I must have dropped her off on a different part of the beach." Julian reached for Scarlett's hand again, but she pulled away. "We need to keep moving or we're both going to freeze. Once we warm up, we can find your sister."

"But what if she's freezing too? Dona—tella!" Scarlett yelled between chattering teeth. The snow beneath her toes and the wet fabric clinging to her icy skin left her colder than she had been the night her father made her sleep outside after he discovered Tella had kissed her first boy. Still, Scarlett was not going to leave without finding her sister. "Donatella!"

"You're wasting your breath." Dripping wet and shirtless, Julian looked more dangerous than usual as he glared at Scarlett. "When I dropped your sister off, she was dry. She had on a coat and gloves. Wherever she is, she's not going to freeze, but we will if we stay here. We should head for whatever's between those trees."

Past where the beach's mantle of snow met lines of thick green trees, a spire of sunset-orange smoke twisted into the sky. Scarlett could have sworn it hadn't been there a minute ago. She didn't even remember seeing the trees. Different from the bony shrubs on Trisda, all of these trunks looked like thick braids, twisted together and covered in snowy blue-and-green moss.

"No—" Scarlett shivered. "We—"

"We can't keep walking around like this," Julian cut her off. "Your lips are turning purple. We need to locate the smoke."

"I don't care. If my sister is still out there—"

"Your sister probably left to find the entrance to the game. We have only until the end of the day to make it inside Caraval, which means we should follow the smoke, and then do the same." He marched ahead, bare feet crunching the snow.

Scarlett's eyes darted around the untouched beach a final time. Tella had never been good at patiently waiting—or even impatiently waiting. But if she had gone into Caraval, why were there no signs of her?

Reluctantly, Scarlett followed Julian into the forest. Bits of piney needles stuck to toes she could no longer feel as a chestnut dirt path replaced the snow. But while her feet left damp footprints, she saw no marks from Tella's heeled boots.

"She probably took a different route from the beach." Julian's teeth didn't chatter, yet his brown skin was taking on an indigo hue, matching the trees' distorted shadows.

Scarlett wanted to argue, but the wet fabric of her clothes was turning to ice. The forest was colder than the coastline had been. She wrapped frigid arms across her chest, but all that did was add to her chill.

A flicker of concern crossed Julian's features. "We need to get you somewhere warm."

"But my sister—"

"—is smart enough to already be inside the game. If you freeze out here you're not going to find her." Julian's arm wrapped around Scarlett's shoulders.

She stiffened.

His dark brows formed an offended line. "I'm just trying to keep you warm."

"But you're freezing too—" *And practically naked.*

Scarlett pulled away, half stumbling, as the forest of trees came to an end and the soft dirt floor transformed into a firmer road paved with opalescent stones, smooth as polished sea glass. The cobbled road stretched farther than she could see, multiplying into a maze of twisting streets. All were lined with mismatched, rounded shops, painted shades of jewels or pastels, and piled on top of one another like sloppily stacked hatboxes.

It was charming and enchanting, but it was also unnaturally still. The shops were all closed and the snow on their rooftops rested like dust on abandoned storybooks. Scarlett didn't know what sort of place this was, but it was not how she imagined Caraval.

Sunset smoke still streamed in the air, but it looked as far away as when they were on the beach.

"Crimson, we need to keep moving." Julian urged her down the curious street.

Scarlett didn't know if it was possible for the cold to make her hallucinate, or if there was just something wrong with her head. On top of being strangely quiet, none of the signs on the hatbox-shaped shops made any sense. Each was printed in a variety of languages. Some said *Open: Sometime Around Midnight.* Other signs said *Come Back Yesterday.*

"Why is everything closed?" she asked. Her words came out in fragile puffs. "And where is everyone?"

"We just need to keep going. Don't stop walking. We need to find somewhere warm." Julian pressed forward, past the most peculiar shops Scarlett had ever seen.

There were bowler hats covered in taxidermy crows. Parasol holsters. Women's headbands studded with human teeth. Mirrors that could reflect the darkness in a person's soul. The cold was definitely toying with her vision. She hoped Julian was right and Tella was someplace warm. Scarlett continued searching for glimpses of her sister's honey-blond hair, listening for echoes of her vibrant giggles, but every store was empty, silent.

Julian tried a few doorknobs; nothing budged.

The following row of abandoned shops boasted a series of fantastical things. Fallen stars. Seeds to grow wishes. Odette's Ocular sold eyeglasses that saw the future. (*Available in four colors.*) "Those would be nice," Scarlett muttered.

Next door to Odette's, a banner claimed its shop proprietor could fix broken imaginations. That message floated above bottles of dreams and nightmares and something called *daymares*, which Scarlett imagined she was experiencing that moment as icicles formed in her dark hair.

Beside her Julian cursed. Beyond several more blocks of hatbox-shaped shops, they could almost see where the smoke came from, and now it was twisting into a sun with a star inside and a teardrop inside of the star—the symbol for Caraval. But the cold had reached into Scarlett's bones and her teeth; even her eyelids were turning frosty.

"Wait—what—about there!" With a trembling hand, Scarlett waved Julian toward Casabian's Clocks. At first she thought it was just the brass window lining, but behind the glass, past a forest of pendulums and weights and shiny wooden cabinets, a fireplace blazed. And a sign on the door said *Always Open*.

A chorus of tick-tocks, cuckoos, second hands, and windup gears greeted the frozen couple as they dashed inside. Limbs Scarlett had stopped feeling prickled from the sudden warmth, while the heated air scorched her lungs as it went down.

Her frozen vocal chords cracked as she called, "Hello?"

Tick-tock.

Tock-tick.

Only gears and cogs answered back.

The shop was round, like a clock's face. The floor was tiled in a mosaic of different styles of numbers, while various timepieces covered almost every surface. Some ran backward; others were full of exposed wheels and levers. On the back wall several moved like puzzles with their pieces drawing together as the hour approached. A heavy glass locked box in the center of the open room claimed that the pocket watch inside wound back time. Another day Scarlett would have been curious, but all she cared about was getting closer to the roaring circle of warmth coming from the fireplace.

She would have gladly melted into a puddle in front of it.

Julian pulled the grate away and stoked the logs with a nearby poker. "We should get out of our clothes."

"I—" Scarlett stopped her protest when Julian crossed over to a rosewood grandfather clock. Two sets of boots rested at its feet and two hangers of garments were swinging from the pediments on each side.

"Looks like *someone* is watching out for you." The mocking lilt had returned to Julian's voice.

Scarlett tried to ignore it as she inched closer. Next to the clothes, on top of a gilded table covered in moon dials, a curvy vase of red roses sat next to a tray laden with fig bread, cinnamon tea, and a note.

For Scarlett Dragna, and her companion.

I'm so pleased you could make it.

—Legend

The message was written on the same gold-edged paper as the letter Scarlett had received on Trisda. She wondered if Legend went to such pains for all his guests. It was difficult for Scarlett to believe she was special, yet she couldn't imagine the master of Caraval bestowed personalized greetings and bloodred roses upon every visitor.

Julian coughed. "Do you mind?" The sailor reached past Scarlett, pulled off a hunk of bread, and yanked down the set of clothes meant for him. Then he started undoing the belt holding up his pants. "You going to watch me undress, because I don't mind."

Immediately embarrassed, Scarlett looked away. He had no decency.

She needed to dress as well, but there was no place to do it safely concealed. It seemed impossible that the room had grown smaller since they'd arrived, yet she could now see how truly minuscule it was. Less than ten feet of space lay between her and the front door. "If you turn your back to me, we can both change."

"We can both change facing each other too." There was a smile in his voice now.

"That's not what I meant," Scarlett said.

Julian chuckled under his breath. But when Scarlett brought her head up, his back was to her. She tried not to stare. Every inch of it was muscled, just as his torso had been, but that wasn't the only part that captivated her attention. A thick scar disfigured the space between his shoulder blades. Two more crossed his lower back. As if someone had stabbed him multiple times.

Scarlett swallowed a gasp and felt instantly guilty. She shouldn't have been looking. Hastily she grabbed the clothes meant for her and focused on dressing. She tried not to imagine what could have happened to him. She wouldn't want anyone seeing her scars.

Mostly her father just left bruises, but for years she'd dressed herself without the help of a maid so no one would see. She had imagined that experience would come in handy now, but the dress Legend left her would require no assistance; it was rather plain, disappointing. The opposite of how she'd imagined clothes from Caraval. There was no corset. The bodice fabric was an unappealing shade of beige, with a flat skirt. No petticoats or underskirts or bustles.

"Can I turn around now?" Julian asked. "It's nothing I haven't seen before."

The firm way he'd gripped her waist while he'd sliced off her dress instantly came to mind, making her tingle from her breastbone down to her hips. "Thank you for that reminder."

"I wasn't talking about you. I barely even saw your—"

"Not making it better. But you can turn around," she said. "I'm buttoning my boots."

When Scarlett looked up, Julian was in front of her, and Legend definitely had not given him an unattractive set of clothes.

Scarlett's eyes traveled from the midnight-blue cravat around his throat to the fitted burgundy waistcoat it tucked into. A deep-blue tailcoat emphasized strong shoulders and a narrow waist. The only item reminiscent of the sailor was the knife belt slung over the hips of his slender pants.

"You look—different," Scarlett said. "It no longer appears as though you've just come from a brawl."

Julian stood a little straighter, as if she'd complimented him, and

STEPHANIE GARBER

Scarlett wasn't sure she hadn't. It didn't seem fair that someone so infuriating could look so close to perfect. Although despite his crisp clothes, he still appeared far from gentlemanly—and it wasn't just his unshaven face or the choppy waves of his brown hair. There was simply something wild about Julian that could not be tamed by Legend's garments. The sharp planes of his face, the shrewd look in his brown eyes—they weren't minimized because he now wore a cravat, or . . . a pocket watch?

"Did you steal that?" Scarlett asked.

"Borrowed," Julian corrected, twirling the chain around his finger. "Same as the clothes you have on." He looked her over and nodded approvingly. "I can see why he sent *you* tickets."

"What's that supposed to me—" Scarlett broke off as she caught her reflection in the glass of a mirrored clock. No longer dull shades of bland, the dress was now a rich cerise—the color of seduction and secrets. A stylish row of bows ran down the center of a fitted bodice with a scooped neck, set off by a matching ruffled bustle. The skirts beneath were scalloped and fitted to her form, five slender tiers of different fabrics, alternating between cerise silk and tulle, and bits of black lace. Even her boots had changed, from dull brown to an elegant combination of matching black leather and lace.

She ran her hands over the material of her dress to make sure it wasn't just a trick of the mirror or the light. Or maybe in her frozen state she'd only thought the dress had been drab before. But deep down Scarlett knew there was only one explanation. Legend had given her an enchanted gown.

Magic like this was only supposed to live in stories, but this dress was very real, leaving Scarlett unsure what to think. The child inside her loved it; the grown-up Scarlett wasn't sure she felt quite comfortable in it—whether it was magical or not. Her father would never have let her wear something so eye-catching, and even though he wasn't there, attention was still not a thing she craved.

Scarlett was a pretty girl, though she often liked to hide it. She'd inherited her mother's thick dark hair, which complemented her olive skin. Her face was more of an oval than Tella's, with a petite nose and hazel eyes so large she always felt they gave away too much.

For a moment she almost wished for the drab beige frock. No one noticed girls in ugly clothes. Maybe if she thought about it, the dress would shift again. But even as she visualized a simpler cut and a plainer color, the cherry gown remained vibrant and tight, clinging to curves she'd rather have concealed.

Julian's cryptic words came to mind—*I can see why he sent you tickets*—and Scarlett wondered if she'd found a way to escape her father's deadly games on Trisda, only to become a well-costumed piece on a new game board.

"If you're finished admiring yourself," said Julian, "should we search for that sister you're so eager to find?"

"I would think you'd be worried about her as well," said Scarlett.

"Then you think too highly of me." Julian started toward the door as every chime in the shop rang out.

"You might not want to exit that way," said an unfamiliar voice.

8

The rotund man who had just entered the shop looked a bit like a clock himself. The mustache on his dark, round face stretched out like a minute and hour hand. His shiny brown frock coat reminded Scarlett of polished wood, his brass suspenders of cable pulleys.

"We weren't stealing," Scarlett said. "We—"

"You should only speak for yourself." The man's baritone voice fell several octaves as he focused two narrowed eyes on Julian.

From dealing with her father, Scarlett knew it was best not to appear guilty.

Don't look at Julian.

Yet she couldn't help but glance.

"I knew it!" said the man.

Julian reached for Scarlett, as if to push her toward the door.

"Oh no, don't run out! I'm only kidding," the stranger called. "I'm not Casabian, I'm not the owner! I'm Algie, and I don't care if your pockets are stuffed with clocks."

"Then why are you trying to stop us from leaving?" Julian's hands were on his belt, one reaching for his knife.

"This boy's a bit paranoid, isn't he?" Algie turned to Scarlett, but she was feeling sage-shaded colors of suspicion as well. Was it just her, or were the clocks on the wall ticking faster than before?

"Come on," she said to Julian. "Tella's probably worried to death about us by now."

"You'll find whoever you're looking for faster this way." Algie stepped over to the rosewood grandfather clock, opened its glass door, and tugged on one of its weights. As he did, the metallic puzzle clocks on the wall shifted. *Click. Clack.* Their pieces snapped together, rearranging into a magnificent patchwork door with a notched count wheel in place of a handle.

Algie waved an arm theatrically. "Today only! For a bargain price the two of you can use this entrance—a shortcut into the heart of Caraval."

"How do we know it's not just an entry into your basement?" asked Julian.

"Does this feel like a door to a cellar? Look with all of your senses." Algie touched the door's notched wheel and at once every clock in the shop went quiet.

"If you leave this shop the other way, you'll be spit into the cold and you'll still have to pass through the gates. This will save you precious time." He released the handle and all the timepieces started moving once more.

Tick-tock. Tock-tick.

Scarlett wasn't sure she believed Algie, yet there was obviously something magical about the portal on the wall. It felt a bit like the dress she wore, as if it took up a little more space than everything else around it. And if it were a shortcut into Caraval, then she would find her sister faster. "What will it cost us?"

Julian's dark brows slanted up. "You're actually considering his offer?"

"If it will get us to my sister faster." Scarlett would have expected the sailor to be all for shortcuts, but instead his eyes darted around almost nervously. "You think it's a bad idea?" she asked.

"I think the smoke we saw is the entrance to Caraval, and I'd rather keep my currency." He reached for the front door.

"But you don't even know the price," said Algie.

Julian threw a look at Scarlett, pausing for the click of a second hand. Something unreadable flickered in his eyes, and when he spoke again she would have sworn his voice sounded strained. "Do whatever you want, Crimson, but just a friendly warning for when you do get inside: be careful who you trust; most of the people here aren't who they appear." A bell chimed as he stepped outside.

Scarlett hadn't expected him to stay with her forever, yet she found herself more than a little bit unnerved by his abrupt departure.

"Wait—" Algie called as she started to follow. "I know you believe me. Are you just going to chase that boy and let him decide for you, or make a choice for yourself?"

Scarlett knew she needed to leave. If she didn't hurry, she'd never find the sailor, and then she'd be utterly alone. But Algie's use of the word *choice* made her pause. With her father always telling her what to do, Scarlett rarely felt as if she had any genuine choices. Or maybe she paused because the part of her that had not quite let go of all her childhood fantasies wanted to believe Algie.

She thought of how effortlessly the door had formed and how every clock had gone silent when Algie had touched the door's peculiar handle. "Even if I was interested," she said, "I don't have any money."

"But what if I'm not asking for money?" Algie straightened the tips of his mustache. "I said I'm offering a bargain; I'd just like to borrow your voice."

Scarlett choked on nervous laughter. "That doesn't sound like a fair trade." *Was a voice even a thing someone could borrow?*

"I only want it for an hour," Algie said. "It will take you at least that long to follow the smoke and make it into the house and start the game, but I can let you inside right now." He pulled a watch from his pocket, and wound both the hour and minute hands to the top. "Say yes, and this device will take your voice for sixty minutes, and my door will lead you right inside the heart of Caraval."

She could find her sister right now.

But what if he was lying? What if he took more than an hour? Scarlett was uncomfortable trusting a man she'd just met, even more so after Julian's warning. The idea of losing her voice terrified her as well. Her cries had never stopped her father from hurting Tella, but at least Scarlett had always been able to call out. If she did this and something happened, she'd be powerless. If she saw Tella from a distance, she'd be unable to yell her name. And what if Tella was waiting for Scarlett at the gate?

Scarlett only knew how to survive through caution. When her

father made deals, there was almost always something awful he failed to mention. She couldn't risk that happening now.

"I'll take my chances with the regular entrance," she said.

Algie's mustache drooped. "Your loss. It really would have been a bargain." He pulled open the patchwork door. For a brilliant moment Scarlett glimpsed the other side: a passionate sky made of melting lemons and burning peaches. Thin rivers that shined like polished gemstones. A laughing girl with curly spires of honey—

"Donatella!" Scarlett rushed for the door, but Algie slammed it shut before her fingers grazed the metal.

"No!" Scarlett grabbed the notched wheel and tried to turn it, but it dissolved into ash, falling into a gloomy pile at her feet. She watched hopelessly as the puzzle pieces shifted again, clicking apart until the door was no more.

She should have made the trade. Tella would have done it. In fact, Scarlett figured that was how her sister had gotten inside in the first place. Tella never worried about the future or consequences; it was Scarlett's job to do that for her. So while she should have felt better knowing Tella was definitely in Caraval, Scarlett could only worry about what kinds of trouble her sister would find. Scarlett should have been in there with her. And now she had lost Julian as well.

Hurrying out of Casabian's shop, Scarlett rushed onto the street. Whatever warmth she'd felt inside immediately vanished. She hadn't thought she'd been there very long, yet the morning had already disappeared along with early afternoon. The hatbox shops were now obscured in a din of leaden shadows.

Time must move faster on this isle. Scarlett worried she would blink and the stars would be out. Not only had she been separated from Tella and Julian, but she'd wasted valuable minutes. The day was almost over, and Legend's invitation said she only had until midnight to make it inside Caraval's main gates.

Wind danced along Scarlett's arms, wrapping cold white fingers around the parts of her wrists her dress didn't cover. "Julian!" she cried out hopefully.

But there was no sign of her former companion. She was totally alone. She wasn't sure if the game had started yet, but she already felt as if she were losing.

For a panicked moment she thought the smoke had disappeared as well, but then she spied it again. Past the darkened storybook shops, sweet-smelling rings of it still made their way into the sky, rising out of a massive brick chimney, attached to one of the largest houses Scarlett had ever seen. Four stories high, with elegant turrets, balconies, and flower boxes full of bright and pretty things—white candytuft flowers, magenta poppies, tangerine snapdragons. All somehow untouched by the snow, which had started falling again.

Scarlett hurried toward the house, a new chill sliding over her as footsteps approached and she heard a low chuckle emerge from the flurry of white. "You didn't take Grandfather Clock up on his offer?"

Scarlett jumped.

"No need to be scared, Crimson, it's just me." Julian emerged from the shadows of a nearby building, just as the sun finished setting.

"Why haven't you gone in yet?" She pointed toward the turreted house. Half relieved not to be alone, half nervous to see the sailor again. A few minutes ago he'd rushed out of the clock shop. Now Julian sauntered closer as if he had all the time in the world.

His tone was warm and friendly when he said, "Maybe I was hoping you'd show up?"

But Scarlett found it difficult to believe he'd just been standing there, waiting for her, especially after the abrupt way he'd left her. There was something he wasn't telling her. Or maybe she was paranoid from having lost Tella in the clock shop. She told herself she'd be with her sister soon enough. But what if Scarlett couldn't find her once they were inside?

The wooden mansion appeared even larger close up, sprawling toward the sky as if its wooden beams still grew. Scarlett had to crane her neck to see the entirety of it. A fifty-foot-tall iron fence curled around it, formed into shapes both vulgar and innocent: They seemed to move, even to perform. Prancing girls being chased by naughty boys. Witches riding tigers and emperors atop elephants. Chariots pulled by winged horses. And in the center of it all hung a brilliant crimson banner embroidered with the silver symbol of Caraval.

If Tella were there they might have giggled together, the way only sisters could. Tella would have pretended not to be impressed, though secretly she would have been delighted. It was not the same with this strange sailor, who looked neither delighted nor impressed.

After how he'd helped her that day, Scarlett had to admit he wasn't quite the scoundrel he seemed, but she also doubted he was the simple sailor he appeared. He eyed the gate suspiciously, the set of his shoulders tense, the lines of his back rigidly straight. All of the laziness she'd witnessed on the boat had vanished; Julian was now a boxed coil, tightly wound as if preparing for some sort of fight.

"I think we should go farther down and look for a gate," he said.

"But see that flag?" Scarlett said. "This has to be where we get in."

"No, I think it's farther down. Trust me."

She didn't, but after her last blunder, she also didn't trust herself. And she didn't want to be left alone again. About twenty yards down they found another flag.

"This looks exactly like where we were before—"

"Welcome!" A dark-skinned girl on a unicycle pedaled out from behind the banner, cutting Scarlett off. "You're here just in time." The girl paused, and one by one, glass lanterns hanging from the tips of the gate lit up with flames. Brilliant gold-blue sparks—*the color of childhood dreams*, thought Scarlett.

"I always love it when that happens." The girl on the unicycle clapped. "Now, before I can let either of you fine people through, I need to see your tickets."

Tickets. Scarlett had forgotten all about the tickets. "Ah—"

"Don't worry, love, I have them." Julian placed an arm around Scarlett, tucking her unexpectedly close. And had he called her "love"?

"Go along with it, please," he whispered in her ear as he reached into his pocket and retrieved two slips of paper, both a little wilted and wrinkled from their dip in the ocean.

Scarlett held back from saying anything as her name appeared on the first. Then the unicyclist held the other note up to one of the gate's candlelit lanterns.

"That's unusual. We don't normally see tickets without names."

"Is there a problem?" Scarlett asked, suddenly uneasy.

The unicyclist looked down at Julian, and for the first time her bright demeanor faded.

Scarlett was about to explain how she'd received the tickets, but Julian broke in first, his arm pressing harder against her shoulders in what felt like a warning. "Caraval Master Legend sent it. The two of us are getting married. He gifted the tickets to my fiancée, Scarlett."

"Oh!" The cyclist clapped again. "I know all about the two of you! Master Legend's special guests." She looked at Scarlett more closely. "I should have recognized your name. I'm sorry. So many names, sometimes I forget mine." She laughed at her own joke.

Scarlett tried to muster a chuckle as well, but all she could think about was the arm wrapped around her and Julian's use of the word *fiancée*.

"You'll want to make sure you hold on to these." The unicyclist reached through the gate, passing the tickets back to Julian, and for a moment her eyes fastened on him as if there was something else she wanted to say. Then she seemed to think better of it. Breaking her gaze, she reached into the pocket of her patchwork vest and pulled out a scroll of black paper. "Now, before I can let you two in, there's one more thing." She quickened the pace of her pedaling, kicking up milky slivers of snow from the ground.

"This will be repeated again once you're inside. Master Legend likes everyone to hear it twice."

She cleared her throat and peddled even faster. "Welcome, welcome to Caraval! The grandest show on land or by sea. Inside you'll experience more wonders than most people see in a lifetime. You can sip magic from a cup and buy dreams in a bottle. But before you fully enter into our world, you must remember it's all a game. What happens beyond this gate may frighten or excite you, but don't let any of it trick you. We will try to convince you it's real, but all of it is a performance. A world built of make-believe. So while we want you to get swept away, be careful of being swept too far away. Dreams that come true can be beautiful, but they can also turn into nightmares when people won't wake up."

She paused, pedaling her cycle faster and faster until the spokes of the wheel seemed to disappear, vanishing in front of Scarlett's eyes as the wrought-iron gate parted.

"If you're here to play the game, you'll want to take this path." A curving lane to the girl's left lit up with puddles of burning silver wax that made the way glitter against the dark. "If you're here to watch . . ." She nodded right, and a sudden breeze swayed hanging paper lanterns to life, casting a pumpkin-orange glow above a sloping trail.

Julian dipped his head closer to Scarlett. "Don't tell me you're considering just watching."

"Of course not," Scarlett said, but she hesitated before taking a step in the other direction. She observed the candles flickering against the full night, the shadows hiding behind the darkened trees and flower bushes that lined the sparkling route into the game.

I'm only staying for a day, she reminded herself.

THE NIGHT OF
CARAVAL EVE

9

The sky was black, the moon visiting some other part of the world, as Scarlett took her first step into Caraval. Only a few rebel stars held posts above, watching as she and Julian crossed the threshold of the wrought-iron gate, into a realm that for some would only ever exist in wild stories.

While the rest of the universe had gone suddenly dark, the grand house blazed with light. Every window shimmered with buttery illumination, turning the flower boxes below into cradles full of stardust. The citrus scent from before was gone. Now the air was syrupy and thick, still much sweeter than the air on Trisda, yet Scarlett only tasted bitter.

She was too aware of Julian. Of the heavy weight of his arm around her shoulders, and the way he'd used that arm to sell his lies. She'd been too nervous to argue at the gate, too eager to get inside and find her sister. But now she wondered if she hadn't gotten herself into another mess.

"What was that all about?" she finally asked, pulling away when they were past the unicyclist but not quite at the mansion's great doors. She stopped right outside its ring of alluring light, next to a fountain, where its tinkling water would mute their words in case anyone else started down the path. "Why didn't you just tell the truth?"

"Truth?" Julian made a dark sound that wasn't quite a laugh. "I'm fairly certain she wouldn't have liked that."

"But you had a ticket?" Scarlett felt as if she were missing a joke.

"I'm guessing you think that girl seemed nice, and she would have eventually let me in." Julian took a meaningful step closer. "You cannot forget what I told you at the clock shop: most of the people here are not who they appear. That girl gave a performance, meant to make you drop your guard. They say they don't want us to get too carried away, but that is the point of this game. Legend likes to—play." The word rolled out unevenly, as if Julian had meant to say something else and changed his mind at the last moment.

"Every guest is chosen for a reason," he continued. "So, if you're wondering why I lied, it's because your invitation was not meant for a common sailor."

No, Scarlett thought, *it had been meant for a count.*

A panicked vermillion moved inside of her chest as she recalled how specific Legend's letter had been. The other ticket was meant for her fiancé. Not the wild boy who stood across from her, untying his cravat. Scarlett was risking enough by deciding to stay and play the game for one day. Pretending to be engaged to Julian made her feel as if she were asking to be punished. Who knew what she and Julian might be pushed to do together as part of the game?

Even if Julian had helped her earlier, lying for him had been a mistake, and there were always consequences for that. Her entire life was evidence of this. "We need to go back and tell the truth," she said. "This isn't going to work. If it gets back to my fiancé or my father that I've behaved as if we're—"

In a flash, Scarlett's back was pressed against the fountain, and Julian's hands were spread out on either side of her, so much larger than her own. "Crimson, relax." His voice sounded uncommonly soft, although as he spoke, relaxing instantly felt impossible. With every word he leaned in closer, until the house and lights had disappeared and all she could see was Julian. "None of this will reach your father, or your devoted count. Once we enter that house, the game is all that matters. No one here cares about who anyone is when they're not on this isle."

"How do you know that?" Scarlett asked.

Julian flashed a wicked smile. "I know because I've played before." He pushed away from the fountain. The bright lights of the turreted house reappeared, but a chill descended on Scarlett's shoulders.

No wonder he seemed to be such an expert. She should not have been shocked. From the moment she'd first spied him on Trisda, she had sensed he wasn't to be completely trusted, but it seemed he was hiding even more than she'd thought behind Legend's tailored clothes. "So that's why you helped me and my sister make it to this isle? Because you wanted to play again?"

"If I said no, and that I did it because I wanted to rescue you from your father, would you believe me?"

Scarlett shook her head.

With a shrug, Julian leaned back, pulled his cravat off, and tossed it over Scarlett's shoulder. A gentle splash sounded as it landed in the fountain.

It now made sense, why he'd seemed so sure of himself. Why he'd crossed the isle full of purpose rather than wonder.

"You're looking at me as if I've done something wrong," he said.

Scarlett knew she shouldn't have been upset, they were nothing to each other, but she despised being deceived; she'd had enough of that to last a lifetime. "What's your reason for coming back to Caraval?"

"Do I need to have a purpose? Who doesn't want to see the magical Caraval players? Or win one of their prizes?"

"For some reason I don't believe that." She might have thought he was there for this year's prize—*the wish*—but something in her core told her that wasn't true. Wishes were things of wonder that took a certain amount of faith, and Julian seemed the type to trust only what he saw.

The game was different each year, but a few things were rumored to be the same. There was always some sort of treasure hunt involving a supposedly magical object—a crown, a scepter, a ring, a tablet, or a pendant. And the winners from previous years were always invited back with a guest. Though Scarlett didn't imagine that would be a draw for Julian either, not when he was so good at finding people to help him get in.

If Scarlett wasn't even sure she believed in wishes, she could not fathom Julian was after one. No, it was not dreams of wishes, or of the magical and fantastical that drew him to this isle. "Tell me the real reason you're here," she said.

"Trust me when I say you're better off not knowing." Julian affected a concerned expression. "It will only spoil your good time."

"You're just saying that because you don't want to tell me the truth."

"No, Crimson, this time, I am telling the truth." His eyes locked onto Scarlett's, unmoving and unflinching, a gaze that required complete control. With a shudder, she saw that the lazy sailor from the boat had partially been an act, and if he'd desired, she realized Julian could have kept that performance up, continued to play the part of a boy who'd happened upon her and her sister and this entire game by accident. But it was as if he wanted Scarlett to see there was more to his story, even if he refused to say what it was.

"I'm not going to argue with you about this, Crimson." Julian straightened, stretching taller while he flexed his back and his shoulders, as if he'd arrived at a sudden decision. "Believe me when I say I have good reasons for wanting inside that house. If you want to go and turn me in I won't stop you or hold it against you, even though I did save your life today."

"You only did that so that I could be your ticket into the game."

Julian's face went dark. "Is that really what you think?" For a moment he looked truly wounded.

Scarlett knew he was trying to manipulate her. She'd had enough experience to recognize the signs. Unfortunately, despite her lengthy history of being used by her father, or perhaps *because* of it, she was never good at evading it. No matter how much she wanted to avoid Julian, she couldn't ignore the fact that he *had* saved her life.

"What about my sister? This lie might affect your relationship with her."

"I wouldn't call what we had a 'relationship.'" Julian flicked a piece of lint off the shoulder of his tailcoat, as if that was how he pictured Tella. "Your sister was using me as much as I used her."

"And now you're doing the same with me," Scarlett said.

"Don't look so put out about it. I've played this game before. I can help you. And you never know, you might actually enjoy it." Julian's voice took on a flirtatious rhythm as he turned back into a careless sailor once more. "A lot of girls would feel lucky to be you." He brushed a cool finger against Scarlett's cheek.

"Don't." She backed away, her skin tingly where he'd touched her. "If we do this, there can be no more of . . . *this*, unless absolutely necessary. I still have a real fiancé. So just because we're saying we're engaged doesn't mean we need to behave like it when no one is watching."

The edge of Julian's mouth tipped up. "Does this mean you're not going to turn me in?"

He was the last person Scarlett wanted to partner with. But she also didn't want to risk staying on the isle longer than one day. Julian had played before, and Scarlett had a feeling she would need his help if she wanted to find her sister quickly.

Just then, a new party of people arrived at the gate. Scarlett could hear the dim clamor of their distant chatter. The echo of the girl on the unicycle clapping.

Inside the house, violin music, richer than the darkest chocolate, started playing. It seeped outside and whispered to Scarlett as Julian's smile turned seductive, all shameless curves and immoral promises. An invitation to places that proper young ladies didn't think about, let alone visit. Scarlett didn't want to imagine what sorts of things this smile had convinced other girls to do.

"Don't look at me like that," Scarlett said. "It doesn't work on me."

"That's why it's so fun."

10

Scarlett loved her nana, but she thought of her as one of those women who never quite got over growing old. She'd spent the last years of her life boasting about the grandness of her youth. How she'd been beautiful. How she'd been adored by men. How she'd once worn a purple dress during Caraval that was the envy of every girl.

She'd shown Scarlett the dress on many occasions. When Scarlett was still small—before she began hating the color purple—she believed it was indeed the most beautiful gown she'd ever seen.

"Can I wear it?" she'd asked one day.

"Of course not! This dress is not a plaything."

After that her nana put the gown away. But it remained in Scarlett's memories.

Scarlett thought of the gown that night, as the doors to the turreted house swept open. And in that moment, she wondered if her grandmother had ever actually been to a Caraval performance, for

Scarlett could not imagine her purple gown being of notice in such a spectacular place.

Lush red carpet cushioned her steps, while soft golden lights licked her arms with gentle kisses of warmth. Heat was everywhere, when a blink ago the world had been covered in cold. It tasted like light, bubbly on her tongue and sugary as it went down, making everything from the ends of her toes to the tips of her fingers tingle.

"It's—" Words failed her. Scarlett wanted to say it was beautiful or marvelous. But those sentiments seemed suddenly too common for such an uncommon sight.

For the turreted mansion was not what it had seemed from the outside. The doors Scarlett and Julian stepped through led them not into a house, but onto a balcony—although the balcony was probably the size of a small home. Roofed by a canopy of crystal chandeliers, carpeted in plush cranberry rugs, and lined with gilded golden rails and spindles that arched around heavy red velvet drapes.

The drapes swished shut a moment after Scarlett and Julian entered, but it was long enough for Scarlett to glimpse the grandeur that lay beyond.

Julian appeared unimpressed, though he managed a dark laugh as Scarlett continued to fumble for words. "I keep forgetting you've never left your little isle before."

"Anyone would think this is incredible," Scarlett argued. "Did you see all the other balconies? There are at least—dozens! And below, it looks like an entire miniature kingdom."

"Did you expect it was just going to be a normal house?"

"No, of course not; it obviously looked much bigger than a normal building." But not nearly large enough to contain the world beneath the balcony. Unable to control her excitement, she drew closer to the rim, but hesitated at the edge of its closed, thick red curtains.

Julian stepped in and drew a bit of it back.

"I don't think we're supposed to touch those," Scarlett said.

"Or maybe that's the reason they shut when we walked in, because they want us to open them." He pulled the curtain back wider.

Scarlett was certain he was breaking some sort of rule, yet she couldn't help but lean closer and marvel at the unbelievable realm resting at least ten stories below. It resembled the cobbled streets Scarlett and Julian had just ventured through, only this hamlet was not abandoned: it looked like a storybook come to life. She peered down at bright pointy rooftops, moss-covered towers, gingerbread cottages, gleaming gold bridges, blue-brick streets, and bubbling fountains, all lit by candled lamps that hung everywhere, giving an appearance of time that was neither day nor night.

It was about the same size as her village on Trisda, but it felt spectacularly bigger, the way a word feels bigger with an exclamation point tacked onto it. The roads looked so alive, Scarlett swore they were moving. "I don't understand how they fit an entire world inside here."

"It's just a very elaborate theater." Julian's tone was dry as his eyes cut from the scene below up to the dozens of different balconies, all overlooking the same curious sight.

Scarlett hadn't realized it before, but Julian was right. The balconies formed a circle—an enormous circle. Her spirits took a significant dip. Sometimes it took her an entire day to track down Tella on their father's estate. How would she ever find Tella here?

"Take it in while you can," Julian said. "It will make it easier to get around on the ground. After this, there will be no coming back up here unless—"

"Ahem." From the back of the balcony someone cleared his throat. "You need to step away and shut those curtains."

Scarlett turned immediately, briefly terrified they'd be kicked out for breaking a rule, but Julian took his time letting go of the drape.

"And who are you?" Julian stared down the intruder, as if this new young gentleman were the one who'd just done something wrong.

"You can call me Rupert." He looked at Julian with equal disdain, as if he knew Julian wasn't supposed to be there. Pompously, the man straightened his top hat. Without it he probably would have been shorter than Scarlett.

At first glance he had looked like a gentleman, in his crisp gray pants and a suit coat with tails, but as he stepped closer Scarlett realized he was merely a boy, dressed up like a man, with cheeks that still had baby fat and limbs that didn't look as if they'd finished growing, despite how he dressed them up in fancy clothes. Scarlett wondered if his costume was homage to Legend, who was known for his top hats and finery.

"I'm here to go over the rules and answer any questions before you officially begin the game." Without any flourishes, Rupert repeated the same speech given by the girl on the unicycle.

Scarlett just wanted to be let in. Knowing Tella, she'd already fallen in love with some new form of trouble.

Julian nudged her in the ribs. "You need to listen."

"We've already heard this."

"Are you certain?" Julian whispered.

"Once inside, you will be presented with a mystery that must be solved," said Rupert. "Clues will be hidden throughout the game to help you on your way. We want you to get swept away, but be careful of being swept too far away," repeated Rupert.

"What happens if someone does get swept too far away?" asked Scarlett.

"That's usually when people die or go mad," Rupert answered, so calmly she wondered if she'd misheard him. With equal composure, he took off his top hat and pulled out two pieces of parchment. He held out the creamy papers for Scarlett and Julian, as if for them to read, but the script was impossibly small.

"I'll need one drop of blood at the bottom of each," said Rupert.

"For what?" asked Scarlett.

"These confirm you've heard the rules, twice, and that neither the Caraval Estate nor Master Legend is responsible in the event of any untimely accidents, madness, or death."

"But you said nothing that happens inside is real," Scarlett argued.

"Occasionally people confuse fantasy with reality. Accidents sometimes result. It rarely happens," Rupert added. "If you're worried, you don't have to play. You may always simply observe." He looked almost bored as he finished, making Scarlett feel as if she were fretting over nothing.

If Tella were there, Scarlett could imagine her saying, *You're only staying one day. If you sit and watch, you'll regret it.*

But the idea of a contract sealed in blood did not sit well with Scarlett.

Though if Tella was playing and Scarlett chose not to, maybe she'd be unable to find her, making it impossible to leave the next day and get home in time to marry the count. Despite Rupert's instructions, Scarlett was still a bit unsure as to the particulars of the game. She had tried to learn everything she could from her grandmother, but the woman had always been vague. Rather than actual facts, she'd given Scarlett romantic impressions that were beginning to feel a bit off. Pictures painted by a woman who saw the past as she wished it had been rather than as it actually was.

Scarlett looked at Julian. Without hesitation he let Rupert prick his finger with some sort of thorn and pressed the bloody tip to the bottom of one contract.

Scarlett remembered a few years ago when Caraval had stopped traveling for a time. A woman had been killed. Scarlett didn't know the details as to why. She had always assumed it was just a tragic accident, unrelated to the game, but now Scarlett wondered if the woman had become too caught up in the illusion of Caraval.

But Scarlett had played her father's distorted games all these years. She knew when she was being deceived and she couldn't imagine she'd become so confused about reality that she would lose her life or go insane. Still, it didn't mean she wasn't nervous as she stretched out her hand. She knew better than to assume any type of game came without a cost.

Rupert pricked her ring finger, so quickly Scarlett barely noticed, though when she pressed her finger to the bottom of the delicate page, it was as if all the lights went out for a moment. When she took it away, the world became even brighter. She felt as if she could taste the red of the curtains. Chocolate cake drenched in wine.

Scarlett had only ever had a sip of wine, but she imagined that not even a whole bottle could bring this much iridescent euphoria. Despite her fears, she felt an uncustomary moment of pure elation.

"The game officially begins at sunset tomorrow and ends at sunrise on the nineteenth. Everyone has five nights to play the game," Rupert continued. "You will each receive one clue to start you on your journeys. After that you will need to find the other clues on your own. I recommend acting quickly. There is only one prize, and many who will be searching for it." He stepped closer and handed them each a card.

It read *LA SERPIENTE DE CRISTAL.*

The Glass Serpent.

"Mine's the same," Julian said.

"Is this our first clue?" Scarlett asked.

"No," Rupert answered. "You'll find lodgings prepared for you there. Your rooms will contain your first clues, but only if you manage to check in before daybreak."

"What happens at daybreak?" Scarlett asked.

As if he didn't hear her, the boy pulled a cord near the edge of the balcony, parting the curtains. Gray birds had taken flight in the sky, and beyond them the colorful streets were fuller than before, while the balconies were emptier—their hosts were letting everyone out at the same time.

Another silver rush of excitement swept over Scarlett. This was

Caraval. She had pictured it more often than she'd dreamed of her own wedding. Even though she could only afford to stay a day, she already imagined it would be difficult to leave.

Rupert tipped his hat. "Remember, don't let your eyes or feelings trick you." He stepped up to the balcony's rail and jumped.

"No!" Scarlett screamed, all the color draining from her face as she watched him plummet.

"Don't worry," Julian said. "Look." He pointed over the edge of the rail, as the boy's suit coat transformed into wings. "He's fine, he just made a dramatic exit."

A swath of gray fabric, he continued to glide until he looked like one of the large birds in the sky.

It seemed the tricks on Scarlett's eyes had already begun.

"Come on." Julian strode from the balcony, a purpose to his step that said he expected her to follow. "If you'd been listening, you'd have heard him say that everything locks at dawn. This game has a reverse curfew. Doors close at sunrise and don't unlock until after sunset. We don't have much time to find our rooms."

Julian stopped walking. At his feet, a trapdoor was open. Most likely it was how the boy had entered unseen. It led to a winding black marble staircase, spiraling down like the inside of a dark seashell, lit by waxy sconces dripping crystal candles.

"Crimson—" Julian stopped her at the threshold. For a moment his expression looked torn, the way it had during the tense seconds before he'd left her in the clock shop.

"What is it?" Scarlett asked.

"We need to hurry." Julian let Scarlett go first, though after a few flights she wished that the sailor had gone before her, or that he'd just left her to her own devices as she imagined he'd been about to at the top of the stairs. According to Julian, every step she took was too slow.

"We don't have all night," he repeated. "If we don't get to the Serpent before dawn—"

"We'll be out in the cold until tomorrow night. I know. I'm going as fast as I can." Scarlett had thought the balcony was ten stories high, but now it seemed more like one hundred. She was never going to get to Tella.

It might have been different if her dress weren't so clingy. Once more Scarlett tried to will it into another shape, but the gown remained determinedly unchanged. Her legs were shaking and a fine layer of sweat coated her thighs as she finally exited with Julian.

Outside, the air was crisper and a little bit damp, though thankfully there was no snow on any of the streets. The dampness came from the canals. Scarlett hadn't realized it while above, but every other street was made of water. Striped boats swam about, as bright as tropical fish and shaped like half-moons, all helmed by young men or women around her age.

But there were no signs of Donatella.

Julian flagged down a boat right away, aquamarine with red stripes, steered by a young sailor girl dressed to match. Her lips were painted red as well, and Scarlett couldn't help but notice how wide they parted as Julian strode closer.

"What can I do for you, lovelies?" she asked.

"Oh, I think you're the lovely one." Julian ran his fingers through his hair, flashing her a look made of lies and other sinful things. "Can you reach La Serpiente de Cristal before sunup?"

"I'll take you wherever you need to go, as long as you're willing to pay." The red-lipped girl emphasized the word *pay*, reinforcing what Scarlett assumed back in the clock shop—coins were not the primary currency used in this game.

Julian was unfazed. "We were told our first ride of the night would be free. My fiancée here is a special guest of Master Legend."

"Is that so?" The girl narrowed one eye as if she didn't believe him, but then to Scarlett's surprise, she beckoned them on board. "I'm not one to disappoint special guests of Legend."

Julian hopped on nimbly and motioned for Scarlett. The boat appeared sturdier than their last ride, with tufted cushions on the benches, yet Scarlett couldn't bring herself to leave the cobbled street.

"This one isn't going to sink," Julian said.

"That's not what I'm worried about. My sister, what if she's out here looking for us?"

"Then I hope someone tells her the sun's about to come up."

"You really don't care about her at all, do you?"

"If I didn't care, then I wouldn't hope someone has told her it's almost sunup." Julian motioned impatiently for Scarlett to enter the boat. "You don't need to worry, *love*. They've probably placed her at the same inn as us."

"But what if they haven't?" Scarlett said.

"Then you're still more likely to find her by boat. We'll cover distance faster this way."

"He's right," said the girl. "Daylight is approaching fast. Even if you did find your sister, you wouldn't be able to walk to La Serpiente before it arrives. Tell me what she looks like, and I can keep an eye out for her as we go."

Scarlett wanted to argue. Even if she couldn't find her sister before sunup, she wanted to do everything in her power to try. Scarlett imagined this to be the sort of place where a person could be lost and never found.

But Julian and the sailor girl were right; they'd move faster in the crescent boat. Scarlett didn't know how much time had passed since the isle's curious sun had disappeared, but she was certain time moved differently in this place.

"My sister is shorter than me, and very pretty, with a bit of a rounder face and long spirals of blond hair."

Scarlett had their mother's darker coloring while Tella had received their father's fair curls.

"The lighter hair should make her easier to find," said the sailor girl, but as far as Scarlett could tell, she spent more time with her eyes on Julian's handsome face.

Julian was just as unhelpful. As they glided over midnight-blue waters she sensed he was searching for something, but it wasn't her younger sister.

"Can you row any faster?" Julian asked, a muscle ticking in his jaw.

"For someone who's not paying, you're rather demanding." The sailor girl gave him a wink but Julian's harsh expression remained unchanged.

"What's wrong?" Scarlett asked.

"We're running out of time."

A shadow fell over him as several of the lanterns lining the water flickered out. The boat sailed farther and more candles died, their fading smoke casting haze over the water and the few remaining people who still lingered about the cobbled streets.

"That's how you tell time here? The lanterns go out as it gets closer to dawn?" Scarlett's eyes anxiously shot around as Julian nodded grimly and another set of candles turned from flames to smoke.

The boat finally came to a rocking halt in front of a long, rickety dock. At the end of it, a searing green door watched Scarlett like a glowing eye. Ivy clung to the walls around it, and though most of the building was swallowed by the night, two dying lanterns illuminated the sign above the entrance—a white serpent coiled around a black cluster of grapes.

Julian was already out of the boat. He grabbed Scarlett's wrist, hauling her onto the dock. "Faster!" One of the lanterns above the entrance snuffed out and the color of the door seemed to dim as well. It was barely visible as Julian wrenched it open and pushed Scarlett forward.

She stumbled inside. But before Julian could follow, the door slammed shut. Wood crashed against wood as a heavy bolt slid into place, trapping him outside.

N o!" Scarlett tried to pry the door back open, but a plump woman in a stocking cap was already placing a heavy lock through the bolt.

"You can't do that. My—" Scarlett hesitated. Somehow the lie seemed more real if she was the one to say it; it made her feel as if she were somehow being unfaithful to the count. Julian had promised her what happened in the game would never get back to her father or her real fiancé, but how could she be sure? And it wasn't as if he was *really* being left out for the night.

But the days on this isle seemed as if they could be worse than the nights. Scarlett remembered the cold abandoned village they'd crossed through to get to the turreted house. If Julian remained locked outside, it was because he'd pushed her in ahead of himself. He risked what he'd wanted so she would be all right. Scarlett couldn't abandon him.

"My fiancé," Scarlett said. "He's out there, you have to let him in."

"I'm sorry," said the innkeeper. "Rules are rules. If you don't make it in by the end of the first night, you don't get to play."

Don't get to play?

"Those weren't the rules I heard." Though she hadn't listened to all the rules. She realized this was why Julian had been so anxious on the boat.

"I'm sorry, dearie." And the innkeeper truly did look apologetic. "I hate to separate couples, but I cannot break the rules. Once the sun's up and the door's locked for the day, no one comes in or gets out until the sun—"

"But it's not up yet!" Scarlett objected. "It's still dark. You can't leave him out there."

The innkeeper continued to look at Scarlett with pity but the set of her mouth was unyielding. It was obvious she was not going to change her mind.

If the situation were reversed, Scarlett tried to think of what Julian would have done. Briefly, she imagined he might not have cared. But although he'd left her on the raft and in the clock shop, he'd also come back—and even if it had only been so he could use her to get into the games, she still felt thankful he'd returned.

Mustering courage she mostly reserved to protect her sister, Scarlett stood a little straighter. "I think you're making a mistake. My name is Scarlett Dragna, and we're special guests of Caraval Master Legend."

The innkeeper's eyes widened almost as fast as her hands reached out to unlock the bolt. "Oh, you should have said that sooner!"

The door flew open. The other side was the hopeless shade of black that only takes over before the sun is about to rise.

"Julian!" Scarlett expected to find him on the other side of the door but all she saw was the relentless darkness.

Her heart pounded. "Julian!"

"Crimson?"

Scarlett still couldn't see him, but she heard Julian's boots hitting the dock, thumping in rhythm with her own pounding pulse.

Her heart continued to race even after Julian was safely inside. The fire that lit the vestibule was dim, a few smoldering logs provided barely enough light to see, but she swore the sailor looked haunted, as if those moments outside had cost him something valuable. She could feel the night still hovering around him. The tips of his dark hair were damp with it.

Somewhere in the distance, bells began to ring in the dawn. If she'd waited a few more seconds it would have been too late to save him. Scarlett fought the unexpected urge to reach out and hug him. He might have been a scoundrel and a liar, but until she found her sister, he was all she had in the game.

"You scared me," Scarlett said.

And it appeared she wasn't the only one.

The innkeeper's face was paler as she locked up the door for a second time.

Julian moved a little closer to Scarlett, his hand gently pressing the small of her back. "How did you convince her to let me in?"

"Um." Scarlett felt reluctant to tell Julian the truth about what she'd said. "I just told her it wasn't daybreak yet."

Julian raised a skeptical brow.

"I might have also told her that we were getting married," Scarlett added.

My little liar, Julian mouthed, his lips parted slightly as he slowly leaned in closer.

Scarlett stiffened. For a moment she thought he was going to kiss her, but instead he whispered, "Thank you." His lips lingered near her ear, tickling her skin, and she shivered as his hand pressed a little harder against the small of her back.

Something about the gesture felt very intimate.

Scarlett inched away, but Julian's hand remained against her spine, keeping her close as he turned to the innkeeper. She bustled behind the large olive-green desk that took up most of the low-ceilinged room.

"And thank you," said Julian. "I appreciate the kindness you've shown us tonight."

"Oh, it wasn't really a problem," said the innkeeper, though Scarlett swore she was still shaken. Her fingers trembled as she adjusted her stocking cap. "Like I told your fiancée, I hate to break up couples. I actually have special arrangements for you two."

The innkeeper rummaged back through her desk before producing two glass keys, one etched with a number eight, and the other with a nine. "Easy to find, just go up the stairs to your left." She winked as she handed them the keys.

Scarlett hoped the wink was just a tic. She had never been overly fond of them. Her father liked to wink, usually after he'd done something nasty. Scarlett didn't imagine this plump innkeeper had done anything nefarious to their rooms, but the little glass keys paired with the odd little gesture left Scarlett with an icy-blue nervous hum.

It was probably just in her head, she told herself. Maybe the keys were part of the game as well. Perhaps they unlocked something other than rooms eight and nine and that was what she'd meant by "special arrangements."

Or perchance they just had a rather good view of the canals.

The innkeeper explained that each hall had a water closet and a tub room for washing. "To your right is the Glass Tavern, closes one hour after sunrise, opens one hour before sunset."

Inside the barroom, jade light fell from emerald chandeliers, hanging over tables of glass that clinked with goblets and the crush of dull chatter. It smelled of stale beer and staler conversation. It was about to close for the day. Only a handful of patrons remained, all of them with different colorings and features, which made it seem they'd come from across the continents. None of them had curly blond hair.

"I'm sure you'll find her tomorrow," said Julian.

"Or maybe she's already in her room?" Scarlett turned back to the innkeeper. "Would you be able to tell us if a young lady named Donatella Dragna is staying here?"

The innkeeper hesitated. Scarlett swore she recognized the name.

"I'm sorry, dearies, I can't tell you who else is staying here."

"But it's my sister."

"I still can't help." The woman divided a slightly panicked look between Julian and Scarlett. "Rules of the game. If she's here, you'll have to find her on your own."

"Can't you—"

Julian's hand pressed against Scarlett's back, then his lips were at her ear again. "She's already done us one favor tonight," he warned.

"But—" Scarlett started to argue, yet Julian's expression stopped her. Something in it went beyond caution and looked much closer to fear.

Dark hair fell over his eyes as he leaned near to her once more and whispered, "I know you want to find your sister, but on this isle secrets are valuable. Be careful about giving yours away too freely. If people know what you want the most, it can be used against you.

"Come on." He started toward the stairs.

Scarlett knew it was dawn, but the crooked halls of La Serpiente smelled like the end of the night, sweat and fading fire smoke mixed with lingering breath from words whose ghosts still haunted the air. The doors didn't seem to be in any particular order. Room two was on the second floor, while room one was on floor three. Room five's teal door came after eleven's raspberry entry.

The halls of the fourth floor were all covered in velvet paper striped with thick lines of black and cream. Scarlett and Julian finally found their rooms, in the middle of the hall. Neighbors to each other.

Scarlett hesitated in front of the rounded door to room eight, while Julian waited for her to go inside.

It felt as if they'd spent more than just one day together. The sailor had not been a horrible companion. Scarlett knew she might not have made it this far without his help.

"I was thinking," she started, "tomorrow—"

"If I see your sister, I'll tell her you're looking for her." Julian's tone was polite, but it was clearly a dismissal.

So that was it.

She shouldn't have been surprised or upset that this was the end of their partnership. Julian had claimed he would help her out, but she'd learned enough of him to know that if he wanted something, he said whatever needed to be said to get it. She didn't know when she started expecting more. Or why.

She recalled what he'd told her in the clock shop, about how she thought too highly of him if she believed he cared for her sister. He used people. His use of her had been mutually beneficial, but he'd used her all the same. She remembered her first impression of him, tall, roughly handsome, and dangerous, like poison dressed up in an attractive bottle.

It was better for her to stay away from him. Safer. He might have helped her today, but she couldn't drop her guard; he was clearly here for his own purposes. And after she found her sister the next night, she wouldn't be alone, or staying much longer.

"Good-bye," Scarlett said as curtly as he'd spoken to her, and without another word she swept into her room.

A fire was already lit in the hearth, warm and glowing, throwing shades of copper against walls covered in flowered wallpaper—roses, white with ruby tips, in various states of bloom. The wood crackled as it burned, a soft lullaby that pulled her toward a massive canopy bed, the most enormous one Scarlett had ever seen. It must have been why the room was considered special. Sheltered by gauzy drapes of white that hung from carved wooden posts, the bed was covered in silk pillows made of fluff and thickly quilted blankets, tied with rich currant-red bows. She couldn't wait to fall on the bed's downy mattress and—

The wall moved.

Scarlett froze. The room grew suddenly hotter and smaller.

For a moment she hoped it was a trick of her imagination.

"No," she said, watching as Julian strode through a narrow door, next to the wardrobe, which until that moment had been camouflaged by the room's papered wall.

"How did you get in here?" she asked. Though even before he answered, Scarlett knew exactly what had happened.

The wink. The keys. The special arrangements. "She gave us the same room on purpose!"

"You did a very good job convincing her we're in love." Julian's eyes cut to the lavish bed.

Scarlett's cheeks blazed with red, the color of hearts and blood and shame. "I didn't say we were in love—I only said we're engaged."

Julian laughed but Scarlett was aghast. "This isn't funny. We can't sleep in here together. If anyone finds out, I'll be utterly ruined."

"There you go being dramatic again. You think everything is going to destroy your life."

But if anyone found out, it would destroy her engagement to the count. "You met my father. If he ever discovered I—"

"No one will find out. I imagine that's why there are two doors with different numbers." Julian crossed over to the enormous bed and threw himself on top of it.

"You can't sleep on that bed," Scarlett protested.

"Why not? It's very comfortable." Julian pulled off his boots, dropping them to the floor with loud thumps. Then he took off his waistcoat and went for the buttons of his shirt.

"What are you doing?" Scarlett said. "You can't do that."

"Listen, Crimson." Julian stopped unbuttoning his shirt. "I told you I won't touch you, and I promise to keep my word. But I am not sleeping on the floor or on that tiny lounge just because you're a girl. This bed is big enough for the both of us."

"You really think I'd get in a bed with you? Are you mad?" A ridiculous question, because clearly he was. He continued to unbutton his shirt, and she was certain he did so only because he knew it made her uncomfortable. Or maybe he just liked showing off.

Scarlett got another glimpse of his smooth muscles as she pivoted for the door. "I'm going back down to see if she has another room."

"And what if she doesn't?" Julian called.

"Then I'll sleep in the hall."

A gentleman would have protested, but Julian was not a gentleman. Something soft hit the floor. Most likely his shirt.

Scarlett reached for the glass doorknob.

"Hold on—"

A square lined with gold landed at her feet. An envelope. Her name written across the front in an elegant script.

"Found that on the bed. I'm imagining it's your first clue."

12

Scarlett's nana used to say the world of Caraval was Master Legend's great playground. No words were spoken that he didn't hear. Not even a whisper could escape his ears, no shadow went unseen by his eyes. No one ever saw Legend— or if they did, they didn't know it was him—but Legend saw all during Caraval.

Scarlett swore she felt his gaze on her as she stepped into the hall. She sensed it in the way the candlelit lanterns seemed to glow brighter, like eyes perking up, as she examined her message.

The envelope looked the same as every one Legend had sent her before, gold and cream and thick with mystery.

When she opened it, several red rose petals fell onto her palm, along with a key. Delicate green glass. Similar to the one she'd been given for her room, only this key had a number five etched into it, and attached to it was a tiny black ribbon, which held a wide slip of paper with one name: Donatella Dragna.

Scarlett knew this was supposed to be her first clue. But to her it felt more like a gift from Legend, just like the dress and the invitations to the isle. Scarlett had found it difficult to believe she was special in the clock shop, but maybe she was feeling a touch of Caraval magic, for she found herself daring to hope that Legend was indeed treating her differently, taking care of her again by showing her where her sister was. For a moment Scarlett felt as if everything was going to be right and bright.

She flew down the hall until she reached the steps to the third floor. Room five came after room eleven: a square teal door with a green glass handle that looked a bit like a giant gemstone. Gaudy and magnificent. Perfect for Tella.

Scarlett started to use her key, but the breathing on the other side of the door sounded a little too loud for Tella. A smoky-ginger prickle of discomfort crawled down Scarlett's neck as she put her ear closer to the door.

Thud.

Something heavy dropped to the floor.

Followed by a groan.

"Tella—" Scarlett reached for the handle. "Are you all right?"

"Scarlett?" Tella's voice sounded strained, out of breath.

"Yes! It's me, I'm coming in!"

"No—don't!"

Another loud thud.

"Tella, what's going on in there?"

"Nothing—just—do *not* come in."

"Tella, if there's something wrong—"

"Nothing's wrong. I'm—just—busy—" Tella broke off.

Scarlett hesitated. Something *was* wrong. Tella didn't sound like herself.

"Scarlett!" Tella's voice rang loud and clear, as if she could see her sister reaching for the knob. "If you open that door I will never speak to you again."

Her tone was low, and this time it was echoed by a deep voice. A young man's voice.

"You heard your sister," he said.

The words ricocheted through the crooked hall, hitting Scarlett like a burst of unwanted wind, reaching into all the places her clothing couldn't protect.

She felt five different shades of berry-colored foolish as she walked away. All this time she had been worried about Tella, but obviously her sister had not been concerned about her. She probably hadn't even thought about her. Not when she had a young man in her bed.

Scarlett shouldn't have been surprised. Her sister had always been wilder; Tella liked the taste of trouble. But it wasn't the wildness that hurt Scarlett. Tella was the most important person in the world to Scarlett, but it always broke Scarlett to know her sister did not feel the same way.

When their mother, Paloma, had abandoned them, all the soft parts of Scarlett's father seemed to disappear along with her. His rules went from strict to severe, and so did the consequences for failing to obey. It would have been so different if Paloma had just stayed on Trisda. Scarlett vowed she'd never leave Tella alone the way their mother had left them. She would protect her. Even though Scarlett was only one year older, she didn't trust anyone else to take care of her sister, and as Tella grew up, Scarlett didn't trust Tella to take care of herself. But while she had sheltered Tella, she'd also spoiled her. Tella too often thought only of herself.

At the end of the hall, Scarlett slumped to the floor. Rough wooden boards rubbed awkwardly beneath her. It was colder on this lower level than it had been up the stairs. Or maybe she only felt chilly because of Tella's dismissal. She'd chosen someone else over Scarlett. A young man whose name Tella probably didn't even know. While Scarlett often feared men, Tella was the opposite, always chasing after the wrong ones, hoping one might give her the love their father withheld.

Scarlett thought about returning to her room, warmed with fire and full of blankets. But all the heat in the world would not entice her to share a bed with Julian. She could have gone down and asked the innkeeper for another room, but something told her that was not a wise idea, not after making such a fuss about how Julian needed to be let in. Stupid Julian.

Stupid. Stupid. Stupid. . . . She repeated the word in her head until her eyes drifted shut.

"Miss—" A warm hand rocked Scarlett's shoulder, returning her to wakefulness.

Scarlett startled, clutching her hands to her chest as her eyes shot open, only to quickly close again. The young man in front of her held a lantern rather close to her face. She could feel its warmth licking her cheek, though he stood a safe distance away.

"I think she's drunk," said a young woman.

"I'm not drunk." Scarlett opened her eyes again. The young man with the lantern appeared a few years older than Julian. But unlike the sailor, this young man was made of polished boots and neatly tied-back hair. He was attractive, and the care he took with his appearance made Scarlett think he knew this as well.

Dressed entirely in sleek black, he was the type of boy Tella would have called uselessly pretty, while secretly thinking of ways to gain his attention. She noticed all the ink covering his hands and moving up his arms. Tattoos, carnal and intricate, arcanists' symbols, a mourning mask, lips curved into an alluring pout, bird talons and black roses. Each of them was at odds with the rest of his refined appearance, which made Scarlett more curious than she ought to have been.

"I was accidentally placed in a room with someone else," Scarlett said. "I was on my way to ask the innkeeper for another suite, but then—"

"You just fell asleep in the hall?" This from the girl who had called Scarlett drunk. She was farther away from the lantern, and the rest of the hall's lights had gone out, so Scarlett couldn't clearly see her face. She imagined her to be sullen and unattractive.

"It's complicated." Scarlett faltered. She could have easily told them about her sister, but even if this couple never met Tella, Scarlett didn't want to expose her sister's indiscretions. It was her job to protect Tella. And Scarlett wasn't sure she really cared about what either of these people thought of her, even if her eyes kept falling on the young man with the tattoos. He had the sort of profile meant for sculptors and painters. Full lips, strong jaw, coal-dark eyes sheltered by thick, dark brows.

Being cornered by a young man like this, in a dimly lit hall, ought to have made her uncomfortable, but his expression was concerned rather than predatory.

"You don't have to explain," he said. "I'm sure you had a good reason for sleeping out here, but I don't think you should stay. I'm in room number eleven. You can sleep there."

From the way he said it, Scarlett was fairly certain he didn't intend to stay in the room with her—unlike another young man she knew—yet Scarlett was so used to hidden danger, she couldn't help but hesitate.

She studied him again in the lamplight, eyes falling on the black rose that inked the backside of his hand, elegant and lovely and a little bit sorrowful. Scarlett didn't know why, but she felt as if that tattoo somehow defined him. The elegant and lovely part might have scared her away—she had learned that this too often disguised other things—but the sad part drew her in. "Where will you sleep?"

"My sister's room." He nodded to the girl at his side. "There are two beds in her suite. She doesn't need them both."

"Yes I do," said the girl, and although Scarlett still couldn't see her clearly, she swore the girl looked Scarlett over with disgust.

"Don't be rude," said the young man. "I insist," he added, before Scarlett could protest again. "If my mother found out I let a shivering young lady sleep on the floor, she would disown me, and I wouldn't blame her." He held out an inked hand to help Scarlett up. "I'm Dante, by the way, and this is my sister, Valentina."

"Scarlett, and thank you." She spoke tentatively, still surprised he wanted nothing in return. "This is very generous of you."

"I think you're giving me too much credit." Dante held Scarlett's hand a beat longer. Briefly his dark eyes traveled below her neck, and she swore his cheeks pinked, but he brought his gaze back up before it could make her uncomfortable. "I glimpsed you from the tavern earlier, but it looked as if you were with someone else?"

"Oh, I—" Scarlett hesitated. She knew what he was asking. But she couldn't discern if Dante's curiosity was because of the game, or something that involved actual interest in her. All she knew was that the steady way Dante gazed at her warmed up the chilly parts of her limbs, and she imagined if Julian were in the hall with a pretty girl, he'd not claim Scarlett as his fiancée.

"So, you'd be free to meet me at nightfall for dinner?" he asked. Valentina groaned.

"Shut it," said Dante. "Please ignore my sister; she had too much to drink tonight. It makes her a little more unlikable than usual. I promise, if you meet me for dinner, she will not be coming along." He continued to smile at Scarlett, the way Scarlett always hoped a boy would, as if he wasn't just attracted to her, but he wanted to protect and take care of her. Dante's eyes stayed on her as if he couldn't turn away.

The count will look at me the same way, Scarlett assured herself. For although she wasn't truly involved with Julian, she was still engaged, and behaving otherwise was dangerous. "I'm sorry. I—can't. I—"

"It's all right," Dante interrupted quickly. "You don't have to explain." He smiled again, wider but not nearly as sincere. Silently he walked her to his room before handing her an onyx key.

For a tense moment they both lingered near the door—narrow and pointed. Scarlett feared that despite his word Dante was going to try to go inside with her. But he merely waited for her to make sure the key worked before whispering, "Sleep well."

Scarlett started to say good-bye, but she broke off as she entered the room. An oil lamp sat on the short wardrobe, illuminating the mirror above it. Even in the dim, Scarlett's image was clear. Dark hair fell past shoulders barely covered in thin ruffles of gauzy white fabric.

She gasped. The evil gown had transformed again, turning sheer and lacy and far too scandalous to be worn in a public hall or while talking to a strange young man.

Scarlett slammed the door without finishing her good-bye. No wonder Dante had been unable to take his eyes off her.

Scarlett did not dream well.

As she slumbered, she dreamed of Legend. She was back in the gilded balcony, wearing little more than an exposed black corset with a red petticoat and trying to cover up with the curtains.

"What are you doing?" Legend swaggered in, sporting his signature blue velvet top hat and a gaze full of wayward intent.

"I was just trying to watch the game." Scarlett wrapped herself deeper into the curtains, but Legend pulled her away. His hand was as cold as snow, his youthful face concealed by a shadow.

Frost nipped Scarlett's naked shoulders.

Legend laughed and wrapped both hands around her waist. "I didn't invite you here to watch, precious." His mouth moved closer to hers, as if he was about to kiss her. "I want you to play the game," he whispered.

Then he threw her off the balcony.

NIGHT ONE
OF CARAVAL

13

Scarlett woke up covered in cold sweat. It drenched her hairline and the space underneath her knees.

She knew it was only a dream, but for a moment she wondered if the magic of Caraval—if *Legend's* magic—had somehow sneaked into her thoughts.

Or maybe the dream was made of her thoughts? Twice she'd been told these experiences were all just a game, yet she was behaving as if everything were real. As if her every action would be discovered and judged and punished.

I didn't invite you here so you could watch.

Scarlett wasn't even doing that, though.

Yesterday she'd seen incredible things, but the entire time she'd been controlled by fear. She reminded herself her father wasn't there. And if she were only going to stay for one night, she would regret it later if she spent the entire time too frightened to enjoy anything. Tella would probably sleep for another hour at least; Scarlett could go that long without worrying about her. And it wouldn't kill Scarlett to have a little fun in the meantime.

Her thoughts fled back to Dante, to the black rose tattoo on his hand and the warm, wanted way he'd made her feel. She should have said yes. It was only a dinner—not nearly as scandalous as talking with him in a darkened hall while only in a nightdress. And even that had not turned out as terribly as she would have imagined.

Her borrowed room had only one tiny octagonal window, but it was enough to see the sun leisurely setting, and the canals and streets returning to life. The world was on the cusp of nightfall. The hour of smoke before everything turned fully dark. Perhaps if she headed to the Glass Tavern fast enough it wouldn't be too late to find Dante and accept his dinner invitation. Though she felt as if she should be eating breakfast. She'd adjusted to sleeping during the day with surprising ease, but the idea of waking up and going to supper still felt unnatural.

Before leaving she gave her appearance a quick check in the mirror. As she'd washed her face, she'd felt her gown shifting, the thin fabric of her nightdress turning to heavy layers of silk.

She'd hoped for something less noticeable, a dress that would blend into the night, but this gown definitely had a mind of its own.

A giant wine-red bow sat atop her bustle, its two thick ties streaming down her backside to the floor. The rest of her dress was pure white, except for the bodice, which was wrapped in red ribbons, leaving only glimpses of the snowy fabric beneath. Her shoulders were bare, though long sleeves covered her arms. Like the bodice, they were threaded with ruby ribbons, which tied on top of her hands, leaving their ends to dance between her slender fingers.

Tella would love it. Scarlett could already imagine how her sister would squeal at the sight of Scarlett in such a bold gown.

Even though Scarlett had vowed not to worry about her sister for the first hour of the night, she still could not help but think of Tella as she passed by room five.

The door was cracked. Emerald-green light, the color of the gem-shaped doorknob, seeped from the other side like fog.

Scarlett told herself to keep walking. To find Dante, who actually wanted to spend time with her. But something about the light and the crack and the ever-present pull of her sister drew Scarlett closer.

"Tella—" Scarlett knocked quietly. The door creaked open a little farther, spilling out more green light, the color of malevolent things. Scarlett's ill feeling from before returned.

"Tella?" She pushed open the door the rest of the way. "Oh my—" Scarlett covered her mouth.

Tella's room was a shambles. Feathers covered the carnage, as if a rebel angel had gone mad. They mixed with the splinters of wood that snapped under Scarlett's boots and the clothes ripped from the torn-apart wardrobe. The bed was damaged as well. Its quilt was torn in half, and one of its posts had been completely removed, like a roughly severed limb.

This was all Scarlett's fault. Tella had been in her room with a man, but not for the reasons Scarlett thought. She should have known. She should have gone in despite Tella's protests. It was Scarlett's job to take care of her sister. Tella was far too reckless with men. And Scarlett had been foolish to think they could stay here, even for a day. She should have departed the island with Tella the moment she'd found her. If Scarlett had left right away, this—

"God's teeth!"

Scarlett spun at the sound of her sister's familiar curse, uttered by an unfamiliar voice.

"Hector, look—it's another clue." The woman who marched into the room was silver-haired and slight, and definitely not Donatella. "This is superb!" She pulled an older man with spectacles through the door.

"What are you doing?" Scarlett asked. "This is my sister's room. You can't be in here."

The couple looked up as if they'd just noticed Scarlett.

The silver-haired woman smiled, but it wasn't kind. It was as greedy and green as the light that dusted the room. "Is your sister Donatella Dragna?"

"How did you know that?"

"When did you last see her?" asked the silver-haired woman. "What does she look like?"

"I—she—" Scarlett started to answer, but the interrogation felt foul, like a bathtub filled with dirty water. The silver-haired woman's tone was as eager as her pale eyes and clutching hands. And then Scarlett saw it, in the woman's wrinkled palm. A green glass key.

Exactly like the one Scarlett had received, etched with a number five, and attached to a slip of paper bearing Donatella's name.

Julian's words rushed back. Her sister's name was Scarlett's first clue. And other people had been given the same exact clue.

It's all a game. Scarlett remembered the warning from the girl on the unicycle. This wasn't real.

But it felt that way. The dresses strewn about the room were really Donatella's. And when her sister had warned her away from the room, that had been her voice, and she had genuinely sounded upset, although now Scarlett feared it wasn't for the reason she originally thought.

Several feathers took flight as the woman plucked one of Tella's lacy light-blue nightdresses from the ground and her companion stole a piece of costume jewelry from the floor.

"Please, don't touch those," Scarlett said.

"Sorry, dear, just because she's *your sister* doesn't mean you get all the clues."

"These aren't clues! These are my sister's things." Scarlett raised her voice, but all that did was draw in more people. As eager as vultures, men and women, both young and old, ripped through the room like beasts sucking meat off bones. Scarlett felt powerless to stop them. How had she ever thought this was a magical game?

Some of them tried to ask her questions—as if she might lead them to another clue—but when Scarlett wouldn't answer they hastily moved on.

She tried to seize what she could. She grabbed dresses and under-things, ribbons and jewelry and picture cards. Tella must have been sincere about never returning to Trisda, for it wasn't only her clothes strewn about the room. All her favorite possessions were there, and a few of Scarlett's as well. Scarlett wasn't sure if these were things Tella had taken selfishly, or if she'd brought them to the isle for Scarlett because she'd not planned on either of them returning to Trisda.

"Excuse me." A pregnant girl with rosy cheeks and strawberry-blond hair approached Scarlett, her voice the one quiet sound amid the chaos. "You look as if you could use some help. I can't exactly bend over well." She motioned to her full, rounded stomach. "Maybe I could hold on to those things while you keep gathering?"

Scarlett was reaching the point where she couldn't pick up more, but she didn't want to let go of what she'd managed to grab.

"It's not as if I can run off," the girl added. She was young, about Scarlett's age, and from the size of her it appeared she could have her baby any minute.

"I'm not sure—" Scarlett broke off as a man in cheap velveteen pants and a brown bowler hat kicked a piece of stained glass. Something glittery red sparkled beneath it.

"No! You can't take those." Scarlett lunged toward the man, but the moment he saw her interest, his own ignited into something stronger. He snatched the precious earrings from the floor and bolted to the door.

She ran after him, but he was quick and her arms were burdened. She was only halfway down the hall when he made it to the rickety stairs.

"Here, let me hold those." The pregnant girl was beside her in the hall. "I'll be right here when you get back," she promised.

Scarlett didn't want to let go of what she'd gathered, but she really couldn't lose those earrings. Dropping her things in the girl's open arms, Scarlett clutched the bottom of her snowy skirt and tried to catch up with the man. She caught a glimpse of his brown bowler hat when she reached the staircase, but then it vanished from sight.

Out of breath, she burst downstairs, seeing the door to La Serpiente swing shut as if someone had just raced through. Scarlett chased after it, grabbing its garish green edge. Outside, the world was nightfall and daybreak all at once. Stars winked above like evil eyes, while hosts of lanterns set the streets ablaze with lustrous candlelight. An accordion's jaunty tune rang over the streets, and people moved to its music, swaying skirted hips and swinging jacketed elbows. But there were no bobbing bowler hats. The man had disappeared.

It shouldn't have mattered. They were only earrings. But they weren't only earrings. They were scarlets.

Scarlet stones for Scarlett, her mother had said. A final present before she had left. Scarlett had known there was no such thing as a scarlet stone, that they were really just colored bits of glass, but that had never mattered. They were a piece of her mother, and a reminder that Governor Dragna had once been a different man. *Your father gave me these,* she said, *because scarlet was my favorite color.*

It was difficult to picture her father being thoughtful like that now. He'd been so different before. After Paloma had run off and he'd been unable to find her, he'd destroyed everything that reminded him of her, leaving Scarlett with only the earrings, but only because she'd hidden them from him. That's when Scarlett swore to always stay with her sister, to never leave Tella with nothing but a piece of jewelry and faded memories the way their mother had. Even years later, Paloma's disappearance clung to Scarlett like a shadow that no amount of brightness could erase.

Scarlett's eyes burned with tears. Again, she tried to remember this was only a game. But it was not the game she thought it would be.

Back in the crooked hallway of La Serpiente, Scarlett was not surprised to find the pregnant girl had made off with all her things. Nothing remained in the hall of her sister's precious belongings. All Scarlett found was a glass button and a picture card that either the girl or someone else must have dropped.

"Those vultures."

"I didn't know you were the sort who ever cursed." Julian leaned against the opposite wall, brown arms crossed lazily over his chest, making Scarlett wonder if he'd been there all along.

"I didn't know the word *vulture* was a curse," said Scarlett.

"The way you used it made it sound like one."

"You'd curse too if you had a sister who was kidnapped as part of this game."

"There you go again thinking too highly of me, Crimson. If I had a sister who was kidnapped for this game, I'd use it to my advantage. Stop feeling sorry for yourself and come on." Julian pushed off the wall and started toward Tella's ransacked room.

The vultures were gone but everything important was cleaned out. Even the green glass doorknob had been absconded with.

"I tried to collect all her things but—" Scarlett's voice cracked as she entered the room, reminded of all the greedy eyes and hands grabbing at Tella's possessions, as if they were segments of a puzzle rather than pieces of a person.

She looked up at Julian, but there was no pity in his hooded gaze. "It's just a game, Crimson. Those people were only playing. If you want to win you have to be a little bit ruthless. Nice is not what Caraval is about."

"I don't believe you," Scarlett said. "Just because your moral compass is broken doesn't mean everyone here is unscrupulous."

"The ones who come close to winning are. Not everyone comes here just for fun. Some only play so they can sell what they gather to the highest bidder. Like the mate who ran off with your earthings."

"He won't get much money for those," Scarlett said bitterly.

"You'd be surprised." Julian picked up a knob from the broken wardrobe. "People are willing to spend a lot of money, or give up their deepest secrets, for a bit of Caraval magic. But those who don't play fairly usually pay an even higher price." Julian tossed the knob into the air and let it fall to the ground before quietly admitting, "Legend has a sense of justice that way."

"Well, I don't want to play at all," Scarlett said. "I just want to find my sister and get home in time for my wedding."

"That's a problem, then." Julian picked up the knob once again. "If you want to find your sister before you leave, you have to win the game."

"What are you talking about?"

"Let me guess, you didn't look at the clue I gave you?"

"All my clue said was Donatella's name."

"Are you certain?" he challenged.

"Of course. I just didn't realize it was a clue. I thought Legend—" Scarlett caught her mistake too late.

Julian's lips were curving into that same mocking twist that appeared whenever she mentioned Legend's name—even though she hadn't finished her witless thought.

Scarlett double-checked the note attached to her key. The only words on the note were her sister's name, but below that was a wide swath of empty space. Crossing over to the closest stained-glass candled lamp, Scarlett held the page up as Tella had done with the tickets from Legend. Sure enough, new lines of elegant script appeared.

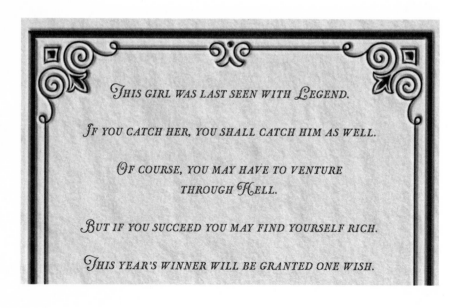

This girl was last seen with Legend.

If you catch her, you shall catch him as well.

Of course, you may have to venture through Hell.

But if you succeed you may find yourself rich.

This year's winner will be granted one wish.

After a moment the poem disappeared, and a new set of words took its place.

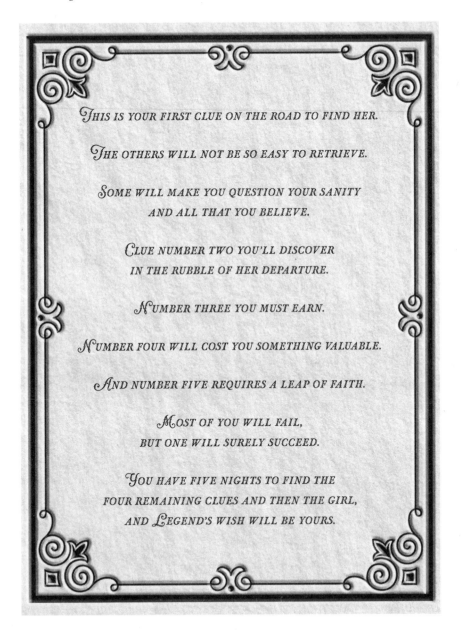

THIS IS YOUR FIRST CLUE ON THE ROAD TO FIND HER.

THE OTHERS WILL NOT BE SO EASY TO RETRIEVE.

*SOME WILL MAKE YOU QUESTION YOUR SANITY
AND ALL THAT YOU BELIEVE.*

*CLUE NUMBER TWO YOU'LL DISCOVER
IN THE RUBBLE OF HER DEPARTURE.*

NUMBER THREE YOU MUST EARN.

NUMBER FOUR WILL COST YOU SOMETHING VALUABLE.

AND NUMBER FIVE REQUIRES A LEAP OF FAITH.

*MOST OF YOU WILL FAIL,
BUT ONE WILL SURELY SUCCEED.*

*YOU HAVE FIVE NIGHTS TO FIND THE
FOUR REMAINING CLUES AND THEN THE GIRL,
AND LEGEND'S WISH WILL BE YOURS.*

Scarlett's dream must have been more than just a delusion. Legend really wanted her here. She recalled what the boy in the balcony had said: *Once inside, you will be presented with a mystery that must be solved.*

Figuring out where Tella had been taken must be this year's mystery. That's why so many people had been rummaging through her room; they were all searching for Tella as well. The note didn't say what would happen to Tella if no one found her, but Scarlett knew her sister didn't plan on going back to Trisda once the game ended.

If Scarlett didn't find her, Tella would vanish just like their mother had. If she wanted to see her sister again, Scarlett really did have to remain and play.

But Scarlett couldn't stay for the entire game. She was supposed to marry the count in six days, on the twentieth. There were five nights of Caraval, but it would take two full days of travel to return to Trisda. For Scarlett to make it home in time for her wedding, she would have to solve all the clues and find Tella before the last night of the game.

"Don't look so distressed," said Julian. "If your sister is with Legend, I'm sure she's being treated well."

"How do you know that?" Scarlett said. "You didn't hear her; she sounded so frightened."

"You saw her?"

"I only heard her voice." Scarlett explained what had happened.

Julian looked as if he were holding back a chuckle. "You keep forgetting this is a game. She was either acting, or someone else was pretending to be her. Either way, I don't think you need to worry about your sister. Trust me when I say Legend knows how to take care of his guests."

Julian's last words should have eased the knots in Scarlett's stomach, but something about the way Julian spoke made them tighten instead. His smile left his eyes cold, untouched.

"How do you know how Legend treats his guests?"

"Look at the room we were given because you're his *special visitor.*" Julian's accent thickened as he said the word *special.* "It makes sense to think he's put your sister somewhere just as nice."

Again, Scarlett should have felt better. Tella was not in any danger. Her sister was merely a part of the game, and an important part at that. Yet that's exactly what made Scarlett so unsettled. Why of all people would Legend choose her sister?

"Ah, I get it," Julian added. "You're jealous."

"No I'm not."

"It would make sense if you were. You were the one who wrote him letters all those years. No one would blame you if you felt bad he chose her instead."

"I'm not jealous," Scarlett repeated, but this only made the sailor smile wider as he continued to toy with the knob from the broken wardrobe, making it disappear and reappear between his deft fingers. A cheap magic trick.

She tried to think of Tella's disappearance this way, a simple sleight of hand—she wasn't gone for good, just out of Scarlett's reach.

She reread her first clue again. *Number two you'll discover in the rubble of her departure.* As Tella's sister, Scarlett should have had an advantage. If something in the room did not belong to Tella, Scarlett would know, but there were hardly any items left. Except for the glass button and the picture card in her hand, which upon second glance no longer looked quite so ordinary as before.

"What is it?" Julian asked. When Scarlett didn't answer right away his tone turned charming. "Come on, I thought we were a team."

"Being teammates has mostly benefitted you, not me."

"I wouldn't say 'mostly.' You forget, if it wasn't for me you wouldn't even be here."

"I could claim the same," Scarlett argued. "Last night, I saved you from being kicked out of the game, but you were the one who slept in our room!"

"You could have slept in the bed as well." Julian toyed with the top button of his shirt.

Scarlett scowled. "You know that was never an option."

"All right." He put his hands up in an exaggerated surrender. "From now on it will be a more even partnership. I'll keep telling you what I know about the game. We share with each other what we learn, and we trade days for the room. When you sleep in there, I promise I will not. Though you are welcome to join me whenever you want."

"Scoundrel," Scarlett muttered.

"I've been called much worse. Now, show me what's in your hands."

Scarlett looked out toward the hall, making certain no one was lingering outside the door. Then she turned the picture card in her hand toward Julian. "This did not belong to my sister."

14

When Scarlett was eleven, she'd been wildly in love with castles. It didn't matter if they were made of sand or stone or bits of imagination. They were fortresses, and Scarlett imagined if she lived in one, she'd be protected and treated like a princess.

Tella had no such romantic notions. She did not want to be cosseted, or spend her days locked away in some musty old castle. Tella wanted to travel the world, to see the ice villages of the Far North and the jungles of the Eastern Continent. And what better way to do that than with a beautiful emerald-green fish tail.

Tella never told Scarlett, but she wanted to be a mermaid.

Scarlett had laughed so hard she'd cried when she'd discovered Tella's hidden cache of picture cards. All of them with glittering mermaids—*and mermen*!

After that, whenever they fought, or Tella teased Scarlett, Scarlett was tempted to taunt her about being a mermaid. At least castles were real, but even Scarlett, who at the time still had impractical dreams and an untethered imagination, knew mermaids did not exist. But Scarlett never said a word. Not when Tella teased her about her castles, or about her growing fixation with Caraval. Because Tella's fantasy of being a mermaid gave Scarlett hope—that despite their mother's abandonment, and their father's lack of love, her sister could still dream, and that was something Scarlett never wanted to destroy.

"My sister's picture cards were a very particular collection," she told Julian. "Tella would not have had a picture card with a castle on it."

"I believe that's actually a palace," said Julian.

"It's still not a picture she would have had. This must be the next clue."

"You're positive?" Julian asked.

"If you don't trust my knowledge of my sister, then you can find someone else to work with."

"Believe it or not, Crimson, I like working with you. And I think I remember seeing that palace after we caught the boat last night. If you're right, and the card is the second clue, the palace is where we should look for the third one. When I played before—" Julian quieted at the sound of boot steps. Heavy. Confident. They stopped just outside the door to Tella's room.

Scarlett peeked into the hall.

"Why, hello there," Dante greeted her, with a smile a little too crooked to be perfect. Again he was dressed in all black, matching the darkness of his tattoos, but he seemed to brighten at the sight of

Scarlett. "I was just going by to check on you. Did you sleep well in my room?"

Coming from Dante, the words *sleep* and *my room* sounded more than a little scandalous.

"Who's at the door, my love?" Julian moved behind Scarlett. He didn't actually touch her, but the way he slid close was just as proprietary. She could feel the coolness of his body caressing hers as he placed one hand on the frame and the other on the door right behind her.

Dante's charming expression vanished. His eyes darted from Scarlett to Julian. He didn't say a word, but Scarlett could clearly read his hardening face. She felt something shift in Julian as well.

Julian's chest brushed her back, and when it did, every muscle was hard and rigid, at odds with his careless tone. "Isn't someone going to introduce me?"

"Julian, this is Dante," said Scarlett.

Dante stuck out a hand. The one with a rose inked on the back.

"He was kind enough to give up his room for me," Scarlett explained, "since there was a mix-up involving mine."

"Well, then it's very good to meet you." Julian shook Dante's hand. "I'm so glad you could help my fiancée. When I heard about what happened I felt sick. I wish she'd come to me." Julian turned to Scarlett, all false affection and infuriating looks.

She was wrong about him being disturbed. He was enjoying this. Playing the part of concerned fiancé, just to scare away Dante, when really he couldn't have cared less.

Scarlett looked back up at Dante, hoping to find a good way to explain she hadn't really lied. But he no longer looked at her, and his handsome face had shifted from upset to a disturbing shade of indifferent, as if she had ceased to exist.

"Come on, love," Julian whispered. "We should move aside so he can get a look."

"That's all right," Dante said. "I think I've seen what I needed." He took off down the hall without another word.

Scarlett whirled on Julian the moment Dante was out of sight. "I am not your piece of property and I don't appreciate your acting like it."

"But you enjoyed the way he was looking at you?" Julian gazed down at Scarlett, blinking thick, dark lashes as he gave her an intentionally lopsided smile. "You think he practices that look in a mirror?"

"Stop it. He didn't look at me like that. He's just a nice person. Unlike some people, he was willing to make a sacrifice to help me."

"He looked as if he was willing to collect on that sacrifice, too."

"Ugh! Not everyone is like you." Scarlett marched out the doorway and down the hall, gripping the second clue—Tella's picture card.

"All I'm saying is, that one's bad news," Julian said. "You should stay away from him."

Scarlett stopped at the top of the stairs, squaring her shoulders as she turned to Julian, clearly recalling the hungry look on his face when she'd caught him in the barrel room with Tella. "As if you're any better."

"I'm not saying I'm a good man," Julian said. "But I don't want any of the things from you that bloke does. If I did, I'd tell you to stay away from me too. He won Caraval last time I played. Remember what I said about this game costing people? Even winning comes with a price, and his triumph cost him, a lot. My bet is he'll do anything to win the wish and try to get back everything he lost. If you think my moral compass is damaged, his doesn't exist."

"Oh, if it isn't the happy couple!" The pretty dark-skinned girl clapped excitedly as Scarlett and Julian climbed into her boat.

The last thing Scarlett felt like doing was pretending to be Julian's blissful bride-to-be, but she managed to add some sugar to her voice. "Weren't you on a unicycle last night?"

"Oh, I do lots of things," the girl said proudly.

Scarlett remembered Julian's warning about her, but as the girl started to row, it was difficult to think she was made of anything other than genuine cheer. Much friendlier than the sailor girl from the night before.

Perhaps Julian just didn't like anyone who seemed pleasant.

Although, he was now amiable enough to this girl; after flashing her the picture card with their destination, he inquired after her name.

"Jovan, but people call me Jo," said the girl. As she rowed, Julian asked more questions and laughed at her jokes. Scarlett was impressed with how polite he could be when he wanted, though she imagined most of it was just to get information. Jovan pointed out all sorts of sights. The canals were circular, like a long apple peel spread out around curving lantern-lit streets, full of pubs piping russet smoke, bakeries shaped like cupcakes, and shops wrapped in colors like birthday presents. Cerulean blue. Apricot orange. Saffron yellow. Primrose pink.

While the canals remained midnight dark, glass lanterns lined the edges of each building, emphasizing the brilliant colors as people bustled in and out. Scarlett thought it looked like a sort of jolly dance to the various kinds of music that played. Harps, bagpipes, violins, flutes, and cellos. Each canal had a different instrumental heartbeat.

"There's a lot to see here," said Jovan. "If you're willing to pay and you look hard enough, you'll find things on the isle you won't come across anywhere else—some people just come here to hunt through shops and don't even bother playing the game."

Jovan continued chattering, but her words were lost as Scarlett spied what seemed to be a commotion on the corner of one street. It looked as if a woman was being dragged out from a shop, forcibly. Scarlett heard a cry, then all she could see was a cluster of people pulling at the woman, made of thrashing arms and kicking legs.

"What's going on over there?" Scarlett pointed. But by the time Jovan and Julian looked, someone on the street had snuffed out all the nearby lanterns, concealing whatever Scarlett had witnessed in a curtain made of night.

"What did you see?" Julian asked.

"There was a woman, in a dove-gray dress, and she was being dragged out of a shop."

"Oh, that was probably just a street show," Jovan said merrily. "Sometimes performers do that to spice things up for the folks who are just observing—probably made it seem as if she'd stolen something or was going mad. I'm sure you'll see more like that as the game goes on."

Scarlett almost whispered to Julian that it looked very real, but hadn't she been warned about that when she'd first entered the game?

Jovan clapped again as she stopped rowing. "Now here we are. The palace on the card. Otherwise known as Castillo Maldito."

For a moment Scarlett forgot about the woman. Lines of gleaming sand stretched up into a palace shaped like a colossal birdcage, covered in curved bridges, horseshoe-shaped arches, and rounded domes, all dusted with gold-like flecks of fallen sunshine. The picture card had not done this place justice. Rather than being lit by candles, the structure itself glowed. It filled everything with light, making it brighter there than everywhere else, as if they'd found a spot of land that managed to bottle streams of daylight.

"What do we owe you for the ride?" Julian asked.

"Oh, for you two, there's no charge," said Jovan, and Scarlett realized this was probably another reason why he'd been so kind to her. "You'll need all you have inside there. Time goes even faster in the Castillo."

Jovan nodded to the two massive hourglasses flanking the sand palace's entrance, each more than two stories high and filled with churning ruby beads. Only a small fraction of the beads were at the bottom.

"If you've noticed, the nights and days on this isle are shorter," Jovan went on. "Certain types of magic are fueled by time, and this place uses a lot of magic, so make sure you use your minutes wisely when you go inside."

Julian helped Scarlett out of the boat. As they crossed over the arched bridge and past the massive hourglasses, Scarlett wondered how many minutes of her life it would take to form one bead. A second in Caraval seemed richer than an ordinary second, like that moment on the cusp of sunset, when all the colors of the sky coalesce into magic.

"We should look for the type of place your sister would be attracted to," said Julian. "I'd wager that's where we find the third clue."

She thought of the note tied to her key. *Number three you must earn.*

Beyond the hourglasses, the path on their right led up into a series of golden terraces, which formed most of the Castillo. From below they looked like libraries, full of the kind of antique books Scarlett felt people were always saying not to touch.

The path straight ahead fed into a massive courtyard, swarming with color and sound and people. A banyan tree grew in the heart of it, teeming with tiny birds made of wonder. Winged zebras and avian kittens, miniature flying tigers wrestling with palm-size elephants that used their ears to keep aloft. A motley collection of gazebos and tents surrounded the tree, music dancing out of some, while laughter tripped out of others, like the jade-green tent selling kisses.

There was no question as to where Tella would have ventured, and if Julian had asked, Scarlett would have confessed she was also mesmerized by what she saw in the tented courtyard. She should not have been tempted.

Scarlett should have been thinking only of Tella, looking for her next clue. But as she watched the jade kissing tent, fluttering with hushed giggles and whispers and the promise of butterflies, she wondered. . . .

Scarlett had been kissed. At the time she'd told herself it was nice, and she had been content with that, but now *nice* seemed like a word people used when they had nothing better to say. Scarlett doubted her nice kiss would compare to a kiss during Caraval. In a place where even the air tasted sweet, she tried to imagine the flavor of someone else's lips pressed to hers.

"Does that strike your fancy?" Julian drew out his words with a throaty rasp, bringing an instant flush to Scarlett's face.

"I was looking next door." She hastily pointed to a tent the unfortunate color of plums.

Julian's grin grew. Obviously he didn't believe her. His smile stretched wider as her cheeks grew pinker.

"No need to be embarrassed," he said. "Although if you need some practice before your wedding, I'm more than willing to help for free."

Scarlett attempted to make a sound of disgust, but it came out more like a whimper.

"Was that a yes?" Julian asked.

She gave him a foul look, meant to serve as a no. But apparently teasing her put him in a good mood.

"Have you even seen your fiancé?" he asked. "He could be really ugly."

"His appearance doesn't matter. He sends me letters every week, and they are kind and thoughtful and—"

"In other words he's a liar," Julian broke in.

Scarlett scowled. "You don't even know what his letters say."

"I know he's a count." Julian began ticking things off with his fingers. "That means he's a noble, and no one holds a position like that and manages to stay honest. If he's looking for an island bride, it's probably because his family is inbred, which also means he's unattractive." Julian's tone turned serious as one of his fingers came to rest beneath the bottom of Scarlett's chin, tilting her face toward his. "Are you sure you don't want to rethink my offer and consider that kiss?"

Scarlett pulled away with a grunt of revulsion, but it was a little too loud, a little too wrong. And to her horror, rather than feeling distaste, a tingle of periwinkle curiosity prickled her senses.

Scarlett and Julian were closer to the kissing tent now. Perfume wafted from it. It smelled like the middle of the night, making Scarlett think of soft lips and strong hands, dark stubble brushing her cheek that reminded her entirely too much of Julian.

Ignoring the way her pulse kicked up speed, she tried to think of something clever to say in retort to Julian's next jibe. But, for once, Julian remained quiet. In a way his sudden silence was more uncomfortable than if he'd teased her again.

She couldn't imagine her response to his offer had offended the sailor, although she noticed he didn't walk as close as before. Even when he made no effort to touch her, he was usually near enough that he easily could, but they continued through the courtyard, a little too far apart and much too quietly, appearing nothing like an engaged couple.

"You wish to know your future?" asked a young man.

"Oh, I—" Scarlett sputtered as she turned and saw a wall of flesh.

She had never looked at a naked man, and while this man was not quite that, he was so close to it she knew it would be improper to even consider entering his russet tent. Yet she didn't back away.

All he wore was a brown cloth that went from his hips to his thick upper thighs, revealing smooth planes of skin all covered in brightly inked tattoos. A fire-breathing dragon chased a mermaid across the forest on his abdomen, while cherubs shot arrows from above his ribs. Some speared coy fish, while others pierced clouds that bled yellow dandelions and peach flower petals. Some of the petals dripped toward his legs, which were covered in detailed circus scenes.

His face was equally decorated; one purple eye looked out from each cheek, while black stars lined his actual eyes. But it was his lips that drew Scarlett's attention. Surrounded by tattoos of barbed blue wire, one side was locked with a golden padlock, while the other was sealed with a heart.

"How much do you charge for a reading?" Julian asked. If he was surprised by the man's unique appearance it didn't show.

"I will uncover your future in proportion to what you give me," said the inked man.

"That's all right," Scarlett said. "I think I'm quite fine discovering my future as it comes."

Julian eyed her. "That's not how it looked yesterday when we passed by those ridiculous spectacles."

"What spectacles?"

"You know, the different-colored ones that could see the future."

Scarlett remembered now: she had been intrigued, but she was surprised he'd noticed.

"If you want to go in, I can keep looking for clues." Julian pressed a hand to the small of Scarlett's back and gave her a gentle shove.

She was about to argue; putting on spectacles was not the same as entering a darkened tent with a half-naked man. But yesterday she'd lost Tella because she'd been too frightened to strike a bargain. If the third clue needed to be earned, maybe she could earn information about the future—about where she would find Tella.

"Do you want to go in with me?" Scarlett asked.

"I'd rather my future remain a surprise." Julian cocked his head toward the kissing tent. "When you're done, I'll meet you over there." He blew her a taunting kiss, which made her think maybe all the earlier awkwardness was just inside of her head.

"I'm not sure if I'd agree with that," said the tattooed man.

Scarlett could have sworn she hadn't spoken aloud; surely this man couldn't have read her mind. Or maybe he'd only guessed that statement could easily apply to whatever it was she'd been thinking, another way to trick her into entering his darkened tent.

15

The tattooed young man told her his name was Nigel as he guided her past the sleek borders of the tent, onto sand steps that led her down into a den covered in pillows and filled with a fog of candle smoke and jasmine incense.

"Sit," instructed Nigel.

"I think I'd rather stand." The sea of pillows reminded Scarlett too much of the bed in her room at La Serpiente. For a moment she flashed back to Julian as he stretched across it and unbuttoned his shirt.

When she looked back at the cushions, Nigel had positioned himself in a similar pose, naked arms spread across the pillows, leaving her with the urge to run back up the stairs.

"Where is your ball of crystal? Or those cards people use?" she asked.

The corner of Nigel's tattooed lips twitched, but it was enough to make Scarlett edge back toward the steps. "You have much fear."

"No, I'm just cautious," Scarlett said. "And I'm trying to figure out how all this works."

"Because you are afraid," he repeated, looking at Scarlett in a way that made her believe he was talking about more than just how hesitant she'd been to enter his tent. "Your eyes keep finding the painted lock on my lips. You feel trapped and unsafe." Nigel pointed to the heart on the other side of his mouth. "Your eyes land here as well. You want love and protection."

"Isn't that what every girl wants?"

"I cannot speak for every girl, but most people's eyes are drawn to other things. Many want power." Nigel drew a finger, inked with a dagger, over the dragon on his abdomen. "Others want pleasure." He ran a hand over the wild circus on his thighs, along with a few more tattoos. "Your eyes passed over all these."

"So is this how you tell the future?" Scarlett inched closer, growing more intrigued. "You use the paintings on your body to read people."

"I think of them as mirrors. The future is much like the past; it is mostly set, but can always be altered—"

"I thought it was the opposite," Scarlett said. "The past is set but the future is changeable?"

"No. The past is only mostly set, and the future is harder to change than you would think."

"So, you're saying everything is fated?" Scarlett was not fond of fate. She liked to believe if she were good, good things would happen. Fate left her feeling powerless, and hopeless, and with an overall feeling of lessness. To her, fate seemed like a larger, omnipotent version of her father, stealing her choices and controlling her life without any regard for her feelings. Fate meant that nothing she did mattered.

"You're too quick to dive into fear," Nigel said. "What you think of as fate only applies to the past. Our futures are only predictable because as creatures of this world we are predictable. Think of a cat and mouse." Nigel revealed the underside of his arm where a tawny cat stretched its clawed paws toward a black-and-white-striped mouse.

"When a cat sees a mouse, it will always chase, unless, perhaps, the cat is pursued by something larger, like a dog. We are much the same. The future knows what things we desire, unless there is something greater in our path that chases us away." Nigel moved his fingers to trace a midnight-blue top hat on his wrist and Scarlett watched, mesmerized. It looked almost exactly like the one Legend had worn in her dream, making her recall the time when all she wanted was a letter from him.

"But even those things that might alter our course, the future usually sees clearly," Nigel went on. "It is not fate, it is simply the future observing that which we crave the most. Every person has the power to change their fate if they are brave enough to fight for what they desire more than anything."

Scarlett tore her eyes from the top hat and caught Nigel smiling at her once more. "You're intrigued by that hat?"

"Oh, I wasn't really looking at that." Scarlett didn't know why she felt embarrassed, except that she should have been thinking about Tella, and not Legend. "I was just looking at the other images on your arm."

Nigel clearly did not believe her. He continued to grin, tiger-wide. "Are you prepared for me to tell you what I see in your future?"

Scarlett shifted her weight, watching as more smoke wove around the pillows at her feet. The lines of the game were beginning to blur again. Nigel made more sense than she wanted him to make. As she looked at the fire-breathing dragon on his abdomen she thought of her father—his destructive desire for power. The wild circus on Nigel's thighs reminded Scarlett of Tella—her need for pleasure to help her forget the wounds she liked to ignore. And he'd been absolutely right about the lock and the heart on his lips. "What will it cost me?"

"Just a few answers." Nigel waved a hand, flicking wisps of purple smoke in her direction. "I will ask you questions, and for every one you respond to truthfully, I will give you an answer in return."

The way he said it made it sound so simple.

Just a few answers.

Not her firstborn child.

Not a piece of her soul.

So simple.

Too simple.

But Scarlett knew nothing was that simple, especially not in a den such as this, a place designed to trap and seduce.

"I'll start with something easy," Nigel said. "Tell me about your companion, the handsome young man you traveled here with. I'm curious, how do you feel about him?"

Scarlett's eyes immediately returned to Nigel's lips. To the barbed wire around them. *Not the heart. Not the heart.* Her feelings for Julian were not like that.

"Julian is selfish, dishonest, and opportunistic."

"Yet you've agreed to play the game with him. Those must not be your only feelings." Nigel paused. He'd seen her look at the heart. Why it mattered, Scarlett wasn't sure, but she could tell it did. She heard it in the way he asked, "Do you find him attractive?"

Scarlett wanted to deny it. Julian was the barbed wire. Not the heart. But while she didn't always like Julian as a person, she couldn't honestly deny he was extremely appealing physically. His rugged face, his wild dark hair, his warm brown skin. And even though she would never tell him, she loved the way he moved, with total confidence, as though nothing in the world could harm him. It made her less fearful when she was around him. As if boldness and bravery did not always end in defeat.

But she didn't want to tell Nigel this, either. What if Julian were listening outside the tent?

"I—" Scarlett tried to say she didn't care for his appearance, but the words stuck to her tongue like molasses.

"Are you having a problem?" Nigel waved his hand over a cone of incense. "Here, this helps loosen the tongue."

Or forces people to tell the truth, thought Scarlett.

When Scarlett opened her mouth again, the words poured out. "I think he's the most attractive person I've ever seen."

She wanted to clap her hand over her mouth and shove the words back inside.

"I also think he's thoroughly full of himself," Scarlett managed to add, just in case the scoundrel was listening outside.

"Interesting." Nigel formed a steeple with his hands. "Now, what two questions would you like to ask me?"

"What?" It alarmed her that Nigel only wanted to know about Julian. "You don't have any more questions for me?"

"We're running out of time. Hours slip by like minutes here." Nigel's hands drifted toward the dying candles lining his den. "You have two questions."

"Only two?"

"Do you wish that to be one of your questions?"

"No, I just—" Scarlett clamped her mouth shut before she accidentally said something she shouldn't.

If it were truly a game, it didn't matter what she asked. Whatever answers she received would be make-believe. But what if parts of it were real? For a moment Scarlett dared to let her thoughts tiptoe into that hazardous place. She'd already witnessed magic in the clock shop, via Algie's clockwork door and the enchanted dress from Legend. And Nigel's incense had made her speak the truth, which evidenced at least some more magic. If the man before her could truly tell the future, what would she want to know?

Her eyes returned to the heart at the corner of his mouth. Red. The color of love and heartache and other things both virtuous and vile. As she looked at it then, she thought of the count, of his lovely letters and whether or not she could believe all the things he'd said. "The person I'm going to marry, can you tell me what sort of man he is—is he a good, honest person?"

Scarlett immediately regretted not asking about her sister first. She should have been thinking only of Tella—that's why she'd gone into the tent in the first place. But it was too late to snatch the question back.

"No one is truly honest," Nigel answered. "Even if we don't lie to others, we often lie to ourselves. And the word *good* means different things to different people." Nigel leaned forward, close enough for Scarlett to feel as if all the scenes on his body were watching her as well. He stared so intently, she wondered if there were images painted on her face that only he could see. "I am sorry, but the man you will marry is not what you would call good. At one time, perhaps, but he has turned from that path, and it is not yet clear if he will turn back."

"What do you mean? How can it not be clear? I thought you said the future was mostly fixed—that we're like cats, always chasing after the same mouse."

"Yes, but every so often there are two mice. It is not yet clear which one he will continue to chase. You would be wise to be careful." Again, Nigel looked at Scarlett as if she were covered in pictures only he could see. Pictures that pulled his face into a frown, as if she too had a heart near her mouth, but it was shattered into pieces.

She tried to tell herself it was all in her head. He was attempting to trick her. To frighten her as part of the game. But her marriage to the count was in no way connected to the game. There was nothing she could gain by Nigel's cryptic warning.

Nigel rose from his cushions and started toward the back of the tent.

"Wait," Scarlett said. "I never asked my second question."

"Actually you asked me three questions."

"But two of those weren't real questions. You never fully explained the rules. You owe me another question."

Nigel looked back at Scarlett. A tower of motley images, topped off by a vicious smile. "I don't owe you anything."

16

lease!" Scarlett chased after him. "I'm not asking for a glimpse into the future. My sister has been taken as part of the game; can you tell me where I'll find her?"

Nigel turned around. A flash of ink and color. "If you really care about this sister, why didn't you ask about her first?"

"I don't know," Scarlett said. But that wasn't quite true. She'd made a mistake yet again, just like in the clock shop. She'd been worried about her own future more than she had cared about finding her sister. But maybe she could fix this error. Nigel had said he'd uncover her future in proportion to what she gave him.

"Wait!" Scarlett called as he started walking again. "It was the heart," she blurted. "Every time I looked at you I saw the heart around your lips and it made me think of my wedding, which is only a week away. I really want to get married, but I've never met my groom, so there are things I don't know about him and—" Scarlett didn't want to admit how she really felt, but she forced out the words: "I'm scared."

Slowly Nigel turned once more. She wondered if he could see how deep her fear went, further down than Scarlett herself had realized. Her eyes found a link of chains around Nigel's throat, and she imagined an invisible bind around her neck as well, always holding her back, formed from years of her father's cruel punishments.

"If you want to win this game," Nigel said, "you should forget about your wedding. And if you want to find your sister, you will not find her in this Castillo. Follow the boy with a heart made of black."

"Is that the third clue?" Scarlett asked. But Nigel was already gone.

When she stepped back into the courtyard the brightness of the Castillo had dimmed. Its arches now looked dull bronze instead of bright gold, casting the palace in distended shadows. She'd used up almost all her time. But she dared to hope that by confessing her fears to Nigel she had *earned* the third clue. Maybe she was one step closer to Tella.

When Nigel said, *Follow the boy with a heart made of black,* her first thought was of Julian, selfish and deceitful. Scarlett could easily imagine his heart to be black.

Unfortunately, she could see no sign of the devious sailor, or the jade kissing tent where he told her to meet him. She saw a furry clover-green tent and a shimmery emerald-green one, but no jade-green anything.

Scarlett felt as if the isle was playing with her.

She crossed over to the emerald tent. Bottles covered every surface: floor, walls, the beams holding up the ceiling. Glass tinkled like fairy dust as she peered inside.

Aside from the female proprietor, the only other people in the tent were a pair of giddy young women. Both hovered in front of a locked glass box full of black bottles with ruby-red labels.

"Maybe if we get to that girl first and find Legend we can slip him some of this," said one young woman to the other.

"They're talking about my romance tonic," said the proprietor. She stepped in front of Scarlett, greeting her with a spritz of something minty. "But I imagine that's not what you're here for. Are you looking for a new scent? We have oils that attract and perfumes that repel."

"Oh, no, thank you." Scarlett stepped back before the woman could spray her again. "What was in that bottle?"

"Just my way of saying hello."

Scarlett doubted that. She turned to leave, yet something pulled her back into the tent, a voiceless call, drawing her to a crude bookshelf in the rear. Piled with burnt-orange apothecary bottles and vials, labeled with things like *Tincture of Forgetting* and *Extract of Lost Tomorrows.*

A voice in Scarlett's head said she was wasting time—she needed to find Julian and follow his black heart. She started to turn to leave once more, but a celestial-blue ampoule on a high shelf caught her eye. *Elixir of Protection.*

For a second Scarlett swore the blue liquid inside pulsed like a heartbeat.

The tent's proprietor retrieved it and handed it to Scarlett. "Do you have enemies?"

"No, just curious," Scarlett hedged.

The woman's eyes were bottle green, an intense concentration of color, and their crinkled edges said, *I do not believe you.* Yet she kindly pretended otherwise. "If someone is about to cause you harm," she went on coolly, "this will stop them. All you need to do is spray a bit on their face."

"Like you did to me?" Scarlett asked.

"My perfume merely opened your eyes so you would see what you might need."

Scarlett rolled the tiny jar in her palm, barely larger than a vial, yet heavy. She imagined the solidly reassuring weight of it in her pocket. "What will this cost me?"

"For you?" The woman looked Scarlett over carefully, taking in her posture, the way she curled into herself or refused to have her back fully to the tent's opening. "Tell me who you fear the most."

Scarlett hesitated. Julian had warned her about giving her secrets away too freely. He'd also told her that to win and find her sister she needed to be a little merciless. She imagined this potion could be ruthless, although that wasn't the entire reason Scarlett pushed out the words in one quick breath. "Marcello Dragna."

With the name came a fearful rush of anise and lavender and something akin to rotted plums. Scarlett looked around the tent, making sure her father wasn't standing at the mouth of it.

"This elixir can be used on a person only once," warned the woman, "and the effects wear off after two hours."

"Thank you." As soon as Scarlett said the words, she thought she glimpsed Julian just beyond the border of the adjacent tent. A blur of dark hair and stealthy movements. She swore he looked right at her, but then he continued in the opposite direction.

Scarlett followed hastily, dashing to the cool edge of the court-yard, where the colorful pavilions no longer grew. But Julian disappeared again. He slipped under the arch to her left.

"Julian!" Scarlett crossed beneath the same shadowed arc, trailing a narrow path that led into a dreary garden. But there was no glimpse of Julian's dark hair behind any of its cracked statues. No sight of his sharp movements near any of its dying plants. He'd vanished, just like all the colors had seemed to fade from the garden, leaving it bleached out and unlovely.

Scarlett searched for another archway Julian might have used to exit, but the small park dead-ended at a shabby fountain spitting out bits of bubbling brown water into a dirty basin containing a few pathetic coins and a glass button. The saddest wishing well Scarlett had ever seen.

It made no sense. Julian's disappearance, or this neglected plot of earth, left to die in the midst of a domain so carefully cultivated. Even the air felt off. Fetid and stagnant.

Scarlett could almost feel the sadness of the fountain infecting her, turning her discouragement into the type of dreary yellow hopelessness that choked out life. She wondered if that's what had happened to the plants. She knew how crippling bleakness could feel. If not for Scarlett's determination to protect her sister at all costs, she might have given up long ago.

She probably should have. What was that saying, *No love ever goes unpunished?* In many ways, loving Tella was a source of constant pain. No matter how hard Scarlett tried to care for her sister, it was never enough to fill the hole their mother had left. And it wasn't as if Tella really loved Scarlett back. If she did, she wouldn't have risked every-thing Scarlett wanted by dragging her to this miserable game against her will. Tella never thought things through. She was selfish and reckless and—

No! Scarlett shook her head and took a deep, heavy breath. None of those thoughts were true. She loved Tella, more than anything. She wanted to find her, more than everything.

This is the fountain's doing, Scarlett realized. Whatever despair she felt was the product of some sort of enchantment, most likely meant to keep anyone from lingering there too long.

This garden was hiding something.

Maybe that was why Nigel had told her to follow Julian and his black heart—because Nigel knew that it would lead her here. This must be where the next clue was hidden.

Scarlett's boots clicked against dull stone as she moved closer to where she'd spied the button. It was the second one she'd seen that night. It had to be part of a clue. Scarlett used a stick to fetch it out. And that's when she saw it.

It was so insubstantial she almost missed it—eyes that cared less might have overlooked it. Beneath the grim brown water, etched into the edge of the basin, was a sun with a star inside and a teardrop in-side of the star—the symbol of Caraval. It did not feel as magical as the silver crest on the first letter Legend had sent her; of course noth-ing felt charmed in this awful garden.

Scarlett touched the symbol with her stick. Immediately, the water started draining, taking every feeling of wretchedness with it, while the bricks of the fountain shifted, revealing a winding set of stairs that disappeared into a dark unknown. It was the type of staircase Scarlett was reluctant to venture down alone. And she was running dangerously low on time if she wanted to get back to the inn before sunrise. But if this was where Julian had disappeared and if he was the boy with the heart made of black, Scarlett needed to follow him to discover the next clue. Either Tella could be the thing Scarlett chased after, or Scarlett's fear could be what chased Scarlett away.

Trying not to worry that she was making an immense mistake, Scarlett darted down the steps. After the first damp set, sand circled around her boots as she spiraled farther down the stairs, which reached much deeper than the steps to the barrel room back home.

Torches lit her descent, casting dramatic shadows against light-gold bricks of sand that grew darker with each flight. She imagined herself to be three stories below; it felt as if she'd entered the heart of the Castillo. A place she was becoming quite certain she did not belong.

The concerns she'd tried to bury resurfaced as she plunged farther down. What if the boy she'd followed wasn't Julian? What if Nigel had been lying? Hadn't Julian warned her about trusting people? Each fear squeezed the invisible chain around her neck, tempting her to turn around.

At the foot of the steps, a corridor stretched out in multiple directions, a snake with more than one head. Dark and tortuous, magnificent and frightening. Cold air blew from one tunnel. Warmth breezed out of another. But no footsteps sounded down any of them.

"How did you get down here?"

Scarlett spun around. Dim light flickered over the mouth of the cold corridor, and the red-lipped girl who'd been unable to keep her eyes off Julian as she'd rowed Scarlett and Julian to La Serpiente the night before stepped out.

"I'm looking for my companion. I saw him come down—"

"No one else is down here," said the girl. "This isn't a place you should—"

Someone screamed. As hot and bright as fire.

A weak voice inside her reminded Scarlett it was only a game, that the shriek was just an illusion. But the red-lipped girl across from Scarlett appeared genuinely scared, and the wail sounded incredibly real. Her thoughts flashed back to the contract she'd signed in blood, and the rumors of the woman who'd died during the game a few years ago.

"What was that?" Scarlett demanded.

"You need to leave." The girl grabbed Scarlett's arm and wrenched her back to the steps.

Another scream rocked the walls, and dust shook off the corridors, mixing with the torchlight, as if flickering to the wretched sound.

It was only for a trembling second, but Scarlett swore she saw a woman being tied up—the same woman in the dove-gray dress who Scarlett had witnessed being carried away earlier. Jovan had told her it was only a performance, but there was no one in this place to hear this woman's wails, aside from Scarlett.

"What are they doing to her?" Scarlett continued struggling with the red-lipped girl, hoping to get to the other woman, but this girl was strong. Scarlett remembered the force she'd used to row the boat the night before.

"Stop fighting me," warned the girl. "If you go deeper into these tunnels, you'll end up mad, just like her. We're not hurting her; we're stopping that woman from hurting herself." The girl pushed Scarlett a final time, knocking her to her knees at the bottom of the staircase. "You will not find your companion down here, only madness."

A fresh scream punctuated her sentence; this one sounded male.

"Who was—" A sand-slate door slammed in front of Scarlett before she could finish. It cut off the girl, the stairs from the corridor, and the screams from Scarlett's ears. But even as Scarlett climbed back up to the courtyard, echoes lingered in her head like damp on a sunless day.

The last scream hadn't sounded like Julian. Or that's what she tried to tell herself as she caught a boat to take her back to La Serpiente. She reminded herself it was only a game. But the madness part was starting to feel very real.

If the woman in gray truly had gone insane, Scarlett couldn't help but wonder: Why? And if she hadn't, if she was just another actor, Scarlett could see how going after her, how believing her cries of pain were real, could make a person mad.

Scarlett thought of Tella. What if she was tied up screaming somewhere? *No.* That type of thinking was exactly what would drive Scarlett mad. Legend had probably provided an entire wing of lush rooms for Tella; Scarlett could picture her ordering around servants and eating strawberries dipped in pink sugar. Hadn't Julian said Legend took excellent care of his guests?

Scarlett hoped she'd find Julian in the tavern, teasing her about how she'd run after someone who looked like him, and how long she'd spent inside of Nigel's silken tent. Scarlett convinced herself Julian had just given up on waiting for her; he'd gotten bored and taken off. She'd not left him screaming in the tunnel. It was a different dark-haired young man she'd seen run into that garden. And Nigel's words had been another trick of the game. She was certain of all this by the time she made it back to La Serpiente. *Almost.*

The Glass Tavern was even more crowded than it had been the day before. It smelled of laughter and boasts, laced with sweetened ale. Half a dozen glass tables were cluttered with windswept women and red-cheeked men all bragging of their finds—or bemoaning their lack of discoveries.

To Scarlett's great pleasure, she overheard the silver-haired woman she'd met in Tella's room talk of how she'd been taken for a fool by a man who claimed to sell enchanted doorknobs.

"We tried the knob," she said. "Put it in the door up there, but it didn't lead us anywhere new."

"That's because it's just a game," a black-bearded man replied. "There's not really any magic here."

"Oh, I don't think—"

Scarlett would have loved to continue eavesdropping in the hopes of learning something, as the lines between the game and reality were starting to blur a little too much for her, but a young man near the corner caught her eye. Dark, chaotic hair. Strong shoulders. Confident. *Julian.*

Scarlett felt a swell of heady relief. He was all right. He wasn't being tortured; in fact, he looked quite well. His back was turned, but the tilt of his head and the angle of his chest made it clear he was flirting with the girl near his table.

Scarlett's relief shifted into something else. If she wasn't even allowed to chat with another young man because of their make-believe engagement, she was not going to let Julian make eyes at some tart in a bar. Especially when this particular tart was the pregnant strawberry blonde who had made off with Scarlett's things. Only now the young woman didn't appear to be with child at all. The bodice of her dress was smooth and flat, no longer curving around a bulging stomach.

Slightly seething, Scarlett placed a hand on Julian's shoulder as she approached. "Sweetheart, who is—"

Scarlett's words broke as he turned around. "Oh, I'm sorry." She should have realized he was wearing all black. "I thought you were—"

"Your fiancé?" Dante provided, in a tone full of nasty innuendo.

"Dante—"

"Oh, so you remember my name. You didn't just use me for my bed." His voice was loud. Patrons sitting at the next tables shot Scarlett looks ranging from disgust to desire. One man licked his lips, while a group of boys made inappropriate gestures.

The strawberry blonde snorted. "This is the girl you told me about? From the way you described her, I thought she'd be much prettier."

"I'd been drinking," Dante said.

Red heat burned Scarlett's cheeks, far brighter than her usual peach embarrassment. Julian might be a liar, but it looked as if he was right about Dante's true nature.

Scarlett wanted to say something back to both Dante and the girl, but her throat was tight and her chest was hollow. The men at nearby tables were still leering, and now the ribbons of her dress were beginning to darken, shifting into shades of black.

She needed to get out of there.

Scarlett turned on her heel and wove back through the tavern, followed by whispers, while black color wept from the ribbons of her dress, spreading like stains all over her white gown. Tears sprang to her eyes. Hot, angry, embarrassed.

This is what she got for pretending as if she didn't have a real fiancé. And what had she been thinking—touching him like that? Calling him "sweetheart"? She'd believed Dante was Julian, but did that make it any better?

Stupid Julian.

She should never have agreed to her arrangement with him. She wanted to be angry with Dante, but it was Julian who had created this mess. She braced herself as she opened the door to her room, half expecting to find him lounging in the great white bed, dark head propped up on a pillow, feet resting on one as well. The room had the feeling of him. Cold wind, wicked smiles, and blatant lies. Scarlett felt the shadow of those things as she stepped inside. But there was no young man to go with it.

The fire quietly roared. The bed lay there, covered in layers of untouched fluff. The sailor had kept his promise about trading days in the room.

Or he'd never left Castillo Maldito.

17

Scarlett did not dream of Legend. She did not dream at all, no matter how hard she chased sleep. Each time she shut her eyes, the snaking corridors beneath Castillo Maldito stretched out, filled with flickering torches and screams.

When she opened her eyes, lurking shadows moved where they did not belong. Then she closed her eyes again and the dreadful cycle repeated.

She told herself it was only in her head, the shadows and the sounds. Wails and footsteps and crackling noises.

Until something cracked that was definitely in her room.

Scarlett sat up carefully. The dying fire buzzed as it tossed bits of light here and there. But the noise she heard was louder than that.

It came again. Another crack, right before the hidden door to her room flew open and Julian stumbled in. "Hello, Crimson."

"What are—" Scarlett couldn't finish her question. Even in the grainy light she could tell something was not right. His uneven steps.

The tilt of his head. Quickly, she escaped her bed, covering herself with a blanket. "What happened to you?"

"It's not as bad as it looks." Julian swayed as if drunk, but all Scarlett could smell was the metallic tang of blood.

"Who did this to you?"

"Remember, it's only a game." Julian smiled, twisted in the firelight, right before collapsing on the lounge.

"Julian!" Scarlett rushed to his side. His entire body was cold, as if he'd been outdoors all this time. She wanted to shake him, to wake him back up, but she wasn't sure that was a brilliant idea given all the blood. So much blood. *Very real blood.* It matted his dark hair and stained her hands as she tried to put him in a better position. "I'll be right back—I'm going to leave and get you help."

"No—" Julian grabbed her arm. His fingers were frosty, like the rest of him. "Don't go. It's only a head wound; they look much worse than they are. Just grab the towel and the basin. Please." His fingers tightened as he said the word *please.* "It will raise too many questions if you bring anyone else up here. The 'vultures,' as you called them, they'll think it's part of the game."

"But it's not?"

Julian wobbled his head as his chilly hand fell away from Scarlett's arm.

Scarlett didn't believe that the vultures were the only reason he wanted to avoid attention, but she hurriedly fetched two towels and the basin. Within a minute the water was red and brown. After a few minutes Julian gained a bit of warmth. He was right about the head wound; it didn't seem to be as bad as it looked.

The gash was shallow, though he tilted to the side as he tried to sit upright.

"I think you should stay lying down." Scarlett placed a gentle hand on his shoulder. "Are you injured anywhere else?"

"You might want to check here." Julian lifted his shirt, revealing perfect rows of golden-brown muscle, so much she might have blushed, if not for all of the blood that stretched across his abdomen.

Using the cleaner of the towels, Scarlett cautiously pressed down against his skin, moving the cloth with slow, circular motions. She'd never touched a young man—or any man—like this. She was careful to touch him only with the cloth, though her fingers were tempted to travel elsewhere. To see if his skin felt as soft as it looked. Would the count have such a flat, lined stomach?

"Julian, you need to keep your eyes open!" Scarlett scolded as she attempted to push thoughts of his body away. She needed to focus on her task.

"I think this cut might need stiches," Scarlett said, yet as her cloth wiped away the blood it revealed a smooth line of unmarked, un-broken flesh. "Wait, I don't see a wound."

"There's not one. But that feels really good." Julian moaned and arched his back.

"You scoundrel!" Scarlett pulled her hands away, resisting the urge to smack him only because he was already injured. "What really hap-pened? And tell me the truth or I will throw you out of this room right now."

"You don't need to make any threats, Crimson. I remember our deal. I'm not planning on staying or stealing your virtue. I just wanted to give you this." He reached into his pocket. She noticed his knuckles weren't bruised or bloody, on either hand. If he'd been in a fight, he hadn't fought back.

Again she was about to ask what happened when he opened his hand.

Sparkling red.

"Were these the things you were fussing about?" Julian dropped her scarlet earrings into her hands unceremoniously, as if he were handing back one of the bloody towels.

"Where did you find them?" Scarlett gasped. Though it truly didn't matter where he'd recovered them. He'd gone to the trouble of retrieving them. Despite his rough handling, not a stone was missing or chipped or broken. During her studies, Scarlett's father had required she learn the proper way to say thank you in a dozen languages, but none of those phrases seemed like quite enough in that moment.

"Is that how you got injured?" she asked.

"If you believe I'd get injured over costume jewelry, you're thinking too highly of me again." Julian pushed up from the sofa and started for the door.

"Stop," Scarlett said. "You can't leave in your condition."

His head cocked to the side. "Is that an invitation to stay?"

Scarlett hesitated.

He was injured.

That still didn't make it appropriate.

She was engaged, and even if she wasn't—

"I didn't think so." Julian grabbed the doorknob.

"Wait—" Scarlett stopped him again. "You still haven't told me what happened to you. Does it have something to do with the tunnels beneath Castillo Maldito?"

Julian paused, his hand hovering over the knob as if suspended by an invisible thread. "What are you talking about?"

"I think you know exactly what I'm talking about." Scarlett distinctly recalled the second set of screams she'd heard. "I followed you."

Julian's expression sharpened; hair dark as wet feathers shadowed a brow pulled tight. "I wasn't in any tunnels. If you were following someone, it wasn't me."

"If you weren't down there, then how did this happen?"

"I swear, I've never heard about these tunnels." Julian dropped his hand from the doorknob and took a step closer to Scarlett. "Tell me exactly what you saw down there."

The fire in the hearth finally died, sending a gray coil of smoke into the air, the color of things better said in whispers.

Scarlett wanted to doubt him. If Julian had been down there it would explain at least a few things. Then again, if he'd been the other person she'd heard screaming, she imagined more than just his head would bear a wound.

"I found the tunnels after I left the fortune-teller's tent." She detailed everything that followed, leaving out the bit about how she'd thought he had a heart made of black. After Julian had given her the earrings she'd stopped believing that was entirely true, though she still watched him carefully for any signs of deception. She wanted to trust him, but a lifetime of mistrust made it impossible. He still seemed unsteady on his feet, but she imagined it was mostly from the cut on his head. "Do you think it might be where they're keeping Tella?" she asked.

"That's not how Legend works. He might lead us through screaming corridors to find a clue to your sister, but I doubt he's keeping her there." Julian flashed his teeth, reminding her of his wolfish look from that first night on the beach. "Legend likes his prisoners to feel like guests."

Scarlett tried to figure out if Julian was just being dramatic. She'd never heard of Legend holding anyone captive. But Julian had said something similar before, and his use of the word *prisoners* left Scarlett with the same uneasy feeling she'd had the first time she'd wondered why Legend had chosen to abduct her sister. "If Legend doesn't have Tella locked up, then what is he doing with her?"

"Now you're finally starting to ask the right questions." Julian's eyes met Scarlett's. There was a flicker of something dangerous, right before they began to shut and he swayed once more.

"Julian!" Scarlett caught both his arms, but he was too heavy to hold, and the couch was too far. She pressed against him. He'd gone from cold to almost feverish. Heat poured from his skin through his shirt, warming her in unexpected ways as she held him up to the door with her body.

"Crimson," Julian murmured as his eyes flickered back open. Light brown, the color of caramel and liquid amber lust.

"I think you need to lie back down." Scarlett started to back away, but Julian's arms wrapped around her waist. As hot as his chest and just as solid.

Scarlett tried to wiggle free, but the look on his face stopped her.

He'd never stared at her like this before. Sometimes he gazed at her as if he wanted to be her undoing, but just then it was as if he wanted her to undo him. It was probably just the fever and the head wound. But for a moment, she swore he wanted to kiss her. Really kiss her, not like when he'd been teasing in the Castillo. Her heartbeat quickened and every inch of her felt sensitive to every part of him as his hot hands roamed up her back. She knew she should have pulled away, but his hands seemed to know exactly what they were doing, and she found herself letting him guide her, gently bringing her closer as his lips parted.

Scarlett gasped.

Julian's hands stopped moving. Her tiny sound seemed to jolt him back. His eyes opened wider, as if he suddenly remembered he thought she was just a silly girl afraid to play a game. He released her and cold air replaced the heat of his hands.

"I think it's time for me to go." He reached for the doorknob. "I'll find you in the tavern right after sunset. We can go take a look at those tunnels together."

Julian slipped out the door, leaving Scarlett wondering what had just happened. It would have been a mistake to kiss him, yet she felt . . . disappointed. It came in cool shades of forget-me-not blue, which wrapped around her like evening fog, making her feel hidden enough to acknowledge that she wanted to experience more of Caraval's pleasures than she would ever have admitted out loud.

It wasn't until Scarlett lay back down that she realized Julian had managed to avoid telling her exactly how he got injured. Or, how he managed to make it back to La Serpiente, long after the sun had come up and the doors had locked.

NIGHT TWO
OF CARAVAL

18

carlett didn't notice the roses at first.

White with ruby-red tips, like the blossoms speckling her room's papered walls. That must have been why she'd not seen them before she'd fallen asleep. She told herself the flowers blended into the room. Someone hadn't come in while she was sleeping.

But what she really meant was, *Legend had not entered her room while she'd slumbered.*

Though his early notes had felt like tiny treasures, something about this latest gift resembled a warning. She wasn't certain the flowers were from Legend. There was no note next to their crystal vase, but she couldn't imagine they were from anyone else. Four roses, one for every night that remained of Caraval.

It was the fifteenth. The game officially ended at dawn on the nineteenth, and her wedding was on the twentieth. Scarlett only had that night and the following night to find Tella, or at the *very* latest by dawn on the eighteenth, if she wanted to leave the island in time for her wedding.

Scarlett imagined her father could keep her *kidnapping* a secret from the count if her fiancé arrived on Trisda early; there were old superstitions about a groom not seeing a bride. However there'd be no salvaging her wedding if Scarlett never showed up for it.

Scarlett reached into her pocket and pulled out the note with the clues once again:

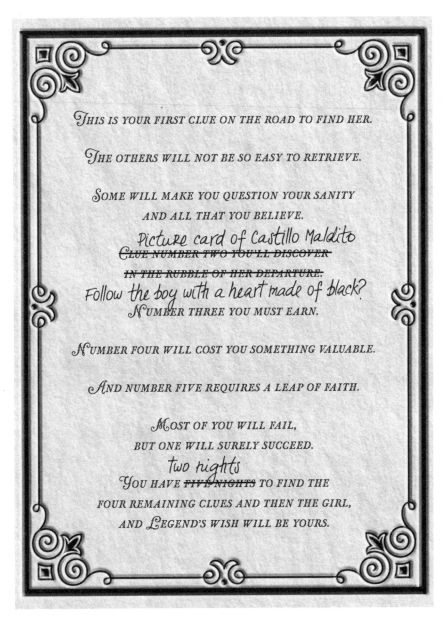

THIS IS YOUR FIRST CLUE ON THE ROAD TO FIND HER.

THE OTHERS WILL NOT BE SO EASY TO RETRIEVE.

SOME WILL MAKE YOU QUESTION YOUR SANITY
AND ALL THAT YOU BELIEVE.

Picture card of Castillo Maldito

~~CLUE NUMBER TWO YOU'LL DISCOVER~~

~~IN THE RUBBLE OF HER DEPARTURE.~~

Follow the boy with a heart made of black?

NUMBER THREE YOU MUST EARN.

NUMBER FOUR WILL COST YOU SOMETHING VALUABLE.

AND NUMBER FIVE REQUIRES A LEAP OF FAITH.

MOST OF YOU WILL FAIL,
BUT ONE WILL SURELY SUCCEED.

two nights

YOU HAVE ~~FIVE NIGHTS~~ TO FIND THE
FOUR REMAINING CLUES AND THEN THE GIRL,
AND LEGEND'S WISH WILL BE YOURS.

Scarlett no longer believed that Julian was the third clue, the boy with the heart made of black. But she couldn't dismiss the feeling he was keeping things from her. She continued to wonder how he'd been wounded, how he'd retrieved her earrings, and about their almost-kiss. Though she couldn't think about the kiss now. Not when she was marrying the count in only five days.

And because all that mattered was finding Tella.

Scarlett hurried to make herself presentable, but her dress seemed to be in less of a rush. It took its time shifting into a lovely cream-and-pink creation, with a milky-white bodice covered in delicate black dots and lined with pink lace, a bustle made of stylish matching bows, and a smart-looking skirt of brushed pink silk. Somehow the dress had managed to fit her with buttoned gloves as well.

Scarlett had a twisting feeling the gown had gone to extra trouble to impress Julian. Or maybe she was only hoping it would have that effect. His abrupt departure the day before had left her with a multitude of battling feelings, and even more questions.

Scarlett prepared to press the sailor for answers. But when she went to meet him, Scarlett found the tavern mostly empty. Soft jade light lit only one patron—a dark-haired girl hunched over a notebook who sat near the glass fireplace. She didn't even look up at Scarlett, though others did, as the hour waxed by and the room began to fill.

There were still no signs of Julian.

Had he taken what she'd learned about the tunnels and left her waiting in the tavern so he could search them for clues all alone?

Or maybe distrust should not always be her first response.

Julian had his faults, but even though he'd left her on a couple of occasions, each time it was only for a short duration and he always came back. Had something happened? She wondered if she needed to search for him. But what if she left and then he appeared?

With every thought she watched her buttoned gloves turn from white to black, and she could feel the neckline of her gown transforming from a heart shape to a high collar. Thankfully it wasn't turning sheer, but the silk was shifting to uncomfortable crepe and she could see the tiny black dots on her bodice growing larger, spreading like stains all over her gown. Reflecting her worries.

She tried to relax, hoping Julian would show up soon and her gown would go back to normal. Glimpsing herself in the table's glass, she looked as if she were in mourning, though that didn't stop people from talking to her.

"Aren't you the sister of that missing girl?" One patron asked the question, and suddenly a small herd of people was upon her.

"I'm sorry, I don't know anything." Scarlett repeated the phrase until one by one they all departed.

"You should try to have some fun with them." The girl who'd been sitting quietly, poring over a journal, appeared at Scarlett's table. As pretty as a watercolor and dressed as bold as a trumpet in a golden gown, daringly sleeveless, with ruffles up to her neck and a bright chartreuse bustle, she folded herself into the glass chair across from Scarlett. "If I were you I'd tell them all sorts of things. Say you saw your sister arm-in-arm with a man in a cape, or that you found a bit of fur on one of her gloves that looked as if it belonged to an elephant."

Were elephants even furry?

For a moment Scarlett just stared at the curious girl. It didn't even seem to occur to her that Scarlett might not want to talk about her sister that way, or that she was waiting for someone else. This girl was that hot sunny day in the middle of the Cold Season, either unaware or uncaring that she did not belong.

"People don't expect the truth here," the girl went on, undeterred. "They don't want it either. A lot of the people here don't expect to win the wish; they come here for an adventure. You might as well give them one. I know it's in you, otherwise you wouldn't have been invited." The girl sparkled, from her metallic skirt to the matching gold lines of paint around her angular eyes.

She didn't look like a thief, but after Scarlett's experience with the strawberry blonde the night before, she wasn't feeling particularly trusting.

"Who are you?" Scarlett asked. "And what do you want?"

"You can call me Aiko. And maybe I don't want anything."

"Everyone who's playing wants something."

"Then I suppose it's a good thing I'm not actually playing—" Aiko cut off as a new couple approached.

Barely older than Scarlett, and obviously newlywed, the young man held his young bride's hand with the care of a man not used to holding such an important thing.

"'Scuse me, miss." He spoke with a foreign accent that took a bit of concentration to discern. "We's were wonderin', are you really Donatella's sister?"

Aiko nodded encouragingly. "She is, and she'd be delighted to answer your questions."

The couple brightened. "Oh, thank you, miss. Yesternight when we made it to 'er room everything was picked clean. We's were jus' hopin' for some bit o' a clue."

The mention of Tella's scavenged room set something ablaze inside of Scarlett, yet the couple looked so sincere. They didn't seem to be mercenaries who would sell things to the highest bidder. Their threadbare clothes were in worse shape than Scarlett's blackened dress, yet their clasped hands and hopeful expressions reminded her of what the game was meant to be. Or what she'd thought it was meant to be. Joy. Magic. Wonder.

"I wish I could tell you where my sister was, but I haven't seen her since I—" Scarlett hesitated as their faces fell, and she remembered how Aiko had said people at Caraval didn't expect or want the truth: *They come here for an adventure. You might as well give them one.*

"Actually, my sister asked me to meet her—near a fountain with a mermaid." The lie sounded ridiculous to Scarlett's ears, but the couple lapped it up like a bowl of sweetened cream, their faces alighting at the prospect of a clue.

"Oh, I think I know dat statue," said the young woman. "Is it da one with a 'ottom all covered in 'earls?"

Scarlett wasn't sure exactly what the woman was trying to say, but she sent them off with a nod and wished them the best of luck.

"See?" said Aiko. "Look how happy you just made them."

"But I lied to them," said Scarlett.

"You're missing the point of the game," said Aiko. "They didn't travel here for truth, they came for an adventure, and you just sent them on one. Maybe they won't find anything, but perchance they will; the game sometimes has a way of rewarding people just for try-ing. Either way that couple is happier than you. I've been watching, and you've been sitting here as sour as rotten milk for the past hour."

"You would be too if your sister was missing."

"Oh, poor you. Here you are on a magical isle and all you can think of is what you don't have."

"But it's my—"

"Your sister, I know," said Aiko. "I also know you'll find her at the end when all of this is over and you'll wish you'd not spent your evenings sitting in this stinking tavern feeling sorry for yourself."

It was the exact sort of thing Tella would have said. A masochis-tic part of Scarlett felt she owed her sister some sort of tithe made of misery, but maybe it was the opposite. Knowing Tella, she would have been more disappointed in Scarlett for not enjoying Legend's isle.

"I'm not going to sit here all night," Scarlett said. "I'm waiting for someone."

"Is that someone late, or are you just very early?" Aiko raised two painted brows. "I hate to inform you of this, but I don't think who-ever it is you're waiting for is going to be showing up."

Scarlett's eyes darted to the door for the hundredth time that evening, still hoping to see Julian walk through. She had been so sure he would come, but if there was a respectable time to wait for someone, she'd surpassed it.

Scarlett pushed up from her chair.

"Does this mean you've decided not to sit around anymore?" Aiko rose elegantly from her own seat, clutching her notebook close, as the back door to the tavern swung open once more.

A pair of giggling young women stepped in, followed by the last person Scarlett wanted to see. He stormed inside like a foul wind made of messy black clothes and mud-caked boots, more disheveled than he'd been the last time she'd seen him—Dante's dark pants were rumpled, as if he'd slept in them, and his tailcoat was gone.

Scarlett remembered how Julian had said Dante wanted Legend's wish to fix something that had happened during an earlier Caraval. Right now Dante looked more desperate than ever to win it.

Scarlett prayed his eyes would pass over her. After their last encounter she wasn't ready for another confrontation with him; waiting for Julian had already sliced her nerves to ribbons and turned her dress black. But even as Scarlett hoped Dante wouldn't notice her, her eyes continued to fall on him. On the sleeves he'd bunched up around his forearms, and the tattoos they exposed.

Specifically, a black tattoo shaped like a heart.

ollow the boy with a heart made of black.

F Nigel's words rushed back to Scarlett right as Dante's eyes fell on her. The look he gave her was pure loathing. But rather than frightening Scarlett, it ignited something inside her; she imagined this was the game's way of testing her resolve to play without Julian's help.

When Dante disappeared out the tavern's back door, Scarlett dashed outside after him. She didn't realize how toasty it had been in the tavern until she escaped into the brittle evening. Crisp, like the first bite of a chilled apple, smelling just as sweet, with hints of burnt sugar weaving through the charcoal night air. Around her, the people on the street were as thick as a murder of crows.

Scarlett thought she glimpsed Dante slip onto a covered bridge, but once she reached the bridge it contained nothing but lantern light, and led to a disappointing dead end. All Scarlett found after she crossed it was an alley made of brick walls, and a cider cart manned by a cute boy with a monkey on his shoulder.

"Can I interest you in some burnt-sugar cider?" asked the boy. "It will make you see things more clearly."

"Oh, no—I'm looking for someone, with tattoos all over his arms, all black clothes, and an angry look on his face."

"I think he might have bought some cider last night, but I haven't seen him tonight. Good luck!" called the boy as Scarlett darted back onto the bridge.

Once she reached the other side, she spied a number of young men with untidy black clothes—at this point in the game, everyone was starting to appear a bit ragged around the edges—but no one had arms covered in ink. Scarlett continued weaving through the crowd, until she caught sight of someone with what looked like a black heart tattoo heading up a set of emerald stairs a few shops past the Glass Tavern.

Picking up the hem of her skirt, Scarlett rushed to follow her black-hearted boy. She tore up the stairs and onto another covered bridge. But when she reached the other side of the bridge, all she found was another dead end and another cute boy, again with a cider cart and a monkey.

"Wait—" Scarlett paused. "Weren't you just over there?" She motioned vaguely, no longer quite sure of where "over there" was anymore.

"I haven't gone anywhere all night, but that bridge you just crossed moves quite often," said the boy. He flashed his dimples and the monkey on his shoulder nodded.

Scarlett craned her neck back toward the bridge, its lights fluttering as if winking at her. Two days ago she would have said it was impossible, but now the thought didn't even cross her mind. She wasn't sure exactly when it happened, but she'd stopped doubting the magic.

"Are you sure you don't want any?" The boy stirred his cider, sending fresh streams of apple-scented steam into the air.

"Oh—" Scarlett was about to say no, her standard response, but then she remembered something. "Did you say this would help me to see things more clearly?"

"You'll not find a brew like this anywhere else." The monkey on his shoulder nodded again in agreement.

A welcome chill raced over Scarlett. What if this was the reason Nigel had told her to follow the boy with the heart made of black? Maybe if she drank the cider her eyes would be sharp enough to spot the clue she needed.

Scarlett snuck a peek at the game's instructions: *Number four will cost you something valuable.*

"What will I have to pay?" Scarlett asked.

"Not much—the last lie you told."

It didn't seem like much of a price. But even if the cider was not the next clue, it would most likely give her some sort of edge, which she definitely needed.

Feeling fortunate she'd taken Aiko's advice in the tavern, Scarlett leaned close and whispered her story about the mermaid fountain. The boy looked disappointed at not being told a juicier lie, but he handed her the cup.

Browned sugar and melted butter with hints of cream and toasted cinnamon. It tasted like the best parts of the Cold Season, mixed with just a hint of heat. "It's delicious, but I don't see anything different. . . ."

"It takes a minute or two to kick in. I promise, you won't be disappointed." The boy nodded a parting good-bye, and his monkey saluted her as he began pushing his cart in the direction of the tricky bridge.

Scarlett took another sip of cider, but now it tasted too sweet, as if it were trying to mask a harsher flavor. Something wasn't right. Scarlett's emotions were swirling into messy grays and dull whites. Normally Scarlett just saw flashes of color attached to her feelings, but as she watched the boy depart, she could see his skin shifting to ashy gray, while his clothes turned black.

Scarlett blinked, unsettled by the image, only to be more disturbed when she opened her eyes once more.

Now *everything* was shades of black and gray. Even the candlelight lining the bridge was foggy gloom instead of golden. She tried not to panic, but her heart beat faster with every step as she crossed back over the bridge and returned to a world no longer full of color.

Caraval had shifted to black and white.

Scarlett dropped the cider, buttery gold liquid splashing over gray walkways, the only puddle of bright amid the awful new dull. The boy with the monkey was nowhere to be seen. He was probably laughing at her as he pushed his cart, searching for a new victim.

She looked up and found herself near the Glass Tavern's back exit. Aiko had just stepped outside, her bright dress now charcoal.

"You look dreadful," she said. "I'm guessing you didn't catch the young man you were after?"

Scarlett shook her head. Behind Aiko, the door to the tavern was closing. Scarlett scanned the inside quickly enough to see Julian had still not arrived, or if he had, he'd already left. "I think I've made a mistake."

"Then make it into something better." Aiko strolled down the cobbled street as if the world could crumble around her and she'd just keep going. Scarlett wanted to feel like that, but the game seemed to be constantly working against her, and she imagined it was easy for Aiko, since she was only observing. No one had stolen *her* sister, or the color from *her* world. Scarlett could picture Aiko gliding on air if enough bits of earth fell away. The only thing she held on to securely was the battered notebook in her hand. Brownish green, the color of forgotten memories, abandoned dreams, and bitter gossip.

It was an unattractive thing, yet—

Scarlett's thought broke off. The journal was in color! An ugly color. But in a world made of black and white, it called to Scarlett. Maybe this was how the cider worked? It took away the colors of everything so Scarlett could clearly see the things that really mattered—or find the next clue.

Number four will cost you something valuable.

Nigel's advice really had been clue number three. After Scarlett followed the boy with a heart made of black, he had led her to the boy with the cider, which had taken away her ability to see colors— costing her something valuable.

Her chest now fluttered with excitement, rather than panic. She hadn't been tricked; she'd been given what she needed to find the fourth clue.

Scarlett followed as Aiko paused in front of a busy waffle-maker. He dipped one of his pastries in the darkest chocolate before passing it to Aiko in exchange for a glimpse at a page in her journal.

Carefully, Scarlett tried to take a look as well.

Aiko snapped the book shut. "If you want to see what's inside, you'll have to give me something like everyone else."

"What sort of something?" Scarlett asked.

"Do you always focus on what you're giving up, rather than what you'll be gaining? Some things are worth pursuit regardless of the cost." Aiko beckoned Scarlett onto a street lined with hanging lanterns, smelling of flowers and flutes and long-lost love. The road narrowed, a watery canal hugging one side as the other curved around a carousel made of roses.

"A song for a donation." A man in front of a pipe organ held out a thick hand.

Aiko dropped something, too small for Scarlett to see, in his palm. "Try to make it pretty."

The organist began to play a melancholy tune, and the carousel started to move, spinning slowly at first. If Tella were there, Scarlett imagined she would have hopped up on it, plucked its red roses, and put them in her hair.

Red!

Scarlett watched as the rosy carousel continued to twirl, shedding brilliant red petals onto the path. A few landed on Aiko's waffle as well, sticking to the chocolate.

Scarlett couldn't tell if her senses were coming back, or if the carousel was somehow important, for at the same moment that Scarlett realized she could see the rich red of its petals, a gentleman with an eye patch walked by. Like everything else he was painted in shades of gray and black, except for the crimson cravat around his neck. It was the deepest hue of red she'd ever seen. His face was equally hypnotic. He possessed the kind of dark good looks that made Scarlett wonder why everyone else wasn't staring as well.

She debated following him. He was mystery and unanswered questions. But something about him made her feel perilous shades of silky black. He moved through the crowd like a wraith, graceful but with an edge that felt a little too dangerous for her liking, and even though she felt a pull toward him, Aiko's journal called to her just as strongly.

The pipe organist's song picked up speed, and the carousel spun faster and faster. Petals landed on more than just Aiko's dessert. They flew until the path in front of them turned to red velvet and the canal beside them transformed into blood, leaving the carousel naked save for its thorns.

The few other people on the street clapped.

Scarlett felt as if there were a deeper lesson there, but she couldn't quite grasp it. Her vision was back to full color. The gentleman with the patch had almost disappeared from view, yet Scarlett continued to feel an unwanted pull toward him. If he'd been wearing a top hat, she might have wondered if he was Legend. Or maybe this enigmatic young man was a decoy Legend had placed in the crowd to lure her away from the actual clue. Earlier that night, as she looked at the winking bridge, Scarlett would have sworn she'd felt Legend's eyes on her, spying on her attempts to figure out his clues.

Scarlett only had a moment left to make her decision—if she was going to follow the young man, or try to look in Aiko's journal, the only thing untouched by red petals. If Scarlett's theory about the cider was right, both the young man and the journal were significant, but only one could lead her closer to Tella. "If I do make this trade to look in your notebook, what is it I'll be gaining? Is it the fourth clue?"

Aiko swayed, humming cryptically. "It's possible; lots of things are."

"But the rules said there are only five clues."

"Is that really what they said? Or is that just how you interpreted them?" asked Aiko. "Think of the instructions as a map. There's more than one way to get to almost every destination. Clues are hidden everywhere. The guidelines you received just make it easier to spot them. But keep in mind, clues are not the only thing you need to win. This game is like a person. If you truly want to play it right, you need to learn its history."

"I know all about its history," Scarlett said. "My grandmother has been telling me tales since I was a little girl."

"Ah, tales passed on from your grandmother, I'm sure they're very accurate." Aiko took a bite of her waffle, white teeth sinking into the red petals on top of it, as she started down a new path.

Scarlett looked a final time for the man with the eye patch. But he was already gone. She'd missed her chance. She couldn't lose Aiko as well.

The pretty girl was now in the middle of buying edible silver bells, and coin-size cakes dipped in glitter. As Scarlett followed, she imagined the girl was about to burst from all she had eaten, but she continued to buy from every vendor who asked her to make a trade. Scarlett discovered Aiko believed in saying yes whenever possible. Conversation paused as she bought confetti candies that glowed like fireflies, a glass of drinkable gold, and everlasting hair dye—*for those silver hairs you want to be rid of forever*—though Aiko looked far too young for it.

"So," Scarlett started as they wove onto a street full of shops with pointy roofs but blessedly free of vendors. She felt ready to make a deal, but she wasn't about to jump into it blind, as she had done before. "Caraval's history is written in your notebook?"

"In a manner," Aiko said.

"Prove it to me."

To her astonishment, Aiko offered her the book.

Scarlett hesitated; it almost seemed too easy. "But I thought you'd only let me see if I gave you something in return."

"Don't worry, you won't be bound to any deal unless you decide you wish to see more. The pictures that would help you are sealed by magic." She said the word *magic* as if it were a private joke.

Scarlett took the book cautiously. Thin and light but somehow full of pages, every time Scarlett turned one, two more seemed to appear behind it, all of them painted with fantastical pictures. Queens and kings, pirates and presidents, assassins and princes. Grand ships the size of islands and tiny slips of wood that looked like the boat she and Julian had—

"Wait—these are pictures of me." Scarlett flipped the next few pages. Aiko's art showed her on the boat with Julian. Trudging half naked to the clock shop. Arguing behind the gates of the turreted house.

"These were private moments!" Thank the saints there were no compromising pictures of her in her room with Julian, but there *was* a very vivid piece of art showing her fleeing from Dante as every eye in the tavern looked on in judgment.

"How did you get these?" Red-faced, Scarlett turned back to the picture of her in the boat with Julian. She remembered an eerie feel of being watched when she'd first arrived on the isle. But this was far worse than that. "Why are there so many pictures of me? I don't see drawings of other people."

"This year's game is not about other people." Aiko's gold-rimmed eyes met Scarlett's. "Other participants aren't missing their sister."

When she'd first arrived to the isle, the idea of being Legend's special guest had made Scarlett feel privileged. For the first time in her life, she'd felt special. Chosen. But once again, rather than feeling as if she were playing the game, it seemed as if the game were playing with her.

Sour shades of yellow-green made her stomach roil with trepidation. Scarlett didn't like being toyed with, but what made her even more uneasy was the question why, out of all the people in the world, Legend would choose to make this game about her and her sister. The day in the clock shop Julian's comment made it seem as if it had something to do with her appearance, but now Scarlett felt there was much more to it.

"In the tavern you started to ask me who I was," Aiko went on. "I'm not a player. I'm a histographer. I record the history of Caraval through pictures."

"I've never heard of a histographer."

"Then you should feel lucky to have met me." Aiko plucked back the journal.

Scarlett didn't imagine luck had much to do with their meeting. She couldn't deny that what she'd seen in the journal's pages had been disturbingly accurate, but even if this girl really was a *histographer*, Scarlett wasn't sure she believed she'd only come there to observe.

"Now you have seen a glimpse of my book," Aiko went on, "and while I may show occasional peeks to vendors on the streets, what I offer you is a rare opportunity. I'm not the only artist who has stained its pages. Every true story from every Caraval in the past is in here. If you choose to examine all the stories inside, you will see who has won and how they did it."

As Aiko spoke, Scarlett thought of Dante, then Julian. She wondered what had happened when they'd each played before. Other stories came to mind as well, like the woman who was killed years ago. Scarlett's grandmother, who'd claimed to have charmed everyone with her purple dress. Scarlett doubted she'd actually find her nana in the book, but there was one person she did not doubt she would see. *Legend.*

If this book detailed the true history of Caraval, then Legend was certain to be pictured in it. Rupert, the boy from the first night, described the game as a mystery to be solved. And the first clue said: *This girl was last seen with Legend.* It made sense that if Scarlett found

Legend, she would then find Tella as well, without having to search for the next two clues.

"All right," Scarlett said. "Tell me what you want for another look in the journal."

"Excellent." Aiko appeared to sparkle a little more than usual. She guided Scarlett past a button-lined path leading to a hatter and haberdashery shaped like a top hat. Then she stopped in front of a dress shop.

Three stories high, made of all glass to better display brightly lit gowns in every material and shade. The color of late-night laughter, early-morning sunshine, and waves crashing around ankles. Each gown seemed to speak of its own rare adventure, with unique prices to match:

> *the thing you regret the most,*
>
> *your worst fear,*
>
> *a secret you've never told a soul.*

One dress only cost a recent nightmare, but it was plum, the one color Scarlett couldn't stand to wear.

"That's your price, you want me to buy you a dress?"

"No. I want you to purchase three dresses for yourself. One for the next three evenings of the game." Aiko pulled open the door, but Scarlett did not cross its threshold.

A funny thing happens when people feel as if they are paying less for something than they ought: suddenly the worth goes down. Scarlett had glimpsed the book so she knew it was valuable—this had to be some sort of trick. "What are you getting out of this? What do you really want from me?"

"I'm an artist. I don't like that your gown has a mind of its own." Aiko's nose wrinkled as she looked over Scarlett's dress, which appeared to still be in mourning: it had even managed to sprout a small dark train. "When it gets emotional, it changes, but anyone who opens the pages of my book might not know that. They'd just think I'd made a mistake, giving you a new gown mid-scene. I also despise the color black."

Scarlett wasn't a fan of black either. It reminded her of too many unpleasant emotions. And, it *would* be nice to have more control over her clothes. But since she could stay only two more nights, at the most, there was no need for three dresses.

"I'll do it for two dresses," Scarlett said.

Aiko's eyes shined like black opals. "Done."

Silver bells chimed as the girls stepped into the shop. They made it two feet before encountering a hanging, jewel-encrusted sign that said: *Thieves Will Be Turned to Stone.*

Below the beautiful warning, a young woman made of granite stood frozen in place, her long hair flowing behind as if she'd been trying to run.

"I know her," Scarlett muttered. "She was pretending to be pregnant last night."

"Don't worry," Aiko said. "She'll be back to normal once Caraval is over."

A piece of Scarlett felt as if she should pity the girl, but it was overshadowed by the thought that Legend had a sense of justice after all.

Beyond the granite girl, every creation in the shop glimmered with Caraval magic. Even the garish ones that looked like parrot feathers or holiday packages with too many bows.

Tella would adore this, thought Scarlett.

But it seemed the enchanted dress Scarlett wore didn't like the shop at all. Every time she selected something, her gown would shift as if to say, *I can look like that too.*

Finally, she settled on a gown of cherry-blossom pink, oddly reminiscent of the first garment her magical dress had formed into. Full of tiered skirts, but with a bodice lined in buttons instead of bows.

At Aiko's insistence she also chose a more modern, corsetless gown. Sleeves that dipped off her shoulders attached to a sweetheart neckline lined with champagne and pale-orchid beadwork—the colors of infatuation. The ornamentation grew denser as it trailed down a slightly flared skirt, which ended in a graceful train that was very impractical but terribly romantic.

"No returns or exchanges," said the shopgirl, a shiny-haired brunette who looked no older than Scarlett. She made her statement without emotion, yet as Scarlett stepped closer she had a prickly sort of feeling that told her she'd reached the point in the game that marked no returns as well.

In front of her, a pincushion, along with an equal-arm brass scale, sat on the edge of a polished mahogany counter. The scale's pan for the goods was empty but the tray for weights contained an object that looked disturbingly close to a human heart. Scarlett had the alarming vision of her own heart being taken from her chest and placed on the empty pan.

The shopgirl continued, "For the dresses, that will be your worst fear and your greatest desire. Or you can pay using time."

"Time?" Scarlett asked.

"We're having a deal. Tonight it's only two days of your life per dress." The brunette spoke matter-of-factly, the same as if she were asking for ordinary coins. But Scarlett felt sacrificing four days of her life was no simple matter. She knew she shouldn't have been keen to give up her secrets, either, but her fear and desire had been used against her already.

"I'll answer your questions," Scarlett said.

"When you're ready," the shopgirl instructed, "remove your gloves and hold the base of the scale."

A few of the shop's other patrons pretended not to watch while Aiko looked on eagerly from the edge of the counter. Scarlett wondered if this was perhaps what Aiko was really after. Of course, if she'd been watching Scarlett, she should have already known her answers.

Scarlett took off her gloves. The brass felt surprisingly warm and soft under Scarlett's fingers. Fleshy, almost, as if it were a living thing. Her hand grew clammy and the surface grew slick.

"Now say your greatest fear," the shopgirl prompted.

Scarlett cleared her throat. "My greatest fear is that something bad will happen to my sister, and I won't be able to protect her."

The brass scale creaked. Scarlett watched with marvel as the chains shifted and the side containing the heart slowly rose while the empty pan mysteriously lowered until the two were perfectly even.

"It's always nice when it works," said the shopgirl. "Now, let go."

Scarlett did as instructed, and the scale reset, returning to an unbalanced state.

"Now grab hold again and tell me your greatest desire."

Scarlett's hands didn't sweat this time, though the scale still felt too alive for her liking. "My greatest desire is to find my sister, Donatella."

The scale shook. Chains rattled gently. But the side with the heart remained firmly weighed down.

"There's something wrong with the scale," Scarlett said.

"Try again," said the shopgirl.

"My greatest desire is to find my younger sister, Donatella Dragna." Scarlett squeezed the stem of the scale, but it made no difference. The empty pan and heart both remained unmoved.

She squeezed harder, but this time the scale didn't even wobble. "All I want is to find my sister."

The shopgirl grimaced. "I'm sorry, but the scale never lies. I'll need another answer, or you can pay with two days of your life."

Scarlett turned to Aiko. "You've been watching me; you know finding my sister is all I want."

"I believe it's something you want," Aiko said. "But there are many things to want in life. It's not a bad thing if there are other things you desire a little more."

"No." Scarlett's knuckles were turning white—the game was playing with her. "I would die for my sister!"

Chains rattled and the scale moved again, balancing until it evened out. This statement was true. Unfortunately, this was not a viable form of payment.

Scarlett ripped her hands away before she was robbed of any more secrets.

"So, two days of your life it will be," said the shopgirl.

Scarlett felt as if she'd been tricked. This must be what they had been after all along. She thought about backing out. Giving up two days of her life left her with a feeling of indescribable unease; the same sensation she experienced whenever she made a deal with her father. But if Scarlett backed out now, it would further prove finding her sister was not what she desired most. She wouldn't get a glimpse into Aiko's secret notebook, either.

"If you take two days of my life, how does it work?" asked Scarlett.

The shopgirl pulled out a miniature sword from her pincushion. "Slice your finger with the tip of this, then squeeze three drops of blood over the scale." She pointed to the shriveled heart.

"If you want, I can cut it for you," Aiko said. "Sometimes it's easier to let someone else wound you."

But Scarlett had had enough of other people hurting her.

"No, I can do it myself." She ran the tiny sword over the tip of her ring finger.

Drip

drip

drip.

Only three dots of blood, yet Scarlett felt each one, and the pain went beyond her finger. It was as if a hand dug nails into her heart and squeezed. "Is this supposed to hurt?"

"A little light-headedness is normal. You didn't expect losing two

days of your life to be painless, did you?" The shopgirl laughed as if
it were a joke.

"I'll let you take the buttoned dress now," she went on, "but the
beaded gown won't be delivered until two days from now, once your
payment is fulfilled. After that—"

"Wait," Scarlett interrupted. "Did you just say you want my debt
paid now?"

"Well, it's not going to do me any good next week, once the game
is over, is it? But don't worry, I won't take the full payment until the
sun is up, which gives you enough time to get somewhere safe."

Somewhere safe?

"I think there's been a mistake." Scarlett gripped the edges of the
counter. Was it just her imagination or had the heart in the scale
started beating? "I thought I'd lose two days at the *end* of my life."

"How should I know when your life is going to end?" The shopgirl chuckled, a harsh sound that seemed to make the world quake
beneath Scarlett's feet. "Don't worry, as long as nothing happens to
your body, you'll come back to life at dawn on the eighteenth just
fine."

That was only two days before her wedding. Scarlett fought
against a new surge of panic. It came in shades of hemlock green—
the color of poison and terror. She had only lost three drops of blood,
but it felt as if she were hemorrhaging. "I can't die for two days—I
need to *leave* in two days!"

If Scarlett died now, she'd never be able to find her sister and
make it home in time for her wedding. And what if someone else,
like Dante, found her sister while she was dead? Or the game ended

early and Tella found Scarlett dead? The field of Scarlett's vision was narrowing, going black around the edges.

Aiko and the shopgirl exchanged a look Scarlett didn't like. Still gripping the shiny counter, she turned to Aiko. "You tricked me—"

"No I didn't," Aiko said. "I didn't know you wouldn't be able to answer the questions."

"But I *did* answer the questions," Scarlett tried to yell, but the effects of her trade were growing stronger, dulling her senses, making the world feel thicker, while she felt thinner. Powerless. "What happens if someone harms my body?"

Aiko grabbed Scarlett's arm to steady her as she swayed. "You need to get back to your inn."

"No—" Scarlett tried to protest. She couldn't go back to La Serpiente; it was Julian's day to use the room. But now Scarlett's head felt like a balloon, trying to detach from her shoulders.

"You need to get her out of here." The shopgirl cast a sharp glance at Scarlett. "If she dies on the street she'll probably find herself buried underground."

Scarlett's horror spiked, turning shades of quicksilver. Her hearing was almost as fuzzy as her vision, but she could have sworn it sounded as if the girl wished this might happen. Something acidic and moldy and burnt bubbled up through Scarlett's throat—the taste of death.

She barely felt strong enough to stand, let alone walk all the way back to the inn. When she woke, she'd have to choose between finding her sister—or leaving to make it back to Trisda in time for her wedding. Scarlett knew it might come down to this, but she wasn't ready to make the choice yet. And what would Julian do if he returned to their room and found her dead body?

"Scarlett!" Aiko shook her again. "You need to stay alive until you make it to safety." She pushed Scarlett toward the door and shoved a sugar cube inside her mouth. "So you'll have the strength. Don't stop walking no matter what."

Scarlett's leaden legs quaked with lines of sweat. She could barely stand; she wouldn't make it back. Aiko's sugar had dissolved into rot in her mouth. "Why can't you walk with me?"

"I have places I need to be," said Aiko. "But don't worry, I'll keep my word. When someone takes days of your life, your body dies, but your mind exists in a sort of dream world. Unless your body is destroyed."

Again, Scarlett tried to ask what would happen in that case, but her words came out garbled, as if she'd bitten them into pieces before spitting them out. She swore the whites of Aiko's eyes shifted to black as she said, "You'll be fine as long as you make it back to your room. I'll find you in the dream world and show you my book."

"But"—Scarlett swayed—"I usually forget my dreams."

"This you will remember." Aiko steadied her, and thrust another sugar cube into her mouth. "But you must promise not to tell anyone. Now"—Aiko gave Scarlett a final shove as she put the cherry-blossom dress in her hands—"get out of here before you die."

20

Scarlett would remember only one thing clearly about her journey from the dress shop. She would not remember her limbs feeling as light as feathers, her bones turning to dust, or either of her attempts to lie down in the boats. She would not remember being prodded out of those same boats, or dropping her cherry-blossom gown. Though she would recall the young man who picked it up, and then took her arm to help her walk the rest of the way back to La Serpiente.

The words *uselessly pretty* came to mind, though as she looked up at her attractive companion, his face no longer looked quite so pretty. Hard lines and harsh angles highlighted dark eyes shadowed by even darker hair.

This person did not like her. She not only knew it, she could feel it in the rough way he handled her. The way he held on to her arm as she attempted to pull away.

"Let me go!" she tried to yell. But her voice was feeble, and the passersby who might have heard were too busy scurrying to their own snake holes. A quarter of an hour was all that remained until the sun rose and erased the magic of the night.

"If I let you go, you'll just crawl into another boat." Dante dragged her through La Serpiente's rounded back door. Noise from the tavern circled around them. Mugs of cider clinking against glass tables. Snorts of amusement mixed with grunts of satisfaction, and groaned tales of things unsatisfying.

Only a sharp-looking gentleman with an eye patch and a crimson cravat noticed her being dragged onto a set of stairs, where the air darkened and the noise quieted. Later Scarlett would remember him watching, but just then her main concern was escaping from Dante.

"Please," Scarlett begged. "I need to get to my room."

"First we need to talk." Dante cornered her in the stairwell, long legs and tattooed arms boxing her against the wall.

"If this is about the other day . . . I'm sorry." It took what felt like all of Scarlett's strength to force the words out coherently. "I didn't mean to trick you. I shouldn't have lied to you."

"This isn't about your lies," Dante said. "I know people lie in this game. Yesterday—" He broke off, sounding as if it were a struggle to keep his tone even. "I was upset because I thought you were different. This game, it changes people."

"I know," Scarlett said, "that's why I need to get to my room."

"I can't let you do that." Dante's voice hardened, and for a rare moment of terrifying clarity, Scarlett could see he'd fallen apart even more than the last time she'd seen him. His eyes were lined in dark shadows as if he hadn't slept in days. "My sister is missing; you have to help me find her. I know your sister is missing too, and I don't think it's just a part of this game."

No. Scarlett couldn't be hearing this now. Tella's disappearance was simply another magic trick. Dante was trying to frighten her. Hadn't Julian said he'd been cruel to win the game before? "I can't talk about this right now."

She needed to make it back to her room. It no longer mattered if it was Julian's for the night. She could not die right there. Not in front of Dante, as crazed as he was. Somehow she managed to pull her dress from his hands. "Why don't we meet in the tavern—after we've both gotten some sleep?"

"You mean after you *die* for two days?" Dante's hand formed a fist against the wall. "I know what's happening to you. I can't lose another night! My sister is gone and you—"

Smack!

Before he could get another word out, Dante flew backward. Scarlett didn't fully see the blow, but it was enough to knock him halfway down the stairs.

"You need to stay away from her!" Heat poured off of Julian as he gently peeled Scarlett from the wall. "Are you all right? Did he hurt you?"

"No . . . I just need to get up to the room." She could feel the minutes slipping away, draining her of life, turning her limbs into flimsy strands of gossamer.

"Crimson—" Julian caught her as she started to fall. He was so much warmer than she was. Scarlett wanted to curl into him like a blanket, weave her arms around him as firmly as he'd wrapped his arms around her.

"Crimson, you need to talk to me." Julian's voice was no longer gentle. "What happened to you?"

"I . . . I think I made a mistake." Her words came out sticky and thick like syrup. "Someone, a girl with very shiny hair and a girl with a waffle . . . I needed to buy dresses and they made me pay with time."

Julian uttered several colorful curses. "Tell me they didn't take a day of your life."

"No. . . ." She fought to stay standing. "They took two days."

Julian's handsome face twisted, turning lethal, or maybe the whole world was twisting into something lethal. Everything spiraled sideways as Julian picked her up, tossing the cherry-blossom gown over his shoulder. "This is all my fault," he muttered.

Julian held her close as he carried her up the stairs, down a very wobbly hall, and into what Scarlett took to be their room. All she could see was white. Endless white, except for Julian's brown face, hovering over her as he gently laid her down onto the bed.

"Where were you . . . earlier?" she asked.

"In the wrong place."

Everything was hazy around the edges, like dusty early-morning sun, but Scarlett could see the dark fringe of lashes around Julian's concerned eyes.

"Does that mean—"

"Shh," Julian murmured. "Save your words, Scarlett. I think I can fix this, but I need you to stay with me a little longer. I'm going to try to give you a day of my life."

Scarlett's head was so muddled, so broken by whatever magic worked its way through her body, that at first she thought she must have misheard him. But that look in his eyes was back, as if he wanted her to be his undoing.

"You would really do this for me?" she asked.

In answer, Julian pressed the pad of a finger to her parted lips.

Metallic and wet and just a little sweet. Bravery and fear and something else she couldn't distinguish. Dimly, she knew she tasted his blood. It was like no other gift she'd ever received. Strangely beautiful, alarmingly intimate. And she wanted more of it. More of him.

She licked the tip of his finger, but Scarlett hungered to taste his lips as well. To feel them against her mouth and her throat. To experience the solid touch of his hands on her body. She craved the heavy weight of his chest crushed to hers, to find out if his heart beat equally fast.

Julian's finger lingered a moment longer, pressing her lips back together, but the taste of his blood remained. And her desire for him intensified. He hovered over her, and she could hear the rhythmic beat of his pulse. She'd been sensitive to his presence before, but never more than this. She was mesmerized by his face, the dark freckle beneath his left eye, the subtle sharpness of his cheekbones, the line of his chiseled jaw, the coolness of his breath on her cheek.

"Now I need some of your blood." His voice was so gentle, made of gentle, the same way his blood had been made of everything he was feeling.

Scarlett had never felt so close to another person. She knew she would give him what he asked for—whatever he asked for—that she would eagerly let him drink a part of her the way she had him. "Julian," she said in a whisper, as if anything louder would destroy the delicacy of the moment, "why are you doing this?"

His amber-flecked eyes met hers, and something in them made her breathing hitch. "I'd think that answer was obvious." He took one of her cool hands and held it near to his knife, but she imagined he waited for her permission. And she knew, he wasn't doing this because of the game; this felt like something entirely separate, existing only for the two of them.

Scarlett pressed down on the tip of the blade. A single drop of ruby blood welled. Carefully Julian brought her finger to his mouth, and when his soft lips touched her skin the entire world shattered into a million shards of colored glass.

Her dying heart beat faster as his tongue gently drew her finger between his teeth. For a moment she could feel his emotions again, as close as if they were her own. Awe mixed with fierce protectiveness, and a thread of pain so intense she wanted to take the hurt from him. Her finger dipped deeper in, pressing against one of his sharp incisors. Days before, she'd stiffened at his touch, but now she wished she were strong enough to wrap her arms around him.

Not quite sure how far she'd already fallen, she imagined loving him would feel like falling in love with darkness, frightening and consuming yet utterly beautiful when the stars came out.

He licked her finger a final time; a shiver coursed through her so painfully cold it felt hot. Then he was lying beside her on the bed, weighing it down as he brought her into the cradle of his arms. Her back fit perfectly against his chest, solid and strong. She burrowed against him, attempting to fight off death for another minute and hold on to him instead.

"You're going to be fine." Julian stroked her hair as her vision went dark.

"Thank you," she whispered.

He said something else, but all she felt was his hand brush her cheek. So soft she thought she imagined it, along with the tender press of his lips to the back of her neck, right before she died.

21

Death was the color purple. Purple wallpaper and purple temperatures. Her nana's purple gown—only the honey-blond young woman wearing the gown, and sitting in the purple chair, looked much more like Donatella.

Her cheeks were full of color, her smile full of mischief, and the bruise that had marred her face days ago was healed, leaving her looking healthier than she had in ages. If Scarlett's heart had been beating, it would have stopped. "Tella, is that really you?"

"I know you're dead right now," Tella said, "but you should try to come up with better questions. We don't have much time."

Before Scarlett could respond, her sister opened the ancient book on her lap. Much larger than the journal Aiko carried around in life, this book was the size of a tombstone, and the color of dark fairy tales—black ice covered with tarnished gold script. It swallowed Scarlett with its leather-bound mouth, and spit her onto a chilly sidewalk.

Donatella materialized beside her, though she looked less corporeal than before, transparent around the edges.

Scarlett didn't feel very solid herself; her head was fuzzy from dreaming and dying and all that came with it, but this time she managed to ask, "Where can I find you?"

"If I told you, that would be cheating," Tella sang. "You need to watch."

In front of them, a purple sun fell behind a grand home, similar to the turreted building that housed Caraval, but smaller, and painted dark plum with violet trim.

The girl inside it wore a shade of purple as well. Again, it looked like her nana's purple dress. In fact it *was* that gown, only this time the woman who wore it *was* her nana, a much younger version, almost as pretty as she had claimed, with golden-blond curls that reminded Scarlett of Tella.

Her arms were wrapped around a dark-haired young man who seemed to think she would look better without the purple dress on. He also looked a great deal like her grandfather, before his body went to fat and his nose filled with blue veins. The young man's fingers fumbled with the purple gown's laces.

"Ugh," Tella said. "I don't want to see this part." She vanished again as Scarlett scrambled to find anywhere else to look. But everywhere she turned she saw the same window.

"Oh," her young grandfather mumbled, "Annalise."

Scarlett had never heard her grandmother called that name; she'd always been just Anna. But something about the name Annalise rang familiar.

Then bells were ringing everywhere. Bells of mourning, in a world covered in mist and black roses.

The purple house was gone and Scarlett was on a new street, surrounded by people wearing black hats and even gloomier expressions.

"I knew they were full of evil," said a man. "Rosa would never have died if they hadn't come."

Black rose petals rained on a funeral procession, and without being told who *they* were, Scarlett knew the man referred to the players of Caraval. A woman had died during Caraval's long history. The year Caraval had stopped traveling, after rumors started that Legend had murdered her.

Rosa must have been that woman, thought Scarlett.

"This dream is just awful, isn't it?" Tella reappeared once again, though now her image was ghostly sheer. "I've never really liked black. When I die, will you please tell everyone to wear brighter clothes at my funeral?"

"Tella, you're not going to die," Scarlett scolded.

Tella's image flickered like a candle lacking confidence. "I might if you don't win this game. Legend likes to—"

Tella vanished.

"Donatella!" Scarlett called for her sister. "Tella!" But she seemed to be gone for good this time. No more traces of her purple dress or blond curls. Just a funeral of endless gloom.

Scarlett could feel the gray press of everyone's grief as she continued to listen, hoping to learn what Tella had been unable to say, as words of mourning switched to gossip.

"Sad, sad story," whispered one woman to another. "When Rosa's fiancé won the game, his prize was finding her in bed with Legend."

"But I heard she was the one who called off their wedding," said the other woman.

"She did, right after her fiancé caught them. Rosa said she was in love with Legend and wanted to be with him instead. But Legend laughed and said she'd gotten too carried away with the game."

"I thought no one ever saw Legend," said the other woman.

"No one sees him more than once; they say he wears a different face every game. Beautiful but cruel. I heard he was there when Rosa flung herself out the window, and he didn't even try to stop her."

"Monster."

"I thought he pushed her," said a third woman.

"Not physically," said the first. "Legend likes to play twisted games with people, and one of his favorites is making girls fall in love with him. Rosa jumped the day after he discarded her, after her parents found out and refused to let her return home. Her fiancé blames himself, though. His servants say he moans Rosa's name in his sleep every night."

The three women turned as a young man trudged by at the very rear of the procession. His dark hair was not so long and his hands contained no ink from tattoos—no rose for Rosa—but Scarlett recognized him right away. *Dante.*

This must have been why he wanted to win the wish so badly, to bring his fiancée back to life.

Just then, Dante's head cocked in Scarlett's direction. But his wounded eyes did not fall on her. They roamed the crowd as if hunting. Searching through the thickening curtain of black flower petals. A soft puddle of them formed around Scarlett's feet, and several petals covered Dante's eyes as he walked past her. The flowers blinded him from seeing the one person whom Scarlett imagined he'd been looking for, a young man in a velvet-rimmed top hat only a few paces from where she stood.

All the air raced from Scarlett's lungs. In every other dream Legend's face had not been clear, but this time she could see him perfectly. His handsome face held no emotion, his light-brown eyes were void of warmth, no hint of a smile curved his lips; he was a shadow of the boy she'd come to know. *Julian.*

DAY FOUR
OF CARAVAL

22

The world tasted like lies and ashes when Scarlett woke. Damp blankets clung to sweaty skin, wet with nightmares and visions of black roses. At least Aiko had not lied about remembering the dreams. Scarlett's memories of her last moments alive were still blurry but her dreams were vivid. They felt as solid and real as the heavy arms encasing her.

Julian.

His hand rested just above her breast. Scarlett sucked in a sharp breath. His fingers were cool against her skin while the marble ice of his chest pressed to her back with an unbeating heart inside. Her body shuddered, but she didn't so much as whimper, afraid it might wake him from his deadly slumber.

She could picture the way he'd looked in her dream, wearing that top hat. A callous expression. Exactly the type of look she would have pictured on Legend, and Julian was certainly as attractive as she'd always imagined Legend to be.

She recalled the innkeeper's frightened eyes when she'd first seen

Julian. Scarlett had thought it was because they were Legend's guests, but what if it was because Julian really *was* Legend? He knew so much about Caraval. He'd known what to do when she'd been dying. And Julian could have easily put the roses in her room.

A sudden heartbeat pressed against her back.

Julian's heart.

Or was it Legend's heart?

No.

Scarlett closed her eyes and took a steadying breath. She'd been warned about this, the game playing tricks on her. It couldn't be true. She didn't know when it had happened, but somewhere, at some point, in this strange world full of impossible, Julian had started to mean something to her. She'd begun to trust him. But if Julian really was Legend, everything significant to her had only been part of a game to him.

Julian's solid chest rose and fell against her back, as heat slowly returned to him. Scarlett felt warmth wherever their bodies aligned. The space behind her knees. The small of her back. Her breath came out in uneven wisps as he leaned farther into her, his fingers drifting up to her collarbone.

A prick of blue on the tip of one of his fingers brought a flush to her cheeks as she remembered his blood on her tongue and the way his lips had felt as he'd tasted her. The most intimate thing she'd ever done. She needed that to be real. She wanted Julian to be real.

But . . .

This wasn't just about what she wanted. Scarlett remembered every time Julian had told her that Legend knew how to take care of his guests. According to her dream, he did more than just *take care* of them. He'd made that woman fall so madly in love, it had driven her to suicide. *Legend likes to play twisted games with people, and one of his favorites is making girls fall in love with him.* The words from her dream gurgled up like vomit in Scarlett's throat. If Julian was Legend, he'd been enticing Tella before the game even started. Perhaps he'd even seduced them both.

Nausea coated Scarlett's stomach at that awful possibility. With disturbing clarity, she recalled those last moments before she'd died, and how she would have given him more than just her blood if he'd only asked.

She needed to escape from Julian's arms before he woke. She was still trying to hold on to the hope he wasn't Legend, but it was too much of a risk to assume otherwise. She would never throw herself out of a window for any man, but her sister was more impulsive. Scarlett had learned to temper her feelings, yet Tella was driven by her volatile emotions and desires. Scarlett could see how both Legend and this game could easily drive Tella to the same unhappy ending as Rosa, if Scarlett did not save her.

Scarlett needed to leave and find Dante. If Rosa had been his fiancée, she imagined he would know if Julian was really Legend.

Holding her breath, Scarlett took Julian's wrist and carefully pried one hand from her waist.

"Crimson," he murmured.

Scarlett sucked in a gasp as the fingers that had been on her collarbone lingered up the column of her neck, leaving a prickly trail of ice and fire. He was still asleep.

But he would wake up soon.

No longer bothering with caution, Scarlett slid off the bed and landed in a heap on the floor. Her clothes now looked somewhere between a mourning dress and a nightgown, black lace and not enough fabric, but she didn't have time to change into her new dress, and in that moment she didn't care.

As she pushed up from the ground, she calculated that it must be exactly one day since she had died. It was the cusp of sunup on the seventeenth, giving her only one night to find Tella before she had to leave for her wed—

Scarlett froze as she caught her reflection in the mirror. Her thick dark hair now had a slender streak of gray ripping through it. At first she thought it a trick of the light, but it was there: her fingers shook as she touched it—right near the temple, impossible to hide with a braid. Scarlett had never thought of herself as vain, but in that moment she wanted to cry.

The game was not supposed to be real, but it was having very genuine consequences. If this was the price of a dress, what else would it cost her to get Tella back? Would she be strong enough?

Red-eyed, and still looking half dead, Scarlett didn't feel particularly tough. The chain of fear around her throat choked her as she thought of how little time she had. But if Nigel, the fortune-teller, was right about fate, then there was no omnipotent hand determining her destiny; she needed to stop letting her worries control it. She might have felt weak, but her love for her sister was not.

The sun had recently risen, so she couldn't leave the inn, but she could make the most of her day by searching La Serpiente for Dante.

As she stepped out of her room, candlelight flickered across the crooked hall, buttery and warm, but something about the space felt wrong. The scent. The usual hints of sweat and fading fire smoke were mired with heavier, harsher scents. Anise and lavender and something akin to rotted plums.

No.

Scarlett had only a blink to panic as she watched her father step around the corner.

She darted back into her room, locked the door, and prayed to the stars—if there was a god or saints, they hated her. How had her father gotten there? If he found her and Tella now, Scarlett had no doubt he would kill her sister as punishment.

Scarlett wanted to think the sight of her father was a cruel hallucination, but it made more sense to believe he'd figured out her sister's kidnapping ruse. And maybe the master of Caraval somehow managed to send him a hint. *Tell me who you fear the most,* the woman had said, and Scarlett had been foolish enough to answer.

What had she done to make Legend hate her so? Even if Julian wasn't Legend, it felt very personal now, though Scarlett couldn't fathom why. Perhaps it was all the letters she'd sent? Or maybe Legend just had a sadistic sense of humor and Scarlett was an easy person to torment? Or maybe—

The beginning of Scarlett's dream rushed back in awful shades of purple, followed by one name, *Annalise*. During the vision she'd been unable to make the connection, but now she remembered her nana's stories about Legend's origin. How he'd been in love with a girl who'd broken his heart by marrying another. Had her grand-mother been Legend's Anna—

"Crimson?" Julian sat up in the bed. "What are you doing against the door like that?"

"I—" Scarlett froze.

His wild dark hair framed a face cloaked with convincing con-cern, but all she could see was the soulless look Julian had worn as he watched the funeral procession of the girl who'd killed herself after he'd made her fall in love with him.

Legend.

Her heartbeat pounded. She told herself it wasn't true. Julian wasn't Legend. Yet she pressed harder against the door as Julian pushed up off the bed and stalked toward her, his steps surprisingly sure and even for someone who'd just awoken from death.

If he was Legend, somewhere in this magical world he'd built was her sister. Scarlett wanted to demand an answer. She wanted to smack him in the face once again. But tipping her hand right now would not help. If Julian really was Legend, and this twisted game was all some way to get back at her grandmother for breaking his heart, the only advantage Scarlett had was that he did not know she'd discov-ered him.

"Crimson, you're not looking too good. How long ago did you wake up?" Julian lifted his hand and brushed cool knuckles to her cheek. "You have no idea how much you scared me, I—"

"I'm fine," Scarlett cut him off, and slid to the side. She didn't want him touching her.

Julian clenched his jaw. All his earlier concern was gone, replaced with—Scarlett wanted to think it was anger, but it wasn't. It was hurt. She could see the sting of her rejection in shades of stormy blue, ghosting over his heart like sad morning mist.

Scarlett had always seen her own emotions in color, but she'd never seen another person's. She didn't know what shocked her more, that she could now see the color of Julian's feelings, or that those feelings were so wounded.

She tried to imagine how Julian would be feeling if he weren't Legend. Before she'd died, they'd shared something extraordinarily special. She remembered how gently he'd carried her up to their room. How he'd given up a day of his life for her. How strong and safe his arms had felt as he'd cradled her on the bed. She could even see the evidence of his sacrifice; in the midst of the dark stubble lining his jaw, there was a thin silver streak—matching the new stripe in her hair. And now Scarlett wouldn't even touch him.

"I'm sorry," Scarlett said. "It's just—I think I'm still shaken up from what happened. If I'm acting strange, I'm sorry. I'm not thinking clearly. I'm sorry," she repeated, which may have been too many *sorry*s.

A muscle ticked in Julian's neck. He clearly didn't believe her. "Maybe you should lie back down."

"You know I can't get back in that bed with you," Scarlett snapped. It was what she would have said before, but her words came out harsher than she intended.

Julian wiped every emotion from his face, yet the turbulent colors hovering over his heart told Scarlett he was far from unfeeling. His hurt now mingled with a shade of something Scarlett had never seen. The color was indiscernible, not quite silver or gray, but she swore she could feel the sharp emotion behind it—maybe it was because they'd shared blood?

Her lungs were tight, and so was her throat. Every breath hurt as Julian strode over to the other door. "I wasn't planning on getting back in bed with you," he said.

Scarlett tried to respond, but now her vocal cords were closed and her eyes were stinging. It wasn't until Julian stepped out of the room that she could breathe once more, and she realized: when he left, it felt as if he was closing the door on her as well.

Scarlett stood with her body pressed against the wall, fighting the urge to run after Julian, to apologize for acting so strange and awful. When he walked out the door, she would have sworn he wasn't Legend, but she couldn't risk trusting him and being wrong.

No, Scarlett corrected herself.

She *could* risk being wrong.

Everything Scarlett had done since arriving at Caraval involved risk. Some of those things had not ended well, but others had pleasantly surprised her—*like the intimate moment she'd shared with Julian.* He'd never have given her such a precious gift if she hadn't first made a mistake by losing two days of her life.

Maybe taking a chance right now was exactly what she needed to do. If not for her own sake, she needed to do it for Tella. Julian had been her ally since she'd arrived, and Scarlett might need his help more than ever, with her father on the island now.

Oh, saints, her father! Scarlett hadn't even told Julian he was there. She definitely had to find him now and warn him.

Anxiously, Scarlett opened the door. The wretched scent of her father's perfume still lingered, but the only person in the hall was the vile man with the bowler hat who'd stolen her earrings. He paid no attention as she darted past him and onto the stairs. She didn't know where Julian had gone, but she hoped he hadn't left—

Scarlett froze at the next landing.

Julian, as confident as if he really was the master of Caraval, strode out of Dante's room, opened Tella's cracked door, and stepped inside.

What is he doing?

Julian hated Dante. And why Tella's demolished room? What was—

Above her, the inn creaked with the weight of multiple footsteps. Three sets. As they drew closer to the stairwell above, she could hear the words of one man echoing down in her direction.

The first half of his sentence she couldn't make out, but she recognized her father's voice and caught what he said next. "You saw her walk by just now?"

A tremor worked its way through Scarlett's body.

"Less than a minute ago. Now, where's my coins?" It must have been the miserable man with the bowler hat speaking.

Suddenly she was back on Trisda, curling into stairwell shadows, afraid to move lest she get caught. But she had to move. Any moment her father would be down the stairs. Scarlett couldn't afford to be afraid, or debate what she should do. Her boots barely tapped the floor as she scurried down the path Julian had taken into Tella's room. She tried to latch the door, but the lock was broken.

The room was empty.

No sign of Julian anywhere.

But he'd definitely come in here.

Scarlett told herself there was a reasonable explanation. And then she remembered.

The dying garden she'd found in Castillo Maldito. Neglected and abandoned. The garden had been carefully cultivated as a place people would not linger—much like Tella's room. Scarlett imagined Julian entering, pushing aside bits of wreckage, finding a floorboard with the symbol of Caraval, and then pressing his finger against it until another board slid open, leading him into a hidden tunnel.

A tunnel she needed to find.

Outside, the sound of footsteps grew louder, a harsh chorus to her frantic search. Dropping to her hands and knees, she scanned for an entrance. Splinters dug into her fingers as she crawled across the floor. Somehow the battered space still managed to smell like Tella. Sharp molasses and wild dreams. Scarlett moved with more urgency; she had to find her sister before their father caught either one of them.

Inside the fireplace, all the bricks were covered with soot, but her eyes latched on to a lighter smudge, as if someone had just pressed his thumb to it. Underneath, the symbol etched into the firebox wall was dirty, hard to see, but the tip of Scarlett's finger tingled as she touched the same spot. For a panicked second nothing happened.

Then, slowly, the fireplace shifted, bricks grinding apart to reveal a set of rich mahogany stairs. The sconces lining them burned with glowing orange coals, revealing a well-worn path down the center, as if someone traveled them often. Scarlett imagined Julian taking these steps every time he'd snuck away or disappeared.

It still doesn't mean he's Legend.

But Scarlett was having a harder time believing that now. If he wasn't Legend, why else did he have so many secrets? Even if he wasn't seducing Tella whenever he was away from Scarlett, Julian was definitely hiding something.

A damp chill wrapped around Scarlett's exposed calves as she started down. Even though she was very much awake, her dress remained thin as a nightgown and fell barely past her knees. Two flights of smooth stairs led to three diverging pathways. On the right a trail of petal-pink sand. In the middle, one of polished glowing stones creating dim puddles of light. To her left, brick.

Torches covered in white flames lit the open mouths of all her options. Each route contained multiple sets of boot prints in a variety of sizes. She imagined any tunnel could hide her from her father, but only one could lead to Julian—and possibly to Tella, if Julian really was Legend.

The tunnels could also lead to madness, Scarlett thought. But she would rather face that possibility than her father.

Closing her eyes, Scarlett listened. To her left, trapped wind beat against walls. To her right, water rushed. Then, down the middle, larger, heavier steps beat forward. Julian!

Quickly, she followed, relying on the steady press of his footfalls to guide her. They seemed to grow louder as the temperature of the path became colder.

Until the footsteps stopped.

Vanished.

Wet chills licked the back of her neck. Scarlett spun, afraid someone was behind her, but it was only the silent corridor, full of stones that were rapidly losing their glow. Scarlett started running faster, but her foot caught on something. Tripping forward, she reached out to steady herself against a damp wall, only to lose her balance once more as she caught sight of the object she'd stumbled upon.

A human hand.

Bile rose in her throat. Acid and acrid.

Five tattooed fingers stretched out as if reaching for her.

Somehow she managed to hold back her scream, until she looked down the hall and saw Dante's twisted dead body, and Julian standing over it.

23

S carlett tried to convince herself what she was seeing wasn't real. The tunnels were trying to drive her mad. She told herself the putrid smell was manufactured. The hand wasn't Dante's; it was someone else's. But even if somehow a body had been stolen and tattoos had been carved into it as part of a game, there was no mistaking the rest of Dante, the pallor of his skin, or the angle of head, only barely attached to his bloody neck.

Julian's head whipped around. "Crimson, it's not what it looks—"

Scarlett started to run, but he was faster. Sprinting forward, he caught her in a heartbeat, banding one strong arm across her chest and another around her waist.

"Let me go!" She squirmed.

"Scarlett, stop! These tunnels intensify fear—don't let yours control you. I swear, Dante and I were working together, and if you stop fighting me I can prove it." Julian adjusted his grip, pinning her hands behind her. "I've been dead for the past day. You really think I killed him?"

If he was Legend, he could have had someone else murder him. "Why did you pretend you didn't know Dante if you were working together?"

"Because we were afraid something like this would happen. We knew Legend would recognize Dante and Valentina from the last time they played, but I mostly watched, so Legend doesn't know me. We thought it wise to keep our partnership a secret in case Legend figured out what Dante was really here to do."

Julian cut two eyes farther down the corridor toward Dante's dead body, but his face remained emotionless. Not the look of someone who'd just found a murdered friend. The same cold look he had worn at the funeral. *Legend.*

Scarlett smothered a whimper, and though each of her instincts battled against it she forced her body to go limp. Not to scream as she felt the press of Julian's chest. Not to hit as he slowly released her wrists. The only thing she fought against was her growing fear, until Julian removed his arm from around her waist.

And then she—

Julian pressed her up against the wall, a few short feet after she attempted to run. "You're going to get both of us killed if you don't stop this," he growled.

Then he ripped open the buttons of his shirt. They skittered across the ground as he arched back and stepped away, just enough for the torchlight to reveal what Scarlett had thought was a scar above his heart. But it wasn't. Fainter than year-old memories, a tattoo in white ink curled near the top of his ribs. *A rose.*

"It's a different color, but I'm sure you've seen this on Dante," said Julian.

"That doesn't prove anything. I've seen roses all over Caraval." Legend was obsessed with them. Further proof the dream sent by Aiko was right. A distant part of Scarlett warned it wasn't wise to reveal her last card to the player holding all the cards. But Scarlett was done playing games. A few feet away lay the body of a dead man; this game had gone far enough. "You can stop lying to me. I saw you at the funeral. I know you're really Legend!"

Julian's dark expression froze. For a moment he looked stunned, then his features softened into subtle amusement. "I don't know what funeral you think you saw, but I've only ever attended one funeral, for my sister Rosa: Dante's fiancée. I'm not Legend. I'm here because I want to stop him from destroying anyone else the way he destroyed her."

Rosa was his *sister*? Scarlett's conviction wavered. But had she begun to believe him because she desperately wanted to, or because Julian really was telling the truth? She tried to see the color of his emotions, but there was nothing over his heart. Her connection to his feelings must have already faded.

"I saw pictures," Scarlett said. "If she was your sister, why were you just standing there? I saw you wearing a top hat."

"You think I'm Legend because you looked at pictures and saw me wearing a top hat?" Julian sounded as if he wanted to laugh.

"It wasn't just the top hat!" Though that might have been most of it. But there were still other things he wasn't telling her. "How did you know what to do when I was dying?"

"Because I heard people talk about it when I watched the game before. It's not any secret, but most people aren't willing to give up their life for someone else, even small pieces of it." He gave Scarlett a pointed look. "I get that you have problems with trust," Julian went on roughly. "After meeting your father, I don't blame you. But I swear, I'm *not* Legend."

"Then how did you get back to La Serpiente the other day after you'd been hurt? And why didn't you meet me in the tavern when you were supposed to?"

Julian let out a frustrated groan. "I don't know how this will prove that I'm not Legend, but I didn't meet you at the tavern because the night before I'd been bashed in the head. I slept in, and when I got to the tavern you were already gone." He smirked, but something about it was off. Too forced.

Even if Julian wasn't Legend, he wasn't being entirely honest. His hands were clenched, holding his secrets the way Scarlett so often clutched her fear, as if letting go would unravel him.

"If you're really here to stop Legend, I can't imagine you'd just sleep in one night. And it still doesn't explain how you got back into La Serpiente that day."

"Why are you so obsessed with that?" A frustrated shake of his head. "All right, fine. You want to know the truth?" Julian leaned in close, until his cool breath was on her neck, the cool scent of him all over her skin, and the tunnel seemed to be made of nothing but him.

"I didn't sleep at all. I left you sitting in the tavern on purpose because after being with you in the room the day before I didn't think it was a good idea for me to see you again." His eyes dropped to her lips, and Scarlett shivered. In the dim tunnels it was too dark to make out their color, but when he looked back up she pictured two hungry pools of liquid amber fringed by dark lashes. It was the exact same way he'd stared at her before, when his back had been against the door and she'd been pressed against him.

"I started this game with a simple mission." Julian paused, swallowed thickly, and when he spoke again his voice was rough and low, as if it was hard for him to get out the words. "I came here to find Legend and avenge my sister. My relationship with you was meant to end right after you got me into the game. So yes, I haven't been completely honest about things, but, I swear, I am not Legend."

Scarlett imagined he could have crumbled stone with the force of his words. Julian always seemed to be covering up how he truly felt, but his last six words had been stripped bare. His tone may not have been sweet, but Scarlett heard nothing but truth in it.

Taking an intentional step back, Julian slowly reached in his pocket and lifted out a note. "I found this in Dante's room. I was down here to meet him, not kill him."

> J—
>
> Valentina is still missing. I think Legend is onto us.

A flicker of a memory.

Valentina was Dante's sister.

Scarlett shook as she recalled the last time she'd seen Dante alive. He'd been frantic with worry in the stairwell. Maybe if Scarlett hadn't lost that day, she would have been able to help him find her. "I should have done something," she muttered.

"There was nothing you could have done," Julian said flatly. "Valentina was supposed to meet us here the night I got my head bashed, but she never showed up."

Julian explained that the tunnels ran under everything. Maps were embedded at the mouth of each one, and they were mainly used for the Caraval performers, to easily get from one place to another. "And sometimes they're used for murder," Julian added wryly. His eyes were hooded, cheekbones sharper than usual, an expression made of shattered things.

Scarlett wished she knew how to fix him, but it seemed as if he was almost as damaged as she was. "Are you still set on revenge?" she asked.

"Would you try to stop me if I was?" He cast his gaze down the hall toward Dante's dead, twisted body.

Scarlett felt as if her answer should have been yes. She liked to believe there were always options besides violence. But Dante's murder and Valentina's disappearance took away any illusions that Caraval was merely a game.

Scarlett had thought her father was vicious, but Legend was just as much of a monster. It seemed her nana hadn't lied when she'd said the more Legend played the role of a villain, the more he'd become one in reality.

Tentatively, Scarlett reached out and took Julian's hand. His fingers were tense, cold. "I'm sorry about your—"

The echo of footsteps cut her off. Steady, determined, and close.

She couldn't hear any voices, but she swore she recognized the gait. Instinctively, she pulled her hand from Julian's. "I think that's my father!"

Julian's head jerked toward the sound. In a flash his sorrow was gone. "Your *father's* here?"

"Yes," Scarlett said.

They both started running.

24

T his way." Julian tugged her toward a corridor lined in bricks and lit with glowing spiderwebs.

"No." Scarlett urged him left. "I used a path with stones." She didn't recall the walls being speckled with radiant rocks as well, but she'd not really been paying attention to that.

Behind them the crush of boots was getting louder.

Julian scowled but followed her. His elbow brushed hers as the tunnel walls grew narrow and knobby stones dug into both their sides. "Why didn't you tell me your father was here?"

"I was going to tell you, but—"

Julian's hand clamped over Scarlett's mouth, salt and dirt pressed against her lips as he whispered, "Shh—"

He grabbed one of the glowing stones dotting the wall, twisted it like a doorknob, and pulled her into a darkened nowhere. The walls hugging Scarlett's back were like ice, moist and cold. She could feel them soaking through her thin dress while she tried to remember how to breathe.

Anise and lavender and something akin to rotted plums were replacing Julian's cool scent, moving like smoke under the odd door he'd just pulled her through.

"I'll keep you safe," Julian whispered. His body pressed close to hers, as if to shield her, while boot steps landed hard just outside their hiding spot, which seemed to be growing smaller. The frigid walls were digging into Scarlett, pushing her closer and closer to Julian. Her elbows hit his chest, forcing her to twine her arms around his waist as his taut body molded against hers.

Scarlett's heart raced irregularly. The coarse stubble of Julian's jaw grazed her cheek as his hands wove low around her hips. Through the insubstantial fabric of her dress she could feel every curve of his fingers. If her father opened the door and discovered her like this she would be dead.

Scarlett tried to push away, her breath coming out quick and fast. The ceiling now seemed to be sinking too, moving closer, dripping cold onto the top of her head.

"I think this room is trying to kill us," Scarlett said. Outside she heard her father's steps retreat, until the sound of them faded to nothing. She would have liked to stay hidden another minute or more, but her lungs were being squashed, sandwiched between Julian and the freezing wall. "Open the door!"

"I'm trying." Julian grunted.

Scarlett sucked in a gasp. Her flimsy gown rose up above her knees as Julian's knuckles roamed over her backside, his palms searching for their exit. "I can't find it," he ground out. "I think it's on your side."

"I can't feel anything." *Except for you.* Her fingers brushed places she knew she shouldn't have been touching, while her hands tried to explore the wall. But the harder she fought, the more the room seemed to push back.

Like the ocean off the island.

The more Scarlett had kicked against it, the more frightened she had been, the more the waters had punished her.

Maybe that was it.

Julian said the tunnels heightened fear, but maybe they fed off of it as well.

"The room is connected to our emotions," Scarlett said. "I think we need to relax."

Julian made a strangled sound. "That's not easy at the moment." His lips were in her hair, and his hands were just below her hips, clinging to her curves.

"Oh," Scarlett said. Her pulse kicked up again, and as it did, she could feel Julian's heart rushing against her chest. A week ago she could never have relaxed in this situation; even now it was difficult. But despite his lies, somehow she knew that she was safe with him. He'd never hurt her. She forced herself to take a calming breath, and as she did the wall stopped moving.

Another breath.

The room grew slightly bigger.

Outside there were still no sounds of her father. No footsteps, no breathing. None of his noxious stench.

A moment later the walls against her back were warmer, a bright contrast to the now damp parts of her dress. As the room expanded, she could feel Julian relax as well. Most of Scarlett's body still touched his, but not so closely as before. His chest moved in rhythm with hers, slow and even as the walls continued to scale back.

With every breath they took, the chamber heated. Soon there were tiny pinpricks of light, dotting the ceiling like dust from the moon and illuminating a glowing knob above Scarlett's right hand.

"Wait—" Julian warned.

But Scarlett had already opened the door. The minute she did the room disappeared. Before and behind them, a low passageway stretched out, embedded with broken seashells that glowed like the stones had, the ground covered by a trail of petal-pink sand.

Julian cursed. "I hate this tunnel."

"At least we lost my father," she said. No footsteps sounded in any direction. All Scarlett could hear were crisp ocean waves colliding in the distance. Trisda didn't have pink beaches, but the echoing push and pull of the water reminded her of home, along with something else.

"How did you know I could get you into the game?" Scarlett asked. "I didn't receive my tickets until after you arrived on Trisda."

Julian kicked up more sand with his boots as he walked a little faster. "Don't you think it's strange you don't even know the name of the man you're marrying?"

"You're changing the subject," Scarlett said.

"No, this is part of your answer."

"All right." She lowered her voice. She still didn't detect any other footsteps, but she wanted to be safe. "It's a secret because my father's controlling."

Julian toyed with the chain of his pocket watch. "What if there was more to it?"

"What are you getting at?"

"I think your father may have actually been trying to protect you. Before you get upset, just hear me out," he rushed on. "I'm not saying your father is good. From what I've seen I'd call him a dirty bastard, but I can understand his reasons to be secretive."

"Go on," Scarlett said tightly.

Julian explained what Scarlett already knew, about Legend and her grandmother Annalise. Though Julian's version of the story was different from her grandmother's. In his tale, Legend started out with more talent and far more innocence. All he cared about was Annalise. She was the entire reason he transformed into Legend; it had nothing to do with a desire for fame. Then before his first performance, he found her in the arms of another, wealthier man, whom she'd planned to marry all along.

"After that, Legend went a little mad. He vowed to destroy Annalise, by hurting her family the way she'd wounded him. Since Annalise crushed his heart, Legend swore he would do the same to any daughters, or granddaughters, unfortunate enough to be a part of her line. He would ruin their chances at having happy marriages or finding love, and if they went mad in the process, even better. "

Julian tried to say the last part as if he weren't altogether serious, but Scarlett could still clearly remember her dream. Legend didn't just make women fall in love, he drove them mad with it, and she had no doubts he was doing the same thing to Tella right now.

"So, when my friends and I learned of your engagement," Julian went on, "we knew it was only a matter of time before Legend invited you to Caraval so he could break it off."

Again, he made it sound so much less harmful than it was. But Scarlett's engagement was her entire future. Without this marriage, she'd be doomed to a life on Trisda with her father.

As the sandy path grew steeper, she struggled to walk up it, thinking back to the foolish letters she'd sent. She'd never signed her full name until the very last one, when she'd written about her wedding— the one Legend had chosen to respond to.

Scarlett could see Julian's story making sense, but she wondered how a simple sailor would know all this. She narrowed her eyes at the dark-haired boy beside her, and asked the question that had visited her thoughts on more than one occasion. "Who are you really?"

"Let's just say my family is well connected." Julian flashed a smile that might have looked charming to some, yet Scarlett could see there was nothing remotely happy about it.

She recalled the gossip she'd overheard in her dream. Julian's family had turned his sister away after learning of her illicit relationship with Legend. From what Scarlett knew of Julian she couldn't imagine him to be so judgmental, but he must have felt the guilt all the same. It was an emotion Scarlett was far too familiar with.

For several beats they walked in silence, until she finally gained the courage to say, "It's not your fault, you know, what happened to your sister."

For a fragile moment, as thin and long as a stretched-out spider-web, there was only the waves in the distance, and the crush of Julian's boots in the sand. Then: "So you don't blame yourself when your father beats your sister?" His words were whisper-soft, but Scarlett felt each one acutely, reminding her of every time she'd failed Tella.

Julian stopped walking and slowly turned to face her. His steady gaze was even softer than his voice. It reached out to the broken parts of her like a caress. The type of touch that moves through damaged flesh, past fractured bones and into a person's wounded soul. Scarlett felt her blood go hot as he watched her. She could have been wearing a dress that covered every inch of her skin and she would have still felt exposed to Julian's eyes. It was as if all her shame, her guilt, the awful secret memories she tried to bury, were laid bare for him to see.

"Your father is the one to blame," he said. "You've done nothing wrong."

"You don't know that," Scarlett argued. "Whenever my father hurts my sister it is because I have done something wrong. Because I failed—"

"Help!" A scream tore through their conversation like a gust of wind. "Please!" A familiar shriek followed.

"Tella?" Scarlett started running, kicking up a flurry of pink sand.

"Don't!" Julian warned. "That's not your sister."

But Scarlett ignored him. She knew her sister's voice. It sounded only a few feet away; she could feel it vibrating. Louder and louder, it echoed off the sandstone walls until—

"Stop!" Julian's arm snaked around Scarlett's waist, pulling her back as the sandy path abruptly ended. A few unfortunate grains skittered off the edge, falling into foamy blue-and-green waters churning more than fifty feet below.

All the air rushed out from Scarlett's lungs.

Julian's cheeks were flushed with color, hands shaking as he continued to steady her. "Are you all—"

But the end of his words were sliced off by evil laughter. A sour sound of nightmares and other foul things. It poured out of the walls as pieces of it twisted into tiny mouths.

It was another trick of the maddening tunnels.

"Crimson, we should keep moving." Julian gently touched the edge of her hip, guiding her back to a safer path, while the tunnels continued cackling, a warped version of her sister's precious laugh.

For a moment Scarlett had felt so close to finding Tella. But what if she was already too late to save her sister? What if Tella had fallen so madly in love with Legend, given herself to him so completely, that once the game ended she would want her life to end as well? Tella loved danger the same way candlewicks loved to burn. It never seemed to scare her that some of the things she lusted for might consume her like a flame.

As a girl, Scarlett had been drawn to the idea of Legend's magic. But Tella always wanted to hear about the master of Caraval's darker side. A part of Scarlett couldn't deny there was something seductive about winning the heart of someone who'd vowed to never love again.

But Legend wasn't just jaded; he was demented, adept at making people fall not only in love but also into madness. Who knew what sort of twisted things he was leading Tella to believe? If Julian hadn't stopped Scarlett just now, she might have run straight off that cliff, and crashed to her death before she even realized her mistake. And Tella leaped forward without thinking far more often than Scarlett.

Tella had been only twelve the first time she'd tried to run off with a boy. Thankfully Scarlett had found her before their father noticed her absence, but ever since then Scarlett had feared that one day her sister would run into trouble that Scarlett could not rescue her from.

Why couldn't it be enough for him to ruin Scarlett's engagement?

"We'll find her," Julian said. "What happened to Rosa won't happen to your sister."

Scarlett wanted to believe him. After everything that had just occurred, she ached to break down and fold into him, to trust him again like before. But the words he meant as reassuring forced to the surface a question she'd been too afraid to think about since he had made his earlier confession as to why he was there.

She peeled away from Julian's hand, forcing herself to create distance. "Did you know when you brought us to Caraval that Legend would take Tella the way he took your sister?"

Julian hesitated. "I knew there was a chance."

In other words, *yes.*

"How much of a chance?" Scarlett choked out.

Julian's caramel eyes filled with something like regret. "I never said I was a good person, Crimson."

"I don't believe that." Scarlett's thoughts raced back to Nigel, the fortune-teller, how he'd told her a person's future could shift based on what he wanted most. "I believe you could be good if you wanted to be."

"You only believe that because you're so good. Decent people like you always believe other people can be virtuous, but I'm not." He cut off. Something painful crossed his face. "I knew what would happen when I brought you and your sister here. I didn't know Legend would kidnap Tella, but I knew that he would take one of you."

25

Scarlett's legs were boneless, thin skin wrapped around useless muscles. Her lungs ached with the pressure of unshed tears. Even her gown looked tired and dead. The black fabric had dulled to gray, as if it no longer had the strength to hold color. She didn't remember ripping the lace, but the hem of her bizarre mourning-nightdress hung in tatters around her calves. She didn't know if its magic had stopped working or if it just reflected how exhausted and unraveled she felt. She'd left Julian at the base of the mahogany stairs, asking him not to follow.

When she returned to her guestroom with its roaring fire and massive bed, all she wanted was to lose herself underneath the covers. To tumble into oblivious sleep until she was able to forget the horrors of the day. But she couldn't afford sleep.

When she'd first arrived on the isle she'd only been concerned about making it home in time for her wedding. But now that Legend had killed Dante and her father was here, the game had changed. Scarlett felt the press of time, heavier than the crush of all the red beads in Castillo Maldito's hourglasses; she had to get to Tella before her father found her, or Legend consumed her like a flame burning a candle. If Scarlett failed, her sister would die.

In less than two hours, the sun would set, and Scarlett would need to be ready to start searching again.

So, she only gave herself one minute. One minute to cry for Dante and sob for her sister and rage because Julian was not who she thought he was. To fall on the bed and whine and moan over all the things that had churned out of her control. To pick up Legend's stupid vase of roses and dash them against the mantel of the fireplace.

"Crimson—are you all right in there?" Julian knocked and burst through the door in the same moment.

"What are you doing here?" She fought back her tears as she scowled at him. She could not bear having him see her cry, though she was fairly certain it was too late for that.

Julian fumbled for words as he cast around for a threat that wasn't there, clearly distressed to find her sobbing and no other danger to deal with. "I thought I heard something."

"What did you think you heard? You can't just burst in here! Go! I need to finish changing."

Instead of leaving, Julian quietly shut the door. His eyes took in the shattered vase and the puddle on the floor before returning to her tearstained face. "Crimson, don't cry because of me."

"You think too highly of yourself. My sister's missing, my father has found us, and Dante's dead. These tears are not for you."

Julian at least had the decency to look ashamed. But he stayed in the room. He sat gingerly on the bed, making the mattress dip beneath his weight as more drops fell down her cheeks. Hot and wet and salty. Scarlett's outburst had purged some of her pain, but now the tears wouldn't stop, and maybe Julian was right: maybe a few *were* because of him.

Julian leaned closer and brushed them away with his fingertips.

"Don't." Scarlett pulled back.

"I deserve that." He dropped his hand and edged farther away, until they were on opposite sides of the bed. "I shouldn't have lied, or brought you here against your will."

"You shouldn't have brought us here at all," Scarlett snapped.

"Your sister would have found a way, with or without me."

"Is this supposed to be an apology? If it is, it's not very good."

Julian answered cautiously. "I'm not sorry for doing what your sister wanted: I believe people should have the freedom to make their own decisions. But I *am* sorry for every time I've lied to you." He paused, and when he looked at her his warm brown eyes were softer than she'd ever seen them, and open, as if he wanted her to view something he usually kept hidden.

"I know I don't deserve another chance, but earlier you said you think I can be good. I'm not, Crimson, or at least I haven't been. I'm a liar and I'm bitter and sometimes I make terrible choices. I come from a prideful family that's always playing games with one another, and after Rosa"—he hesitated, his voice taking on the rough, strangled, hard-to-speak edge that came whenever he mentioned his sister—"after she died, I lost faith in everything. Not that it's an excuse. But if you give me another chance, I swear, I'll make it up to you."

Across from them the fire crackled, its heat shrinking the puddle of water on the floor. Soon it would just be the roses and shattered glass. Scarlett thought of Julian's rose tattoo. She wished he really had been just a sailor who'd happened by her isle, and she hated that he'd lied to her for so long. But she could understand devotion to a sister. Scarlett knew what it was like to love someone so irrevocably, no matter the cost.

Julian leaned against the bedpost, all kinds of tragic and lovely, dark hair hanging over tired eyes, his wicked mouth turned down, and rips marring his once pristine shirt.

Scarlett had made mistakes because of this game as well. But Julian had never held those against her, and she didn't want to punish him, either.

"I forgive you," she said. "Just promise me, no more lies."

With a heavy breath, Julian closed his eyes, forehead knotted into a look somewhere between gratitude and pain. He spoke hoarsely, "I promise."

"Hullo?" A knock on the door startled them both.

Julian jumped up before Scarlett could move. *Hide,* he mouthed.

No. She'd done enough hiding already that day. Ignoring his angry looks, Scarlett grabbed the fireplace poker and followed him as he crept toward the door.

"I have a delivery," said a feminine voice.

"For who?" asked Julian.

"It's for the sister of Donatella Dragna."

Scarlett gripped the poker tighter, her heart hitting an extra beat.

Tell her to leave it at the door, Scarlett mouthed. She wanted to hope it was a clue. But all she kept thinking of was Dante's severed hand.

With a shudder, she imagined Legend chopping off Tella's hand and delivering it to her room.

After the messenger girl's footsteps faded, she let Julian open the door.

The box on the other side was flat black, the color of failure and funerals. It stretched in front of her doorway, long, and almost as wide across as Scarlett. Next to it rested a vase with two red roses.

More flowers!

Scarlett kicked over the vase, spilling the flowers across the threshold of her room before pulling the box inside. She couldn't tell if it felt heavy or light.

"You want me to open it?" Julian asked.

Scarlett shook her head. She didn't want to open the black box either, but every second she wasted was a second they could be searching for Tella. Carefully she lifted the lid.

"What is that?" Julian's brows formed a sharp V.

"It's my other dress from the shop." Scarlett released a relieved laugh as she pulled the gown from the box. The girl had said it would be delivered in two days.

But something about the dress was off. It looked different from how Scarlett remembered. The color was much lighter, almost pure white—wedding-gown white.

26

The dress seemed to mock her. With sleeves that were nonexistent, and a deep, heart-shaped neckline that looked far from sweet, this piece of clothing was more scandalous than the one Scarlett had chosen in the shop.

The creamy buttons gleamed like ivory in the room's warm light. At the bottom of the box Scarlett found a small note, attached to a broken pin. "It must have fallen off the gown."

On one side was the image of a top hat, on the other a brief message:

I imagine this will look lovely on you.

Warm regards,

—D

"Who's 'D'?" Julian asked.

"I think someone wants me to believe it's from Donatella." But Scarlett knew this gift was not from her sister. The mockery of a wedding gown could only be from one person, and the top hat on the note could only mean one thing. *Legend.*

Invisible spiders crawled over her skin, such a different feeling from the bright colors his first letter had summoned. "I think this is the fifth clue."

Julian grimaced. "Why would you think that?"

"What else would it be?" Scarlett said. She pulled out her note with all the clues.

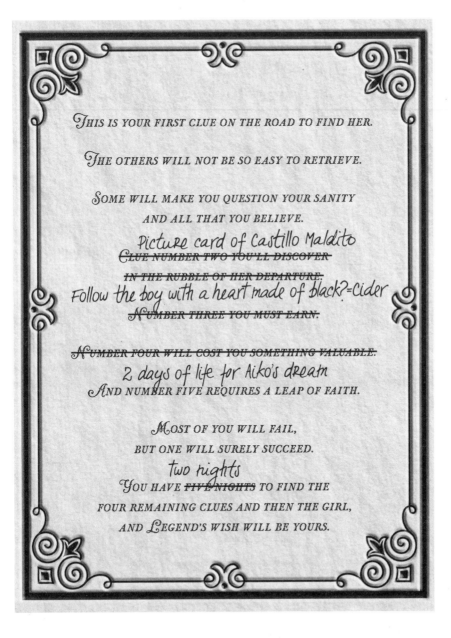

THIS IS YOUR FIRST CLUE ON THE ROAD TO FIND HER.

THE OTHERS WILL NOT BE SO EASY TO RETRIEVE.

SOME WILL MAKE YOU QUESTION YOUR SANITY
AND ALL THAT YOU BELIEVE.

Picture card of Castillo Maldito
~~CLUE NUMBER TWO YOU'LL DISCOVER~~

~~IN THE RUBBLE OF HER DEPARTURE.~~
Follow the boy with a heart made of black?=cider
~~NUMBER THREE YOU MUST EARN.~~

~~NUMBER FOUR WILL COST YOU SOMETHING VALUABLE.~~
2 days of life for Aiko's dream
AND NUMBER FIVE REQUIRES A LEAP OF FAITH.

MOST OF YOU WILL FAIL,
BUT ONE WILL SURELY SUCCEED.
two nights
YOU HAVE ~~FIVE NIGHTS~~ TO FIND THE
FOUR REMAINING CLUES AND THEN THE GIRL,
AND LEGEND'S WISH WILL BE YOURS.

"See, I've already figured out the first four clues," Scarlett said. "All that's left is number five."

"But how is this the fifth clue?" Julian asked, still looking at the dress as if it were covered in something far more offensive than buttons.

That's when Scarlett unpuzzled it. Buttons and a top hat were both symbols.

"Legend is known for his top hats, and I've been finding buttons all over the game," she said. "I didn't know if the buttons meant anything or not, but after seeing this dress covered entirely in buttons, I'm almost certain they do. When I bought the gown, next door to the shop was a path of buttons that led to a hatter and haberdashery shop shaped like a top hat."

"I still don't see how that means anything." Julian's scowl remained in place as he read Scarlett's note with all the clues. "'And number five requires a leap of faith.' How does this place fit with that?"

"I don't know. I think that's where the faith part comes in. Maybe it's some sort of challenge from Legend and we need to go to the hat shop and face whatever is waiting for us." Scarlett wasn't fully convinced of this, but she'd begun to learn that no matter how logically she tried to reason, there were always variables she'd be unable to see. Sometimes caution held her back rather than kept her safe.

But it seemed as if Julian was starting to feel the opposite. He had a look on his face that suggested he wanted to toss her over his shoulder and keep her locked away and hidden from the rest of the world.

"The sun will go down in less than an hour," Scarlett said firmly.

"If you come up with something better before then, I'm open to suggestions. If not, the minute it's dark out, I think we should go to the shop and see what we find."

Julian looked at the dress once again, his mouth opening as if he wanted to say something, but then he snapped it shut, and nodded. "I'll check the halls to see if your father is anywhere before we leave."

After he left, Scarlett changed into the gown, and grabbed the buttons she'd collected. They felt like a flimsy offering, but maybe there was something magical about them she had yet to realize.

NIGHT FOUR
OF CARAVAL

27

As Scarlett left the inn, she didn't smell even a hint of her father's foul perfume. Right before they'd stepped outside, Julian had sworn he saw her father leave the building. But Scarlett continued tossing glances behind her, wondering if her father were somehow following, waiting for the right moment to pounce.

The delights of Caraval continued to dance all around her. Girls on sidewalk stages dueled with parasols, while bands of zealous participants continued to hunt for clues. Yet Scarlett felt as though the night had been knocked askew. The air was damper than usual. And the light felt unnatural as well. The moon was only a sliver, but it cast a silver glow over the usually colorful shops and turned the water into liquid metal.

"This plan still doesn't feel right." Julian lowered his voice as they entered the curving lane that wove around the carousel made of roses.

"A song for a donation?" asked the organist.

"Not tonight," Scarlett said.

The man started playing just the same. This time the carousel didn't turn. Its red flowers stayed in place, but the music was enough to muffle Julian's words as he went on, "I think this hat shop you told me about is too obvious to be the final clue."

"Maybe it's so bold, everyone else has missed it." Scarlett's feet moved faster as they neared the triple-tiered dress shop where she'd purchased her gowns.

Heavy storm clouds had moved over the moon, and unlike the last time Scarlett was there, all the shop windows were dim. The hatter and haberdashery next to the dress shop was almost too dark to see. Yet its outline was unmistakable.

Rimmed in a wide moat of black flower boxes that circled the rounded two-story building like a brim, the place was shaped exactly like a top hat, with a path of buttons leading to its black velvet door.

"This really doesn't feel like Legend," Julian insisted. "I know he's known for those ridiculous top hats, but he wouldn't be this blatant."

"It's almost too dark to see the shop. I'd hardly call this obvious."

"Something about this is wrong," Julian spoke under his breath. "I think I should go in alone and check it out first."

"Maybe neither of you should go in." Aiko suddenly appeared by Scarlett's side. Her skirt and blouse were silver this time, with eyes and lips painted to match. Like a teardrop the moon had cried.

"I'm so glad you decided to wear that dress." She glided closer to Scarlett, nodding in approval. "I think it looks even better than the other night."

Julian divided a look between the girls, made of equal parts confusion and distrust. "You two know each other?"

"We went shopping together," Aiko replied.

Julian's expression turned to stone. "You're the one who convinced her to buy the dresses?"

"And you must be the one who left her waiting in a tavern?" Aiko raised two appraising eyebrows threaded with pearls, though she must have already known who Julian was from the drawings in her journal. "If you didn't want her shopping, you shouldn't have abandoned her."

"I don't care if she shops," Julian said.

"Then you don't like her dress?"

"Excuse me," Scarlett interrupted, "but we're in a bit of a hurry."

Aiko made an exaggerated point of looking the haberdashery up and down distastefully. "I recommend you both stay away from the hatter tonight. You won't find any good deals in there."

Thunder clapped above.

Aiko raised her head as drops of shimmering liquid fell from the sky. "I should go. I've never liked the rain; it washes all the magic away. I just wanted to warn you: I think you're *both* about to make a mistake."

Silver rain continued to fall while Aiko glided away.

Drops of wet clung to Julian's dark hair as he shook his head, his expression conflicted. "You need to be careful with that one. Though I do think she's right about this hat shop."

Scarlett wasn't so sure. Aiko's dreams had given Scarlett some answers, but not all of them had been accurate. She had no idea whose side the girl was really on.

The rain fell a little harder as Scarlett marched closer to the doors of the hatter and haberdashery. Julian was right—it didn't feel quite like Legend. There was nothing romantic or magical about it. Yet at the same time it felt like *something*. Scarlett had an emerald-green premonition that she would make a discovery inside.

"I'm going in," Scarlett said. "The fifth clue requires a leap of faith. Even if this doesn't lead me to Legend, it might take me closer to Tella."

A bell tinkled as Scarlett pushed open the door to the unusual shop.

Peach bonnets, lime bowlers, yellow knit caps, velvet top hats, and flashy tiaras covered every inch of a domed ceiling, while pedestals of oddities sprouted up around the shop like bizarre wildflowers. There were bowls of glass shoehorns, lines of invisible thread, birdcages full of ribbons made of feathers, baskets brimming with self-threading needles, and cuff links supposedly made from leprechaun gold.

Julian trudged in after her, shaking rain from his person onto everything in sight, including the boldly dressed gentleman who stood at an angle a few feet from the door.

Even amid so many colors and fine things, this gentleman made a statement. Dressed in a deep red tailcoat and matching cravat, he looked as if he could be a decoration. The type of young man someone invited to a party just because he had a way of looking beautiful and intriguing at once. Underneath his coat, he wore a matching red vest that contrasted with both his dark shirt and snug-fitting trousers, which tucked neatly into tall silver boots. But what drew Scarlett's attention most was his silk-trimmed top hat.

"Legend." She gasped, her heart dropping into her stomach.

"I'm sorry, what did you say?" Ink-dark hair spilled across the corner of the gentleman's forehead and grazed the tip of his black collar as he took off his top hat and set it on a display of identical-looking caps. "I'm flattered, but I think you have me confused with someone else." He cracked an amused smile as he pivoted in Scarlett's direction.

Beside her Julian tensed, and Scarlett froze as well. She'd seen this young man before. His face was not the kind a girl easily forgets. Long sideburns fed into a neatly trimmed beard, shaped like a work of art, outlining lips designed for dark whispers and straight white teeth perfect for biting into things.

Scarlett shuddered, but she didn't look away. Her eyes continued to take him in, traveling upward until they reached his black eyepatch.

It was the same young man she'd seen the night her vision had gone black-and-white. He'd not noticed her then, but he watched her now. Intensely. His right eye as green as a fresh-cut emerald.

Julian edged closer, the damp of his coat sending crisp shivers over her arms. He didn't say a word, but the look he cut toward the other young man was so clearly threatening, Scarlett swore she felt the room shift. The colors in the shop seemed to grow violently brighter.

"I don't think he can help us," Julian muttered.

"Help with what?" The gentleman had a slight accent that Scarlett couldn't place. But even though Julian continued to give him murderous glances, his tone remained inviting. He looked at Scarlett almost as if he'd expected her.

He might not be Legend, but Scarlett sensed he was *someone*. She held out the buttons she'd collected during the game. She wasn't quite sure what to say about them, but she hoped by showing him, he might open up some secret door, like the one she'd found in Castillo Maldito or Tella's bedroom. "We were wondering if you could help us with this," Scarlett asked.

The gentleman took her palm. He wore black gloves, yet Scarlett could feel that beneath the velvety fabric, his hands were soft. He was the sort of aristocrat who let others do his hard work.

He lifted Scarlett's hand to take a closer look at the buttons, though his sharp green eye stayed on hers. Vibrant and elegant and poisonous.

Julian cleared his throat. "You might want to actually look at the buttons, mate."

"I did. But I'm not really interested in trinkets." The gentleman folded Scarlett's fingers over her palm, and before she could pull away he kissed her hand, letting his lips linger much longer than necessary.

"I think we should go," Julian said. His knuckles were white, his own hands clenched at his sides, as if he were holding back from doing something violent.

Scarlett debated leaving with him before anything regrettable happened. But a leap of faith wasn't supposed to be easy. She reminded herself that this young man's cravat had been in color after she'd drunk the cider, which meant he had to be important.

The gentleman watched her as if there was a question he hoped she might ask. His lips curved into another smile that showed off those dangerous white teeth.

Julian wrapped a protective arm around Scarlett. "I'd appreciate it if you stopped looking at my fiancée like that."

"That's funny," the gentleman said. "All this time, I thought she was my fiancée."

28

S carlett's instincts told her to run, but her body refused to
move. Bold colors swirled inside her.

She heard the man say his name—*Count Nicolas d'Arcy*—
as she felt Julian's arm tighten around her shoulder.

"I think you're mistaken," Julian said confidently. "You must have
my fiancée confused with another. She's been getting that all week.
Haven't you, love?" Julian squeezed her shoulder in a way that felt
very much like a warning.

But Scarlett remained in too much shock to move. The buttons
had never been clues. The black box, containing the dress covered in
buttons, had not been from Legend or her sister. *D stood for d'Arcy.*

Like Legend, it seemed her fiancé was also fond of playing games.
Though the longer Julian kept his arm wrapped around Scarlett, the
less amused Count Nicolas d'Arcy looked.

Scarlett could scarcely believe this was the same man who'd written her so many lovely letters. He didn't appear to be mean or anywhere close to unattractive, yet he also didn't feel anything like his

letters. The count she'd corresponded with had seemed as if he couldn't wait until they met so there'd be no more need for secrecy. Now she wondered if he hadn't just written down all the things he imagined she wanted to hear, for this young man seemed far from transparent. He looked like the type who enjoyed keeping secrets.

"I hope you're not disappointed." The count adjusted his cravat as a back door opened behind him and the tailor returned, along with another man. Lavender. Anise. Rotted plums.

"Love, I think we need to leave now." Julian wrenched open the front door at the same moment Scarlett's father came into view.

Every shade of purple flashed in front of her eyes.

But Julian didn't hesitate. The instant the count reached for Scarlett, Julian shoved over a pedestal of glass eyes and used the distraction to pull her under the arch of the door into a curtain of silver rain. Scarlett gripped his hand as her father's angry words chased from behind.

"Do whatever it takes to stop her!" he called.

"Scarlett, you don't need to run!" The count's voice was not as harsh, but he ran fast, especially for a finely dressed gentleman.

Scarlett tugged Julian toward a covered bridge that she hoped was the same tricky bridge from two nights before. But it wasn't. Her father and the count continued to pursue them, through winding streets and brightly lit shops, past people who clapped as if it were part of the show.

"This way—hold on." Julian tore Scarlett from the slippery main road, toward the canals, ripping through a crowd of people all trying to reach shelter. "Hop in."

"But there's lightning!" Scarlett said. "We can't get in a boat."

"You have any better ideas?" Julian grabbed two oars as he leaped inside a crescent vessel.

"Scarlett!" her father shouted through the rain. "Don't do this—" His words were cut off by a strike of lightning and a clap of thunder. In the silver-streaked night, Scarlett witnessed something she'd not seen before.

Her father looked afraid. Raindrops ran down his cheeks like tears. She was sure it was just a trick of the light, but for a moment she imagined her father actually loved her, that maybe deep down he really cared. Beside him, the count's expression was concealed by the dark, but while they'd run, Scarlett would have sworn he'd appeared excited by the challenge she'd presented.

Scarlett looked away and clasped her wet knees to her chest as Julian's oars cut through the water. Even if her father was still capable of kindness, and even if the count had actually seemed like the type of man she'd thought he would be, Scarlett still couldn't have brought herself to go back to either of them.

She'd already made her choice, and she'd made it before she'd run out of the haberdashery with Julian. She didn't know the exact instant when it happened, but an arranged marriage to a man she knew only through letters was no longer something Scarlett wanted. Finally she understood what Tella meant when she'd said there was more to life than being safe.

She watched Julian take another heavy pull with the oars while more lightning spiderwebbed across the sky. Before meeting him, she'd believed she could be content as long as she married someone who could take care of her, but Julian had brought out a desire for something more.

She remembered thinking falling for him would be like falling in love with darkness, but now she imagined he was more like a starry night: the constellations were always there, constant, magnificent guides against the ever-present black.

"Crimson, did you hear what I said?"

Scarlett dropped her gaze from the sky to the soaking-wet boy in front of her. "What?"

"We need to get out of the boat!" Julian shouted through the rain as they bumped against a darkened dock.

"Where are we?"

"Castillo Maldito."

"No—" Threads of violet panic returned. Nigel already told her Tella wasn't in the Castillo. "We need to keep searching for my sister. I was wrong about the buttons, but there has to be—"

"We can't stay on the water," Julian cut in. "The lightning will kill us." As he spoke more bolts of silver-white slashed the sky.

"But if my father finds her first—"

"Do you even know where to look right now?"

When Scarlett didn't answer, Julian grabbed her hand and hauled her onto the dimly lit, shaking dock. The only light came from the Castillo's massive hourglasses and the churning red beads inside them. Aiko must have been telling the truth about the rain washing all the magic away, for the Castillo no longer glowed. It had turned from golden to tarnished. In the courtyard, abandoned tents flapped in the wind, their tuneless beat replacing the vibrant music of the birds from nights before.

"We need to find somewhere to dry off," Julian said.

"I'd rather keep the boat in sight." Scarlett huddled under a nearby arch, where she could see the docks and anyone else who might arrive. "Once the rain stops we need to start searching again."

Julian didn't answer right away. "I think the game, or at least your part in it, should be over. I should never have brought you here. I can take you to a safe place, off the isle—"

"No!" Scarlett cut him off. "I'm not leaving here without my sister. After what I've just done, my father will be even more furious when he finds Tella, and he will take it out on her."

"And what about you? You'll just keep sacrificing yourself? Marry Nicolas d'Arcy?"

Scarlett wished she could just ignore his question. If she stayed in the game and her father caught her, he wouldn't kill her, he'd make her marry the count, in a way that almost felt like death. But if she didn't marry him, how else could she protect her sister? "I don't know what I'm going to do."

Julian made a sound like a growl. "So you're still planning on going through with your engagement?"

"I don't *know* if I am or not! But what other choices do I have?"

Sheets of silver rain fell harder.

Scarlett waited for Julian to say something. To reassure her in some sort of way. To tell her *he* could be her other option. But even as she thought it, she realized how ridiculous it was. Did she really think he was going to say he wanted to sweep her away into another life, or marry her?

When more lightning tore through the night, Scarlett had her answer. Julian stayed close by her side, but his expression was closed off. She recalled the way he'd dusted lint off his shoulder that first night. He might not have wanted her to be the count's bride, but that didn't mean he planned on being with her instead.

"I'm so stupid." Her voice danced a line between breaking and shouting. "None of this means anything to you. You saw my fiancé, got jealous, acted rashly, and now you regret it."

"Is that what you think?" Julian's words came out deep and rough. "You believe I'd risk crossing your father, put you in danger like that, because I'm *jealous*?" He laughed, as if the jealousy were a ridiculous assumption.

"You're such a liar," Scarlett snapped.

Julian flattened his lips into a harsh line. "I've already told you that."

"No," Scarlett said, "you lie to yourself. You pull me to you whenever it seems you're afraid of losing me, but whenever I get too close, you push me away."

"I've only pushed you away once." Julian's voice hardened as he took a step closer. "I was definitely jealous, but that's not the only reason I wanted you out of there."

"Then tell me what your other reasons were," Scarlett said.

He edged forward, until there was almost no space between them. She could feel the wet of his clothes, clinging to hers. Slowly, he wrapped an arm around her waist, as if giving her the chance to pull away. But she'd already made her decision. Her heart beat faster as his other arm encased her, tightening around her upper back, pulling her closer to the hard planes of his chest until their lips were feeling the same cold air.

"Is this close enough for you?" Julian's mouth hovered over hers. A whisper shy of kissing her. "You're sure you want this?"

Scarlett nodded, afraid saying the wrong thing might push him away. With Julian it wasn't about protection—she just wanted to be with him. The boy who'd saved her from drowning in more ways than one.

His hand slid down to the small of her back, gentle and firm, slowly pulling her closer once more, while his other hand slipped under her hair and around her neck, rubbing the tender skin there, before it forged a new path.

"I don't want you to regret any of your choices." Julian's tone almost sounded pained, as if he wanted her to pull away, but everything about the way he continued to touch her made her feel the opposite. His fingers were now at her mouth, tracing the line of her bottom lip. They tasted like wood and rain, damp from running through her wet hair. "There are still things you don't know about me, Crimson."

"Then tell me what they are," Scarlett said. He'd shared about his sister and Legend, but there were obviously more shadows in his life.

Julian's fingers were still at her mouth. Slowly she kissed them, one by one. Just a gentle press of her lips, but she could feel how it affected him by the way his other hand gently dug into her lower back. She had to concentrate to keep her voice from turning breathless as she looked up at his face half eclipsed by darkness and said, "I'm not afraid of your secrets."

"I wish I could say you shouldn't be." Julian stroked her lip a final time, then covered her mouth with his own. Saltier than his fingers and more intense than the hand now moving down her spine or the one tightening around her waist. He held her as if she might slip through his grip, and she clung to him, loving the feel of the muscles that lined his back.

He mumbled words against her lips, too low for her to hear, but she imagined she got a strong impression of what he wanted to say, as he coaxed her lips apart, letting Scarlett taste the coolness of his tongue and the tips of his teeth as he grazed her lower lip. Every touch created colors she had never seen. Colors as soft as velvet and as sharp as sparks that turned into stars.

29

That night the moon stayed out a little longer, watching with silver eyes as Julian took Scarlett's hand and wrapped it carefully in his own. He kissed her once more, gently and deliberately, reassuring her without words that he had no intentions of letting her go.

If this had been another sort of story they would have stayed like this, twined in each other's arms until the sun woke up, casting rainbows across the storm-ravaged sky.

But most of Caraval's magic ran on time, soaking up the hours of the day and turning them into wonders at night. And this night was running out. Nearly all the glowing red beads in both of Castillo Maldito's hourglasses had tumbled through into the bottom. Like drops of falling rose petals.

Scarlett looked up at Julian.

"What's wrong?" he asked.

"I think I know what the last clue is. It's the roses." Scarlett recalled the vase of flowers she'd found next to the box containing her dress. Foolishly she'd assumed they'd been sent together. Scarlett didn't know what they meant, but they were all over the game. It made sense to believe they were part of the fifth clue; they had to symbolize *something* besides a sick homage to Rosa.

"We have to get back to La Serpiente and look at the roses," she said. "Maybe there's something on the petals, or a note attached to the vase."

"What if your father sees us when we go back there?"

"We'll take the tunnels." Scarlett dragged Julian through the courtyard. It was already chilly out, but the air felt even colder when they reached the abandoned garden. Skeletal plants surrounded them, while the dreary fountain in the center dripped a melancholy siren song.

"I don't know about this," Julian said.

"Since when did you become the nervous one?" Scarlett teased, though she felt ochre shades of uneasy as well, and she knew it wasn't from the garden's enchantment.

She'd just made a huge error by going to the haberdashery, and she wasn't eager to make another mistake. But Aiko had been right when she'd said some things were worth the pursuit regardless of the cost. Scarlett now felt as if she were trying to rescue herself as well as Tella. She'd not given much thought to this year's prize—the wish—but she was thinking about it now. If Scarlett did win the game, maybe she really could save them both.

Scarlett removed her hand from Julian's and pressed against the Caraval symbol embedded inside the fountain. Just as before, the water drained and the basin transformed into a set of winding stairs.

"Come on." She waved him forward. "The sun will be up any minute." Scarlett could already picture it, bursting through the darkness, ushering in the dawn of the day she'd originally intended to leave. And for the first time, despite all that had happened, she was glad she'd remained, because now she was determined to win the game and sail away with more than just her sister.

Scarlett reached for Julian's hand again as she stepped onto the stairs.

"Why does it seem as if you're always trying to leave the moment I show up?" Governor Dragna appeared at the other end of the neglected garden, followed by the count, whose dark hair dripped water in his eye; no longer did he appear excited by this challenge.

Scarlett yanked Julian down the damp steps to the tunnel entrance, gripping his hand as her father and the count gave chase. She didn't dare look behind her, but she could hear their pursuit, the thunder of their boots, the shaking of the ground, the pounding of her own heart as she spiraled down the stairs.

"Julian, you need to go ahead of me. Find the lever to shut the tunnel, before—" Scarlett broke off as her father and the count reached the stairs. Their shadows stretched out in the golden light, clawing at her from afar. It was too late to keep them out of the tunnels now.

But Scarlett and Julian were almost at the bottom of the steps. Scarlett could see the tunnels went off in three different directions: one lit by gold, one almost pitch-black, and the other illuminated by silver-blue.

Ripping her arm free from his protective grasp, she pushed Julian toward the darkest tunnel. "We need to split up, and you need to hide."

"No—" He reached for her.

Scarlett danced back. "You don't understand—after tonight, my father will kill you."

"Then we won't let him catch us." Julian wove his fingers through hers and raced with Scarlett into the golden passage on the left.

Scarlett had always liked the color gold. It felt hopeful and magical. And for a brief, shining moment she dared to dream that it was. To hope she could outrun her father, create her very own fate. And she almost did.

But she could not outrun her fiancé.

Scarlett felt his gloved hand band around her arm. A moment later her head snapped back, every piece of her scalp on fire as her father's fists took hold of her hair.

She screamed as both men tore her away from Julian.

"Let her go!" Julian shouted.

"Don't take another step, or this will get worse." Governor Dragna wrapped one hand around Scarlett's throat as he continued pulling her hair.

Scarlett bit back her yelp, a pained tear rolling down one cheek. From the twisted angle of her neck, she could not see her father, but she could imagine the sick look on his face. This would only get worse.

"Julian," Scarlett pled, "please get out of here."

"I'm not leaving you—"

"Not another step," Governor Dragna repeated. "Remember the

last time we played this game? Do something I don't like, and my darling daughter pays."

Julian froze.

"Much better, but just so you don't forget again . . ." Governor Dragna released Scarlett and punched her in the stomach.

Scarlett fell to her knees as the air left her lungs. Her vision blanked as she hit the dirt. She could only feel the pain, the echo of her father's fists, and the dirt she'd fallen into staining her hands as she struggled to stand back up.

Around her, voices bounced off the walls. Angry ones and frightened ones, and when she stood, the world had changed.

"Is that really necessary?"

"Touch her again and I will—"

"I think you missed the point of my demonstration."

One by one she matched the words with the men as she took in the new scene. The count's well-groomed expression had shifted to something cloudy and uncertain as he helped Scarlett stand. Across from them, too far out of her reach, her father stood with a knife to Julian's throat.

"He just won't stay away from you," said Governor Dragna.

"Father, stop this," Scarlett rasped. "I'm sorry I ran away. You have me. Just let him go."

"But if I let him go, how do I know you'll behave?"

"I agree with your daughter," said the count, his arm now curling around her, almost protectively. "I think this is going a little too far."

"I'm not going to kill him." Governor Dragna's eyes crinkled at the edges as if they were all being unreasonable. "I'm only giving my daughter a little extra incentive not to run away again."

A slick mud-colored feeling coated Scarlett's insides as her father adjusted the knife. She thought nothing could be as painful as watching him hit Tella, but the blade, so close to Julian's face, created a whole new world of terror. "Please, Father." She trembled and shook with every word. "I promise, I'll never disobey you again."

"I've already heard that worthless vow, but after this I think you'll finally keep it." Governor Dragna licked the corner of his lips as he flicked his wrist.

"Don't—"

The count clamped a gloved hand over Scarlett's mouth, muffling her screams as her father slashed his dagger across Julian's beautiful face. From his jaw, across his cheek, all the way up to below his eye.

Julian sucked in a cry of pain as Scarlett fought to reach him. But she was powerless to do more than kick, and she feared her father would do more damage to Julian than he already had. She'd probably shown too much emotion as it was.

Scarlett waited for Julian to fight back. To grab the knife. To run away. She remembered his rows of sharply defined brown muscles. She imagined, even bleeding and injured, he could overpower her father. But for a boy who had started out so selfish, he now seemed determined to keep his ridiculous word and stay with her. He stood stoically as a wounded statue while Scarlett crumbled inside.

"Now, I think we're done," said her father.

"You know"—Julian turned to the count, speaking through a

bloody smile—"it's pathetic when you have to torture a man just to get a woman to be with you."

"Maybe I was wrong about being finished here." Governor Dragna lifted his knife once more.

Scarlett tried to break free from the count, but his arms stayed bound around her chest, cutting into her like ropes.

"You're not making this any better," the count hissed. Then louder, to her father, in a tone that sounded bored, "I don't think that's necessary. He's just trying to get a rise out of us." The count smirked as if he couldn't have cared less about Julian's words, yet Scarlett could feel the quickening of his heart and the heat of his rapid breath against her neck, even as he added, "And for the saint's sake, give the man a handkerchief; he's dripping blood everywhere."

The governor tossed Julian a tiny square of cloth, but it was barely enough to soak up the blood. Scarlett could see the droplets fall to the ground as their grim party began trudging forward.

The entire journey back to La Serpiente, Scarlett tried to think of ways to escape. Despite his wound, Julian was still strong. Scarlett imagined he could have easily run away, or at least tried to fight back. But he marched silently by her father's side while the count clutched Scarlett's limp hand.

"It's going to be all right," the count whispered.

Scarlett wondered what type of delusional world he must live in to think such a thing. She almost hoped they'd find a dead body again, giving her the chance to break away. She loathed herself for the idea, but it didn't stop her from thinking it.

When they emerged from the tunnel into Tella's razed room, the count made an effort to dust off his coat, while Scarlett debated the benefits of running. It was clear her father had no intention of letting Julian go. He eyed Julian the way a child might ogle his younger sister's doll right before chopping off all its hair, or its head.

"I'll release him tomorrow, at the end of the night, after you've behaved yourself." Governor Dragna wrapped an arm around Julian's shoulder, while the cloth held to Julian's cheek continued dripping blood.

"But, Father, he needs medical attention!"

"Crimson, don't worry about me," Julian said.

Obviously, he didn't know how much worse this could get.

Scarlett tried a final time. She could see no way out of this for her, but maybe it wouldn't be too late for Julian. If he got away, he could still save Tella, too. "Please, Father, I will do whatever you wish, but you have to let him go."

Governor Dragna grinned. This was exactly what he wanted to hear. "I already said I'd release him, but I don't think he wants to leave yet." He squeezed Julian's shoulder. "Do you feel like leaving us alone, boy?"

Scarlett tried to meet Julian's eyes, tried to beg him to leave with a look, but he was being more stubborn than ever. Scarlett wished he'd turn back into the careless young man she'd met on Trisda. His selflessness would accomplish nothing here unless he had a death wish.

It seemed it was up to her to find a way to end this.

"I've got nowhere else I need to be," Julian said. "Are we all going to go upstairs now, or do you plan to have us sleep in here?"

"Oh, we're not sleeping together—at least, not all of us." Governor

Dragna winked and a tremor went through Scarlett. He was looking at her with the type of expression that might have lit up another person's face before bestowing a gift—but Governor Dragna's presents were never pleasant.

"Count d'Arcy and I have been sharing a suite, but it's too cramped for four people. So the sailor will stay with me in there, and Scarlett"—Governor Dragna drew his words out in slow, unmistakable syllables—"you'll be sleeping in your own room with Count d'Arcy. You'll be married soon enough," he went on. "And your fiancé has paid quite a sum for you. I don't see why I need to make him wait any longer before enjoying what he's bought."

Scarlett's horror escalated as her father's mouth slanted into a new smile. This was so far from how she'd imagined things. It was horrid enough that she'd been purchased like a sheep, that a price had been placed on her, saying this was all she was worth. "Father, please, we're not married yet, this isn't proper—"

"No, it's not," Governor Dragna cut her off. "But we've never been a proper family, and you're not going to complain, unless you want to watch your friend continue to bleed." The governor stroked the unmarred side of Julian's face.

Julian didn't flinch, yet he no longer wore the placid expression he bore in the tunnels. Everything about him had intensified. He caught Scarlett's eyes, a silent fire burning in his. He was trying to tell her something, though she had no clue what it was. All Scarlett could feel was the nearness of Count d'Arcy; she imagined his hands eager to claim her body, as her father's hands were eager to inflict more pain upon Julian.

"Call it an early wedding present that I'm not mutilating him further right now," said Governor Dragna. "But if you say another word aside from *yes*, my generosity ends."

"No," Scarlett said. "You will not touch him again, because I will not do another thing unless you release him this moment."

Scarlett turned to the count. He did not appear as if he was enjoying this. Wrinkles marred his perfect forehead. But he did nothing to stop the governor, and just the sight of him, standing there in his crimson cravat and silver boots, made her ill to her core.

Tella had been right. *You think your marriage is going to save you, but what if the count is as bad as Father, or worse?*

Scarlett didn't know if Count d'Arcy was actually worse than her father, but in that moment he felt just as vile. He no longer held her hand softly as he had in the haberdashery; his grip was firm, assured. The count had more strength than he let on. He had the power to stop this if he desired.

"If you let this happen"—Scarlett paused to meet the count's eye, searching for a trace of the young man she'd exchanged so many letters with—"if you use the threat of his punishment to control me, I will never obey or respect you. But if you let him go, if you show some of the humanity I read in your letters, I will be the perfect wife you paid for." She recalled Julian's words in the tunnel and added, "Do you really want a bride who will only sleep with you because another man will be tortured if she doesn't?"

The count's face flushed. Scarlett's heart beat faster with every darkening shade on his visage. Frustration. Embarrassment. Wounded pride.

"Let him go," the count grit out. "Or our deal is over."

"But—"

"I won't argue this." The count's elegant voice turned rough. "I just want this done."

Governor Dragna did not look pleased to part with a toy he'd barely played with. Yet to Scarlett's surprise, he released Julian without further argument, shoving him toward the door. "You heard him. Leave."

"Crimson, don't do this for me." Julian shot a pleading look toward Scarlett. "You can't give yourself to him. I don't care about what happens to me."

"But I care," Scarlett said, and though she wanted to look at Julian's beautiful face one last time, to show him how she thought he was the furthest thing from a scoundrel or a liar, she didn't dare meet his eyes. "Now, please, leave, before you make this harder."

30

The crooked halls of La Serpiente felt shorter than Scarlett remembered. Already she and Count d'Arcy were on the fourth floor, right outside her door.

There were so many ways her plan could go wrong. The count held her glass key, but he looked down at her before placing it in the lock. "Scarlett, I want you to know, this wasn't how I intended things to be between us. What happened in those tunnels, that wasn't me." His eye met hers, far gentler than the way he'd looked at her in the hat shop. For a moment she could almost see something beneath his over-polished appearance, as if it was just another type of coat he wore for show, and in reality, he was as trapped as she was. "This marriage is very important to me. The thought of losing you made me go a little mad. By the time we were in the tunnels I wasn't thinking clearly. But things will be different once we're married. I'll make you happy, I promise."

With his free hand the count brushed the silver lock of hair from her face, and for a dreadful moment Scarlett feared he was going to lean down and kiss her. It took every ounce of strength she'd gained this last week not to run, or cringe.

"I believe you," Scarlett said. Though no words could have been further from the truth. She knew what happened in the tunnels could drive people to madness, twist their fear to make them do things—or allow things—they might not normally. But even if he kept her safe from this point on and never lifted a finger against her, no universe existed where Count Nicolas d'Arcy would ever make Scarlett happy. Not when the only person she wanted to be with was Julian.

Fear clutched her insides as the count opened the door to her room.

Again, she thought of all the ways her plan could go wrong.

She could have misread Julian.

Julian could have misread her.

Her father could come back and listen on the other side of the door—she'd heard of such deplorable things happening.

Her palms grew sweaty as she followed the count into the heated chamber. The massive bed, which had looked so inviting the first time she'd seen it, now looked like a silent threat. Its four wooden posts made her think of a cage. She imagined the count drawing the curtains and trapping her inside. She glanced at the wardrobe, hoping Julian would appear from the hidden door on the other side, or possibly burst out from inside. It was large enough to hold a person. But the doors were shut, and they remained that way.

It was only Scarlett and the count and the bed.

Now that it was just the two of them, the count moved differently. His overbred sophistication was completely gone, replaced with clinical precision, as if this were a business matter he needed to wrap up.

He took off his gloves first, dropping them on the floor. Then he began undoing the buttons of his waistcoat, creating tiny pops that made Scarlett want to retch. She couldn't do this.

Watching her father hurt Julian, Scarlett had finally understood what Julian had been trying to tell her in the tunnels earlier. She had grown up thinking her father's abuse had been her fault—the result of what happened when she made a mistake. But now she could clearly see: Her father was responsible. Nobody deserved his *punishments*.

This was wrong too. When she'd kissed Julian, it had felt right. Two people choosing to give tiny vulnerable parts of themselves to each other. That's what Scarlett wanted. That's what she deserved. No one else had the right to decide this for her. Yes, her father had always treated her like a possession, but she was not a thing to be bought or sold.

Before, Scarlett had always felt as if she didn't have choices, but now she was starting to realize that she did. She just needed to be bold enough to make the difficult ones.

Another pop. The count had moved on to the buttons of his shirt, and he was looking at Scarlett as if he were getting ready to take off her damp gown as well and complete this transaction.

"It's chilly in here, don't you think?" Scarlett grabbed the fireplace poker and stoked the logs, watching the fire skip over the metal until it turned shades of brilliant orange-red—the color of bravery.

"I think you've stoked it enough." The count placed a firm palm on her shoulder.

Scarlett spun around and aimed the red-hot poker at his face. "Don't touch me."

"Sweetheart." He appeared only mildly surprised, and not nearly as frightened as she would have liked. "We can take things slowly, if you want, but you should put that down before you injure yourself."

"I can manage not to hurt myself." Scarlett inched the fireplace rod closer, stopping right below his bright-green eye. "But you might not be so lucky. Don't move or breathe a word unless you want a scar on your cheek that matches Julian's."

The count's breathing hitched, yet his voice was unnervingly even as he said, "I don't think you realize what you're doing, sweetheart."

"Stop calling me that! I'm not yours, and I'm very aware of my actions. Now get on the bed." Scarlett motioned with the poker, but already its red tip was losing color. She had thought she'd tie him to the bed, but there was no way it would work. The minute she set down her weapon, he would be upon her. And despite her threats, Scarlett didn't know if she could bring herself to use it.

"I know you're frightened," the count said calmly. "But if you stop whatever it is you're doing, I'll forget this ever happened and no harm will be done."

Harm.

The elixir of protection.

The vial she'd bought in the tent at the Castillo had slipped her mind. But it was still in the pocket of her enchanted gown. She just needed to get to the wardrobe.

"Back up all the way against the bedposts." Scarlett backed away as he did as he was told. Then she bolted for the wardrobe. The count leaped up the moment she turned, but Scarlett was already opening the wooden doors.

With a loud tumble, Julian fell out. His skin was gray and bleeding. Scarlett's heart cracked.

"What is he doing here?" The count froze long enough for her to reach inside and grab the elixir. She could do nothing for Julian unless she took care of d'Arcy first.

Scarlett ripped the top off the bottle and splashed its contents all over the count. The spray smelled of daisies and urine.

The count choked and sputtered. "What is this?" He dropped to his knees as he tried to grab Scarlett, but he looked like an infant attempting to catch a bird. The elixir worked fast, dimming his reflexes to a clumsy crawl.

"You're making a mistake." He continued wilting to the floor as Scarlett rushed to Julian's side.

"This is exactly what Legend wants," the count slurred, lips going numb like the rest of his body. "Your father told me the history . . . of your grandmother and Legend. I have no idea who *he* is." The count cut a drooping eye to Julian. "But you're playing right into Legend's hands. He brought you to this isle to destroy our marriage, to ruin your life."

"Well, then it seems he's failed," Scarlett said. "From where I'm standing, it looks as if Legend has done me a favor."

Julian's eyes fluttered open as Scarlett helped him up from the floor, and her ex-fiancé finished crumpling to the ground.

"Don't be too sure about any of that," the count mumbled. "Legend doesn't do anyone favors."

31

"C an you walk?" Scarlett asked.

"Aren't I doing that now?" Julian's voice was playful. But there was nothing humorous about the wound that went from his jaw to his eye. Her arms were wrapped around him, keeping him steady.

"Crimson, don't worry about me, we should get you to your sister."

"You need stitches first." Her eyes returned to the ragged gash on his cheek. It would scar, and while it did not make him any less handsome, it did make her ill to remember how fragile he'd appeared when he'd tumbled out of the wardrobe.

"You're overreacting," Julian said. "It's not half bad. Your father barely scraped me. I doubt he enjoys it unless his victims remain conscious."

"But you were passed out in the closet."

"I've recovered. I'm a quick healer." Julian pulled away from her, as if to prove it, when they reached the bottom floor. Light snuck in through the cracks around the doors, illuminating candles growing inside sconces, preparing for another treacherous night. On the floor, a small group of dedicated participants slept huddled together. Waiting for evening to fall and the doors to unlock.

"I still think we should find a way to bandage it up," Scarlett whispered.

"It only needs a little alcohol." Julian swaggered past the sleeping participants and into the tavern, though Scarlett swore he was still only half himself. His boots scraped the glass floor with an uneven gait as he went behind the bar and poured half a bottle of clear liquor over his cheek.

"See"—Julian winced, shaking his head, making drops of liquid fall to the floor—"not as bad as it looks."

A line still went from near the corner of his eye to the edge of his jaw. It wasn't as deep as Scarlett thought, yet she could not ignore the ill feeling she had.

Amid all that had happened she'd lost track of time, but she imagined the sun would set in about two hours, welcoming the final night of the game.

To win, Scarlett needed to find her sister before anyone else. And after what she'd just done to the count—not only had she knocked him out, she'd tied him to the bed before leaving—Scarlett could all too clearly imagine how furious her father would be when he woke, and the malicious punishments he would inflict on Tella if he found her before Scarlett. He wouldn't just kill her; he'd torture her first.

"When I was in the room, I forgot to look at the roses," Scarlett said.

Julian took a swig of the bottle before putting it away. "You're the one who said they were all over Caraval."

Meaning it would be impossible to figure out which roses were actually clues. There were probably hundreds of roses she'd never seen as well. The first clue she'd received said: *And number five requires a leap of faith*. But Scarlett had no idea how that connected to the flowers. Too many roses and not enough time.

"Crimson, don't fall apart on me now."

Scarlett looked up and Julian was in front of her, drawing her close before she could say the words "I'm not." Though she imagined if Julian were to release her, she would. Fall to the floor. Then fall through it. Fall and fall—

He kissed her, parting her lips with his own until all she could taste or think about was him. He tasted like midnight and wind, and shades of rich brown and light blue. Colors that made her feel safe and guarded.

"It's going to be all right," Julian murmured, and he pressed his lips to her forehead.

Now she was tumbling for altogether different reasons. Sinking into a feeling of security that she'd never known before. As Julian's lips stayed pressed to her temple, his arms wrapped around her as if he wanted to protect her—not possess her or control her. He wouldn't let her crumble. He wouldn't toss her from a balcony as Legend had done in her dream.

"Julian." Scarlett looked up abruptly, as the words from the clue, *leap of faith*, suddenly ricocheted through her thoughts.

"What's wrong?" Julian asked.

"I need to ask you something about your sister."

Julian stiffened.

"I wouldn't ask this if it wasn't important, but I think it might help us find Tella."

"Go ahead," he said, and despite the shuttered look on his face, his voice was soft. "Ask whatever you want."

"I've heard about your sister's death, but the accounts were conflicting. Could you tell me how she actually died?"

Julian took a deep breath. Obviously the subject made him uncomfortable, but he said, "After Legend rejected her, Rosa leaped from a balcony to her death."

A balcony. Not a window, as Scarlett had overheard in her dream. No wonder Julian hadn't appeared more excited at the sight of all the balconies at the beginning of the game. They were fifty cruel reminders of what he had lost. Legend truly was monstrous, and if Scarlett was correct, he'd set this game up for a twisted repeat of history with either Scarlett or her sister. *A leap of faith indeed.*

With a shudder, Scarlett worried that was what it would take— that she would have to jump off a balcony to save her sister.

She kept this suspicion to herself as she told Julian of her dream involving Legend and the balcony. "I think we need to search the balconies to find our last clue."

Julian ripped a hand through his hair. "There are dozens of them, all with different entrances. I don't see how that is a better plan."

"Then we should start searching now." Expecting an argument, Scarlett went on, "I know going out during daylight is against the rules, but I don't think Legend really abides by rules. The innkeeper said that if we didn't make it in before daybreak after the first night we didn't get to play, but she didn't mention the *rest* of the nights."

Scarlett lowered her voice, just in case some of the people over in the hall were actually awake. "All the doors are locked so people think they can't get out, but we can leave using the tunnels. If we go right now we can get a head start on the count and my father, and maybe we can win this game."

"Now you're finally thinking like a player." Julian smiled, but it looked as flat as a line in a painting. She wondered if her fearless Julian now feared her father too, or if he dreaded the same thing Scarlett did, that to save her sister one of them would have to take a deadly leap.

32

Julian's hand was the only thing that felt truly solid as they emerged from the tunnels and entered into a realm that appeared utterly different when lit by the late-afternoon sun.

The Caraval sky was a creamy blur of butter and vanilla swirls. It made Scarlett think the air around her should taste like sweetened milk and sugared dreams, but all she could taste was dust and haze.

"Where do you want to look first?" Julian asked.

The balconies surrounded the entire perimeter of the game. Scarlett craned her neck, searching for a glimpse of movement or anything odd on any of the nearest ones, but the blanket of mist obscured her view. On the ground, shops that looked colorful at night now appeared almost blurry. The elaborate fountains, dotting every other corner of the street, spilled no water. The world was stillness and quiet and milky fog. No colorful boats traveled canals and no other people walked on the cobbled paths.

Scarlett felt as if she'd stepped into a faded memory. As if the magical town had been abandoned long ago, and she was coming back to find nothing quite as she recalled.

"This doesn't even look like the same place." Scarlett walked a little closer to Julian. She'd feared that the moment they stepped outside someone would try to remove them from the game, but this strange, dull reality was almost as frightening. "I can't see any of the balconies."

"Let's not focus on those, then. Maybe the leap of faith means something different," said Julian. "You said before, you thought the clue involved roses. Does anything else here remind you of your dream with Legend?"

Scarlett's first thought was, *Legend has left this place.* She saw no top hats, no rose petals, no colors brighter than palest yellow. But while her eyes were letting her down, her ears picked up a gentle melody.

Subtle. So quiet it almost sounded like a memory, but as Scarlett moved forward with Julian, the soft music grew into something more solid and soulful. It hummed from the street with the rose-covered carousel, the only spot not infected with fog. She remembered it was also one of the few things that had remained in color when her world had turned to black-and-white.

Brighter than freshly spilled blood, the carousel appeared even more alive than when Scarlett had seen it last. It was so vibrant, she almost didn't notice the man sitting at the pipe organ beside it. He was far older than most of the other workers she'd come across, and his face was wrinkled and weatherworn, and a little bit sad, mirroring his music. He stopped playing as Scarlett and Julian approached, but the echoes of his song still hung in the air like lingering perfume.

"Another song for a donation." The man held out a hand and looked up at Scarlett expectantly.

It should have struck her as uncanny the first time she'd seen him that he would beg for coins in a place where people rarely used them.

Scarlett turned to Julian, not wanting to repeat the mistake she'd made at the hatter and haberdashery. "Does this feel like Legend to you?"

"If feeling like Legend means disturbing and creepy, then yes." Julian cast a hooded gaze over the rose-drenched carousel and the ruddy man at the pipe organ. "You think this will lead to the balcony holding your sister?"

"I'm not sure, but I think it will definitely take us somewhere."

Aiko had been right when she warned Scarlett and Julian they were making a mistake by going into the hatter's. It made sense to believe she'd also been trying to help when she'd brought Scarlett to this peculiar carousel. It could have been a coincidence, but even if it was, she doubted it was also a coincidence that when not another person was in sight, they would come back here and find the organ player waiting for them.

"All right, then. Here you go." Julian reached into a pocket and pulled out some coins.

Remembering Aiko's words, Scarlett added, "Can you play us something pretty?"

The song that followed was not pretty; it rasped out of the pipe organ like a dying man's final words. But it did make the carousel spin around. Slowly at first, yet hypnotic in its graceful movements. Scarlett could have stood there and watched forever, but in her dream, just before he tossed her from the balcony, Legend had warned Scarlett not to observe.

"Come on." She let go of Julian's hand and leaped onto the spinning wheel.

Julian looked as if he wanted to stop her, but then he followed as well.

The carousel began to turn faster and soon they were on opposite sides, fingers bleeding as they searched through bushes covered in thorns, for a symbol that would open a passage of stairs.

"Crimson, I'm not seeing anything!" Julian shouted over the music. The tune grew louder and more off-key as the carousel twirled faster, shedding more and more petals that swept up into the sky like a ruby cyclone.

"It's here!" Scarlett yelled back. She could feel it with every prick of her finger. There would not be so many thorns if nothing was hidden beneath them. Thorns protected roses. Again, Scarlett felt as if there was a lesson to be learned from this carousel, but before she could figure it out, she saw a sun with a star inside and a teardrop inside of the star. It was hidden beneath a rosebush, the size of a small pony, shaped to look like a stallion wearing a top hat.

Scarlett gripped the flower stems to keep from falling as she crouched close to press her finger to the symbol for Caraval. One touch and the entire emblem filled with blood.

The carousel spun even faster. Round and round. And as it twirled in a destructive dance the center disappeared, turning into a circle of dark. A hole made of black sky robbed of stars. Unlike the other passages, there were no stairs this time. Scarlett could not see the bottom.

"I think we need to jump." Maybe she'd been wrong about the balcony and this was the leap of faith.

"Wait—" Julian edged around the hole, grabbing one of her bloody hands before she could hurtle herself forward.

"What are you doing?" Scarlett shouted.

"I want you to take this." Julian pulled out a pocket watch on a long, circular chain and pressed it into her palm. "Inside the cover I etched the coordinates of a boat, just off the coast of the isle."

Fresh panic filled Scarlett as Julian's face grew more serious. This felt too much like good-bye. "Why are you giving this to me now?"

"In case we get separated, or something else unexpected happens. The boat's already crewed; it will take you anywhere you want to go and—" Julian broke off, and for a moment it appeared as if the words were trapped in his throat. His face grew pained as the carousel jolted and slowed, and the hole in the center started shrinking. "Crimson, you need to jump now!" He released her hand.

"Julian, what are you not telling me?"

His lips fell into a rough line, making him look sad and regretful all at once. "There's not time for all the things I wish I could say."

Scarlett wanted to ask more questions. She wanted to know why Julian, who moments before held her hand as if he never planned to let it go, was suddenly looking at her as if he feared he would never see her again. But the black hole was already closing.

"Please, don't make me use this without you!" She took the chain and placed it around her neck.

Then she leaped.

She thought she heard Julian shout something about not trusting Legend as she fell. But his words were muffled by the rushing water, roaring as it welcomed her into a river of cold.

Scarlett gasped for air, arms flailing wildly to keep from sinking. She was glad she was in water as opposed to landing on a slab of rock or a bed of knives, but the current was too strong to fight. It sucked her in, dragging her down a path that felt eternally long.

Her entire body was steeped in cold but she forced herself not to panic. She could do this. The water wasn't trying to punish her. She relaxed until the current eased up. Then, with steady, even strokes and pulls she worked her way back to the surface, kicking hard until she reached a wide set of steps.

Slowly, her eyes adjusted as tiny green lights, as infinitesimal as bits of dust, flickered to life. They swarmed the air like fireflies, casting jade illumination over two gray-blue soapstone statues guarding the entrance to the steps.

Twice as tall as Scarlett, and cloaked in robes that disappeared beneath the water, the figures' hands were clasped in silent prayer. But though their eyes were closed, their faces appeared far from peaceful. Their mouths stretched wide, calling out in silent agony as Scarlett pulled herself onto the black soapstone staircase.

"I was starting to lose faith in you." The click of a walking stick pressed against the stairs, as one by one each polished step brightened.

Though it was not the stairs nor the murky places they led, but the young man in the velvet top hat who captured Scarlett's full attention.

She blinked and he was suddenly there in front of her, reaching out a hand to help her to her feet. "I'm so glad you finally made it, Scarlett."

33

Scarlett told herself not to be dazzled.

She knew Legend was a viper. A serpent in a top hat and tails was still a snake. It did not matter that this snake was almost exactly how Scarlett had always pictured him. He might not have been *quite* as handsome as she'd imagined, but still, he was made of dashing elegance, laced with intrigue and illusion, set off by a twinkle in his dark eyes that made her feel as if she were the charmed one, covered in magic only he could see.

He appeared younger than she would have thought, a few years older than she was, without a wrinkle or scar on his face. The rumors that he never aged must have been true. He wore a royal-blue half cape, which he quickly tore off and draped around Scarlett's shaking shoulders. "I'd suggest you take off your wet clothes, but I've heard you're on the modest side."

"I won't say what I've heard about you," Scarlett spit out.

"Oh no!" Legend clapped his hands to his chest in a show of mock offense. "People have been saying nasty things about me?"

He laughed—a rich, spicy sound. It bounced off the cavern's walls as if there were a dozen different Legends hidden behind the stones. The noise continued, even after he stopped laughing. It wasn't until he snapped his fingers that the horrid echoes stopped. But Legend's manic smile remained, twitching and restless, as if he were thinking of a joke he had yet to share.

He's mad.

Scarlett edged back as her gaze quickly cut to the water, where Julian should have been emerging behind her. But now the water wasn't even moving.

"If you're waiting for your friend, I don't think he's going to be joining us. At least not yet." Legend's lips turned cruel around the corners, leaving her drenched in a cold blue-violet feeling that went deeper than the wetness soaking her clothes.

"What have you done to Julian and my sister?"

"It's really too bad," Legend said. "You're so dramatic, you would have made a fantastic performer."

"That's not an answer to my question," Scarlett said.

"Because you're asking the wrong questions!" Legend shouted. Instantly he was right in front of her again, taller than she realized and even madder than he'd been moments before. His eyes were all black, as if the pupils had devoured the whites.

Scarlett reminded herself that the tunnels beneath the game did strange things to people's heads. She stood her ground without flinching, and repeated, "Where are my sister and Julian?"

"I already told you that's not the right question." Legend shook his head, as if she'd disappointed him. "But now that you've brought them up a second time, I'm curious. If you could see only one of them again, Julian or your sister, who would you choose?"

"I'm finished playing games," Scarlett said. "I took your leap of faith, I don't have to answer any more questions."

"Ah, but the rules say you need to find *the girl* before you can officially win." Green lights danced around Legend's head, adding a glittering emerald cast to his fair skin. He was magical to be sure, but in all the wrong ways. "Have you wondered at all why the game is played during the night?"

"If I answer you, will you tell me where to find my sister?"

"If you manage to do it correctly."

"What if I'm wrong?"

"I'll kill you, of course." Legend laughed, but this time it was hollow, like a bell without a clapper inside. "I'm just kidding. No need to look at me as if I'll sneak into your house at night and strangle all your kittens. If you answer incorrectly, I'll reunite you with your male companion, and together you can continue searching for your sister."

Scarlett highly doubted Legend would keep his word, but he was blocking the stairs in front of her, and behind her was a river that she doubted led anywhere good.

She tried to remember what Julian had told her about Caraval their first night there. *They say they don't want us to get too carried away, but that is the point.*

"I imagine the game wouldn't be the same in the light," Scarlett answered. "People think no one sees all the nasty things they do in the dark. The foul acts they commit, or the lies they tell as part of the game. Caraval takes place at night because you like to watch, and see what people do when they think there are no consequences."

"Not bad," said Legend. "Although, I'd think you'd have realized by now that what happens here isn't really just a game." His voice dropped to a whisper. "Once people leave this isle, the things they've done here don't just unhappen, no matter how much they might wish them undone."

"Maybe that should be your warning when people enter," Scarlett said.

Legend chuckled again, and this time it sounded almost real. "It's terribly unfortunate this is going to end so badly. I might have liked you." He brushed her chin with one cool knuckle.

Scarlett slipped a little as she took a nervous step back, shooting another futile glance behind her toward the unmoving waters. "I answered your question. Now where is my friend?"

"It amazes me," Legend said. "I've only told you the truth and you won't even allow me to touch you. Yet you think yourself in love with someone who has done nothing but lie to you this entire game. Your *friend* has told you not to trust me, but you cannot trust him, either."

"Coming from you, I'll take that as an endorsement."

Legend sighed dramatically, tipping his head back. "Oh, to be so hopeful and stupid. Let's see how long that lasts."

Just then, heavy footfalls sounded on the sandstone steps behind him. A moment later, Julian appeared, perfectly dry, and aside from the wound Scarlett's father had inflicted, entirely unharmed.

"We were just talking about you," Legend said. "Would you like to tell her, or should I?" Legend's eyes glittered, and this time there was no madness in them at all. He was the perfect picture of a gentleman in a top hat and tails, fully sane and dreadfully victorious.

Water dripped from Scarlett's hair down the back of her neck, turning hot where it touched her skin. She couldn't believe Legend had kept his word, but more than that, she didn't like the sound of what he'd just said, or the possessive way he was looking at Julian.

"It seems to me your fiancé is meant for decorative purposes only, but he was right about one thing," Legend said. "I don't do anyone favors. It would make no sense to go to all that trouble to put an end to your engagement only to let you leave the isle with someone else. Which is why I've had Julian working with me for the entire game."

No. Scarlett heard Legend's words, but she refused to process them. She didn't want to believe it. She watched Julian, waiting for some sort of signal that this was another part of a greater deception.

Meanwhile the master of Caraval regarded Julian as if he were one of his prized possessions, and to Scarlett's horror Julian smiled back, the straight edges of his teeth flashing in torchlight. It was the same wicked grin she'd first noticed on Del Ojos Beach; the smirk of someone who'd just succeeded in playing a very cruel trick.

"Originally, I'd planned for you to favor Dante," Legend said. "I thought he would be more your type, but I suppose it's good I'm wrong on occasion."

"Dante and his sister were part of the game too?" Scarlett blurted.

"Don't tell me it wasn't a brilliant deception," said Legend. "And try not to look so upset. I had people warn you. Twice, in fact, you were told not to believe anything."

"But—" Openmouthed, Scarlett turned to Julian. "So your sister, Rosa? That was all a lie?"

For a moment it almost looked as if Julian flinched at the name Rosa, but when he spoke again, there was no emotion in his voice. Even his accent was altered. "There was someone named Rosa, and she died the way I told you, but she was not my sister. She was just an unfortunate girl who got too swept away in the game."

Scarlett's hands trembled, but still, she refused to believe it. It could not have all been false, merely a game to Julian. There had been moments she knew were real. She continued to watch him, hoping for some flicker of something, a glimmer of emotion, a glance that told her this act with Legend was really the game.

"I guess I'm better than I thought." Julian's smile turned vicious, the kind made for breaking hearts.

But Scarlett had already been broken. For years her father tore her down. Over and over, she had let him. She'd allowed him to make her feel worthless and powerless. But she was neither of those things. She was done allowing her fear to make her weaker, to eat away at the meat on her bones until she could do nothing but whimper and watch.

"I still say you did me a favor," she said, turning back to Legend. "You said it yourself. My ex-fiancé is more of a decoration than a man, and I'm better off without him. Now give me my sister and let us go home."

"Home? You still have somewhere to go after tomorrow, now that you've thrown your entire future away? Or"—Legend cut another look toward Julian—"are you saying this because you're still under the illusion that he cares for you?"

Scarlett wanted to say it wasn't an illusion. The Julian she knew had let himself be tortured for her. How could that not be real? She refused to believe it, even as Julian looked at her as if she were the most foolish girl in the world. And he was probably right.

She'd not realized something that had been true until that moment. Since Julian had brought her to the island, *the look* had been there, that extra spark; whether frustrated or angry or laughing, there was always something there that said some facet of her touched something inside of him.

Now there was nothing there. Not even pity. For a dangerous moment Scarlett doubted everything she believed to be true.

Then she remembered. *In case something unexpected happens.*

The pocket watch. Scarlett's hand went to the cool piece of jewelry around her neck, her heart beating a little faster as she clutched it and recalled Julian's words on the carousel.

"What do you have there?" Legend asked.

"Nothing," Scarlett said. But her words came out too fast, and Legend's hands moved quicker, spreading the velvety fabric of the royal-blue cape she still wore, his icy fingers pulling out the watch.

"I don't remember seeing this on you before." Legend cocked his head toward Julian. "A recent gift?"

Julian denied nothing as Legend popped the makeshift necklace open. *Tick. Tick. Tick.* The watch's second hand wound its way up to the twelve, and a voice started pouring from the locket. It was barely above a whisper, but Scarlett clearly recognized the timbre as Julian's.

"I'm sorry, Crimson. I wish I could say what I'm sorry for, but the words—" He cut off for several tense clicks as the second hand continued its lap around the numbers. Then, as if it wounded him, Julian's voice ground out, "It wasn't just a game for me. I hope you can forgive me."

The edge of Legend's eye ticked as he snapped the watch shut and addressed Julian. "I don't remember this being part of any plans. Care to explain?"

"I think it's rather self-explanatory," Julian answered. He turned back to Scarlett with the look she'd been searching for, his brown eyes full of all sorts of unspoken promises. He'd wanted to tell her the truth, but it seemed as if he physically couldn't. Some spell or enchantment wouldn't allow him to say the words. But he was still her Julian. Scarlett could feel the pieces of her battered heart daring to move back together. And it might have been a beautiful moment, if Legend had not chosen that same instant to pull out a knife and stab Julian in the chest.

"No!" Scarlett wailed.

Julian staggered and the whole world seemed to tilt and sway with him. The jade lights of the cavern muted to brown.

Scarlett rushed to his side as blood bubbled up from his beautiful lips.

"Julian!" She dropped to her knees as he fell to the cavern floor. Legend hadn't hit his heart, but he must have punctured a lung. There was blood. So, so much blood. This must have been why he'd looked at her so coldly, making no effort to reveal the truth with so much as a glance. He had known Legend would punish him for his betrayal.

"Julian, please . . ." Scarlett put her hands over the wound, soaking her palms in red for the second time that day.

"It's all right." Julian coughed, more blood staining his mouth. "I probably deserved this."

"Don't say that!" Scarlett ripped the cape from her shoulders and pressed it hard against Julian's chest, trying to stop the bleeding. "I don't believe that, and I don't believe this is how it's supposed to end."

"Then don't let it end here. I've already told you—I'm not worth crying for." Julian reached up to brush away one of her tears, but his hand fell before he reached her.

"No! Don't give up," Scarlett begged. "Please, don't leave me." There were so many other things she wanted to say, but she feared that if she said her good-byes, it would make it easier for him to let go. "You can't abandon me. You told me you were going to help me win the game!"

"I lied—" Julian's eyes fluttered. "I—"

"Julian!" Scarlett cried, pushing harder against his chest as more blood soaked through the cape and onto her hands. "I don't care if you lied. If you don't die, I'll forgive you for everything."

Julian's eyes shut, as if he didn't hear her.

"Julian, please keep fighting. You've been fighting me this whole game, don't stop now."

Slowly his eyelids lifted. For a moment it looked as if he was coming back to her. "I lied about how I got bashed in the head," he mumbled. "I wanted you to have your earrings back. But the man was tougher than he looked. . . . I got into a little trouble. But it was worth it to see your face. . . ." A ghost of a smile moved his lips. "I should have stayed away from you . . . but I really wanted you to succeed. . . . I wanted to—"

Julian's head fell back.

"No!" Beneath her hands, Scarlett felt his chest fall a final time.

"Julian. Julian. Julian!" She pressed her hands to his heart but nothing moved.

Scarlett didn't know how many times she repeated his name. She said it like a prayer. A plea. A whisper. A good-bye.

34

Scarlett had never wanted time to stop before, to slip into a crawl so slow that one heartbeat would take a year, a breath would take a lifetime, and a touch could last an eternity. Usually she wanted the opposite, for time to speed up, race ahead, so that she could escape any current pain and move forward into a new, unblemished moment.

But Scarlett knew that when this instant ended the next would not feel fresh, or thick with promise for the future. It would be incomplete, lacking, void, because Julian would not be in it.

Scarlett's tears fell harder as she felt Julian die. His muscles losing tension. His body growing colder. His skin taking on a gray pallor that there was no return from.

She knew Legend was watching. Taking sick pleasure from her pain. But a part of her couldn't bear to let go of Julian, as if he might miraculously take another breath, or manage another heartbeat. She'd once heard emotions and desires fueled the magic that made wishes possible. But either Scarlett didn't feel enough, or the stories she'd heard about wishes were made of lies.

Or, perhaps, she was thinking of the wrong stories.

Hope is a powerful thing. Some say it's a different breed of magic altogether. Elusive, difficult to hold on to. But not much is needed.

And Scarlett did not have much, just the memory of a poorly written poem.

THIS GIRL WAS LAST SEEN WITH LEGEND.

IF YOU CATCH HER, YOU SHALL CATCH HIM AS WELL.

OF COURSE, YOU MAY HAVE TO VENTURE THROUGH HELL.

BUT IF YOU SUCCEED YOU MAY FIND YOURSELF RICH.

THIS YEAR'S WINNER WILL BE GRANTED ONE WISH.

Scarlett had momentarily forgotten about the wish, but if she could find Tella first, and wish for Julian's life, maybe it could end happily after all. That anything could be happy again seemed almost as unreal as a wish, but it was all she had left to hope for.

As she looked up, ready to demand her sister's location again, she realized Legend had vanished. All he'd left was Julian's pocket watch and his own velvet top hat, resting on a dark letter.

Black rose petals drifted to the ground as Scarlett picked up the note. It was rimmed in onyx black leafing, a shadow of the first letter Legend had sent her.

Dear Miss Dragna,

Your presence is requested for the funeral of Donatella Dragna, tomorrow, one hour after sunrise. Unless you manage to prevent her death.

Yours truly,

Legend

P.S. I recommend taking the stairs to your right.

Scarlett's hand fisted around the letter. This was more than madness. This was something perverted that Scarlett did not understand. She wasn't even sure she wanted to understand it.

Again, she was struck with the feeling this was personal to her, that it was about more than just Legend's sordid past with her grandmother Anna.

Behind her the water started rushing again. She didn't know if that meant others were coming. She hated to leave Julian's body—he deserved so much more than to be abandoned in a cave—but if she was going to save him, she needed to end this, find Tella, and get that wish.

Scarlett looked up to see more jade firefly lights dancing in the air, moving like a curtain of glowing smoke to illuminate a fork in the stairs before her.

Legend had recommended the set to her right. She imagined he knew she wouldn't trust him, so there was a good chance he'd told the truth because of that. However, he was cunning enough to know she would have thought that too.

She started toward the stairs on the left, only to change her mind at the last minute, as she remembered what Legend said about telling the truth. Her father seldom told the entire truth, but he also rarely outright lied. He saved his lies for when they would count the most. Scarlett figured Legend was the same way.

She pushed herself to run up the stairs, spiral after spiral after spiral, remembering all the staircases she'd traveled with Julian. With every flight she fought against tears and fatigue. Whenever she managed not to cry over Julian, she imagined finding Tella the same way she'd left him, unmoving body, unbeating heart, unseeing eyes.

The world felt thinner by the time Scarlett reached the top of the steps. Sweat soaked her gown, and her legs burned and shook. If she'd chosen the wrong staircase she didn't imagine she'd have the strength to run back down and then back up again.

In front of her was a spindly ladder leading to a small square trapdoor. Scarlett lost her footing several times as she climbed. She had no idea what she'd find on the other side of the door. She felt heat. There were sounds of crackling as well. Definitely a fire.

Scarlett tottered against the ladder, praying it was just a fire in a hearth, not an entire room ablaze. She sucked in a deep breath as she pulled the trapdoor.

NIGHT FIVE
THE LAST NIGHT
OF CARAVAL

35

tarlight everywhere.

Constellations Scarlett had never seen domed a vast, inky night. The world was made of a rimless balcony, its floor a stretch of luminous onyx, with oversize cushioned lounges in shades of stardust, and small fire pits growing incandescent blue flames.

High above the rest of the world, it should have felt cold, but the air was warm as Scarlett crawled through the opening, the buttons of her dress softly tinkling against the polished floor. Everything about this place reeked of Legend, even the scent of the fire pits, as if the logs were made of velvet and something slightly sweet. The air felt soft and poisonous. Closer to the room's back wall, a massive black bed, piled with pillows as dark as nightmares, mocked her. Scarlett didn't know what Legend used this room for, but her sister was nowhere—

"Scar?" A petite figure sat up in the bed. Honey-blond curls bounced around a face that might have been angelic, if it wasn't for her devil's grin.

"Oh, my love!" Tella squealed, jumping out of the bed and capturing Scarlett in an embrace before she made it halfway across the room. When she hugged Scarlett with her fierce arms, it made Scarlett believe happy endings were possible. Her sister was alive. She felt like softness and sunlight and seeds for growing dreams.

Now Scarlett just needed to bring back Julian.

Scarlett pulled away only to make sure it was really Tella, who often embraced her but not usually with that much enthusiasm.

"Are you all right?" She looked her sister over for signs of any cuts or bruises. Scarlett could not allow her excitement to let her forget why she was there. "Have you been treated well?"

"Oh, Scar! Always the worrier. I'm so glad you're finally here. For once I was starting to fret." Tella sucked in a deep breath, or maybe it was a shiver since she was standing in only a thin, pale-blue nightdress. "I was beginning to fear you were never going to come—not that it isn't so lovely up here."

Tella waved her arms toward all the stars, ones that felt close enough to grab and tuck inside a pocket. Too close, in Scarlett's mind. Like the raised edge around the balcony, so low to the floor it almost wasn't a barrier at all. A prison disguised to look like a master suite with a palatial view.

"Tella, I'm so sorry."

"It's all right," Tella said. "I was just getting awfully bored."

"Bored—" Scarlett choked on the word. She didn't imagine Caraval would have changed her sister as much as it had changed herself, but *bored?*

"Don't mistake me. There have been perks, and I've been treated well—God's teeth!" Tella's round eyes widened as they dropped to Scarlett's bloody hands and dress. "What happened? There's blood all over you!"

"It's not mine." Scarlett's throat felt tight as she looked down at her palms. Just one drop had given her a day of Julian's life. It made her ache to think how many days were splattered all over her body— *days he should have lived.*

Tella grimaced. "Whose blood is it?"

"I'd rather not explain right here." Scarlett stopped, not quite sure what to say. They needed to get out of there, away from Legend, but Scarlett also needed to find him again if she was going to collect her wish and save Julian.

"Tella, we need to leave." Scarlett would move her sister to safety, then she'd come back for the wish. "Dress quickly; don't bring anything that will weigh us down. Tella, why aren't you moving? We don't have much time!"

But Tella didn't budge. She just stood there in her fragile blue nightdress, a rumpled angel, looking up at Scarlett with wide, worried eyes.

"I was warned this might happen." Tella softened her voice, using that awful tone mostly reserved for unreasonable children or old people. "I don't know where you think we need to run to, but it's all right. The game is over. This room, it's the end, Scar. You can sit down and take a breath." Tella tried to guide her to one of the ridiculous cushioned lounges.

"No!" Scarlett pulled away. "Whoever gave you that warning lied. It was never just a game. I don't know what they told you, but you're in danger—we're both in danger. Father's here."

Tella's eyebrows peaked, but she quickly smoothed her expression out, as if she wasn't alarmed at all. "Are you sure it wasn't just some sort of illusion?"

"I'm positive. We need to get out of here. I have a *friend* . . ." Scarlett couldn't say Julian's name—she could barely say the word *friend*—but she forced herself to stay strong for Tella. "My *friend*, he has a boat and it's going to take us where we want to go. Like you've always wanted."

Scarlett reached for her sister, but this time Tella was the one to step back, pursing her lips. "Scar, please, listen to what you're saying. Your eyes have played tricks on you. Don't you remember the warning they gave when we arrived: don't let yourself get swept too far away?"

"What if I told you this year's game is different?" Scarlett said, and as quickly as possible, she tried to explain Legend's history with their grandmother. "He's brought us here for revenge. I know you've been treated well, but whatever he's told you, it's a lie. We need to leave."

As Scarlett spoke, Tella's expression had shifted. She started gnawing on her lower lip, though whether it was fear for their lives or for Scarlett's sanity, Scarlett could not tell. "You really believe this?" Tella asked.

Scarlett nodded and hoped desperately that their sisterly bond would overcome Tella's doubts. "I know how this sounds, but I've seen the proof."

"All right, then. Give me a moment." Tella bustled off, disappearing behind a large black dressing curtain near her bed, while Scarlett worked to push one of the lounges until it covered up the trapdoor, cutting off the stairs she'd used to get there. As she finished, Tella reappeared, wrapped in a blue silk robe, holding a cloth in one hand and a water basin in the other.

"What are you doing?" Scarlett asked. "Why don't you have on proper clothes?"

"Sit down." Tella motioned toward one of the many cushioned things. "We're not in danger, Scar. Whatever you're afraid of, I know you think it's real, but that's the entire point of Caraval. It's all supposed to feel real, but none of it is. Now, sit, and I'll wash off some of the blood. You'll feel better when you're clean."

Scarlett didn't sit.

Tella was using the voice again, the one for crazed children and delusional adults. Not that Scarlett could blame her. If she hadn't come face-to-face with their father, and if she hadn't seen Julian die, if she hadn't felt his heart stop, his warm blood on her hands, or watched as the life drained out of him, she might have been able to doubt it was real.

If only she could doubt it.

"What if I can prove it?" Scarlett pulled out the funeral invitation. "Right before I came up here, Legend left me this." She thrust the note into Tella's hand. "Look for yourself. He plans to murder you!"

"Because of Nana Anna?" Tella scowled as she read. Then she seemed to be fighting a laugh. "Oh, Scar, I think you've taken this letter the wrong way."

Tella smothered another giggle as she handed the note back to her. The first thing Scarlett noticed were the edges. No longer black, they were now lined in gold, and the script was altered as well.

Dear Miss Dragna,

As my special guest, I'd like to invite you and your sister to a party, usually reserved for my Caraval performers. It starts one hour after sunset. I know I'm not the only one who hopes to see you and your sister there.

Yours,

Legend

36

There's nothing threatening about this." Tella laughed. "Not unless you're nervous about the idea of Legend fancying you?"

"No! That's not what it said before. It was an invitation to a funeral, *your* funeral." Scarlett looked at Tella, her eyes pleading. "I'm not crazy," she insisted. "This note was different when I read it in the tunnels."

"The ones beneath the game?" Tella interrupted. "Aren't the tunnels where people go mad?"

"It was a different set. Tella, I swear, I'm not insane. The note said you would die tomorrow unless I could stop it. Please, even if you don't believe me, I need you to try."

Tella must have seen her desperation. "Let me see the paper again."

Scarlett handed it back. Her sister examined the invite with particular care this time, holding it close to one of the fire pits. But no matter what, the script didn't change.

"Tella, I swear, it was for a funeral, not a party."

"I believe you," Tella said.

"You do?"

"Well, I'm guessing it's like the tickets you received on Trisda, it changes in certain lights. But, Scar . . ." That painfully careful voice once more. "Couldn't it be just another part of the game, a device to get you up here, because it was taking you so long, and now that you are here: ta-da! The note has changed from a threat to a reward. Tell me, which makes more sense?"

The way Tella said it sounded so very reasonable. And oh, how Scarlett wanted her to be right. She knew how deceiving the tunnels—and Legend—could be. But Legend was not the only threat.

"Tella, even if you don't believe me about this, I swear, Father's here. He's looking for you, for us both, right now. And trust me when I say his presence is not a magical mirage of Caraval. He's here with Count Nicolas d'Arcy, my fiancé. To escape, I had to knock d'Arcy out with a protection elixir and then tie him to a bed—I'm sure you can imagine how furious Father will be if he finds us now."

"You tied your fiancé to a bed?" Tella snickered.

"This isn't a joke! Did you miss what I said about what will happen if Father finds us?"

"Scar, I didn't know you had it in you! I wonder what else the game has changed about you." Tella grinned wider, looking truly awed and impressed, which might have pleased Scarlett if she hadn't hoped her sister might grow frightened and panicked instead.

"You're missing the point. I had to do that because Father was going to make me—" Shame choked her throat as she tried to get the words out. Thinking of what her father had attempted to force upon her made her feel like not quite a person. More like a thing.

Tella's expression softened. She wrapped her arms around Scarlett, hugging her in a way only a sister could. Fierce as a kitten who'd just gotten claws, willing to shred the whole world to make this right. And for a moment Scarlett thought it would be.

"Do you believe me now?" she asked.

"I believe you've been through a bit of madness this week, but it's over now. None of that was real." Tella gently smoothed a dark lock of hair from Scarlett's face. "You don't have to worry, sister. And," she added, "someday, Father will pay for all his sins. Every night I pray an angel will come down and cut off his hands so he won't hurt anyone again."

"I don't think that's what angels do," Scarlett mumbled.

"Maybe not the kind up in heaven, but there are different kinds of angels." Tella pulled away, pink lips parting into a smile made of hopes and dreams and other treacherous things.

"Don't tell me you're planning to cut off Father's hands yourself."

"After tonight I don't think Father's hands will be a problem anymore, at least not for us." Tella's eyes twinkled with the same dangerous glint as her smile. "I haven't been up here alone this whole time. I've *met* someone. He knows all about our father and he's promised to take care of us. Both of us." Tella beamed, brighter than candlelight and glass-cut glitter, the type of joy that could only mean one terrible thing.

When Tella had first said the word *bored*, Scarlett dared to hope

Legend hadn't gotten to her. But from the pitch of Tella's voice and the way she looked just then, it made Scarlett fear he had—every ounce of reason had left her eyes. Tella's expression had turned dreamy in a way that said she was either in love or insane.

"You can't trust him," Scarlett blurted. "Haven't you been listening to what I've said? Legend hates us. He's a murderer!"

"Who said anything about Legend?"

"Isn't that who you were talking about?"

Tella made a funny face. "I've never even met him."

"But you've been up in this tower. His tower."

"I know," Tella said. "And you have no idea how vexing it's been watching everyone down below, while I've been stuck up here." With a huff, she cast her gaze over the rimless balcony.

They were a good twelve feet away from the edge, but Scarlett did not feel safe. It would still be far too easy to jump. Tella might not have been seduced by Legend, but knowing the master of Caraval had placed both Dante and Julian in Scarlett's path, she could not imagine Tella's new suitor was any different—the perfect boy to drive her mad.

"What's his name?" Scarlett asked.

"Daniel DeEngl," Tella announced. "He's a bastard lord from the Far Northern Empire. Isn't that terribly delicious? You'll love it, Scar, they have castles up there, with moats and towers and all sorts of dramatic things."

"But, if you've been up here all this time, how did you ever meet?"

"I wasn't up here this *entire* time." Tella's cheeks took on the faintest pink blush and Scarlett recalled the man's voice she'd heard coming from Tella's room after the end of that first night. "I was with Daniel when I was abducted for the game. He actually tried to fight them off, but they just took him as well." She smiled as if it were the most romantic thing that had ever happened to her.

"Tella, this is wrong," Scarlett said. "You can't be in love with someone you just met."

Tella flinched, the hue of her cheeks deepening into an angrier red. "I know you've been through a lot. So I'm not going to point out that you were going to *marry* someone you'd never even met."

"That was different."

"I know, because unlike you, I actually know my fiancé."

"Did you say *fiancé?*"

Tella nodded proudly.

"You're not serious," Scarlett said. "When did he ask you to marry him?"

"Why aren't you happy for me?" Tella's expression fell, like a doll Scarlett had dropped.

Scarlett bit back her first five responses.

"Scar, I know I've prayed for some awful things, the types of things angels don't do, but I've also prayed for something exactly like this. I might be able to get a boy to follow me into the barrel room, but until Daniel, no one had ever actually cared about *me.*"

"I'm sure this Daniel person seems wonderful," Scarlett said carefully. "And I want to be happy for you, I really do. But doesn't this seem a little coincidental? I keep thinking, maybe Legend is just playing a different game with you, and what if this Daniel is part of it?"

"He's not," Tella said. "I know you don't have a lot of experience with men, but I do, and trust me when I say my relationship with Daniel is very real." Tella took a sharp step back, feet pale against the dark onyx floor as she plucked a silver bell from one of the cushioned lounges.

"What are you doing?" Scarlett asked.

"I'm ringing for Daniel so you can meet him and see for yourself."

The door opened and Jovan appeared, looking like a rainbow in the same colorful outfit she'd worn the first night, on the unicycle. "Oh, hello." She perked up when she saw Scarlett. "You've finally found your sister."

"You can't trust her," Scarlett whispered to Tella. "She works for Legend."

"Of course she works for Legend," Tella said. "Forgive my sister, Jo, she's still caught up in the game. She thinks Legend is out to kill us both."

"Are you certain she's wrong?" Jovan winked as if she was joking, but when her eyes cut to Scarlett her playfulness vanished.

"Did you see that?" Scarlett said. "She knows!"

Tella ignored her. "Can you fetch Lord DeEngl for me, please?"

Before Scarlett could protest, Jovan nodded and disappeared the way she'd come, through a hidden door tucked into the back wall.

"Tella, please," Scarlett begged. "We need to get out of here. You have no idea how dangerous this is. Even if you're right about Daniel, it's still not safe. Legend won't let you be together."

Scarlett paused and held out her hands, showing her sister all the precious blood once more. "See—this?" Her voice cracked. "This is real. Before I came up here, I watched Legend kill someone—"

"Or you thought you did," Tella interrupted. "Whatever you believe you saw, I'm sure it wasn't real. You keep forgetting, what happens down there is all part of the game. And I'm not running from Daniel because you got too caught up in it."

Tella's mouth formed a soft downward curve. "I know no one loves me more than you do, Scar, I'd be desolate without you. Please, don't leave me now. And do not ask me to leave Daniel." Tella's lips shifted into a deeper frown. "Don't make me choose between the two loves of my life."

Two loves. Scarlett's heart ached at her sister's choice of words. Suddenly she was on the steps again, watching Julian's head fall before his breathing stopped. She needed to find a way to bring him back, but she also had to get her sister safely out of this tower and far away from this balcony.

"Now," Tella said brightly, as if everything were settled, though Scarlett had not uttered a word. "Help me become beautiful for Lord Daniel!" Tella skipped off toward her dressing area. "You might want to clean up as well," she called. "I have some gowns that would look stunning on you."

The night grew even darker as Scarlett remained rooted in place.

She knew she looked halfway to dead, and she was tempted to keep it that way. She liked the idea of frightening Tella's fiancé. Scarlett liked the idea of leaving even more—but Tella was not the sort who'd run after Scarlett if she left. And what if Tella was right? Perhaps it was grandiose to assume the entire game revolved around the two of them. If her sister was correct, and Scarlett ruined this, Tella really would never forgive her.

But if Scarlett wasn't crazy, and Julian was really dead, then Scarlett needed to retrieve her wish and save him.

Behind Tella's dressing curtain, one wardrobe and multiple trunks were opened, overflowing with an assortment of clothes. Scarlett watched as her sister debated between several gowns.

Hopefully after she met this Daniel person, Scarlett could figure out a way to convince Tella to leave with her. In the meantime she would stay by her side and discover a way to collect her wish from Legend.

"The periwinkle," Scarlett said. "Blue is always the most becoming on you."

"I knew you'd stay," Tella said. "Here, this one's for you, it will look so dramatic with your dark hair and that new little streak. Sorry, I don't have any slippers your size, you'll just have to let your boots dry." She gave Scarlett a cranberry dress with a frothy ball-gown skirt, longer in the back than in the front, and covered in teardrop-shaped red beads.

The dress matched the blood on Scarlett's palms. As Scarlett finally washed it away, she vowed to herself once more that she'd find a way to bring Julian back. No more wounds would stain her hands that night.

"Promise me one thing," Scarlett said. "Whatever happens, swear you won't jump off any balconies."

"Only if you promise me not to say strange things like that when Daniel arrives."

"I'm being serious, Tella."

"So am I. Please don't spoil this—"

A knock at the door.

"That must be Daniel." Tella slid into a pair of silver slippers before spinning around in her periwinkle dress. The color of sweet dreams and happy endings.

"You look beautiful," Scarlett said. But even as she dared to hope her sister was the one who'd been right all along, Scarlett could not ignore the bitter yellow puddle of dread in her stomach as Tella swept out from behind the dressing curtain and toward the hidden door against the back wall.

The world swayed as Tella opened it, everything tilting as Scarlett watched the man on the other side reach around her sister's waist and reel her in for a kiss.

Two spots of pink colored Tella's cheeks as she pulled away. "Daniel, we have company." Tella drew the man she called Daniel back toward the cushioned lounges where Scarlett stood, immobile.

"I'd like you to meet my sister, Scarlett." Tella beamed again, so brightly, she didn't notice the way Scarlett had involuntarily taken a step back, or how the young man at her side ran his tongue over his lips when Tella wasn't looking.

"Donatella, step away from him," Scarlett said. "His name is not Daniel."

37

He no longer wore a top hat, and he'd traded his dark tailcoat for a crisp white frock coat, but his eyes still sparked with the same mad gleam, as if there was something unhinged behind them, and he didn't care about hiding it.

"Scar," Tella hissed. *Acting weird again,* she mouthed.

"No, I know him," Scarlett insisted. "That's Legend."

"Scarlett, please stop acting crazy," Tella said. "Daniel's been with me, all night, *every night* of the game. It's not possible for him to be Legend."

"It's true." Legend hooked his arm around Tella's shoulder; she looked childlike under his heavy grip as he possessively pulled her short frame closer.

"Get your hands off her!" Scarlett launched herself at Legend.

"Scar! Stop!" Tella grabbed Scarlett's hair, yanking her away before she managed more than a scratch.

"Daniel, I'm so sorry," Tella said. "I don't know what's gotten into her. Scarlett, end this madness!"

"He lied to you!" Scarlett's scalp burned as she struggled with Tella. "He's a murderer."

Though Legend didn't look like a killer just then. Dressed in white, and without his mad smile, he looked as innocent as a saint. "Maybe we should tie her up before she hurts herself."

"No!" Scarlett shouted.

A flash of unease crossed Tella's face.

"Love, she's wild, she's going to hurt one of us." Legend's brows drew together as if he were truly worried. "Remember the warnings about people who get swept too far away? I'll hold her while you fetch rope. There should be some in a dressing trunk for episodes like this."

"Tella, please, don't listen to him," Scarlett pled.

"Love," coaxed Legend, his voice dripping deceptive concern. "It's for her own safety."

Tella's eyes darted from Legend, in all his pristine glory, to Scarlett, with her knotted hair and tear-stained cheeks. "I'm sorry," Tella said. "I don't want you to get hurt."

"No!" Scarlett thrashed again, ripping the sleeve of her dress and spilling beads on the floor, as Legend took her from her sister. Hands as strong as iron manacles twisted her wrists behind her back, while Tella disappeared behind her dressing curtain.

"See how willing she is to do whatever I suggest?" Legend purred into her ear.

"Please," Scarlett begged, "leave her alone. I'll do whatever you say if you let her go. You want me to jump off the balcony, I will. Just don't hurt her!"

In one sharp motion, Legend spun Scarlett around. Pale skin and harsh cheekbones, and eyes full of unveiled madness. "You would jump for her, to your death?" He released Scarlett with a shove. "Then do it. Now."

"You want me to jump right now?"

"Not right now." His lips twitched at the corners, the demented imitation of a smile. "I wouldn't have invited you to her funeral if I planned on you dying tonight. Just walk to the edge of the balcony, as close as you can get without falling over."

Scarlett couldn't think clearly. She wondered if this was how Tella felt around Legend. Befuddled and bewildered. "If I do this, you promise you won't hurt my sister?"

"You have my word." Legend X-ed a pale finger over his heart. "If you walk to the rim of the balcony, I swear, on my amazing life, I will not touch your sister again."

"And promise me you won't let anyone else?"

Legend raked Scarlett over with his eyes, from the ripped sleeve of her dress to her naked feet. "You're not really in a position to make deals."

"Then why are you making a deal with me?"

"I want to see how far you're willing to go." His tone turned syrupy with curiosity, but the look he gave her was pure challenge. "If you're not willing to do this, you'll never be able to save her."

To Scarlett it sounded as if he said, *If you're not able to do this, you don't love her enough.*

Purposefully, Scarlett started toward the edge of the balcony. Night air swept around her ankles as she drew closer, and even though Scarlett had never feared heights, she felt dizzy as she dared to look down at the specks of light and dots of people, and the solid ground that would show no mercy if she—

"Stop!" Legend yelled.

Scarlett froze, but Legend continued to shout, filling his voice with artificial terror, making it crack in all the right places. "Donatella, hurry, your sister is trying to jump."

"No!" Scarlett hollered. "I'm not—"

A warning look from Legend cut her off. "Say another word, and you have no guarantees from me."

But a promise from him meant nothing. She'd been a fool to believe anything he'd said. He'd driven her to the edge to push her further from Tella, who looked stricken when she reappeared with the rope.

"Scarlett, please, don't jump!" Tella's face was red and splotchy.

"I wasn't going to jump," Scarlett insisted.

"I'm so sorry—she convinced me to let her go," Legend said. "Then she said if she jumped she'd wake up from the game."

"Daniel, it's not your fault," Tella said. "Scar, please, step away from the ledge."

"He's lying!" Scarlett yelled. "He's the one who made me go to the edge—he said if I did, he wouldn't hurt you." Scarlett realized too late this only made her sound more insane. "Tella, please, you know me; you know I wouldn't do something like that."

Tella sucked on her lower lip, looking torn once more, as if deep down Tella believed her sister wasn't suicidal.

"I love you, Scar, but I know this game does strange things to people." Tella handed her coil of rope to Legend. He lowered his head dramatically, as if this pained him, too.

"No!" Scarlett wanted to back away, but the edge of the balcony was behind her. The cruel night hungering to swallow her up if she fell.

She shot forward instead, trying to outrun Legend, but he moved like a viper. One hand wrapped around her wrists. He used the other to shove her into a chair.

"Let me go!" Scarlett tried to kick, but Tella was there as well, working to bind Scarlett's flailing ankles, while Legend secured her arms and chest to the chair. Scarlett could feel Legend's breath against her neck, hot as he whispered too low for Tella to hear, *"Wait until you see what I do next."*

"I will kill you!" Scarlett screamed.

"Maybe we should get her a sedative?" asked Tella.

"No, I think this should hold her long enough." Legend tugged on the rope a final time, slicing through Scarlett's breathing.

A hidden door in the back opened, and Legend's maniacal smile returned as Scarlett's father, along with Count Nicolas d'Arcy, walked through. The governor strode forward purposefully, head high, shoulders straight, as if he were an honored guest. The count appeared interested in only one person—Scarlett.

"Tella!" Scarlett's panic escalated.

For the first time there was a flicker of fear in Tella's face as well. "What are they doing here?"

"I invited them." Legend waved an arm magnanimously toward

Scarlett, who continued struggling against the rope, while the two men stepped closer.

"All tied up and ready to go, as promised," said Legend.

"Daniel, what are you doing?" Tella whispered.

"You really should have listened to your sister." Legend stepped to the side as Governor Dragna and Count Nicolas d'Arcy closed in on Scarlett.

The count had cleaned up since she'd seen him last. His black hair was combed, and he'd changed into a fresh garnet-red tail-coat. He peered down at Scarlett and shook his head as if to say, *I told you so.*

"Can I keep the rope?" the governor asked, his eyes full of retribution.

"Daniel, tell them to stay away from us!" Tella cried.

"Oh, Donatella," Legend said. "Stupid and stubborn until the end. There is no Daniel DeEngl. Though it was enjoyable pretending." Legend laughed perversely. The same awful sound Scarlett had first heard in the tunnels.

Splinters dug into Scarlett's arms while she battled to free herself from the ropes.

Tella didn't say another word, but Scarlett could see her sister crumbling. Growing smaller and younger and turning suddenly fragile as she continued to stare up at Legend the way Scarlett imagined she'd gazed at Julian when she'd first learned the truth about how he'd deceived her. Believing but not accepting. Waiting for an explanation that Scarlett knew would never come.

Even Governor Dragna looked stunned by Legend's confessed

identity. However, the count did not look entirely surprised. He merely cocked his head.

"I don't believe you," Tella said.

"Would you like me to perform a magic trick to prove I'm really him?"

"That's not what I don't believe. You said you loved me," Tella said. "All those things you told me—"

"I lied," Legend answered flatly. And there was something about the flatness. As if Tella didn't even matter enough to hate.

"But . . . but . . ." Tella sputtered, the spell Legend cast upon her finally breaking. If she were made of porcelain—as Scarlett often thought—Tella would have shattered. But she just kept stepping back. Closer and closer to that dangerous edge of the balcony.

"Tella, stop!" Scarlett yelled. "You're almost at the rim."

"I'm not stopping until you step away from her." Tella shot a pointed look at her father and the count. "If either of you take another step toward my sister, I swear I'll jump. And, Father, you know if you don't have me, you'll never be able to control Scarlett. Even if you have her, you won't make this marriage happen."

The governor and the count stopped moving, but Tella continued backing up, silver slippers sliding all the way to the edge of the balcony.

"Tella, stop!" Scarlett fought to free herself from the rope, beads breaking off her dress as she thrashed against the chair. This couldn't be happening. Not after watching Julian die. She couldn't lose Tella like this. "You're getting too close to the edge!"

"It's a little late for that." Tella laughed, a brittle sound, as breakable as she looked. Scarlett wanted to run to her, to grab hold of her where she tottered on the balcony's rim. But the rope wasn't loose enough yet. Her ankles had managed to kick free, but her arms were still bound. Only the stars watched in sympathy as she rocked back and forth, hoping that if she knocked over the chair she'd smash one of its arms and finally break loose.

"Donatella, it's all right," her father said, almost tenderly. "You can still come home with me. I'll forgive you. Both you and your sister."

"You expect me to believe that?!" Tella exploded. "You're a liar, and worse than he is!" She pointed a shaky finger at Legend. "All of you are *liars!*"

"Tella, I'm not." With a crash Scarlett's chair hit the floor, one of its arms splintering, so that she could finally crawl out of the ropes and start for the ledge.

"Stay back, Scar!" Tella moved one foot so her heel was over the rim.

Scarlett froze.

"Tella, please—" Scarlett took another tentative step, but when Tella wobbled, she froze again, terrified one false move would push her sister over the very edge she so badly wanted to rescue her from.

"Please, trust me." Scarlett held out a hand. No longer stained in blood, she hoped she could save Tella in the way she hadn't been able to save Julian in the tunnels. "I will find a way to take care of you. I love you so much."

"Oh, Scar," Tella said. Tears streamed down her pink cheeks. "I love you, too. And I wish I was strong like you. Strong enough to hope it could be better, but I can't do this anymore." Tella's hazel eyes met Scarlett's, as sad as fresh-cut wood. Then she closed them, as if Tella couldn't bear to look at her. "I meant it when I said I'd rather die at the edge of the world than live a miserable life on Trisda. I'm so sorry."

With trembling fingers, Tella blew her sister a kiss.

"Don't—"

Tella stepped off the edge of the balcony.

"*No!*" Scarlett wailed, watching as her sister plummeted into the night.

With no wings to fly her down, she fell to her death.

38

Scarlett would only remember fragments and pieces of what happened next. She would not remember how Tella had looked like a doll, knocked from a very high shelf, until the blood started pooling around her.

Even then Scarlett couldn't look away from her sister's lifeless body. She just kept wishing. Wishing Tella would move. Wishing Tella would get up and walk. Wishing for a clock that could turn back time and give Scarlett one last chance to save her.

Scarlett remembered the time-twisting pocket watch she'd seen her first day there. If only Julian had stolen that watch instead.

But Julian was dead too.

Scarlett choked on a sob. She'd lost both of them. Scarlett cried until her eyes and her chest and parts of her body she didn't know could hurt began to ache.

The count stepped closer, as if to offer some form of consolation.

"Stop." Scarlett held out a shaking hand. "Please." She choked on the word, but she couldn't bear anyone's comfort, especially not his.

"Scarlett," said her father. He approached her as the count backed away. Or rather, her father shuffled. Hunched over, as if an invisible pack were tied to his back, and for the first time Scarlett didn't see a monster but rather just a sad, old bully. She saw how his fair hair had grayed at the edges, and his eyes were shot with blood. A dragon with no fire and broken wings. "I'm sorry—"

"Don't." Scarlett cut him off; he deserved this. "I don't ever want to see you again. I don't ever want to hear your voice, and I don't want you to try to ease your conscience by apologizing. You brought this about. You drove her to this place."

"I was just trying to protect you." Governor Dragna's nostrils flared. His wings might have been broken but he still had his flames after all. "If you'd listened to me, rather than always being such a disobedient, ungrateful wretch of a—"

"Sir!" Jovan, who Scarlett had failed to notice before, boldly stepped in front of Governor Dragna. "I think you've said en—"

"Get out of my way." The governor slapped Jovan across the face.

"Don't touch her!" Scarlett and Legend both spoke at once, though it was Legend who moved forward in a flash. Sharp, pale lines and dark, dark eyes now focused on the governor. "You will not hurt any more of my players."

"Or what are you going to do?" Governor Dragna snarled. "I know the rules. I know you can't harm me as long as the game is in play."

"Then you also know the game ends at sunrise, which is approaching fast. When that happens, I'm no longer bound by those rules." Legend bared his teeth. "Since you have seen my true face, that's even more incentive for me to rid the world of you."

Legend flicked his wrist, and every candled lamp and fire pit throughout the balcony turned brighter, casting a hellish red-orange glow over the obsidian floor.

Governor Dragna paled.

"I may not have cared about your daughter," Legend went on, "but I do care about my players, and I know what you have done."

"What is he talking about?" Scarlett asked.

"Don't listen to him," said the governor.

"Your father thought he could kill *me*," Legend said. "The governor mistakenly believed Dante was the master of Caraval, and took his life instead."

Scarlett looked at her father aghast. "*You* murdered Dante?"

Even the count, who now stood at a distance, looked unsettled by this.

Governor Dragna's breathing turned heavy. "I was just trying to protect you!"

"Maybe you should think about protecting yourself," Legend went on. "If I were you, *Governor,* I'd leave now and never come back, to this place or anywhere else you might find me. Things will not end as favorably next time I see you."

The count backed away first. "I had nothing to do with any murders. I was only here for her." The count's eye cut to Scarlett, holding her gaze far past that initial moment of being uncomfortable. He didn't say another word. But his lips curved just enough to show a flash of white teeth. It was the same way he had looked at her the first time she'd run away from him; as if a game between the two of them had just begun and he was eager to play.

Scarlett got the impression that although Count Nicolas d'Arcy was leaving, their business was far from complete.

The count tilted his head in a mockery of a bow. Then he turned and strode out of the door, silver boots echoing as he disappeared.

"Come on." The governor waved Scarlett forward with an unsteady hand. "We're leaving."

"No." Scarlett was shaking again, but she stood her ground. "I'm not going anywhere with you."

"You stupid—" The governor swore. "If you stay, he's defeated our family. This is what he wanted. But if you want to come with me, he loses. I'm sure the count will—"

"I'm not marrying him, and you cannot make me. *You're* the one who destroyed our family. All you want is power and control," Scarlett said, "but you will not have either over me any longer. You have nothing left to hold me now that Tella is gone."

For a moment Scarlett was tempted to step up on the ledge and add, *Now leave, before you lose both your daughters.* But she would not let him destroy her as he had her sister. She would do what she should have done long ago.

"I know your secrets, Father. I was always too afraid before, but now that you can't use Tella to control me, I have no reason to stay quiet. I know you think you can get away with murder, but I don't imagine your guards will stay loyal much longer when I tell everyone you murdered one of their own sons. I will tell the entire isle how you killed Felipe, drowned him with your own hands, just to frighten me into obeying you. How well do you think you'll sleep once Felipe's father learns about that? And I know other secrets too, ones that will put an end to everything you've built."

Scarlett had never been so bold in all her life. Her heart and her soul and even her memories managed to hurt. Everything ached. She felt hollow and heavy all at once. It pained her to breathe and it took effort to speak. But she was still alive. She was still breathing and speaking and feeling. Most of what she felt was agony, but she also didn't feel afraid of anything.

And for the first time, her father looked afraid of *her*.

He looked more frightened of Legend. But, either way, he was leaving and she didn't imagine he would come after her again. A governor did not live long without loyal guards. The Conquered Isles were not the most prestigious place to rule, but there was always someone looking to usurp power.

So it should have felt like a victory when he walked out the door. Scarlett was finally free. Free of her father. Free to go wherever she wanted—Julian had given her that with the coordinates in his pocket watch.

Julian. The grief she felt for him was different from the loss she felt for Tella: each tore apart a separate half of her, but they weighed her down equally. She could feel fresh sobs building in her chest, swelling like waves about to crash, but at the thought of Julian, she recalled something else. She remembered why she'd abandoned his body in those tunnels.

She'd won the game. She still had her wish and Legend was there to grant it.

For a moment she felt hope, lighter than the weight of her grief. Indescribable and iridescent—*and utterly impossible to hold on to.*

Because it wasn't only Julian she needed to save.

Scarlett's chest ached again. Tella and Julian were both gone. She felt as if it shouldn't even have been a choice. But it was a choice, which made her feel like less of a sister. Or maybe Julian mattered even more than she realized, because although she knew she was going to choose Tella, she couldn't say it right away, as if maybe there was a way to save them both that she hadn't figured out yet.

Her sister, or the boy Scarlett had almost certainly fallen in love with.

Julian had died because of her. He'd risked everything for her by facing her father and then by giving her that pocket watch just before Scarlet would meet Legend. Scarlett thought of how strained his voice sounded as he struggled to tell her the truth. It wasn't his job to protect her, but he'd done what he could. He also made her feel things she never knew she could desire, and for that she would always love him.

But Tella was not only her sister, she was Scarlett's best friend, the one person in the world she should have loved more than anything or anyone else, the person she was responsible to take care of.

Scarlett turned to Legend, her decision made. "I won. You owe me a wish."

Legend snorted, as if amused. "I'm afraid my answer to that is no."

"What do you mean, no?"

Legend responded dryly, "From your tone, I think you know exactly what I mean."

"But I won the game," Scarlett argued. "I solved your confusing clues. I found my sister. You owe me a wish."

"You really expect me to grant you a wish after all of this?" Around Legend the candles flickered, as if they were all laughing along with him.

Scarlett fisted her hands, telling herself she would not cry again, even as tears burned the backs of her eyes. Giving her only one wish, and making her choose between the two people she loved, was cruelty enough, but no wish at all was unspeakable. "What is wrong with you? Don't you care that two innocent people are dead? You're absolutely heartless."

"If I'm so vile, then why are you still here?" Legend said. But when he slid his eyes to her, they were no longer the sparkling gems she'd seen at their first meeting. If it were anyone else, she would have sworn he almost looked sad.

It must have been her grief. Scarlett was seeing things, because Legend now seemed dimmer as well. Duller than he had been in the tunnels or when he'd first arrived at the balcony. As if a glamour had been cast over him, and it was somehow disappearing, making him less of the Legend he had been before. Where his pale skin had glittered in the tunnels, it now appeared dusty, blurry almost, as if she were looking at a rendering of him that had grown dull over time.

For years Scarlett had believed no one could be worse than her father, and no one could be more magical than Legend, but despite his tricks with the fire, the master of Caraval didn't look so magical now. Maybe he said he wouldn't grant her wish because he *couldn't* grant her wish.

But Scarlett had seen enough wonder to believe that wishes had to be real. She tried to remember every story she'd ever been told about magic. Jovan had said different things fueled it, like time. Her grandmother had said it was desire. When Julian had given her a day of her life, he'd used his own blood.

Blood. That was it.

In the world of Caraval, blood possessed some sort of magic. If a drop could give a person a day of life, maybe Scarlett could bring Julian and Tella both back to life if she gave them enough of her blood.

She turned to Jo. "How do I get down to the street?" Scarlett wasn't sure if the girl would give her an answer, but Jo quickly told her how to find exactly what Scarlett sought.

Outside, it was growing darker by the second, as the lamps were burning low, signaling the final hour of the night.

A crowd had gathered around Tella. Precious Tella, who already wasn't Scarlett's Tella anymore. Without her smile and her laugh and her secrets and her teases and all the things that made her Scarlett's beloved sister.

Ignoring the onlookers, Scarlett plunged to her knees, sinking into the puddle of blood around her sister, who looked broken in every possible way. Her arms and legs were skewed at awful angles, her bright honey curls soaked in red.

Scarlett bit down hard on her finger, until blood dripped down to her palm. She pressed it to her sister's blue, unmoving lips.

"Tella, drink!" Scarlett said. Her fingers trembled as she continued holding them to Tella's mouth, but Tella didn't move or breathe.

"Please, you told me there was more to life," Scarlett whispered. "You can't stop living now. I wish you would come back to me."

Scarlett closed her eyes and repeated the wish like a supplication. She'd stopped believing in wishes the day her father had killed Felipe, but Caraval had restored her faith in magic once again. It didn't matter that Legend said he wouldn't grant her wish. It was like her nana had said: *Every person gets one impossible wish, if the person wants something more than anything, and they can find a bit of magic to help them along.* Scarlett loved her sister more than anything; maybe that, combined with the magic of Caraval, would be enough.

She continued to wish, as all around her the candled lamps slowly burned out until there was no more flame, like the unmoving girl in Scarlett's arms.

It hadn't worked.

Fresh tears ran down Scarlett's cheeks. She could have held Tella until they dried up and she and her sister both turned to dust, a warning to any others who dared to get too swept away in the deception of Caraval.

The story could have ended there. In a storm of tears and muttered words. But just as the sun was about to rise, in the black instant before dawn, the darkest moment of the night, a dark brown hand gently rocked Scarlett's shoulder.

Scarlett looked up to find Jovan. The candles and lanterns had almost turned to smoke, so Scarlett could barely see her, but she recognized the light lilt of her voice. "The game's about to officially end. Soon the morning bells will toll, and people will start packing up. I thought you might want to collect your sister's things."

Scarlett craned her neck toward Tella's rimless balcony—no, Legend's rimless balcony. "Whatever is up there, I don't want it."

"Oh, but you may want these items," said Jo.

THE DAY AFTER

CARAVAL

39

When Scarlett arrived at Tella's balcony room she imagined it was a ploy, another way to torment her. The possessions in the suite were all newly acquired. Dresses. Furs. Gloves. None of it truly felt like Tella. The only thing that felt like her sister was Scarlett's memory of the periwinkle gown Tella had died in. The gown that had failed to bring her a happy ending.

Whatever Jo thought—

Scarlett paused at the sight of something. On Tella's vanity sat a long rectangular box made of etched glass and silver edges with a clasp that made Scarlett's heart trip a beat. It was a sun with a star inside and a teardrop inside of the star.

The symbol of Caraval.

Scarlett now hated that crest more than the color purple, but she distinctly knew that box, with its wretched emblem, had not been there before.

Slowly Scarlett raised the lid.

A slip of paper. Carefully, she unfolded the note. It was dated almost a year ago.

1st day of the Hot Season,

Year 56, Elantine Dynasty

Dear Master Legend,

I believe you are a liar, a blackguard, and a villain, and I would very much like your help.

My father is a villain as well, though not the dashing sort like you. He's the kind who likes to beat his daughters. I know this is not your problem, and since you probably have a heart made of black, perhaps you don't care. But I've learned you did actually feel something when that woman threw herself from your balcony after you rejected her during Caraval a few years ago. I heard you were so upset, that was the real reason you stopped traveling.

Helping my sister and me won't completely make up for whatever happened then, but it might help a little. I also think it would create a very interesting game, and I know how you like to play.

Yours truly,
Donatella Dragna

Scarlett reread the letter, again and again. Each time she believed it a little more and a little more, until at last she believed it without a doubt.

The game was not over yet. And it seemed Scarlett was right: this year's Caraval really was about more than just Legend and her grandmother. In fact, it appeared her sister had made some sort of bargain with the master of Caraval himself.

"Jo!" she called. "Jovan!"

The girl appeared with a peculiar bounce to her step the second time her name was shouted.

"Take me to Master Legend," Scarlett said.

40

hat's the meaning of this?" Scarlett demanded. Across from her Legend sat in a tufted champagne chair looking out an oval window. There was no balcony, not in this room. Scarlett imagined these quarters were sick—if it were possible for a room to be ill. The large stretch of space was covered in dull shades of beige, with only two faded chairs.

Scarlett waved the letter in front of Legend, who'd yet to look away from the view. He peered down on all the people below, dragging trunks and carpetbags, as they began their exodus back into the "real" world.

"I was wondering when you'd come," he said airily.

"What type of deal did you make with my sister?" Scarlett asked.

A sigh. "I didn't make any deal."

"Then why did you leave this letter?"

"I didn't do that, either." The master of Caraval finally looked away from the window, yet something about his placid expression was off-kilter—or rather missing.

"Think. Who would want you to have that letter?" he asked.

Again, Legend was her first thought.

"It was not me," he repeated. "And here's a hint, it shouldn't be hard to figure out. Imagine who could have left it for you."

"Donatella?" Scarlett breathed. She could have moved the box when she'd gone to fetch the rope. "But why?"

Ignoring her question, Legend handed Scarlett a short stack of letters. "I'm supposed to give you these, as well."

"Why don't you just tell me what's going on?" Scarlett said.

"Because that's not my role." Legend rose from his chair, moving so close to Scarlett he might have touched her. He was back in his velvet top hat and tailcoat. But he didn't grin, or laugh, or do any of the mad things she'd begun to associate with him. He looked at her not as if he was trying see her, but as if he was trying to show her something about himself.

Again, Scarlett prickled with the feeling something was missing from him, as if the clouds had parted to reveal the sun, only there was nothing but more clouds. In Tella's room, it seemed he'd wanted her to see how unhinged he was; he'd made her believe he might do something crazed at any moment. Now it appeared as if the opposite was true.

The words *my role* replayed in Scarlett's thoughts.

"You're not really Legend, are you?"

A faint smile.

"Does that mean yes or no?" Scarlett was in no mood for riddles.

"My name is Caspar."

"That's still not an answer," Scarlett said. But even as she glared at him, puzzle pieces were clicking together inside her head, creating a complete picture of something she'd been unable to see until that moment. Around her neck, the pocket watch felt hot as she recalled the way Julian's confession had cut off, as if he'd been physically unable to speak the words. The same thing had happened to him on the carousel, right before Scarlett had jumped.

"As a performer, magic prevents you from saying certain things," Scarlett guessed aloud. She remembered something else then, words from a dream she'd been told she would not forget. *They say Legend wears a different face every game.*

Not magic. A variety of actors. It also explained why Caspar had looked dimmer and duller, like a copy of the real Legend, when they'd been up in the balcony—there really must have been some sort of glamour over him. And as Caraval had come to a close, it had begun to fade. The corners of his eyes were now red, the space beneath them puffy. In the tunnels, his fair skin had been eerily perfect, but now she could see tiny scars on his jaw, where she imagined he'd nicked himself shaving. He even had a few freckles on his nose.

"You're not really Legend." This time it was a statement, not a question. "That's why you said you wouldn't grant my wish. You're just an actor, so you're not capable of making wishes come true."

It seemed the game truly wasn't over.

Scarlett should have known better than to assume the real Legend would appear for her. How many years had she written him before ever hearing back?

"Is there really even a Legend?"

"Oh yes." Caspar laughed, as faint as his smile, seasoned with something bitter. "Legend is very real, but most people have no idea if they have met him—including many of his performers. The master of Caraval doesn't go around introducing himself as Legend. He's almost always pretending to be someone else."

Scarlett thought about the myriad people she'd seen during Caraval. She wondered if any of them had been the elusive Legend. "Have you ever met him?" she asked.

"I'm not allowed to answer that."

In other words, he hadn't.

"However," he added, "it seems your sister managed to capture his attention." Caspar nodded toward Scarlett's hand.

Six letters, penned by two different people. Starting a season after Tella's first correspondence.

> 1st day of the Harvest Season,
> Year 56, Elantine Dynasty

Dear Miss Dragna,

You propose an interesting question, though I'm not sure what delusion has led you to believe I could help you. If you know my history, you're aware of what happened between myself and your grandmother Annalise.

—L

16th day of the Harvest Season,

Year 56, Elantine Dynasty

Dear Master Legend,

I am very aware of your history. But I also know you were once told whatever roles you played during Caraval would affect who you are as a person. And I recently heard that after that woman killed herself, you decided you no longer wished to be a villain, and you were keen on becoming more the hero type. This is your chance at redemption.

Donatella Dragna

44th day of the Harvest Season,
Year 56, Elantine Dynasty

Dear Miss Dragna,

I am beyond redemption. However, depending on how far you're willing to go, I've thought about it, and I may be able to work with you.

—L

61st day of the Harvest Season,

Year 56, Elantine Dynasty

Dear Master Legend,

I'm willing to do whatever it takes. I'm willing
to die.

Donatella Dragna

Scarlett cursed her sister for having written such foolish words. Foolish. Reckless. Irrational. Thoughtless—

Scarlett's anger stilled as she read the next letter.

> 76th day of the Harvest Season,
> Year 56, Elantine Dynasty
>
> Dear Miss Dragna,
>
> I take it you believe someone loves you enough to wish you back to life?
>
> —L

1st day of the Cold Season,
Year 56, Elantine Dynasty

Dear Master Legend,

Absolutely.

Donatella Dragna

There were no more letters after that. Scarlett reread them, and every time, her eyes burned with new tears. *What had Tella been thinking?*

"It seems she thought you could wish her back," Caspar said.

Scarlett didn't realize she'd asked the question aloud. And perhaps Caspar's response should have made her feel better.

It didn't.

Scarlett looked down at the letters once again. "How did my sister know all of this?"

"I can't speak for her," Caspar said. "But I can say Caraval is not the only place where people trade secrets for things. Your sister must have bargained away something valuable to learn so much."

Scarlett's hands trembled. All this time Tella had been working to save them both. And Scarlett had failed them. She'd tried to wish Tella back, but she must not have loved her enough.

On the other side of the oval window, the world had faded even more. Whatever magic held Caraval together was quickly turning to dust, taking all the buildings and the streets with it. Scarlett watched everything outside disappear as fresh tears rolled down her cheeks. "Foolish Tella."

"Personally, I think *clever* is a more appropriate word."

Scarlett spun around.

A girl with a devil's smile and a cherub's curls.

"Tella? Is that really you?"

"Oh please, I'd think you could come up with something better than that." Tella's curls bounced as she glided farther into the room. "And please don't cry."

"But I saw you die," Scarlett sputtered.

"I know, and trust me when I say, plummeting to the ground is not a good way to go." Tella grinned again, but her death, no matter how short-lived or how fake, still felt too real—*too soon*—for her to joke about.

"How could you—put me through that?" Scarlett stammered. "How could you pretend to kill yourself while I watched?"

"I think I'll leave you two alone." Caspar edged toward the door with a parting look to Scarlett. "Hope there's no hard feelings about everything. See you at the party?"

"Party?" Scarlett asked.

"Ignore him," Tella said.

"Stop telling me what to do!" Scarlett lost control then, sobbing once more, the sort of hysterical tears that made her hiccup and sneeze.

"I'm so sorry, Scar." Tella closed in and gathered Scarlett into a hug. "I didn't want you to go through that."

"Then why did you do it?" Scarlett pulled away, hiccupping as she moved so one of the tufted chairs stood between her and her sister. No matter how relieved she was to see Tella alive, she couldn't shake how it had felt to see her die. To cradle her dead body. To believe she'd never hear her voice again.

"I knew your love could wish me back to life," said Tella.

"But I didn't bring you back. Legend never gave me my wish."

"A wish isn't something someone can give," Tella explained. "Legend could give you a little extra magic to help you along, but the wish would only work if you wanted it more than anything."

"So you're saying I wished you back to life?" Scarlett still couldn't fathom it. When she first saw her sister, alive and breathing and irreverently joking, she imagined Tella's death had somehow been an elaborate trick. But there was no humor in her sister's expression now. "Tella, what if it had failed?"

"I knew you could do it," Tella said firmly. "No one loves me as much as you do. You would have leaped from the balcony if Caspar had convinced you it'd protect me."

"I don't know about that," Scarlett muttered.

"I do," Tella said. "You might not have been able to see me during the game, but I snuck out to watch you a couple of times. Even when you didn't pass the tests, I knew you would still be able to save me."

"Tests?" Scarlett asked.

"Legend insisted we put you through a few trials. He promised he could provide a bit of magic, but you had to want the wish enough, or it wouldn't happen at the end of the game. That's why the woman in the dress shop asked you what you desired most."

"But I failed that test."

"You didn't fail all of them. You passed the most important one, and that was enough. If you hadn't, I wasn't supposed to jump."

Scarlett remembered what Caspar had said as he made her walk to the edge of the balcony. *If you're not willing to do this, you'll never be able to save her.*

"Please, don't be mad." Tella's heart-shaped mouth pulled into a frown. "I did this for both of us. Like you said, Father would hunt me to the ends of the earth if I ran away."

"But not if you died," Scarlett finished.

Tella nodded grimly. "The night we left, I planted a pair of tickets for him, with a note from Legend saying Father could find us at Caraval."

Scarlett took a shaky breath as she pictured Tella sneaking into their father's study. Scarlett was still tempted to scold her sister for devising such a dangerous and horrible plot, but for the first time Scarlett could see how much she'd always underestimated Tella. Her younger sister was brighter, smarter, and braver than Scarlett ever gave her credit for.

"You could have told me," Scarlett said.

"I wanted to." Tella cautiously stepped around the chair, until the sisters were face-to-face. She'd changed out of the ruined dress she'd died in; she now wore white—a ghostly shade of it, and Scarlett wondered if she'd chosen the gown for that very reason. As if a little more drama was needed.

"You have no idea how hard it was not to say anything before we left Trisda, and when we were up in that balcony, I was scared to dea—I was nervous. But part of the bargain was I couldn't say a word. Legend told me it would put too much pressure on you; he said you might fail out of fear. And that blackguard likes his games." Tella's expression soured.

Scarlett got the impression this game was also more than Tella had bargained for. Not surprising, given everything Scarlett had learned about Legend.

"So this really had nothing to do with Nana Anna?"

Tella nodded. "They did have a romance. It's true that it didn't end well because she chose another man, but Legend never vowed to destroy all the females in her line. After Nana went to the Conquered

Isles to marry Grandfather, a rumor started that she'd fled there to hide because Legend wanted revenge, but that's not entirely true either. I'm fairly certain lots of women have warmed his bed since then."

Scarlett thought about Rosa, and everything Tella had written in her letters. Even though Legend hadn't vowed to destroy her nana, it seemed his broken heart had ruined at least one other woman. Scarlett also imagined Legend toyed with her and Tella more than he might have because they were Annalise's granddaughters.

She would have asked more questions, but though she remained curious about Legend, she could no longer ignore the sharp pain of another death that still weighed heavy on her thoughts.

"I need to know about Julian."

Tella chewed on the corner of her lip. "I was wondering when you were going to ask about him."

"What does that mean?" Scarlett's words came out rough. She wanted to ask more, but she still could not bring herself to question if he was truly alive or dead. Ever since Tella walked in, Scarlett had dared to hope Julian wasn't really dead. But Tella's expression turned unreadable, making Scarlett fear she'd only get one happy ending today. "Did you know he was going to die?"

Tella nodded slowly. "That might have actually been my fault."

41

Scarlett paled, falling into a chair. "You had him killed."

"Please don't be upset. I was trying to protect you."

"By having him murdered?"

"He's not really dead," Tella promised.

"Then where is he?" Scarlett looked around as if he'd suddenly walk through the door. But when it didn't open, and Tella frowned, some of Scarlett's panic returned. "If he's alive, then why didn't he come here with you?"

"If you calm down, I'll explain it all." Tella's voice contained the slightest tremor. "Before the game began, I told Legend I didn't want anyone making you fall in love. I knew how much you wanted to marry the count. I never liked the idea, but I wanted you to choose another path for your own reasons, not because of a Caraval player who was pretending to be someone else. So . . ." Tella paused, drawing the word out before rushing on to say, "I told Legend, if that happened, I wanted the player taken out of the game before it ended, and you made your final choice regarding your fiancé. I can see now how misguided that was. But I swear, I was trying to protect your heart."

"You shouldn't have—"

"You don't need to say it." Tella rocked back on her heels, frowning again. "I know I've made a lot of mistakes. In my head, I saw it all playing out differently. I didn't realize how unpredictable Legend is. He was supposed to take Julian out of the game earlier, and I never imagined Legend would actually have him killed in front of you."

Tella appeared truly apologetic, but it didn't erase the horror roiling around inside of Scarlett. No one should be forced to watch two of the people they love die in the same night. "So, Julian is really alive now?"

"Yes, very much. But why don't you look happier about this?" Tella's brows scrunched up. "From what I heard about the two of you, I would have thought—"

"I'd rather not discuss my feelings right now." Or any of the things her sister had heard. It was starting to feel like too much to take in. Too many real threads mixed with false threads, all of them tangling together. Scarlett wanted to be thrilled Julian was alive, but she could still feel the pain of his death, and knowing that it really was all pretend meant the Julian she had fallen in love with never actually existed—he was just a role one of Legend's performers had played.

"I want to know how it works. I need to know what's real and what's not." Tears were threatening to fall again. Scarlett knew she should have been happy, and a part of her was relieved, but she was also terribly confused. "Was everything that happened scripted?"

"Not at all." Tella plopped down in the chair beside Scarlett. "My kidnapping and your kidnapping were my ideas. And I knew you would be tested before we met on the balcony, where I would have to jump. But most of what happened in between wasn't scripted.

"Before each game, the performers are bound by magic that prevents them from confessing certain truths—like admitting they are really actors." Tella went on, "They're given guidelines to follow, but their actions are not all predetermined. I think you already know this, but during Caraval there's always a bit of real mixed in with everything. There is some free will involved. So, I can't tell you what was real for Julian. And I probably shouldn't tell you that his role was supposed to end shortly after he got you to the isle." Tella paused meaningfully.

Julian had said something similar, but in light of everything else, Scarlett was no longer sure she believed any of the things he'd said to her. For everything she knew, Julian was actually Legend after all.

Still, she had to ask. "What do you mean by that?"

"According to the other players, Julian was meant only to get us to the isle and then take off. I think he was supposed to leave you at a clock shop. But you didn't hear that from me," Tella said. "And in case you were wondering, Julian and I weren't ever really involved. We never even kissed."

Scarlett blushed; this was something she'd tried to avoid thinking about. "Tella, I can explain, I would never have—"

"You don't need to explain," Tella broke in. "I never blamed you for anything. Though I will admit I was surprised whenever I would get reports as to how things were progressing." Her voice went higher, as if she were on the verge of laughter.

Scarlett covered her face with her hands. *Mortified* was not a strong enough word to use. Despite Tella's words, Scarlett felt deceived and humiliated.

"Scar, don't be embarrassed." Tella pulled her sister's fingers from her burning cheeks. "There was nothing wrong about your relationship with Julian. And in case you were worried, it wasn't Julian who told me about what was happening between you two. It was mostly Dante, who seemed quite put out you didn't fancy him more."

Tella made a funny face, giving Scarlett the impression she was pleased about this.

"I'm guessing Dante didn't really die either?"

"No, he died, but also came back, like Julian," Tella said. Then she did her best to explain the truth about death and Caraval.

Tella didn't know the particulars as to how it worked. It was one of those things that people didn't really talk about. All Tella knew was if one of Legend's performers was killed during the game, they really died—but not permanently. They felt all the pain and nastiness that went with death, and they stayed dead until the game officially ended.

"Does that mean you would have come back, no matter what?" Scarlett asked.

Tella paled, turning whiter than her dress, and for the first time Scarlett wondered what death had been like for her sister. Tella was good at concealing her real emotions, yet it seemed she couldn't keep the tremble from her voice as she said, "I'm not a performer. Regular people who die during the game stay dead. Now come on." Tella pushed up from the chair, shaking off her pallor as she filled her voice with cheer. "It's time to get ready."

"Get ready for what?" Scarlett asked.

"The party." Tella said it as if it were obvious. "Remember your invitation?"

"The one from Legend? That was real?" Scarlett couldn't decide if she thought it twisted or terribly clever.

Tella grabbed Scarlett's arm as she started for the door. "I'm not letting you say no to this celebration!"

Scarlett didn't want to leave her sister's side, but attending a party was the last thing she felt like doing. She enjoyed socializing, but just then she could not imagine flirting and eating and dancing.

"Come on!" Tella tugged her harder. "We don't have much time. I'd rather not arrive looking like a specter."

"Well then you should have picked out a different dress," Scarlett snapped.

"I died," Tella said, unfazed. "What's more perfect than this? You'll see; next game, I'm sure you'll get into the drama of it all even more than me."

"Oh, no," Scarlett said. "There's no next game for me."

"You might change your mind after tonight." Tella flashed a cryptic smile, and pushed open the door before Scarlett could argue. Like the tunnels underneath the game, it led to a new hallway, one Scarlett had never seen. Gemstone tiles covered the floor, tinkling softly as Tella dragged Scarlett past halls covered in paintings that reminded her of Aiko's notebook.

Scarlett paused in front of one she'd never viewed, an image of herself in the dress shop, wide-eyed and openmouthed, taking in every creation, as Tella spied in secret from the third floor.

"My room's this way, not the same one where you found me last night." Tella towed Scarlett around several more corners, and past a variety of performers, who exchanged brief hellos, before stopping in front of a rounded sky-blue door. "Sorry if it's not very tidy."

The room inside was a disaster, covered in corsets, gowns, elaborate hats, and even a few capes. Scarlett didn't see any gray hairs upon her sister's head, but she imagined they were hiding somewhere, because her sister must have lost at least a year of her life in order to acquire so many new and fanciful things.

"It's hard when there's not much space to put things away," Tella said, picking up clothes to create a path as Scarlett stepped inside. "Don't worry, the dress I picked out for you is not on the floor."

"I don't think I can go." Scarlett sat on the edge of the bed.

"You have to. I already got you a dress, and it cost me five secrets." Tella marched over to a chest, and when she turned back around her arms held an ethereal pink dress. "It reminds me of a Hot Season sunset."

"Then you should wear it," Scarlett said.

"It's too long for me, and I got it for you." Tella tossed her sister the dress. It felt as indulgent and dreamlike as it looked, with tiny sleeves that dripped off the shoulders and an ivory bodice covered in ribbons that flowed into a gauzy skirt. Silk flowers clung to the ribbons, which Scarlett noticed changed color in the light, a combination of blazing creams and burning pinks.

"Just wear it tonight," Tella said. "If the party ends and you want to leave Caraval and everyone who's part of this world behind, I will go with you. But I'm not letting you miss this. I've been told Legend doesn't extend invitations like this to anyone who's not one of his performers, and I don't think you'll be happy if you leave this business with Julian unresolved."

At the mention of Julian, Scarlett's heart constricted. She was glad he was alive. But whatever there was between them, she was sure it wouldn't be anywhere close to what it had been before. Even though Julian had tried to tell her the truth, it could have just been because he felt sorry for her. Or maybe it was part of the act too. It wasn't as if he'd ever said he loved her.

"I feel as if I don't even know him." Scarlett also felt like a fool, but she felt too ridiculous to admit that.

"Then tonight is your chance to *get* to know him." Tella grabbed her sister's hands and pulled her up from the bed. "I wish I could tell you that whatever you two shared was real."

"Tella, this isn't helping."

"That's because you haven't let me finish. Even if it wasn't what you'd thought it was, you two still experienced something significant this past week. I would think he'd want closure as much as you do."

Closure. Another word for end, conclusion.

It now made perfect sense why Julian had warned her most people she met during Caraval were not who they appeared to be.

But Scarlett could not deny that she wanted to see him again.

"I'll make sure you're the prettiest girl there. Next to me, of course." Tella giggled, soft and pretty, and even though Scarlett's heart felt as if it were breaking once again for Julian, she reminded herself she had her sister, and they were finally, blessedly, gloriously free. This was what she'd always wanted, and it came with a future that had yet to be written, full of hope and possibilities.

"I love you, Tella."

"I know you do." Tella looked up with an indescribably tender expression. "I wouldn't be here if you didn't."

42

It felt like stepping into a world made of ancient fairy tales and dreams come to life. Air smelling of evergreen, dusty with flecks of gold lantern light.

Scarlett didn't know where the snow had gone, but not a flake remained. The ground was dotted with flower petals instead. The forest was shades of green and olive and jade and ivory. Even the tree trunks were covered in rich emerald moss, except for the bits wrapped in gold-and-cream streamers. People sipped golden drinks as rich and thick as honey, while others ate cakes that looked like clouds.

And then there was Julian. Her heart leaped into her throat at the sight of him. Scarlett had been looking for him since the moment she arrived, and suddenly she couldn't move or breathe.

Across the way, under a bow of green leaves and gold ribbons, he stood drinking a flute of honey, looking very much alive and chatting with a shiny-haired brunette, far too pretty for Scarlett's comfort. When he laughed at something the girl said, Scarlett's heart plunged from her throat to her stomach.

"This was a mistake."

"Looks like you need my help again." Aiko appeared between Tella and Scarlett. Unlike the sparkling and colorful outfits she had worn during Caraval, the girl's bustled dress was now sedate and dark. Blue or black, Scarlett couldn't tell. With a floor-length straight skirt, long sleeves, and high neck.

"I get cold," she stated simply. "And you look as if you have a chill as well, though I'm guessing it's not from the temperature." Aiko's eyes went to the brunette, watching as she wrapped her hand around Julian's arm.

"Her name is Angelique. You might recall her from the dress shop. She loves flirting with the ones who have their sights set on someone else." Aiko looked pointedly at Scarlett.

"Is this your way of saying I should go over there and talk to him?"

"You said it, not us," said Tella.

Aiko nodded in agreement.

"Ah!" Tella exclaimed.

Scarlett followed her sister's gaze until it hastily dropped on Dante, who'd just entered the party. He was still dressed in black, but now had both his hands, and a pretty girl on either arm.

"Dante, I'm so glad you're here! I was looking for you, and I believe Aiko was as well." Tella trotted off toward Dante. Without a word Aiko followed, leaving Scarlett all alone.

Scarlett tried to steady herself with a deep breath, but her heart beat faster with every step she took. Dew from the grass dampened her thin gold slippers. Julian still hadn't looked her way and she feared what she would see when he did. Would he smile? Would it be the polite sort or the real sort? Or would he turn back to Angelique and make it clear that whatever he'd shared with Scarlett was really nothing at all?

Scarlett stopped several feet away, unable to move any closer. She could hear the low rumble of his voice now as he told Angelique, "I think that's where we're headed next."

"And are you planning on stealing the show again?" Angelique asked.

A wolfish flash of teeth.

Angelique wet her lips.

Scarlett wanted to melt into the night, wink out of existence like a broken star.

Then he saw her.

Without another word, Julian set down his glass and strode toward her. The leaves above Scarlett shuddered, raining down bits of green and gold as he moved. His gait shifted, wavering between confident and something that looked nothing like it.

Her Julian. Yet, how could he be hers when she didn't know anything real about him?

She said, "Hello," but it came out like a whisper. And for a moment they just stood there, under trees that had gone as still as her heart.

"So, is your name really something else?" she finally asked. "Like Caspar?"

"Thankfully, no, my name is not Caspar."

When Scarlett didn't smile, he added, "It gets too confusing if we all use different names. Only the performer who plays Legend does that."

"So your name really is Julian?"

"Julian Bernardo Marrero Santos." His lips curved slightly, just the corners. Not the wicked twist she recognized. Another sharp reminder that this was not the boy she knew. Shades of the rich ruby love she'd felt during the game mixed with hues of deep-indigo hurt, turning everything just a little bit violet.

"I feel as if I don't know you at all," she blurted.

"Ouch—you're wounding me, Scarlett." He sounded more serious than mocking. Yet all she heard was the way he'd called her Scarlett—not Crimson. The nickname had probably just been part of the game, and it shouldn't have meant anything, yet not hearing it reminded her once more of who he really was, and wasn't.

"I don't think I can do this." She turned to leave him.

"Scarlett, wait." Julian grabbed her arm, spinning her back around. From the distance they might have looked like one of the many dancing couples around them—if one couldn't see the frustration in his face or the hurt in hers.

"Why do you keep calling me Scarlett?" she asked.

"Isn't that your name?"

"Yes, but you've never called me it before."

"I've also never done this before." A muscle ticked in Julian's jaw. "When the game ends, we go, leaving everything behind. I'm not used to talking to participants after it's over."

"Would you rather I go?" Scarlett asked.

"No. I would think that's obvious," Julian ground out. "But I do want you to stop looking at me as if I'm some kind of stranger."

"But you are," she said.

Julian winced.

"Can you deny it? You know so much about me and I don't know anything real about you."

The hurt in Julian's expression deepened. "I know it feels like that, but not everything I told you was a lie."

"But most of it was. You—"

Julian brought a finger to Scarlett's lips. "Please let me finish. It wasn't all a deception. Who we play during Caraval always reflects part of who we are. Dante still thinks he's prettier than everyone else. Aiko is unpredictable, but usually helpful. You might think you don't know me, but you do. What I told you—about my family being well connected and playing games—that was true." Julian waved an arm, gesturing toward all the people around them. "This has been my family for most of my life."

A mixture of pride and some other emotion that Scarlett couldn't place edged his features. And suddenly she recognized one of his names from her nana's stories—*Santos*. "You're related to Legend?"

Instead of answering, Julian scanned the celebration before turning back to her. "Will you walk with me?" He reached out a hand.

Scarlett could still remember kissing his fingers, tasting each one as she pressed them to her lips. A tremor slid across her bare shoulders at the memory. He'd warned her that she should be afraid of his secrets, and now she understood why.

Refusing his hand, she followed him anyway. Her slippers crushed flower petals as he led her toward a willow tree, parting its sweeping branches so she could step through. Some of the leaves gleamed in the dark, casting gentle green light and sheltering them from the rest of the party.

"Almost my entire life, I looked up to Legend," Julian began. "I was like you were, when you started writing him letters. I idolized him. Growing up, I wanted to *be* Legend. And when I became a performer, I never cared if the lies I told hurt anyone. All I cared about was impressing him. Then came Rosa." The way he said her name made something tumble uncomfortably inside Scarlett's chest. She knew Rosa was real, but she'd thought it was Legend who had seduced her.

"You were the performer who was involved with her?"

"No," Julian answered immediately. "I never even met her, but I was telling you the truth when I said I lost faith in everything when she killed herself. After that, I realized Caraval was no longer the game it had once been, meant to give people a harmless adventure, and hopefully make them a little wiser. Legend had changed over the years, and not for the better. He takes on a part of whatever roles he plays, and he'd been playing the role of a villain for so long, he'd become one in real life. Finally, a few months back, I decided to leave, but Legend convinced me to give him another chance and stay."

"So you've actually met him?" Scarlett asked.

Julian opened his mouth, as if there was something he wanted to tell her but the words wouldn't come out. He looked at Scarlett meaningfully. "Remember what you asked me about Legend?"

"Whether you were related to him?"

Julian nodded, but didn't elaborate. The glowing leaves of the willow tree rustled as he quietly went on, "Legend sent me a letter, asking me to play one last game. He claimed he was trying to redeem himself. And I wanted to believe him."

Julian took a deep breath before continuing.

"I was only supposed to bring you and Tella to the isle, but every time I tried to walk away from you, I couldn't do it. You were different than I expected. Most people only worry about their own pleasure during Caraval. But you cared so much about your sister; it reminded me of the way I had always felt about my own brother."

Julian's caramel eyes met Scarlett's as he finished. And suddenly a thought struck her.

"Legend is your brother?" she asked.

A wry smile curved Julian's lips. "I was hoping you'd figure it out."

"But . . ." Scarlett stumbled over what to say next as she tried to make sense of it.

It explained why Julian would have had such a hard time walking away from the game. Scarlett knew how difficult it was to turn away from a sibling, even when they did hurtful things. And the other players *had* treated Julian differently.

Ever since learning Caspar had only pretended to be Legend, and that Julian was alive, Scarlett had wondered once more if Julian was actually the master of Caraval. But maybe Scarlett only thought this because the two were closely related.

"But how is it possible? You're so young."

"I don't age as long as I'm one of Legend's performers," Julian explained. "But I was feeling ready to grow up when I decided to leave."

"So then why did you stay and play this time?"

Julian looked at Scarlett almost nervously, as if she were the one who now had the power to break his heart. "I stayed because I started to care about you. Legend doesn't always play fair, and I wanted to try to help you. But I knew if we grew close, and you found out the truth, it would hurt you. So at first I tried to give you excuses to hate me. But then it became harder to push you away; it pained me every time I lied to you. This game brings out the most selfish parts of many people, but it had the opposite effect on you. Watching you restored my belief that Caraval could be what I believe it used to be—and that my brother could be good once again."

Julian's voice was thick with emotion. "I know I've hurt you, but please just give me another chance." He looked as if he wanted to reach out and touch her. And a part of Scarlett wanted him to, but it was too much to take in all at once. If Julian had been Legend, it would have been easier to hate him for putting her through so much. But knowing Legend was actually Julian's brother left her all kinds of torn.

Before he could reach for her, she pulled away.

Julian's mouth pinched at the corners. He was hurt, but he covered it up, bringing his hand to his face to rub the underside of his jaw. Unlike most of the game, he was clean-shaven, younger-looking, except for—

Scarlett froze.

When she'd first seen him, she hadn't noticed the mark her father had made was still there, a thin, jagged scar that ran from his jaw to the corner of his eye. She'd thought that since he could come back to life, the wound would have somehow vanished as well, and it would be as if that awful night had never happened.

Julian caught her staring and answered her unasked question. "I might not be able to die during the game, but all the injuries I receive throughout Caraval leave scars."

"I didn't know," Scarlett murmured.

She'd been nervous about seeing Julian, because she'd feared the game wasn't as real for him as it had been for her. But perhaps Tella had been right when she'd said, *There's always a bit of real mixed in with everything.*

"I'm so sorry my father did that to you."

"I knew the risks I was taking," answered Julian. "Don't be sorry, not unless it's the reason you're trying so hard to walk away from me."

Scarlett's eyes sought his scar again. Julian had always been handsome to her, but this very real scar down his cheek made him devastating. It reminded her of his bravery and his selflessness, and how he'd made her feel more than anyone else she'd ever met. Maybe he wasn't exactly the same boy she had thought he was during the game, but he no longer seemed like a stranger. And he'd done it all to help his brother. How could she, of all people, hold something like that against him?

"If anything, I think this scar is the most beautiful thing I've ever seen."

Julian's eyes widened. "Does that mean you'll forgive me?"

Scarlett hesitated. This was her chance to walk away. Tella had said that after tonight if she wanted, they could forget all about Caraval. Scarlett and Tella could start new lives for themselves on another island, or even one of the continents. Scarlett used to fear she couldn't take care of herself, but now that challenge excited her. She and Tella could do anything they wanted.

But as Scarlett looked at Julian, she couldn't deny she still wanted him as well. She remembered all of the reasons she'd first fallen for him. It wasn't only his handsome face, or the way his smile made her stomach flutter. It was the way he'd pushed her not to give up, and the sacrifices he'd made. Maybe she didn't know him as well as she'd have liked, but she was fairly certain she was still in love with him. She knew she could walk away, but she'd spent enough of her life fearing the risks that accompanied the things she wanted most.

In answer to his question, Scarlett lifted her hand, slowly bringing her fingers to his cheek. Her skin tingled where it touched his, sending shivers all the way down her arm as she traced the thin line from the edge of his parted lips to the corner of his eyelid. "I forgive you," she whispered.

Julian briefly closed his eyes, brushing the ends of her fingers with his black lashes. "This time, I really promise I won't lie to you again."

"But, don't you have rules about *involvement* with people who aren't a part of Caraval?" Scarlett asked.

"I'm not really too concerned with rules." Julian drew a cool finger along her collarbone as he leaned in closer, sliding his free hand around her neck.

Scarlett's heart raced faster at the promise of his lips, the feeling of his hands, and the memory of a kiss, so flawless and so reckless.

Scarlett wasn't sure who kissed who first. Their lips were almost touching, then Julian's soft mouth was crushing hers. It tasted like the moment before night gives birth to morning; it was the end of one thing and the beginning of something else all wrapped up together.

Julian kissed her as if he'd never touched her lips before, sealing the promise he'd just made as he pulled her against his chest, wrapping long fingers in the ribbons of her gown.

Scarlett reached up and threaded her hands through his satiny hair. In some ways he still felt just as mysterious and unknowable as the first time she met him, but in that moment, none of her questions mattered. She felt as if her story could have ended there, in a tangle of lips and hands, and ribbons of color.

EPILOGUE

As the stars leaned a little closer to earth, watching Scarlett and Julian, in the hopes of witnessing a kiss as magical as Caraval, Donatella began to dance beneath of canopy of spying trees, wishing she had someone of her own to kiss.

She twirled from partner to partner, her slippers barely touching the ground, as if the champagne she'd sipped earlier contained bits of stars that kept her feet floating just above the grass. Tella imagined that in the morning she'd most likely regret having drunk so much, but she enjoyed this sensation of floating—and after everything she'd been through, she needed a night of abandon and forgetting.

Tella continued eating cakes of liquor and draining crystal goblets full of spiked nectar until her head spun along with the rest of her body. She practically fell into the arms of her newest partner. He pulled her closer than the others had. His large hands snaked determinedly around her, bringing with them a new surge of pleasure. Tella liked the confident way he touched her. As he tugged her toward the edge of the party and farther from the crowd, she imagined feeling his hands on places besides her waist. Maybe he could help her take her mind off all of the things she'd been too afraid to share with her sister.

Tilting her head back, Tella smiled up. But the night had grown dark, and her vision was blurry. He didn't look like any of the Caraval performers she knew. When her partner leaned closer, all Tella could see was a shadowy smirk as his hands trailed down. She sucked in a breath when his fingers dug into the folds of her dress, touching her hip bones as he . . .

disappeared.

It happened so rapidly, Tella stumbled back.

One moment the young man had his arms around her, drawing her close as if he might kiss her. Then he was walking away. He moved so fast, it made Tella wish she'd not drunk so much. Before she made it more than two steps, he vanished into the crowd, leaving her cold and alone and—with something rather heavy in her pocket.

A chill swept over Tella's naked shoulders. Her head might have been spinning, but she knew the item weighing down her skirts had not been there before. For a moment she tried to entertain the thought of it being some kind of key—perhaps her stranger was hoping she might follow him back to his room for that kiss they never shared. But if that's what he wanted, Tella didn't imagine he would have run off so quickly.

"I think I need another glass of champagne." Tella mumbled the words to no one in particular as she edged away from the crowd. Aside from being wrapped in paper, she could not tell what the object in her pocket was, though she had a prickly feeling it was meant for her eyes alone.

Music from the party faded as she edged toward a secluded tree, lit by hanging candles that flickered white-blue light as she reached into her pocket.

The object she pulled out fit inside the palm of her hand. Some-one had wrapped a note around a thick coin. But it didn't look like any currency Tella had ever seen. Tella shoved the coin back in her pocket after unwrapping the note.

The handwriting on it was crisp and precise.

Dearest Donatella,

Congratulations on escaping your father and surviving Caraval. I am pleased our plan worked, although I had no doubts you would survive the game.

I'm sure your mother will be quite proud, and I believe you should be able to see her soon. But first you must keep up your end of our bargain. I hope you haven't forgotten what you owe me in exchange for all that I've shared with you.

I plan on collecting my payment very soon.

Truly yours,

A friend

ACKNOWLEDGMENTS

Thank you, God, for being faithful when I was faithless, for your love, and for every miracle that made this book possible.

When I started writing I had no idea how long and difficult my journey to publication would be. *Caraval* was not the first book I'd written, or the second, or the third, or the fourth, or the fifth. Before I finished this book, I'd been confronted with every reason to give up on writing. Thankfully, and in huge part because of everyone I'm about to mention, that did not happen.

A very special thank-you to my parents, who helped support me and allowed me to live with them so I could finish this book. An even larger thank-you because both of you believed in all the unpublished books that came before this. Mom and Dad, I love you so much!

Thank you to my amazing-wonderful-fantastic-fearless agent, Jenny Bent, for all your good advice, for working so hard to get this book in shape, and for finding it so many wonderful homes. I've learned so much from you—and I think you're fun.

Sarah Dotts Barley, my gratitude for you knows no bounds.

Thank you for being such an extraordinary editor and champion of this book. It is a constant joy to work with you. I am so thrilled you fell in love with this story and that you showed me how to take this book to the places I could not have brought it on my own. It's been wonderful to work with you!

Thank you, Amy Einhorn and Bob Miller, my brilliant publishers; I'm so honored that *Caraval* is on Flatiron's list. Amy, thank you for all the extra work you put into this book, especially while Sarah was on maternity leave. I also want to thank Caroline Bleeke, for stepping in to help, and for always being so delightful.

I am incredibly thankful for everyone at Macmillan who has put an imprint on this book. Thank you, David Lott, Donna Noetzel, Liz Catalano, Vincent Stanley, Brenna Franzitta, Marlena Bittner, Patricia Cave, Liz Keenan, and Molly Fonseca.

Erin Fitzsimmons and Ray Shappell, thank you for the magic you've added to this book with your gorgeous cover designs and illustrations. And thank you, Rhys Davies, for bringing my make-believe world to life with your amazing map of Caraval.

Thank you, Pouya Shahbazian, my fantastic film representative, for finding *Caraval* an extraordinary home at Twentieth Century Fox. Thank you, Kira Goldberg, for loving *Caraval* enough to give it a home at Twentieth Century Fox—I'm so glad my book found its way into your hands. Thank you, Nina Jacobson, for believing in this book enough to produce it. And thank you, Karl Austen, for stepping in on such short notice to help make the most exciting day of my life even more amazing.

Thank you to everyone at the phenomenal Bent Agency, with special thanks to Victoria Lowes, for answering my many questions, and for doing a million things that I'm sure I'm unaware of. Molly Ker Hawn, thank you so much for finding such a wonderful home for this book in the UK.

I continue to be filled with gratitude and amazement that *Caraval* is also going to be published across the globe. A tremendous thank-you to all my amazing foreign coagents, scouts, and foreign publishers—Novo Conceito (Brazil), BARD (Bulgaria), Booky (China), Egmont (Czech Republic), Bayard (France), WSOY (Finland), Piper (Germany), Libri (Hungary), Noura (Indonesia), Miskal (Israel), RCS Libri (Italy), Kino Books (Japan), Sam & Parkers (Korea), Luitingh-Sijthoff (The Netherlands), Aschehoug (Norway), Znak (Poland), Presenca (Portugal), Editura RAO (Romania), Atticus-Azbooka (Russia), Planeta (Spain), Faces (Taiwan), Dogan-Egmont (Turkey), Hodder & Stoughton (United Kingdom & Commonwealth)—thank you all for investing in this book and making all of this wonder possible.

At its heart *Caraval* is a book about sisters, and I could never have written it if I didn't have such an incredible sister. Allison Moores, thank you for being my best friend and for always believing that someday I would be published, no matter how impossible it looked, or how often I lost faith.

Matthew Garber, my generous brother, I've always looked up to you, and I am so thankful for all the brilliant advice you gave me when I was making so many difficult decisions regarding this book.

You were there so many times when there was no one else I could talk to, and you always knew just what to say.

Matt Moores, my patient brother-in-law, thank you for taking such lovely author photos and designing my fantastic Web site. (Richard L. Press, thank you for letting me use your bookstore.)

Stacey Lee, my dear friend and amazing critique partner. I think we were always meant to be friends. Thank you for helping me figure out what to do with this concept, for reading my rough draft in less than twenty-four hours, for talking me through revisions on the phone, and for being there through every wild up and down.

I also want to thank my other amazing critique partners and early readers. Mónica Bustamante Wagner, thank you for your willingness to read this book over and over, and for making me work so hard on that query letter. Elizabeth Briggs, thank you for everything you've taught me about writing. I am so grateful Pitch Wars brought us together. Thank you, Amanda Roelofs, for always reading all my first drafts, and putting up with all my questions. Jessica Taylor, thank you for being there when things were horrible, and for your excitement when I first told you about this very vague concept. Julie Dao, thank you for lending me your eyes when I needed a fresh pair to read this book. And a special thanks to Anita Mumm, Ida Olsen, and Amy Lipsky, for all of your invaluable feedback.

Beth Hampson, so often when I felt worthless because I was pursuing a dream that didn't seem to love me back, you encouraged me and made me feel as if what I was doing was truly worthwhile.

Portia Hopkins, thank you for offering to read a book if I ever wrote one, and then for taking a chance on a teacher who'd never taught. Jessica Negrón, although you never read this book, your help with Lost Stars taught me so much.

To the generous and talented authors who were kind enough to read early galleys of this book and write such lovely quotes for it, thank you so much: Sabaa Tahir, Jodi Meadows, Kiersten White, Renée Ahdieh, Stacey Lee, Marie Rutkoski, and Mackenzi Lee.

I also want to give a big hug and a huge thank-you to my dear friends, Katie Nelson, Katie Zachariou, Katie Bucklein, Melody Marshall, Kati Bartkowski, Heidi Lang, Jenelle Maloy, Julie Eshbaugh, Roshani Chokshi, Jen White, Valerie Tejada, Richelle Latona, Denise Apgar, Alexis Bass, Jamie Schwartzkopf, everyone at Pub(lishing) Crawl, the Swanky Seventeens, and the Sweet Sixteens—I am beyond grateful to know all of you.